image comics presents

THE WALKING DEAD™

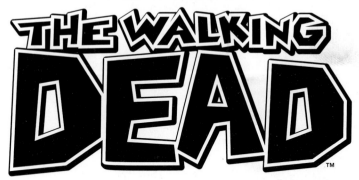

ROBERT KIRKMAN
CREATOR, WRITER

CHARLIE ADLARD
PENCILER

STEFANO GAUDIANO
INKER

CLIFF RATHBURN
GRAY TONES

RUS WOOTON
LETTERER

CHARLIE ADLARD
&
DAVE STEWART
COVER

SEAN MACKIEWICZ
EDITOR

For SKYBOUND ENTERTAINMENT

Robert Kirkman - CEO
David Alpert - President
Sean Mackiewicz - Editorial Director
Shawn Kirkham - Director of Business Development
Brian Huntington - Online Editorial Director
June Alian - Publicity Director
Rachel Skidmore - Director of Media Development
Michael Williamson - Assistant Editor
Dan Petersen - Operations Manager
Sarah Effinger - Office Manager
Nick Palmer - Operations Coordinator
Genevieve Jones - Production Coordinator
Andres Juarez - Graphic Designer
Stephan Murillo - Administrative Assistant

International inquiries: foreign@skybound.com
Licensing inquiries: contact@skybound.com
WWW.SKYBOUND.COM

IMAGE COMICS, INC.
Robert Kirkman – Chief Operating Officer
Erik Larsen – Chief Financial Officer
Todd McFarlane – President
Marc Silvestri – Chief Executive Officer
Jim Valentino – Vice-President

Eric Stephenson – Publisher
Corey Murphy – Director of Sales
Jeremy Sullivan – Director of Digital Sales
Kat Salazar – Director of PR & Marketing
Emily Miller – Director of Operations
Branwyn Bigglestone – Senior Accounts Manager
Sarah Mello – Accounts Manager
Drew Gill – Art Director
Jonathan Chan – Production Manager
Meredith Wallace – Print Manager
Randy Okamura – Marketing Production Designer
David Brothers – Content Manager
Addison Duke – Production Artist
Vincent Kukua – Production Artist
Sasha Head – Production Artist
Tricia Ramos – Production Artist
Emilio Bautista – Sales Assistant
Jessica Ambriz – Administrative Assistant
IMAGECOMICS.COM

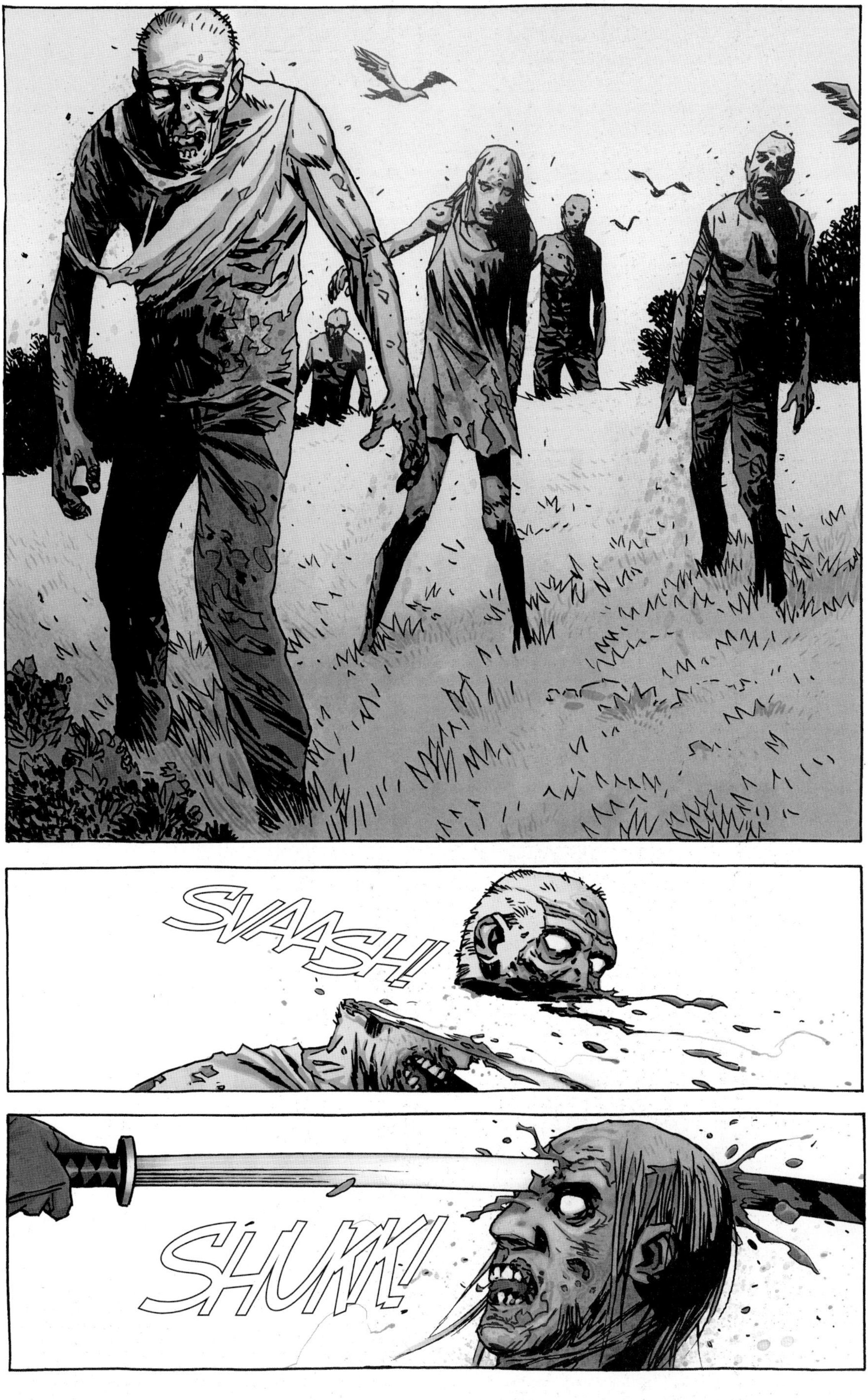
SVAASH!
SHUKK!

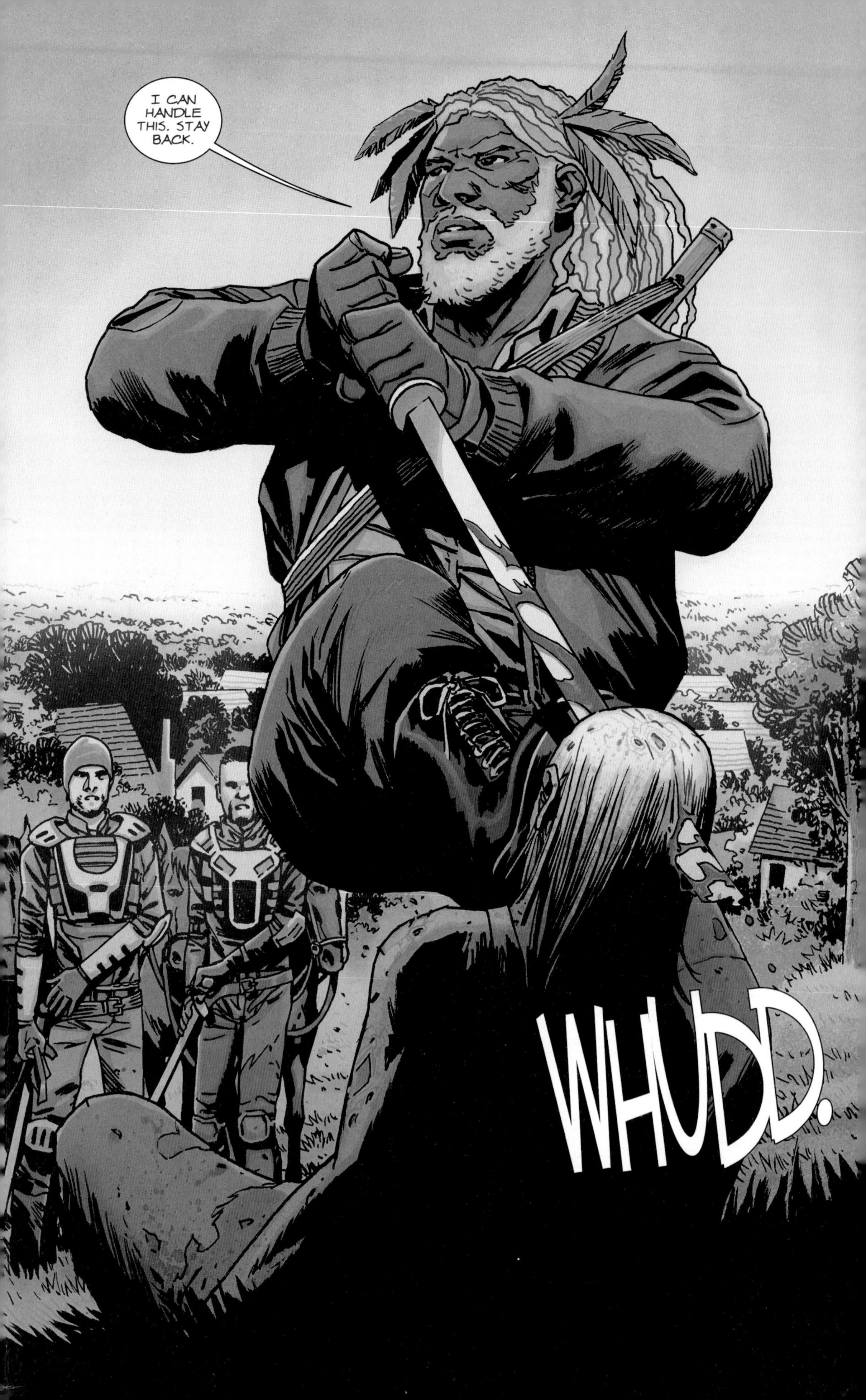
I CAN HANDLE THIS. STAY BACK.
WHUDD.

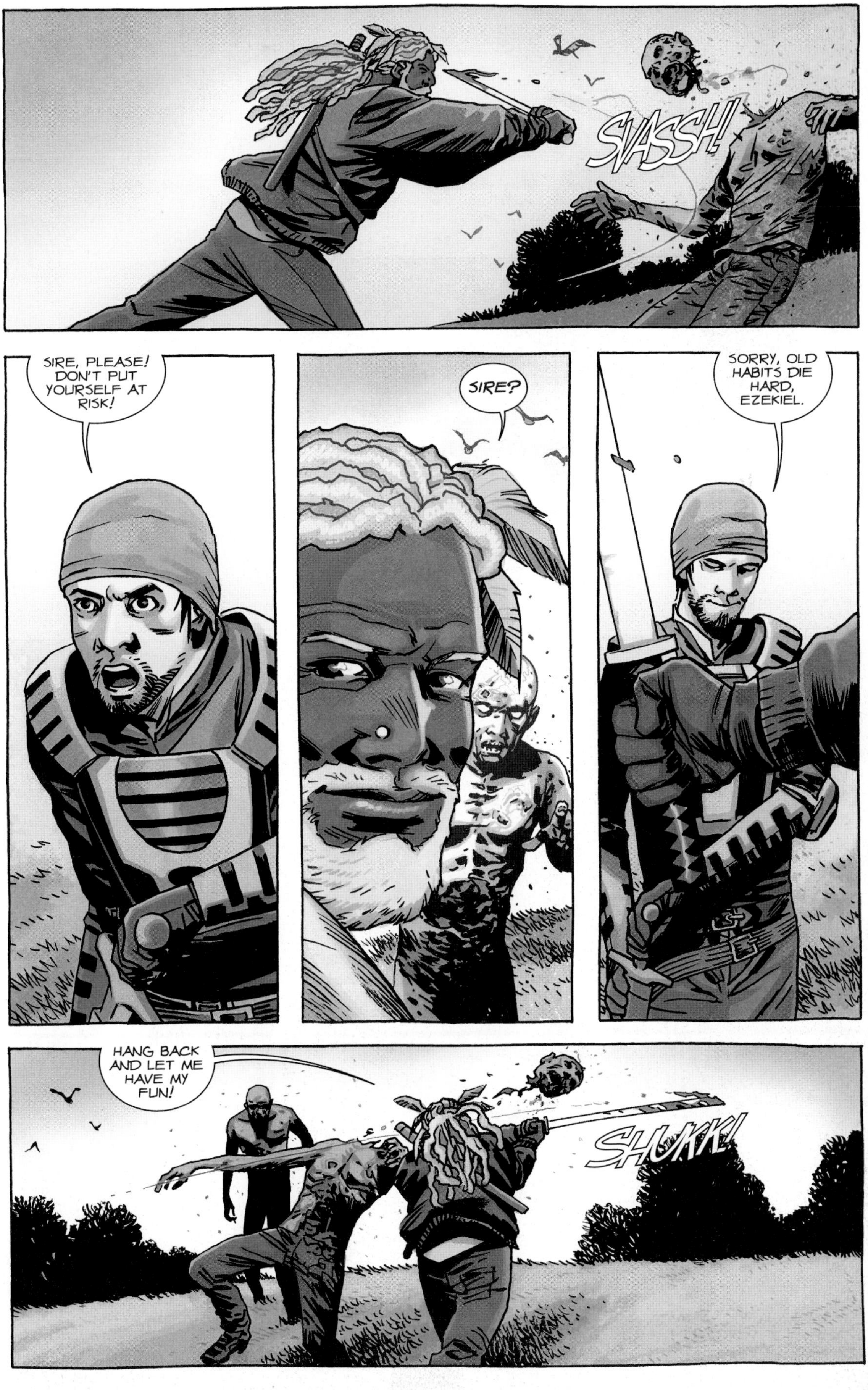
SVASSH!
SIRE, PLEASE! DON'T PUT YOURSELF AT RISK!
SIRE?
SORRY, OLD HABITS DIE HARD, EZEKIEL.
HANG BACK AND LET ME HAVE MY FUN!
SHUKK!

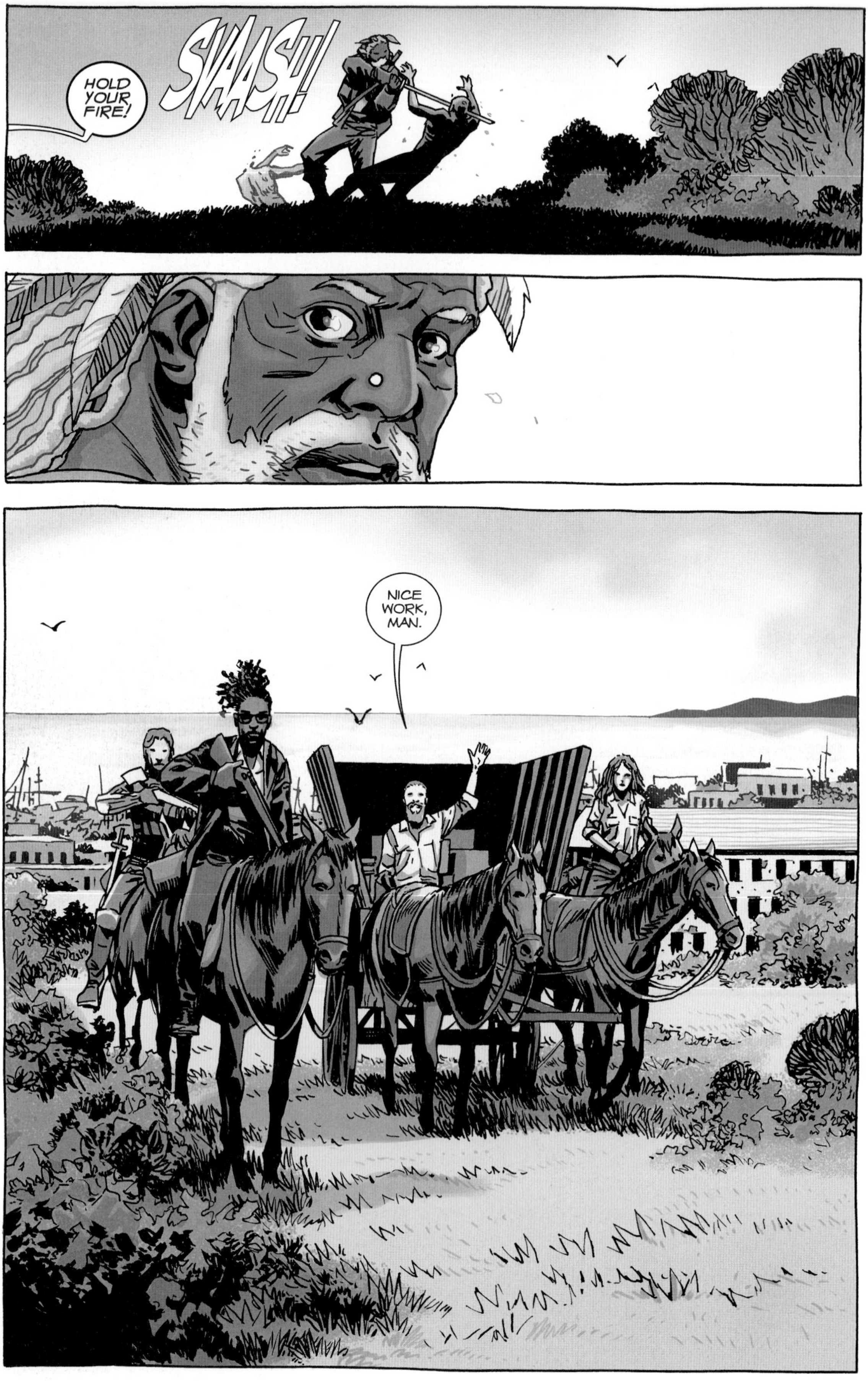
HOLD YOUR FIRE!
SVAASH!
NICE WORK, MAN.

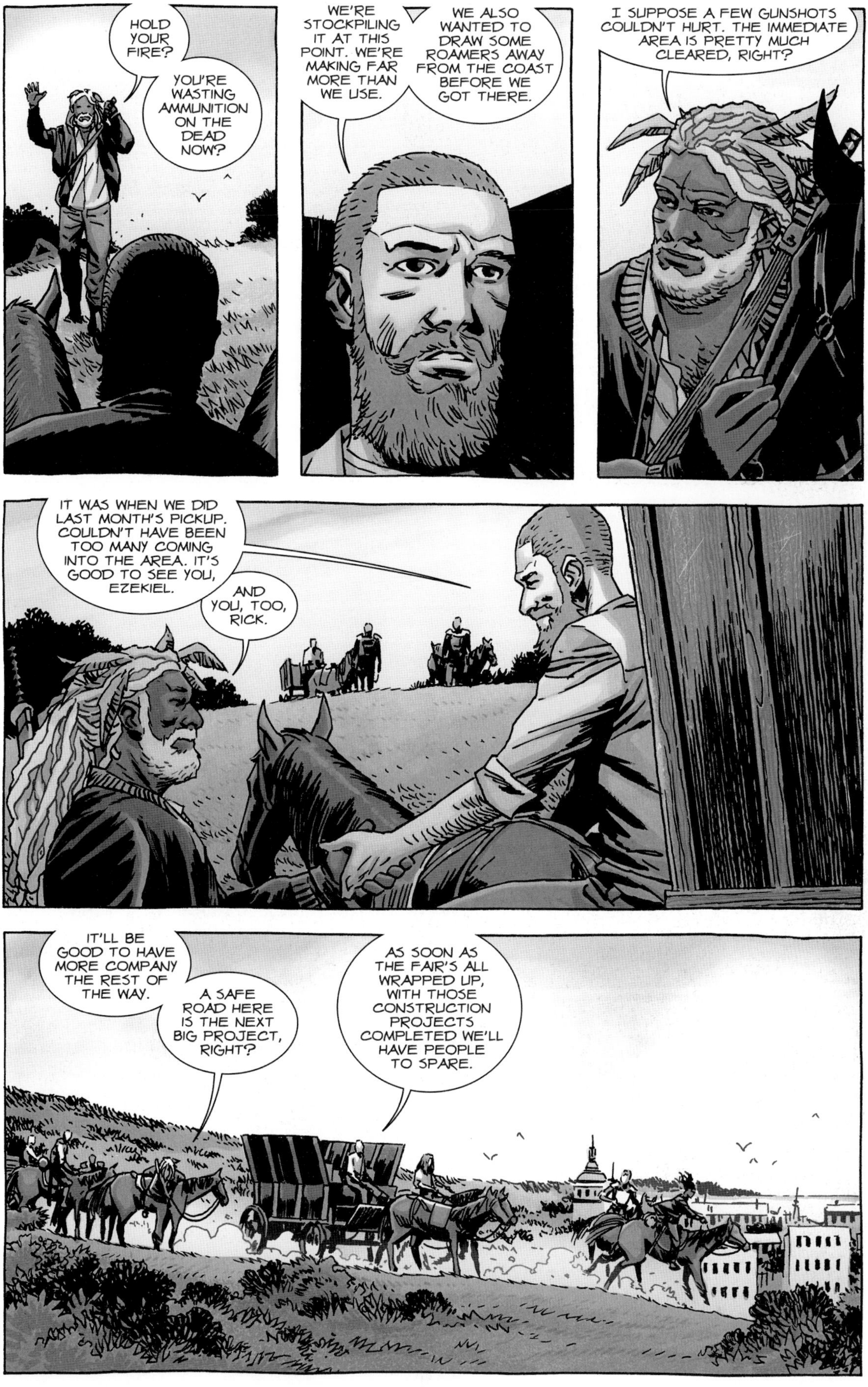
HOLD YOUR FIRE?
YOU'RE WASTING AMMUNITION ON THE DEAD NOW?
WE'RE STOCKPILING IT AT THIS POINT. WE'RE MAKING FAR MORE THAN WE USE.
WE ALSO WANTED TO DRAW SOME ROAMERS AWAY FROM THE COAST BEFORE WE GOT THERE.
I SUPPOSE A FEW GUNSHOTS COULDN'T HURT. THE IMMEDIATE AREA IS PRETTY MUCH CLEARED, RIGHT?
IT WAS WHEN WE DID LAST MONTH'S PICKUP. COULDN'T HAVE BEEN TOO MANY COMING INTO THE AREA. IT'S GOOD TO SEE YOU, EZEKIEL.
AND YOU, TOO, RICK.
IT'LL BE GOOD TO HAVE MORE COMPANY THE REST OF THE WAY.
A SAFE ROAD HERE IS THE NEXT BIG PROJECT, RIGHT?
AS SOON AS THE FAIR'S ALL WRAPPED UP, WITH THOSE CONSTRUCTION PROJECTS COMPLETED WE'LL HAVE PEOPLE TO SPARE.

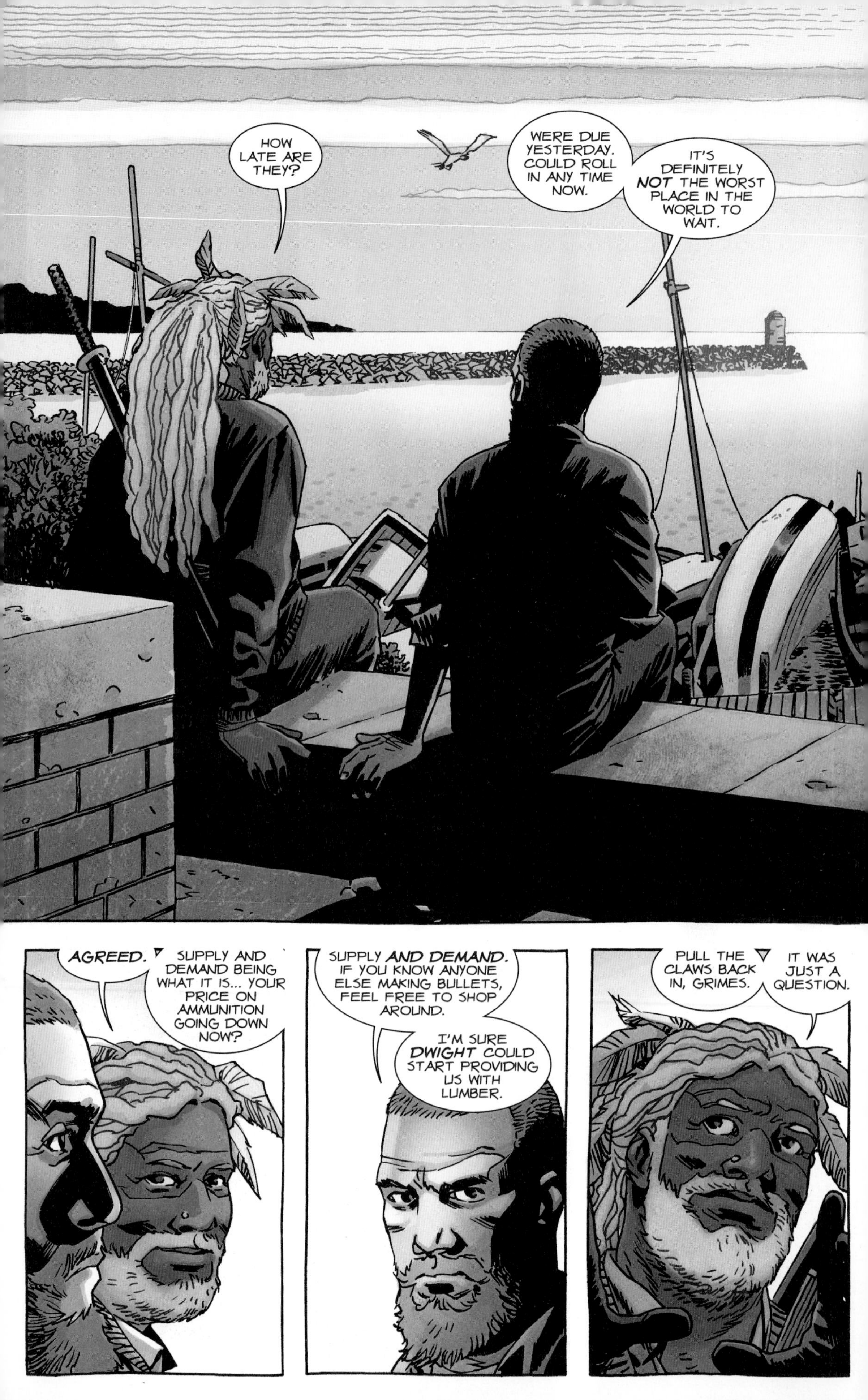

HOW LATE ARE THEY?
WERE DUE YESTERDAY. COULD ROLL IN ANY TIME NOW.
IT'S DEFINITELY NOT THE WORST PLACE IN THE WORLD TO WAIT.
AGREED.
SUPPLY AND DEMAND BEING WHAT IT IS... YOUR PRICE ON AMMUNITION GOING DOWN NOW?
SUPPLY AND DEMAND. IF YOU KNOW ANYONE ELSE MAKING BULLETS, FEEL FREE TO SHOP AROUND.
I'M SURE DWIGHT COULD START PROVIDING US WITH LUMBER.
PULL THE CLAWS BACK IN, GRIMES.
IT WAS JUST A QUESTION.

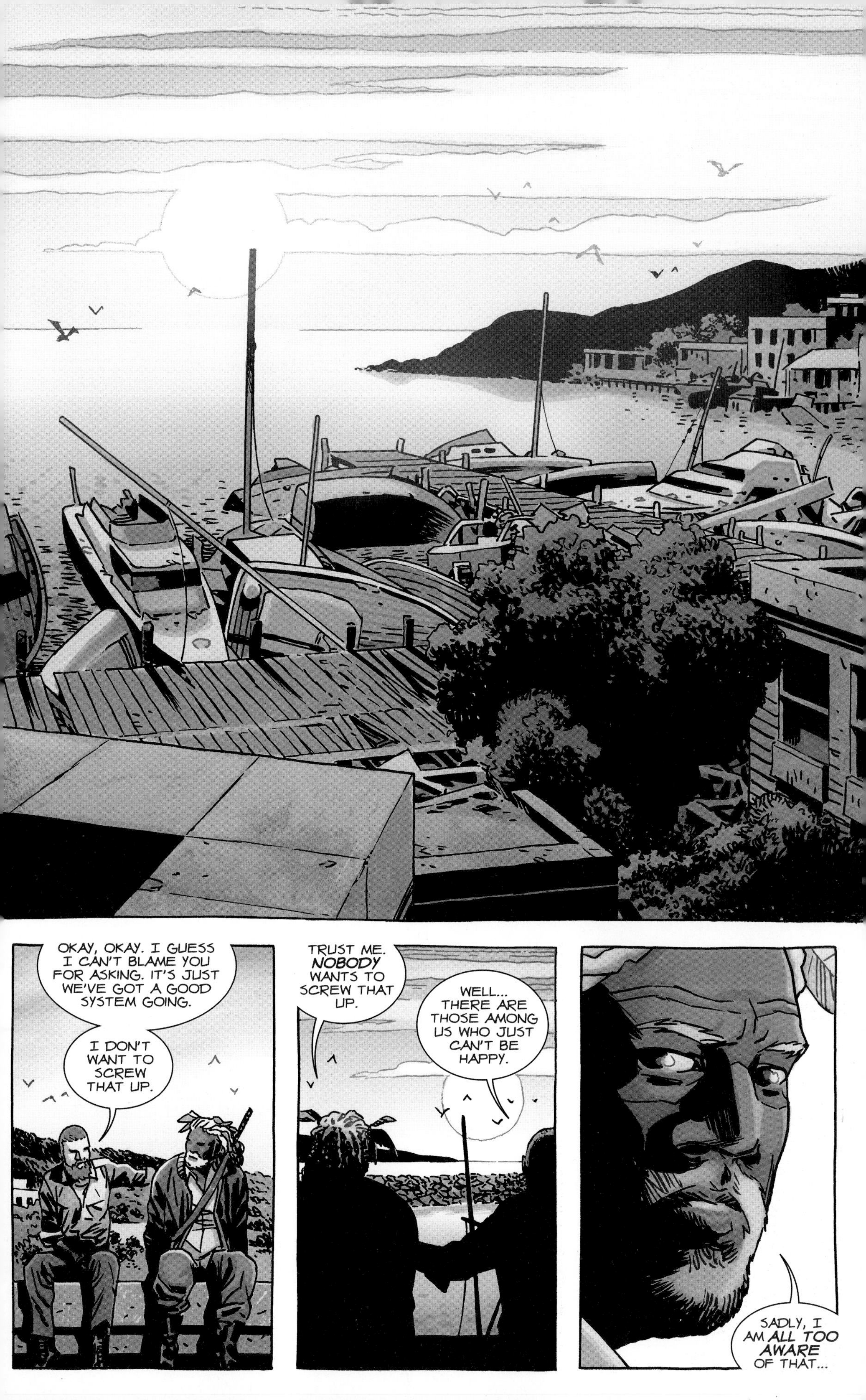
OKAY, OKAY. I GUESS I CAN'T BLAME YOU FOR ASKING. IT'S JUST WE'VE GOT A GOOD SYSTEM GOING.
I DON'T WANT TO SCREW THAT UP.
TRUST ME. NOBODY WANTS TO SCREW THAT UP.
WELL... THERE ARE THOSE AMONG US WHO JUST CAN'T BE HAPPY.
SADLY, I AM ALL TOO AWARE OF THAT...

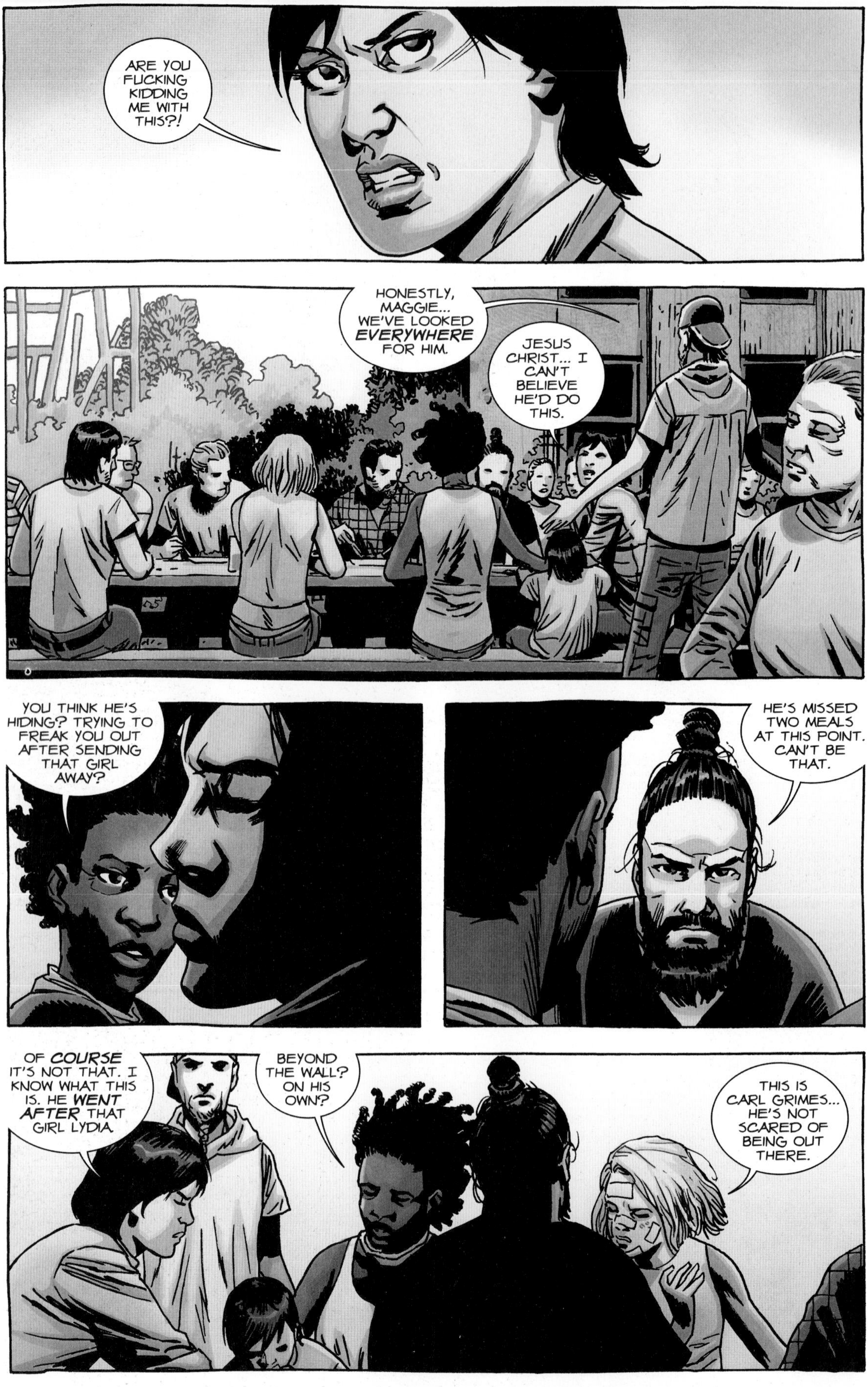
ARE YOU FUCKING KIDDING ME WITH THIS?!
HONESTLY, MAGGIE... WE'VE LOOKED EVERYWHERE FOR HIM.
JESUS CHRIST... I CAN'T BELIEVE HE'D DO THIS.
YOU THINK HE'S HIDING? TRYING TO FREAK YOU OUT AFTER SENDING THAT GIRL AWAY?
HE'S MISSED TWO MEALS AT THIS POINT. CAN'T BE THAT.
OF COURSE IT'S NOT THAT. I KNOW WHAT THIS IS. HE WENT AFTER THAT GIRL LYDIA.
BEYOND THE WALL? ON HIS OWN?
THIS IS CARL GRIMES... HE'S NOT SCARED OF BEING OUT THERE.

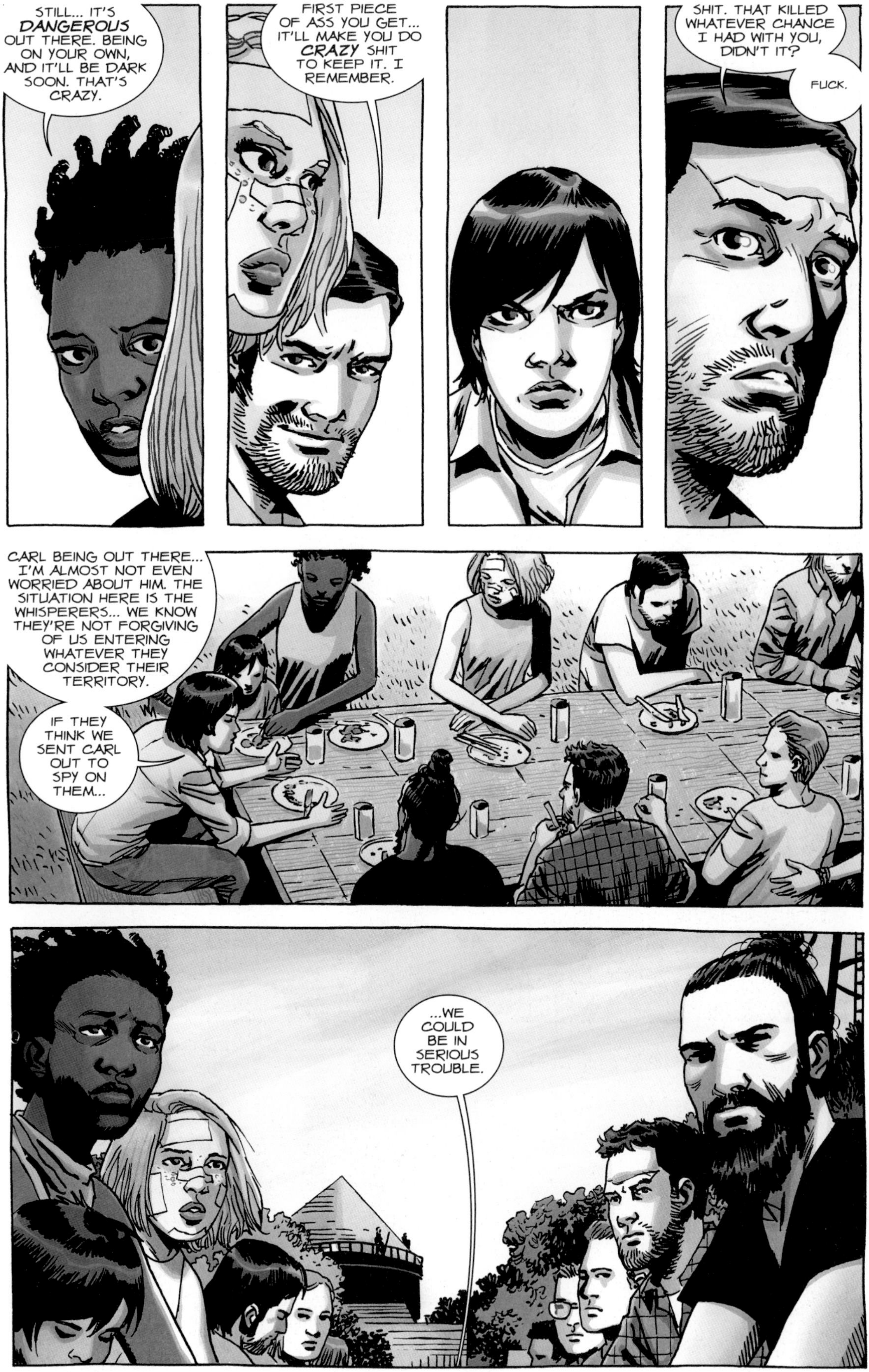
STILL... IT'S DANGEROUS OUT THERE. BEING ON YOUR OWN, AND IT'LL BE DARK SOON. THAT'S CRAZY.
FIRST PIECE OF ASS YOU GET... IT'LL MAKE YOU DO CRAZY SHIT TO KEEP IT. I REMEMBER.
SHIT. THAT KILLED WHATEVER CHANCE I HAD WITH YOU, DIDN'T IT?
FUCK.
CARL BEING OUT THERE... I'M ALMOST NOT EVEN WORRIED ABOUT HIM. THE SITUATION HERE IS THE WHISPERERS... WE KNOW THEY'RE NOT FORGIVING OF US ENTERING WHATEVER THEY CONSIDER THEIR TERRITORY.
IF THEY THINK WE SENT CARL OUT TO SPY ON THEM...
...WE COULD BE IN SERIOUS TROUBLE.

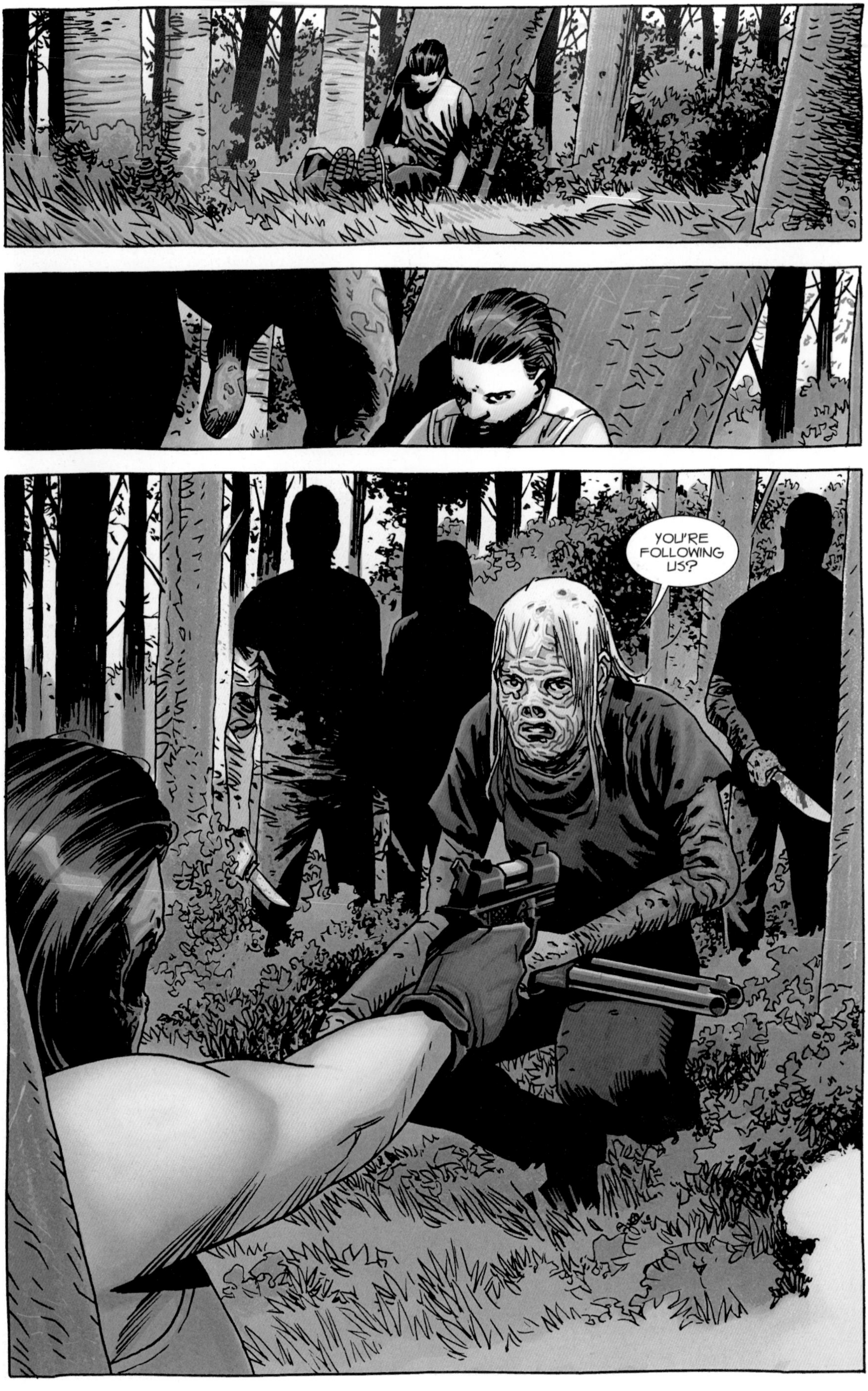
YOU'RE FOLLOWING US?

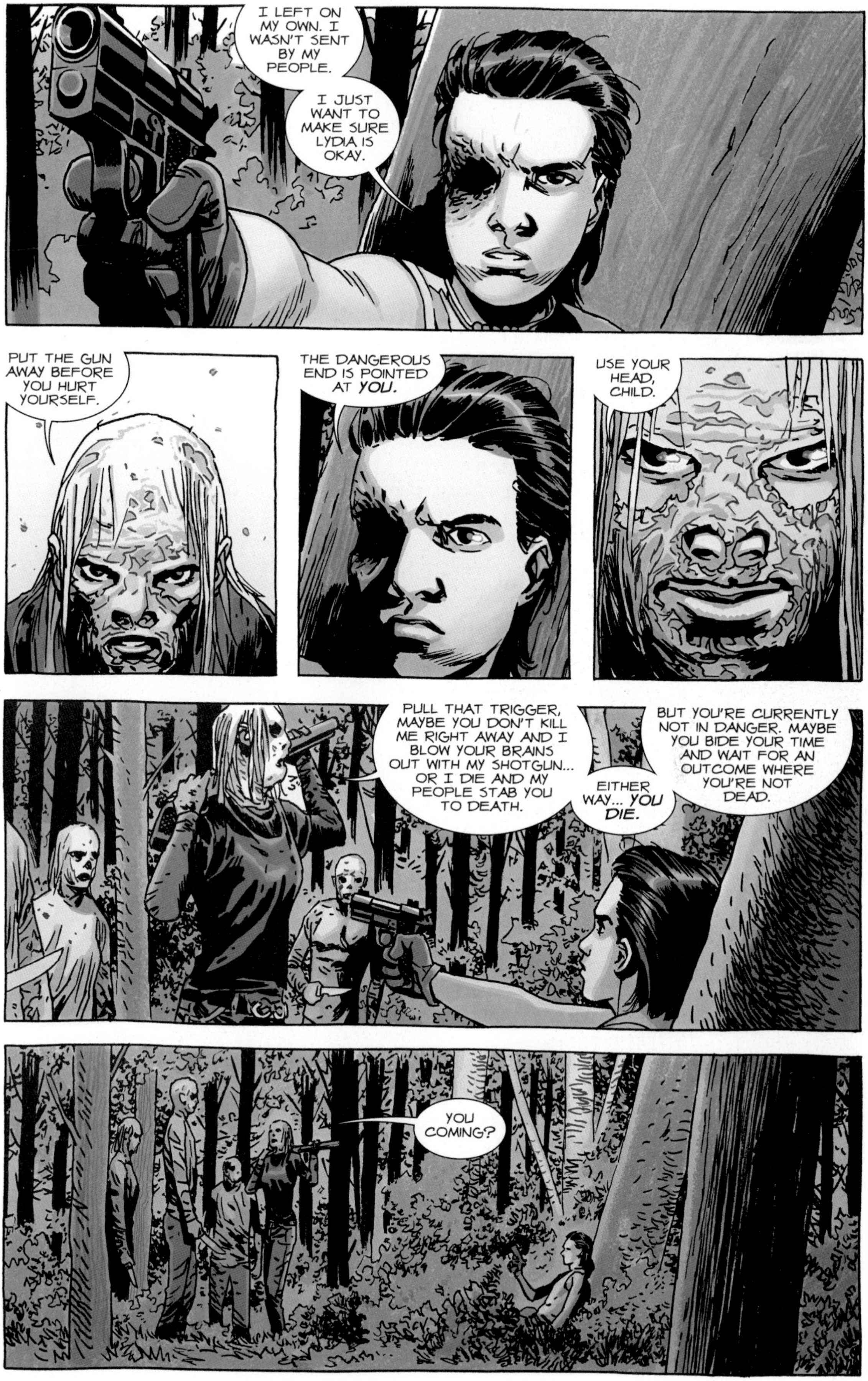
I LEFT ON MY OWN. I WASN'T SENT BY MY PEOPLE.
I JUST WANT TO MAKE SURE LYDIA IS OKAY.
PUT THE GUN AWAY BEFORE YOU HURT YOURSELF.
THE DANGEROUS END IS POINTED AT *YOU.*
USE YOUR HEAD, CHILD.
PULL THAT TRIGGER, MAYBE YOU DON'T KILL ME RIGHT AWAY AND I BLOW YOUR BRAINS OUT WITH MY SHOTGUN... OR I DIE AND MY PEOPLE STAB YOU TO DEATH.
EITHER WAY... *YOU DIE.*
BUT YOU'RE CURRENTLY NOT IN DANGER. MAYBE YOU BIDE YOUR TIME AND WAIT FOR AN OUTCOME WHERE YOU'RE NOT DEAD.
YOU COMING?

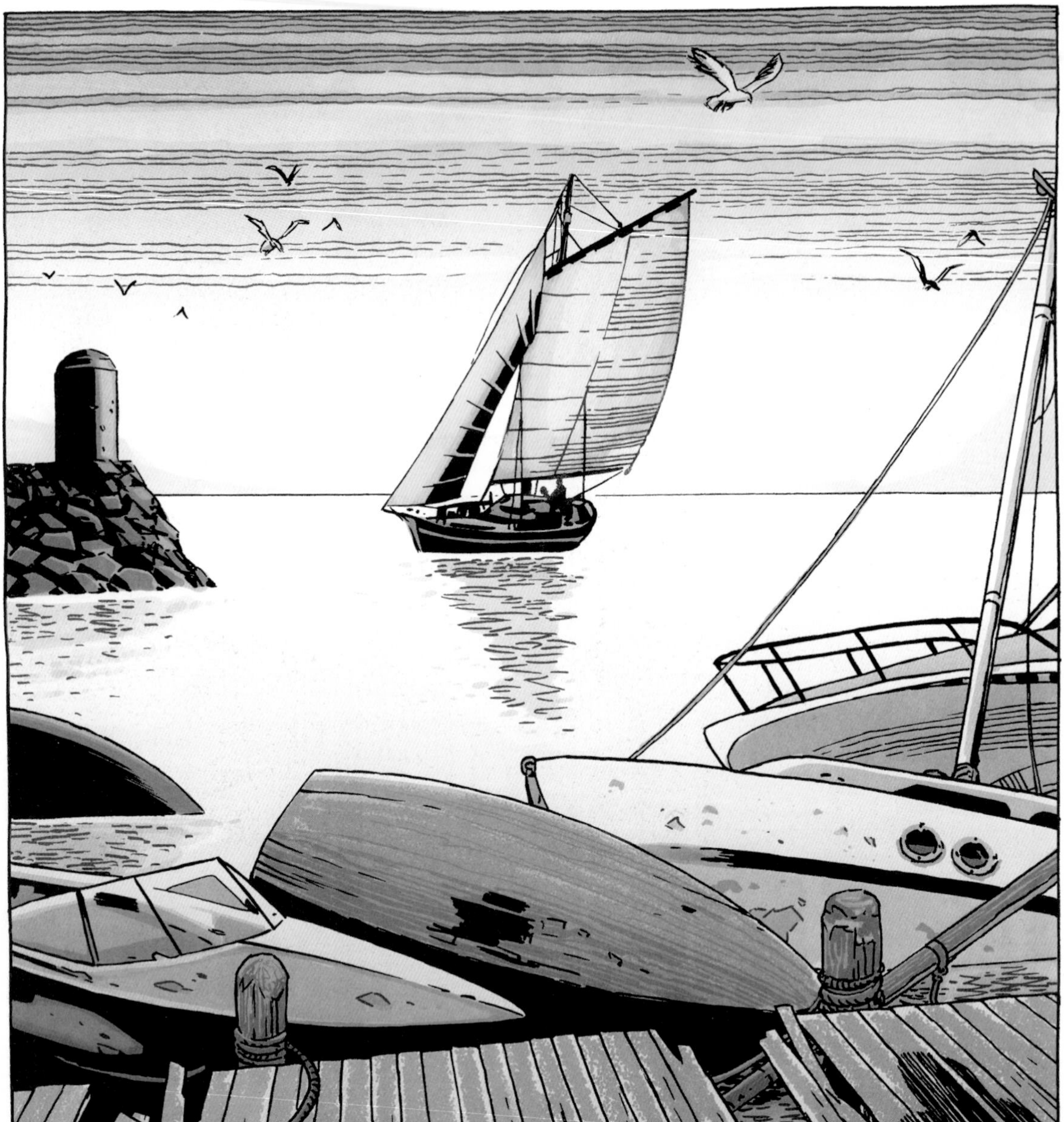

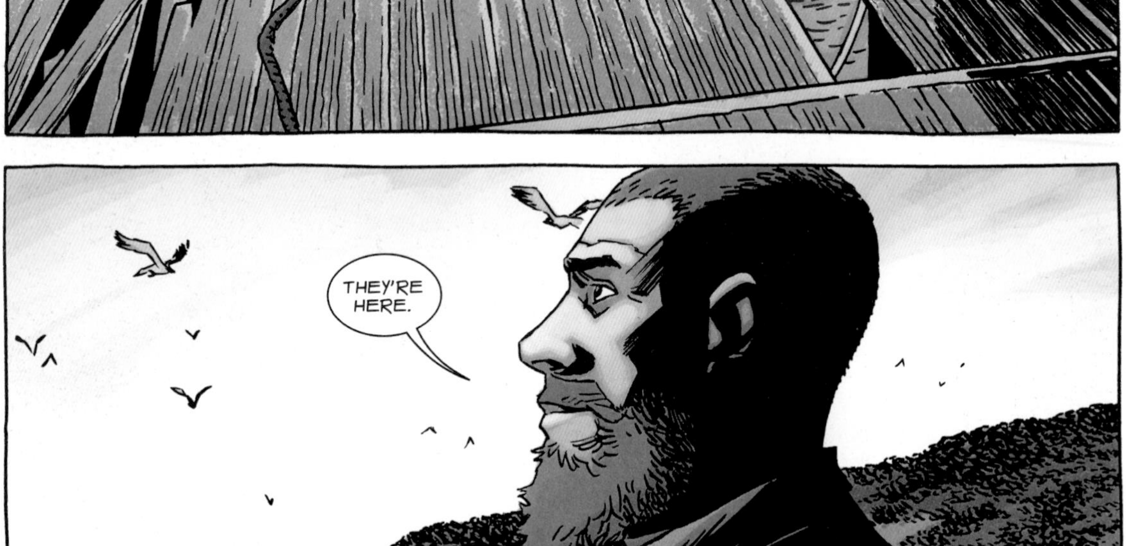
THEY'RE HERE.

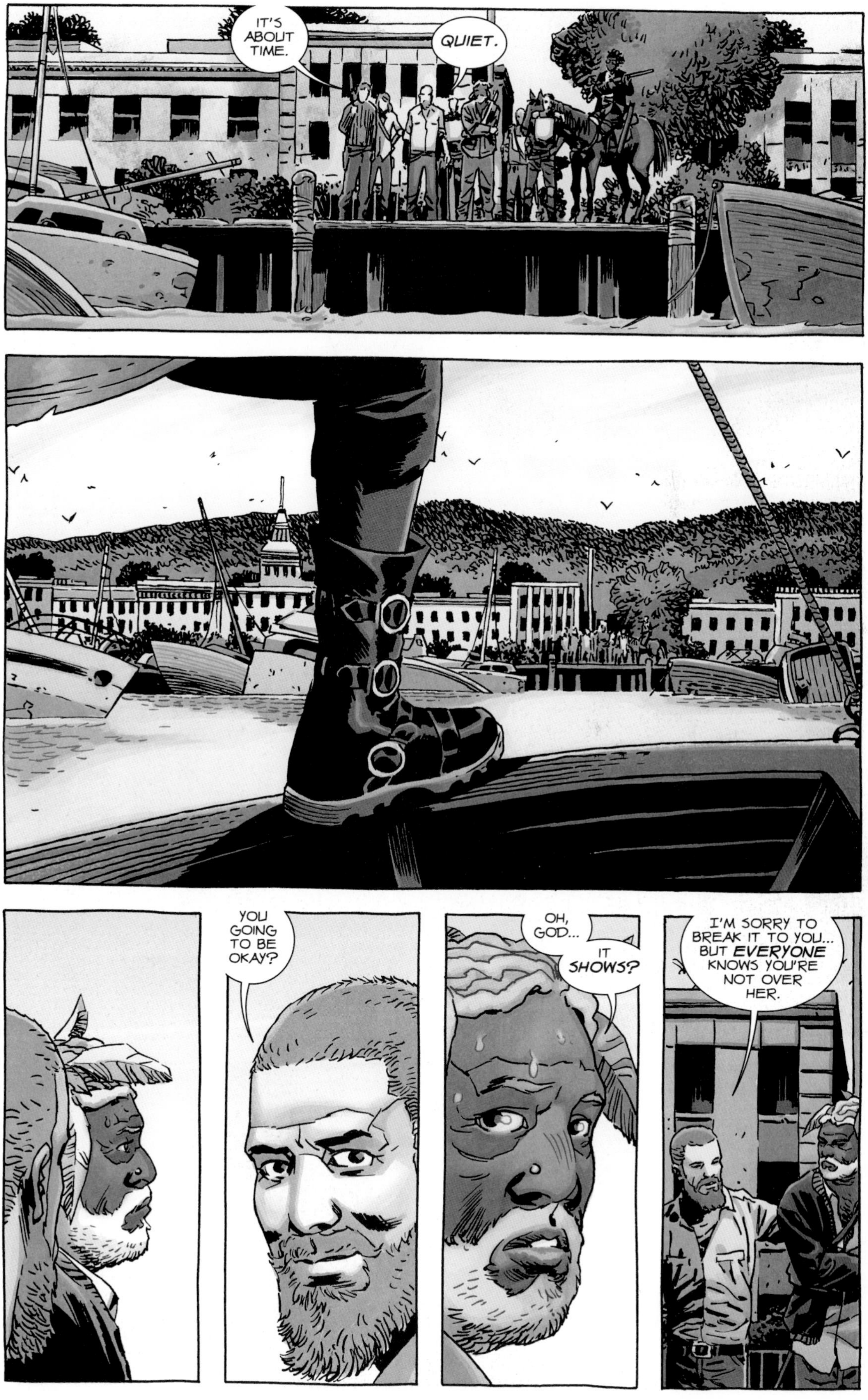
IT'S ABOUT TIME.
QUIET.
YOU GOING TO BE OKAY?
OH, GOD...
IT SHOWS?
I'M SORRY TO BREAK IT TO YOU... BUT EVERYONE KNOWS YOU'RE NOT OVER HER.

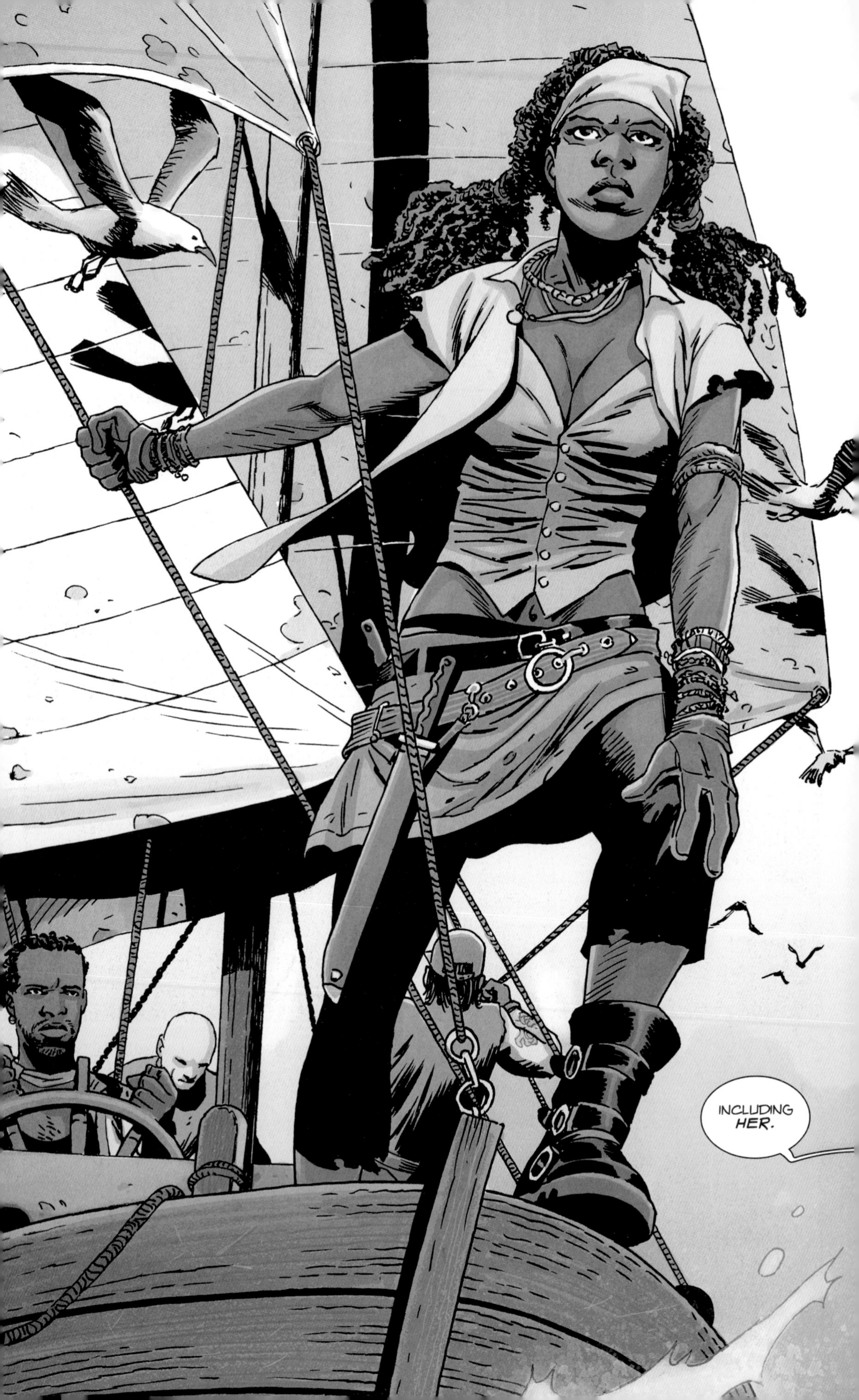
INCLUDING HER.

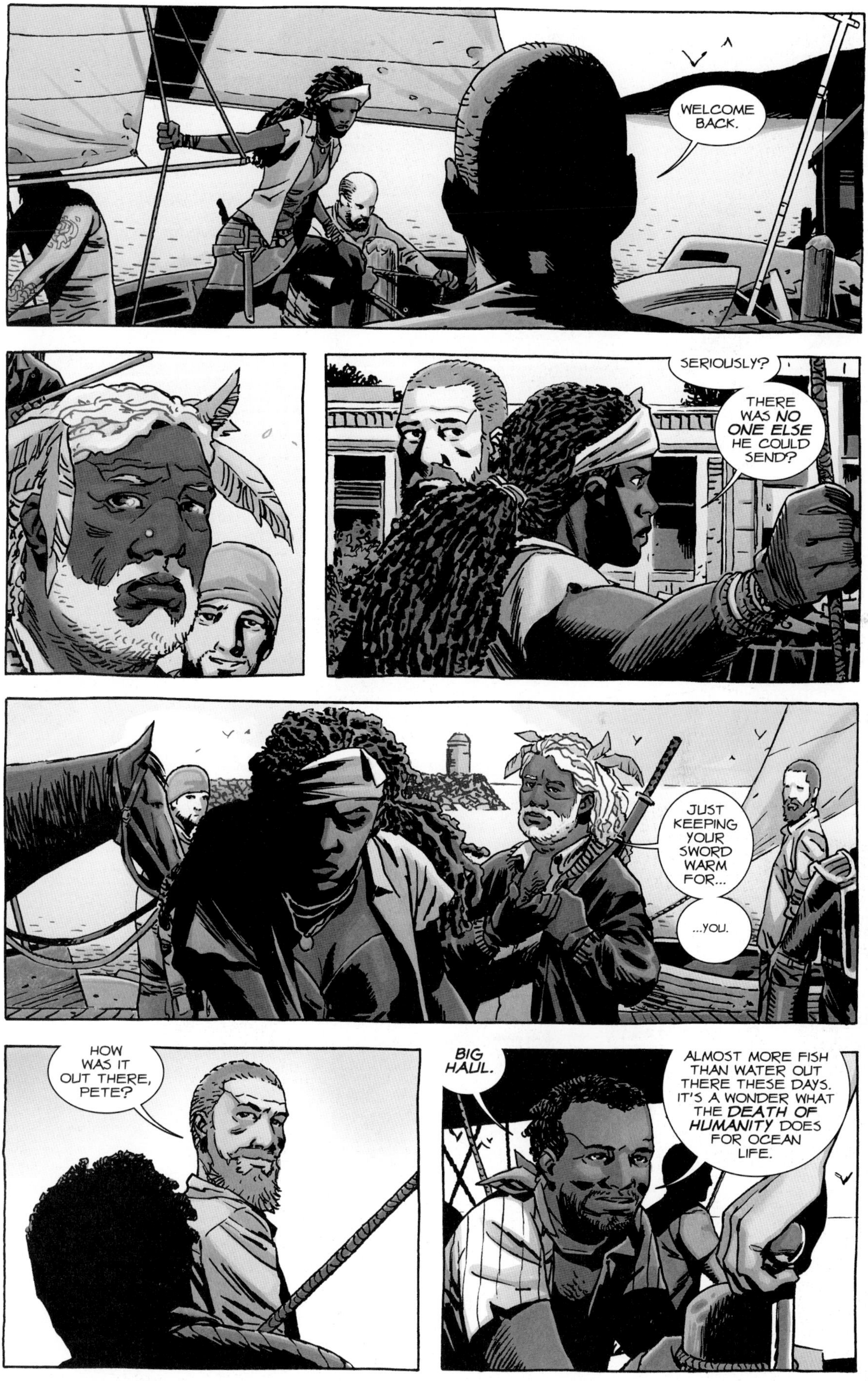
WELCOME BACK.
SERIOUSLY?
THERE WAS NO ONE ELSE HE COULD SEND?
JUST KEEPING YOUR SWORD WARM FOR...
...YOU.
HOW WAS IT OUT THERE, PETE?
BIG HAUL.
ALMOST MORE FISH THAN WATER OUT THERE THESE DAYS. IT'S A WONDER WHAT THE DEATH OF HUMANITY DOES FOR OCEAN LIFE.

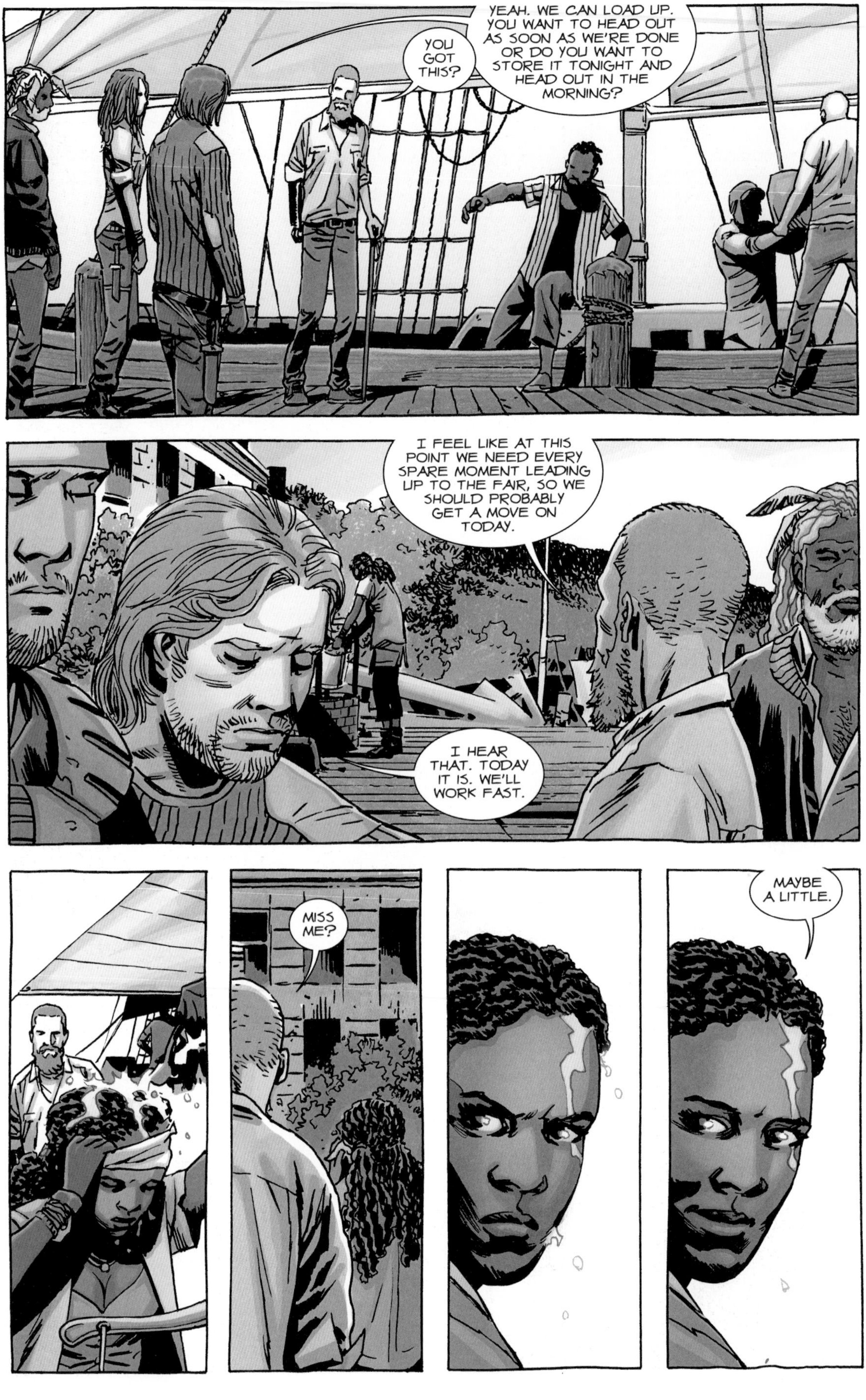
YOU GOT THIS?
YEAH. WE CAN LOAD UP. YOU WANT TO HEAD OUT AS SOON AS WE'RE DONE OR DO YOU WANT TO STORE IT TONIGHT AND HEAD OUT IN THE MORNING?
I FEEL LIKE AT THIS POINT WE NEED EVERY SPARE MOMENT LEADING UP TO THE FAIR, SO WE SHOULD PROBABLY GET A MOVE ON TODAY.
I HEAR THAT. TODAY IT IS. WE'LL WORK FAST.
MISS ME?
MAYBE A LITTLE.

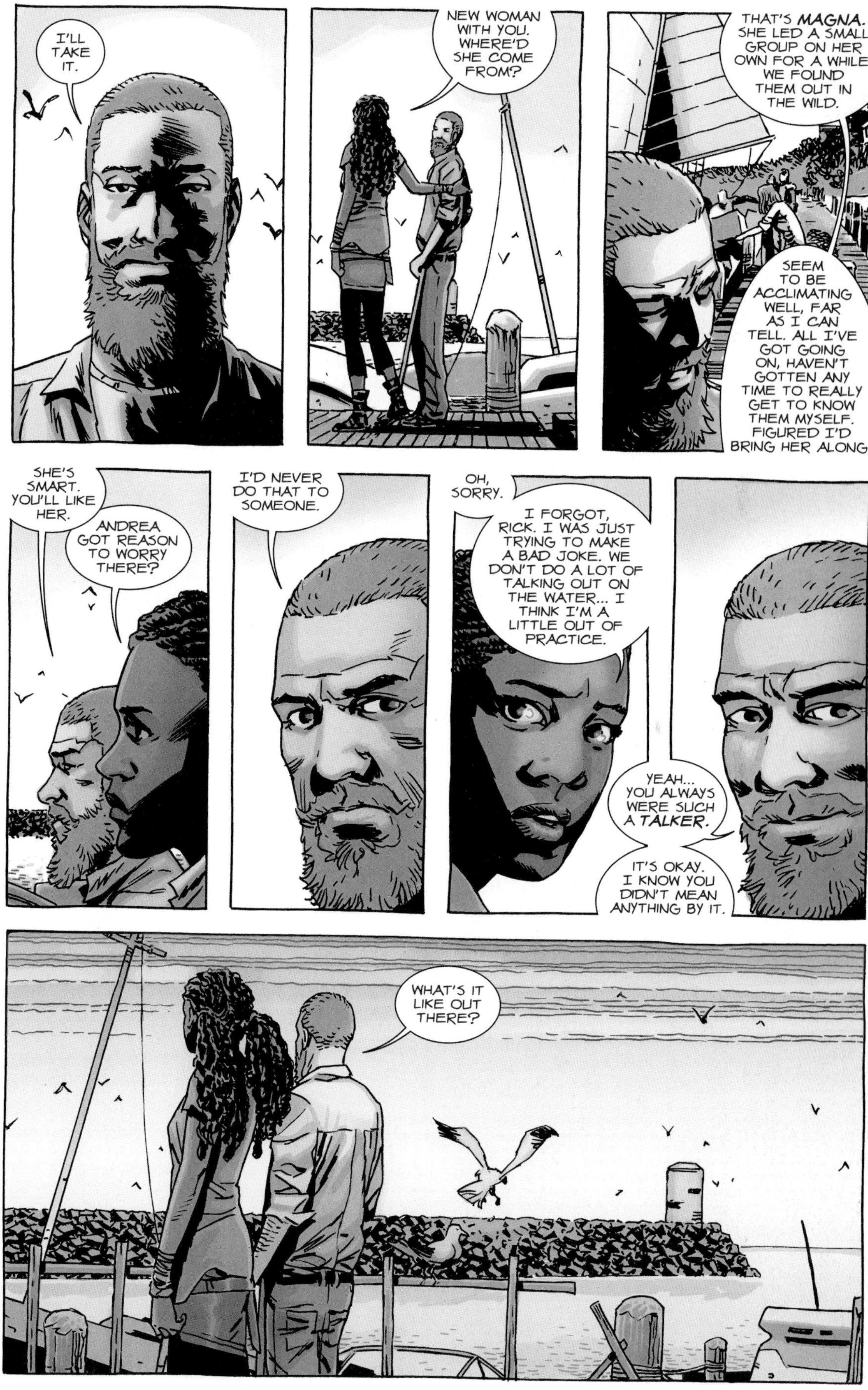
I'LL TAKE IT.
NEW WOMAN WITH YOU. WHERE'D SHE COME FROM?
THAT'S MAGNA. SHE LED A SMALL GROUP ON HER OWN FOR A WHILE. WE FOUND THEM OUT IN THE WILD.
SEEM TO BE ACCLIMATING WELL, FAR AS I CAN TELL. ALL I'VE GOT GOING ON, HAVEN'T GOTTEN ANY TIME TO REALLY GET TO KNOW THEM MYSELF. FIGURED I'D BRING HER ALONG.
SHE'S SMART. YOU'LL LIKE HER.
ANDREA GOT REASON TO WORRY THERE?
I'D NEVER DO THAT TO SOMEONE.
OH, SORRY.
I FORGOT, RICK. I WAS JUST TRYING TO MAKE A BAD JOKE. WE DON'T DO A LOT OF TALKING OUT ON THE WATER... I THINK I'M A LITTLE OUT OF PRACTICE.
YEAH... YOU ALWAYS WERE SUCH A TALKER.
IT'S OKAY. I KNOW YOU DIDN'T MEAN ANYTHING BY IT.
WHAT'S IT LIKE OUT THERE?

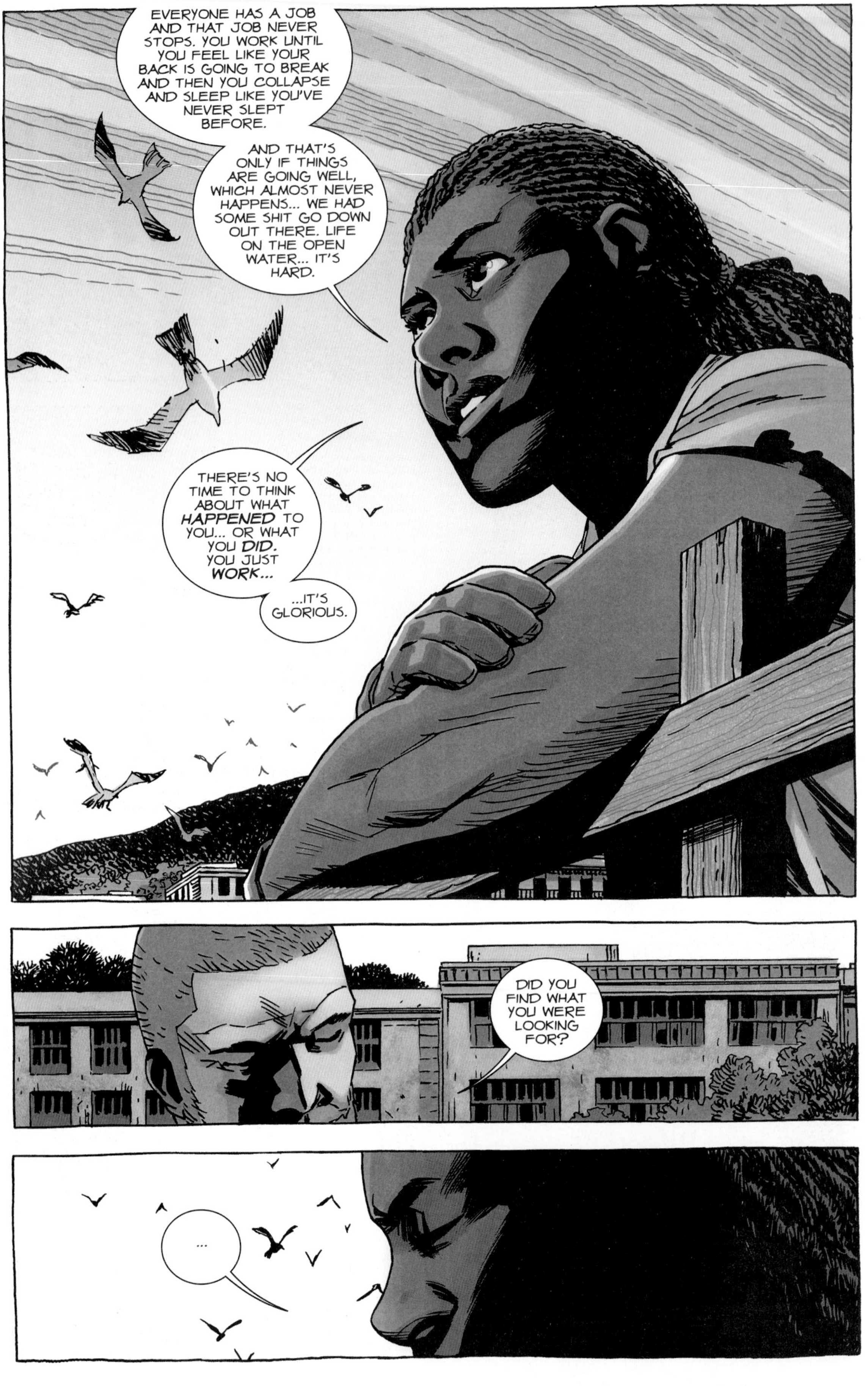
EVERYONE HAS A JOB AND THAT JOB NEVER STOPS. YOU WORK UNTIL YOU FEEL LIKE YOUR BACK IS GOING TO BREAK AND THEN YOU COLLAPSE AND SLEEP LIKE YOU'VE NEVER SLEPT BEFORE.
AND THAT'S ONLY IF THINGS ARE GOING WELL, WHICH ALMOST NEVER HAPPENS... WE HAD SOME SHIT GO DOWN OUT THERE. LIFE ON THE OPEN WATER... IT'S HARD.
THERE'S NO TIME TO THINK ABOUT WHAT HAPPENED TO YOU... OR WHAT YOU DID. YOU JUST WORK...
...IT'S GLORIOUS.
DID YOU FIND WHAT YOU WERE LOOKING FOR?
...

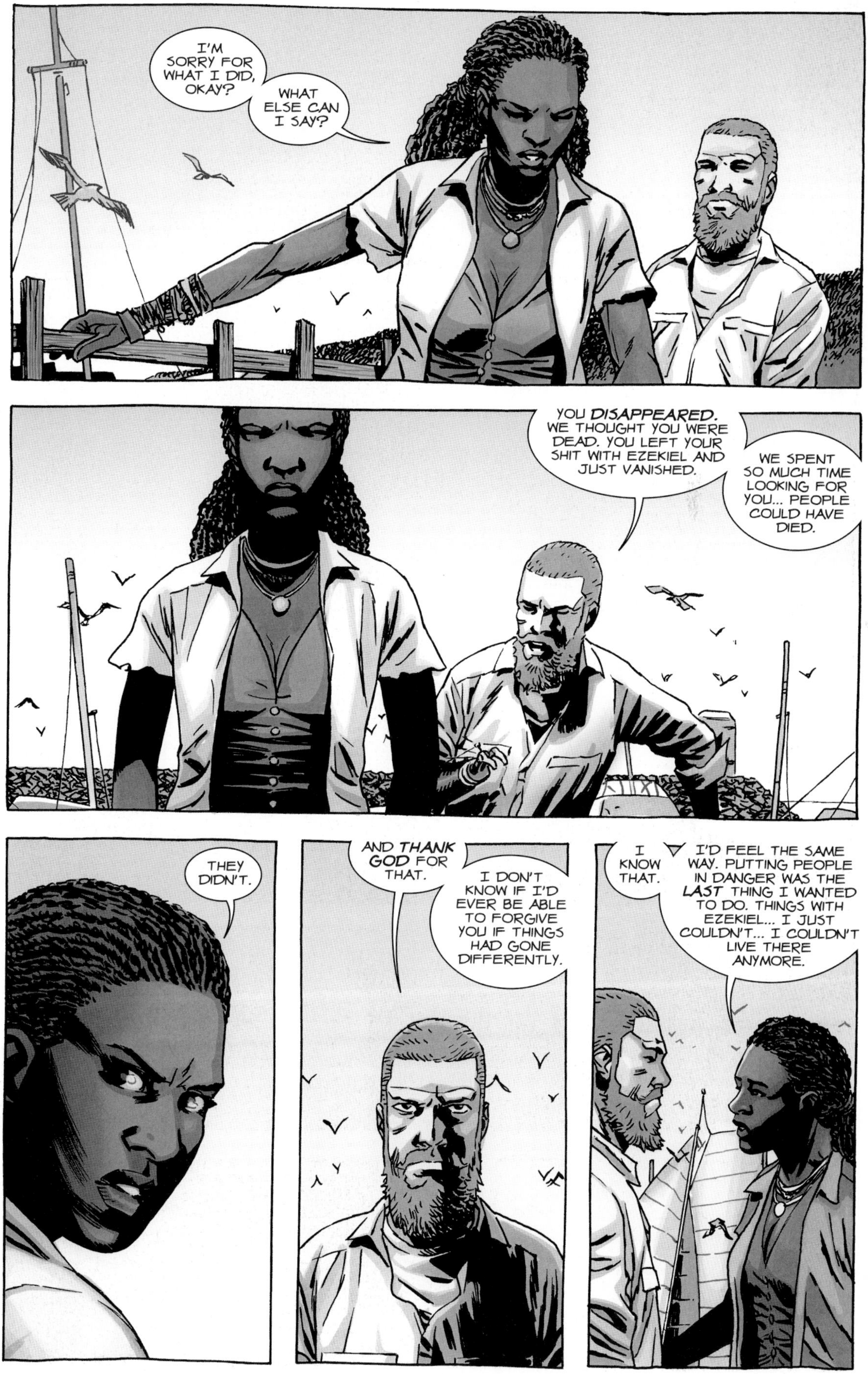

I'M SORRY FOR WHAT I DID, OKAY?
WHAT ELSE CAN I SAY?
YOU DISAPPEARED. WE THOUGHT YOU WERE DEAD. YOU LEFT YOUR SHIT WITH EZEKIEL AND JUST VANISHED.
WE SPENT SO MUCH TIME LOOKING FOR YOU... PEOPLE COULD HAVE DIED.
THEY DIDN'T.
AND THANK GOD FOR THAT.
I DON'T KNOW IF I'D EVER BE ABLE TO FORGIVE YOU IF THINGS HAD GONE DIFFERENTLY.
I KNOW THAT.
I'D FEEL THE SAME WAY. PUTTING PEOPLE IN DANGER WAS THE LAST THING I WANTED TO DO. THINGS WITH EZEKIEL... I JUST COULDN'T... I COULDN'T LIVE THERE ANYMORE.

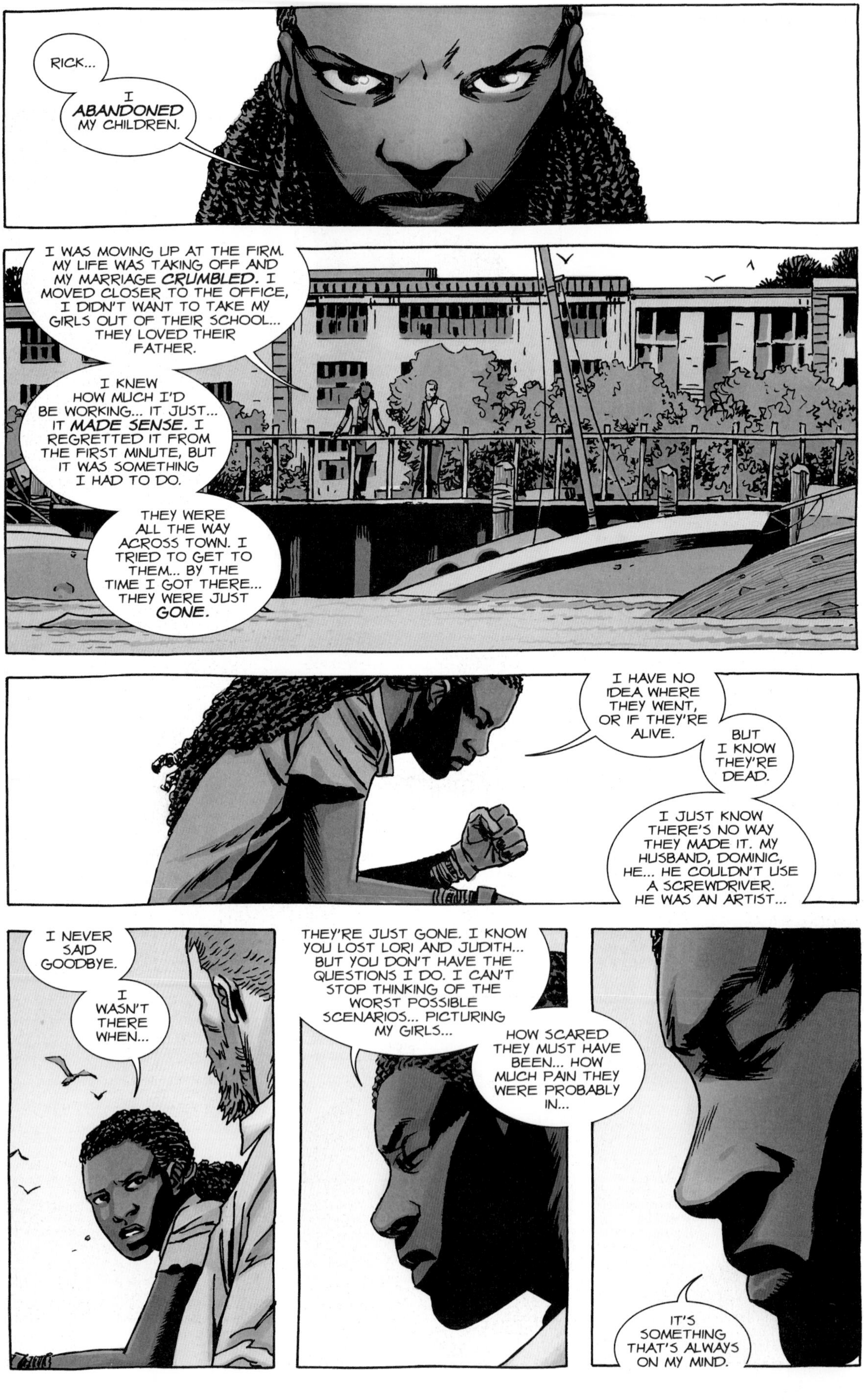
RICK...
I ABANDONED MY CHILDREN.
I WAS MOVING UP AT THE FIRM. MY LIFE WAS TAKING OFF AND MY MARRIAGE CRUMBLED. I MOVED CLOSER TO THE OFFICE, I DIDN'T WANT TO TAKE MY GIRLS OUT OF THEIR SCHOOL... THEY LOVED THEIR FATHER.
I KNEW HOW MUCH I'D BE WORKING... IT JUST... IT MADE SENSE. I REGRETTED IT FROM THE FIRST MINUTE, BUT IT WAS SOMETHING I HAD TO DO.
THEY WERE ALL THE WAY ACROSS TOWN. I TRIED TO GET TO THEM... BY THE TIME I GOT THERE... THEY WERE JUST GONE.
I HAVE NO IDEA WHERE THEY WENT, OR IF THEY'RE ALIVE.
BUT I KNOW THEY'RE DEAD.
I JUST KNOW THERE'S NO WAY THEY MADE IT. MY HUSBAND, DOMINIC, HE... HE COULDN'T USE A SCREWDRIVER. HE WAS AN ARTIST...
I NEVER SAID GOODBYE.
I WASN'T THERE WHEN...
THEY'RE JUST GONE. I KNOW YOU LOST LORI AND JUDITH... BUT YOU DON'T HAVE THE QUESTIONS I DO. I CAN'T STOP THINKING OF THE WORST POSSIBLE SCENARIOS... PICTURING MY GIRLS...
HOW SCARED THEY MUST HAVE BEEN... HOW MUCH PAIN THEY WERE PROBABLY IN...
IT'S SOMETHING THAT'S ALWAYS ON MY MIND.

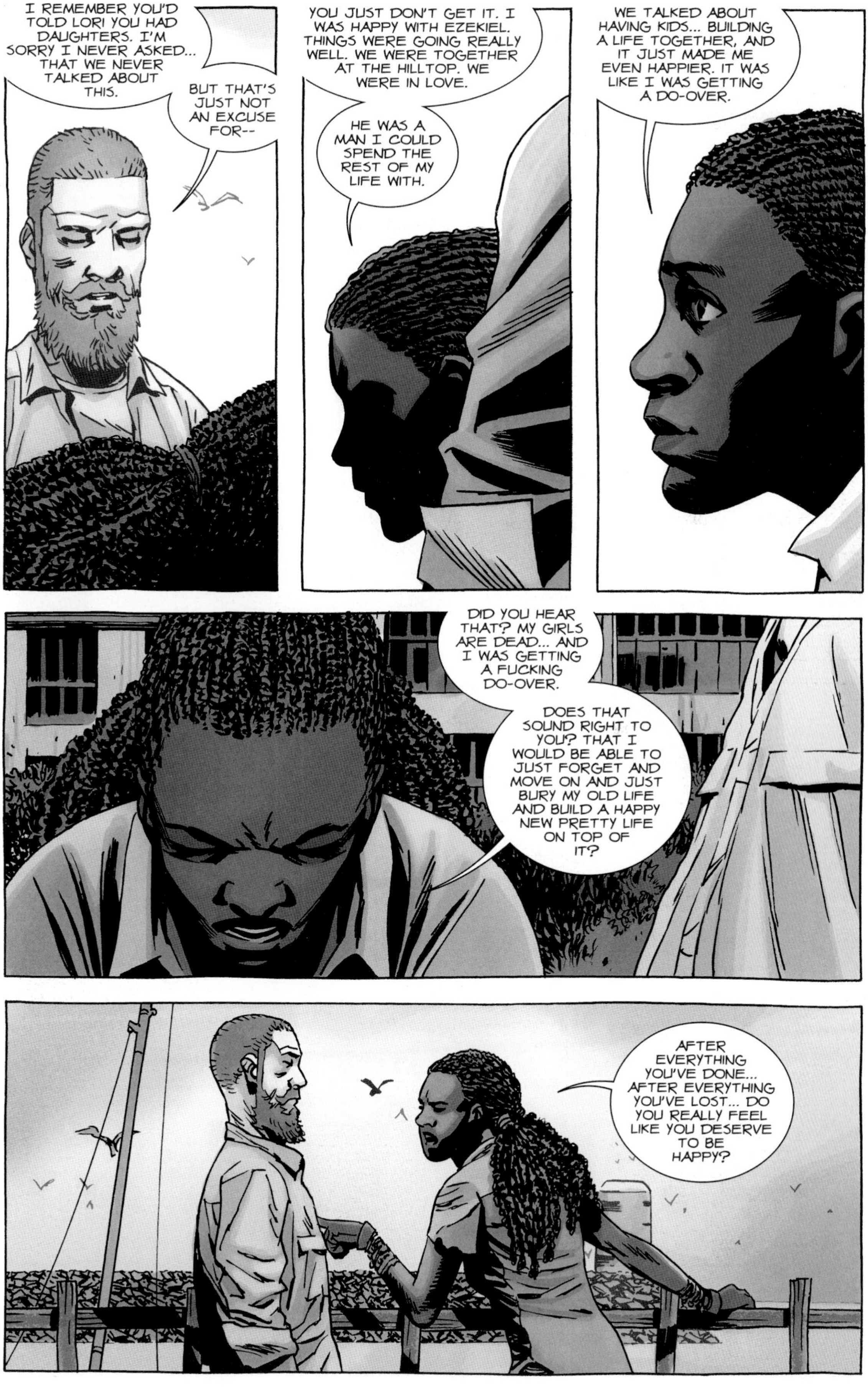
I REMEMBER YOU'D TOLD LORI YOU HAD DAUGHTERS. I'M SORRY I NEVER ASKED... THAT WE NEVER TALKED ABOUT THIS.
BUT THAT'S JUST NOT AN EXCUSE FOR--
YOU JUST DON'T GET IT. I WAS HAPPY WITH EZEKIEL. THINGS WERE GOING REALLY WELL. WE WERE TOGETHER AT THE HILLTOP. WE WERE IN LOVE.
HE WAS A MAN I COULD SPEND THE REST OF MY LIFE WITH.
WE TALKED ABOUT HAVING KIDS... BUILDING A LIFE TOGETHER, AND IT JUST MADE ME EVEN HAPPIER. IT WAS LIKE I WAS GETTING A DO-OVER.
DID YOU HEAR THAT? MY GIRLS ARE DEAD... AND I WAS GETTING A FUCKING DO-OVER.
DOES THAT SOUND RIGHT TO YOU? THAT I WOULD BE ABLE TO JUST FORGET AND MOVE ON AND JUST BURY MY OLD LIFE AND BUILD A HAPPY NEW PRETTY LIFE ON TOP OF IT?
AFTER EVERYTHING YOU'VE DONE... AFTER EVERYTHING YOU'VE LOST... DO YOU REALLY FEEL LIKE YOU DESERVE TO BE HAPPY?

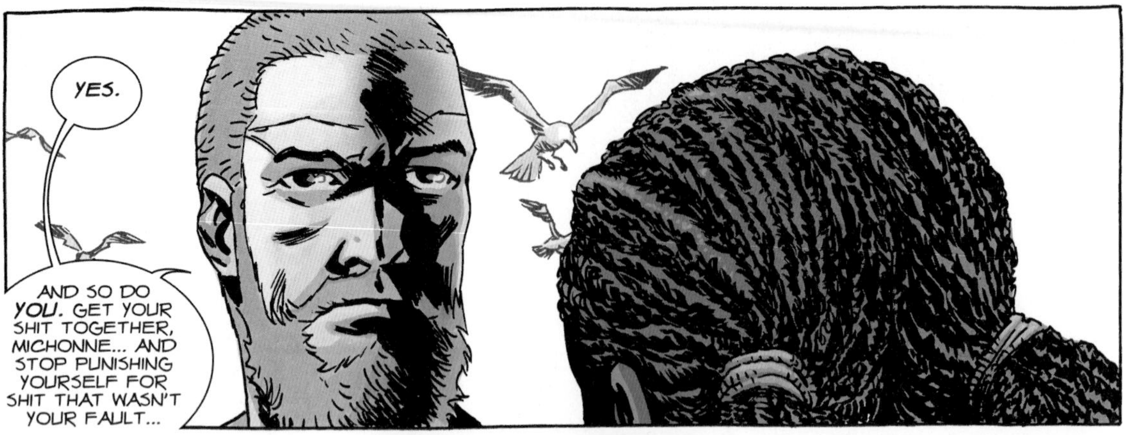
YES.
AND SO DO *YOU.* GET YOUR SHIT TOGETHER, MICHONNE... AND STOP PUNISHING YOURSELF FOR SHIT THAT WASN'T YOUR FAULT...

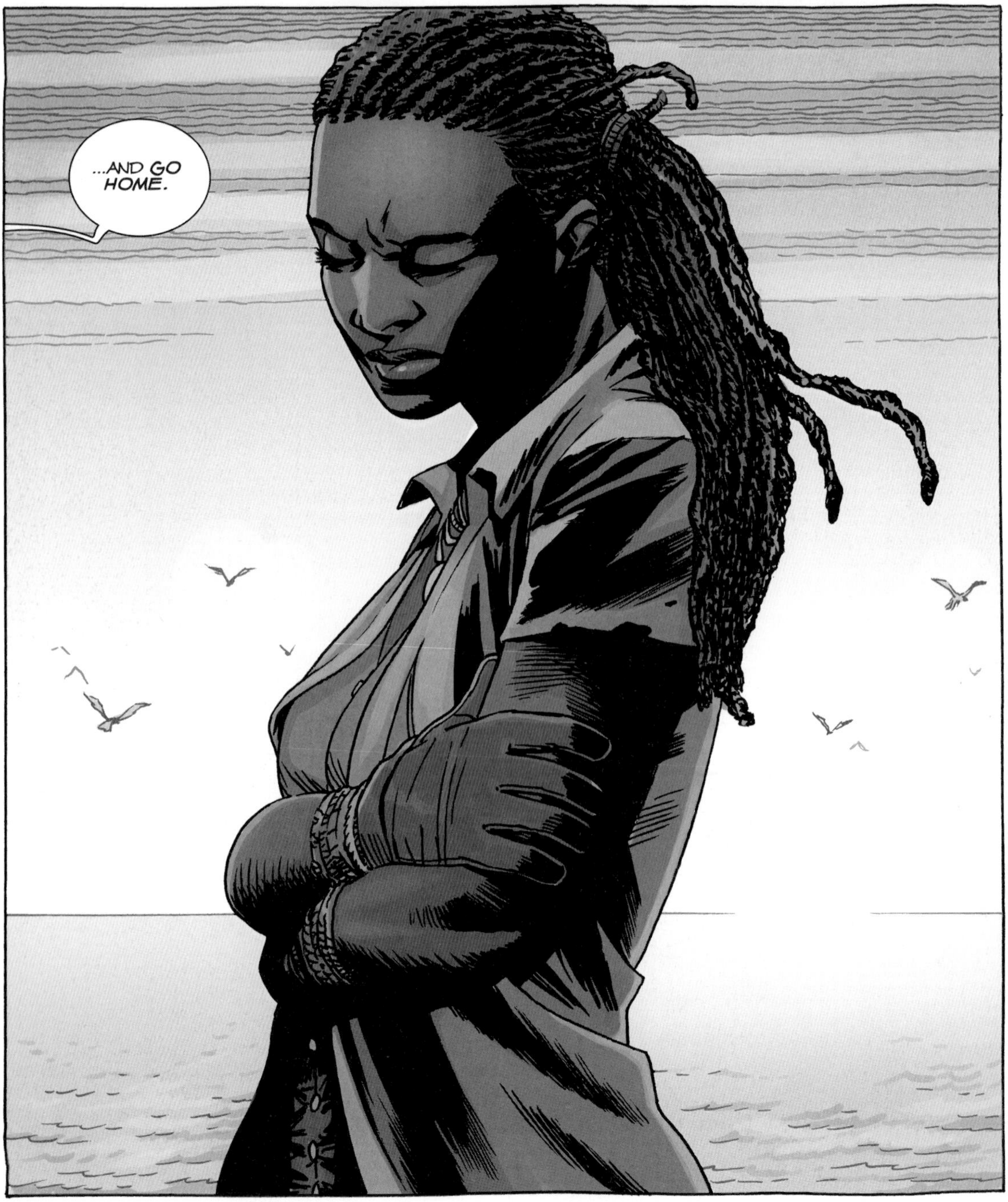
...AND *GO HOME.*

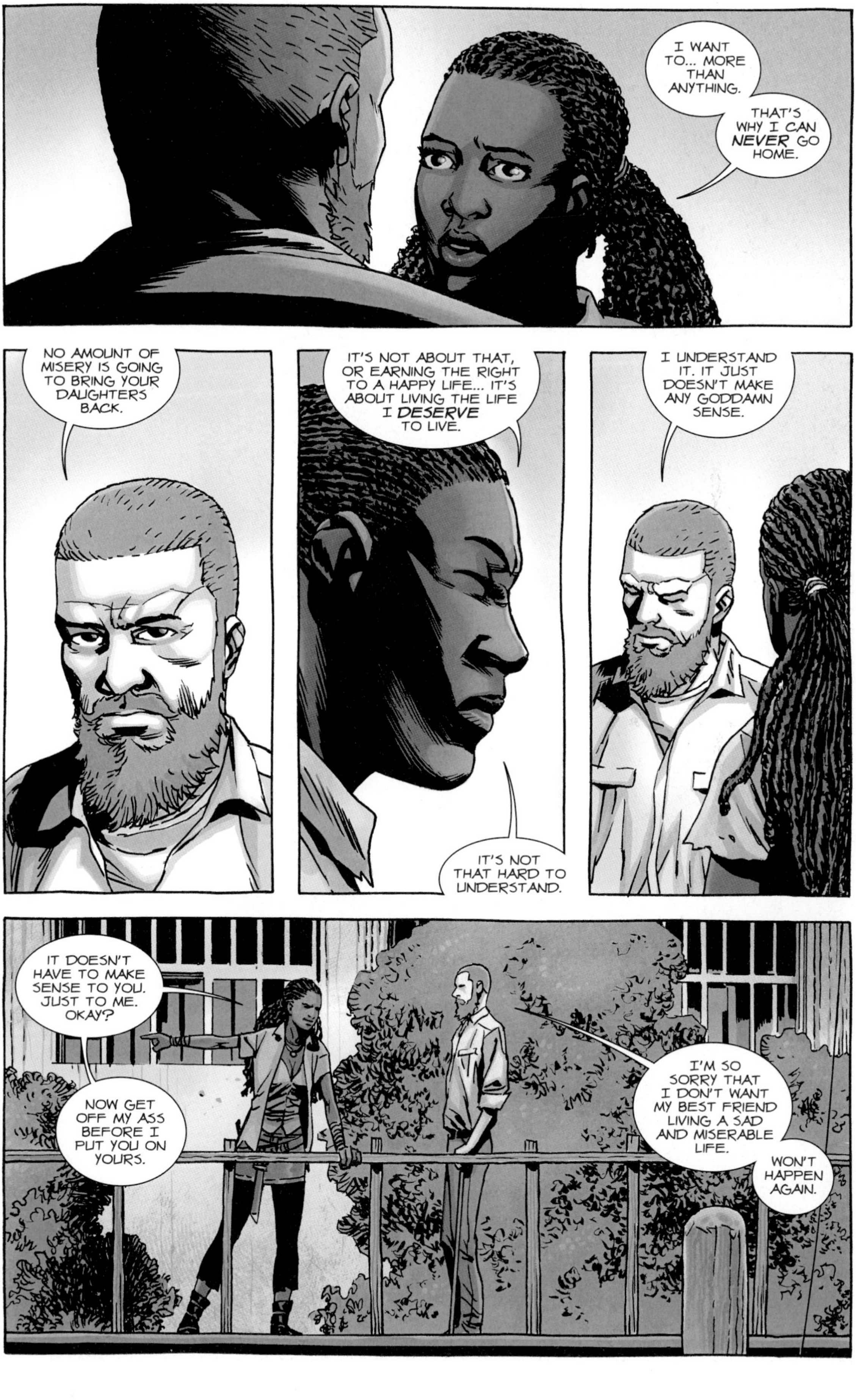
I WANT TO... MORE THAN ANYTHING.
THAT'S WHY I CAN NEVER GO HOME.
NO AMOUNT OF MISERY IS GOING TO BRING YOUR DAUGHTERS BACK.
IT'S NOT ABOUT THAT, OR EARNING THE RIGHT TO A HAPPY LIFE... IT'S ABOUT LIVING THE LIFE I DESERVE TO LIVE.
IT'S NOT THAT HARD TO UNDERSTAND.
I UNDERSTAND IT. IT JUST DOESN'T MAKE ANY GODDAMN SENSE.
IT DOESN'T HAVE TO MAKE SENSE TO YOU. JUST TO ME. OKAY?
NOW GET OFF MY ASS BEFORE I PUT YOU ON YOURS.
I'M SO SORRY THAT I DON'T WANT MY BEST FRIEND LIVING A SAD AND MISERABLE LIFE.
WON'T HAPPEN AGAIN.

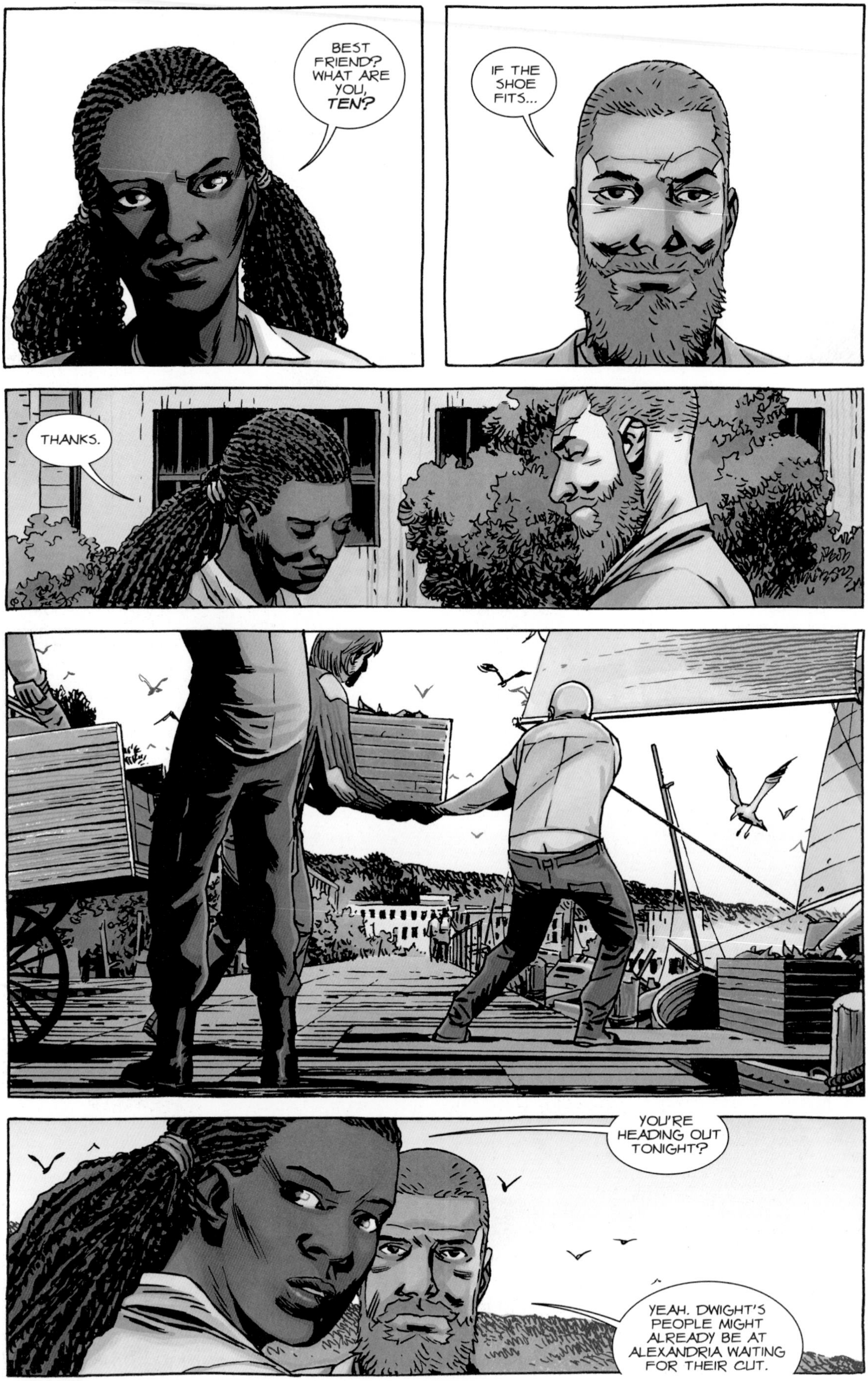
BEST FRIEND? WHAT ARE YOU, *TEN?*
IF THE SHOE FITS...
THANKS.
YOU'RE HEADING OUT TONIGHT?
YEAH. DWIGHT'S PEOPLE MIGHT ALREADY BE AT ALEXANDRIA WAITING FOR THEIR CUT.

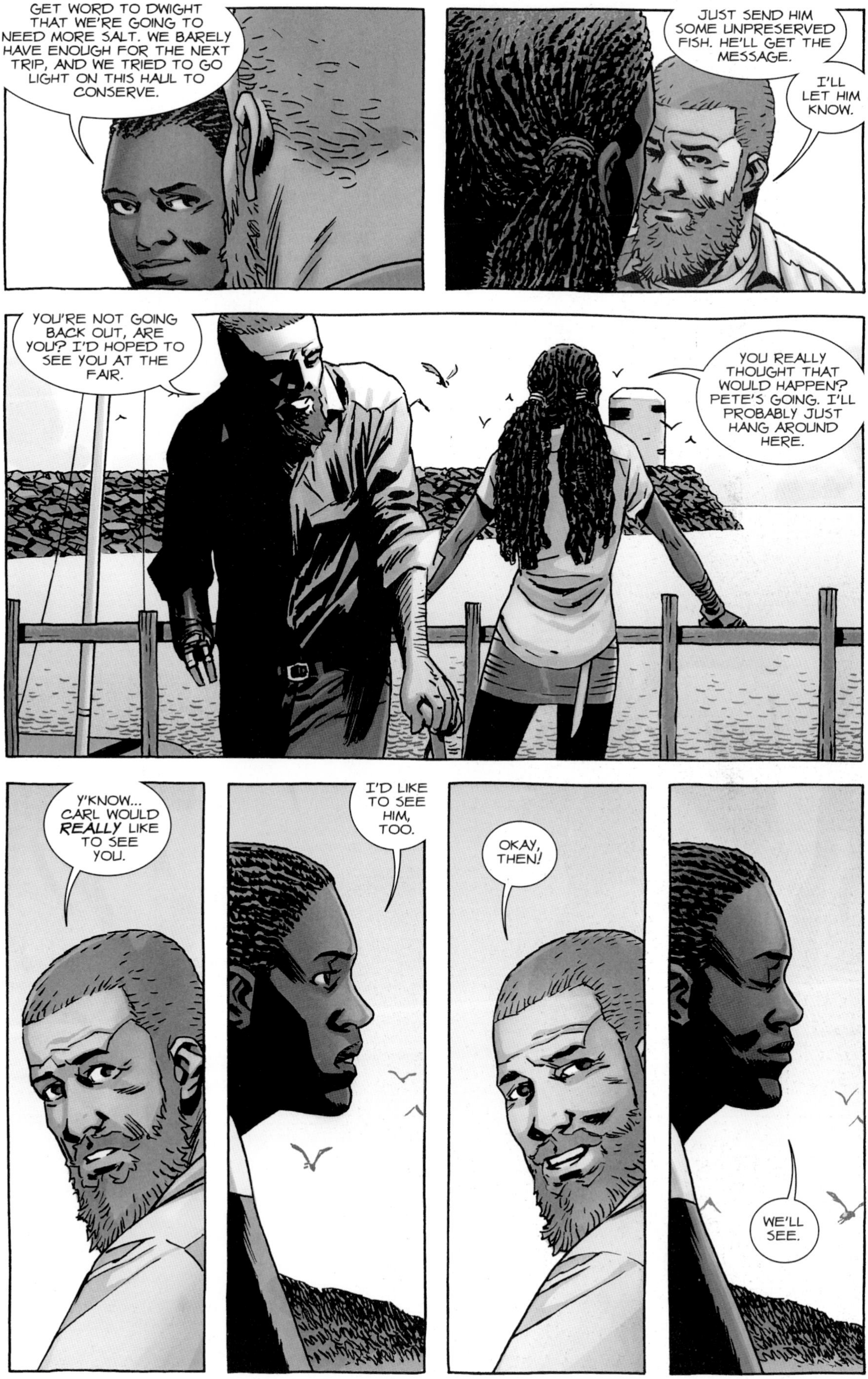

GET WORD TO DWIGHT THAT WE'RE GOING TO NEED MORE SALT. WE BARELY HAVE ENOUGH FOR THE NEXT TRIP, AND WE TRIED TO GO LIGHT ON THIS HAUL TO CONSERVE.
JUST SEND HIM SOME UNPRESERVED FISH. HE'LL GET THE MESSAGE.
I'LL LET HIM KNOW.
YOU'RE NOT GOING BACK OUT, ARE YOU? I'D HOPED TO SEE YOU AT THE FAIR.
YOU REALLY THOUGHT THAT WOULD HAPPEN? PETE'S GOING. I'LL PROBABLY JUST HANG AROUND HERE.
Y'KNOW... CARL WOULD *REALLY* LIKE TO SEE YOU.
I'D LIKE TO SEE HIM, TOO.
OKAY, THEN!
WE'LL SEE.

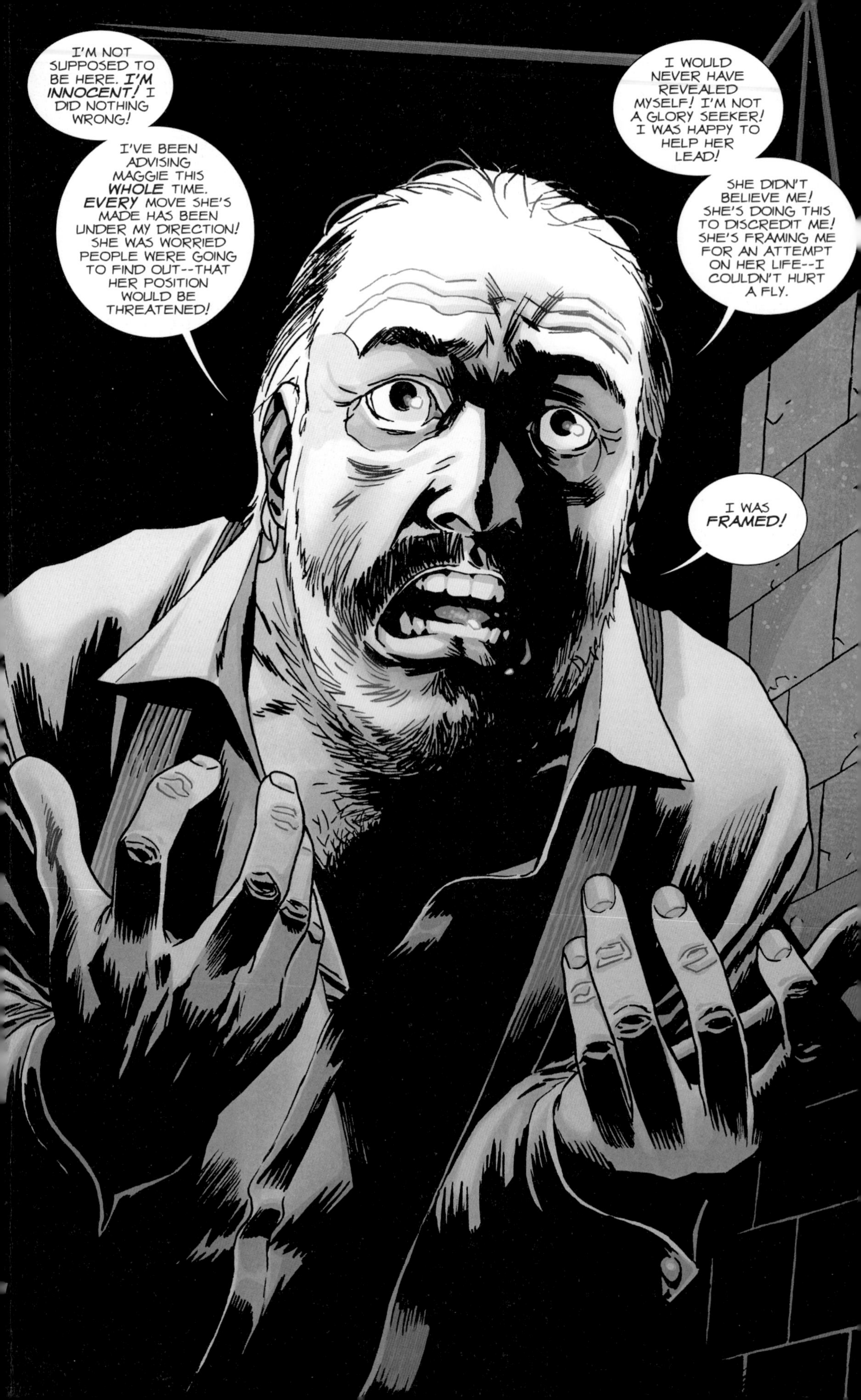
I'M NOT SUPPOSED TO BE HERE. I'M INNOCENT! I DID NOTHING WRONG!
I'VE BEEN ADVISING MAGGIE THIS WHOLE TIME. EVERY MOVE SHE'S MADE HAS BEEN UNDER MY DIRECTION! SHE WAS WORRIED PEOPLE WERE GOING TO FIND OUT--THAT HER POSITION WOULD BE THREATENED!
I WOULD NEVER HAVE REVEALED MYSELF! I'M NOT A GLORY SEEKER! I WAS HAPPY TO HELP HER LEAD!
SHE DIDN'T BELIEVE ME! SHE'S DOING THIS TO DISCREDIT ME! SHE'S FRAMING ME FOR AN ATTEMPT ON HER LIFE--I COULDN'T HURT A FLY.
I WAS FRAMED!

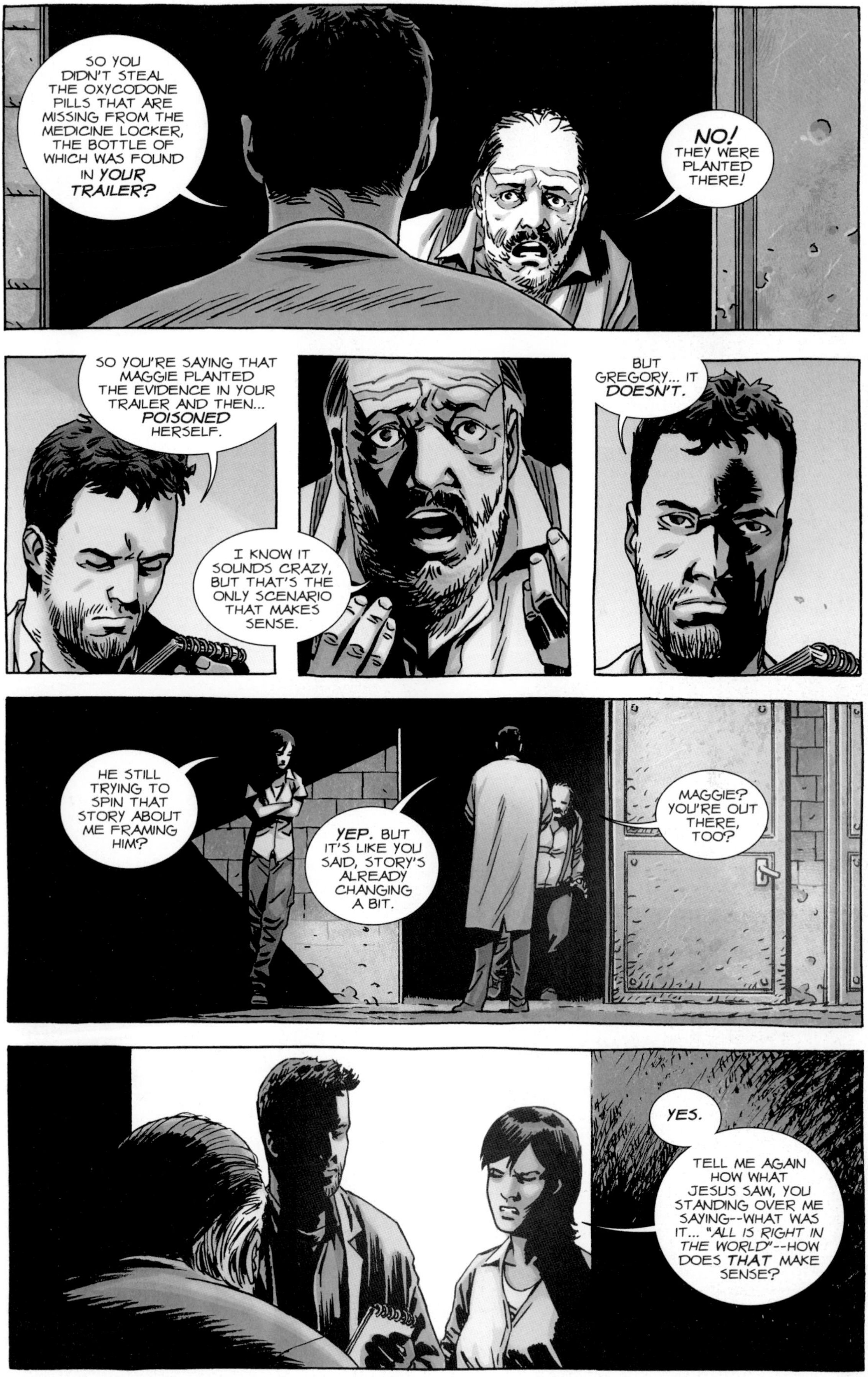
SO YOU DIDN'T STEAL THE OXYCODONE PILLS THAT ARE MISSING FROM THE MEDICINE LOCKER, THE BOTTLE OF WHICH WAS FOUND IN YOUR TRAILER?
NO! THEY WERE PLANTED THERE!
SO YOU'RE SAYING THAT MAGGIE PLANTED THE EVIDENCE IN YOUR TRAILER AND THEN... POISONED HERSELF.
I KNOW IT SOUNDS CRAZY, BUT THAT'S THE ONLY SCENARIO THAT MAKES SENSE.
BUT GREGORY... IT DOESN'T.
HE STILL TRYING TO SPIN THAT STORY ABOUT ME FRAMING HIM?
YEP. BUT IT'S LIKE YOU SAID, STORY'S ALREADY CHANGING A BIT.
MAGGIE? YOU'RE OUT THERE, TOO?
YES.
TELL ME AGAIN HOW WHAT JESUS SAW, YOU STANDING OVER ME SAYING--WHAT WAS IT... "ALL IS RIGHT IN THE WORLD"--HOW DOES THAT MAKE SENSE?

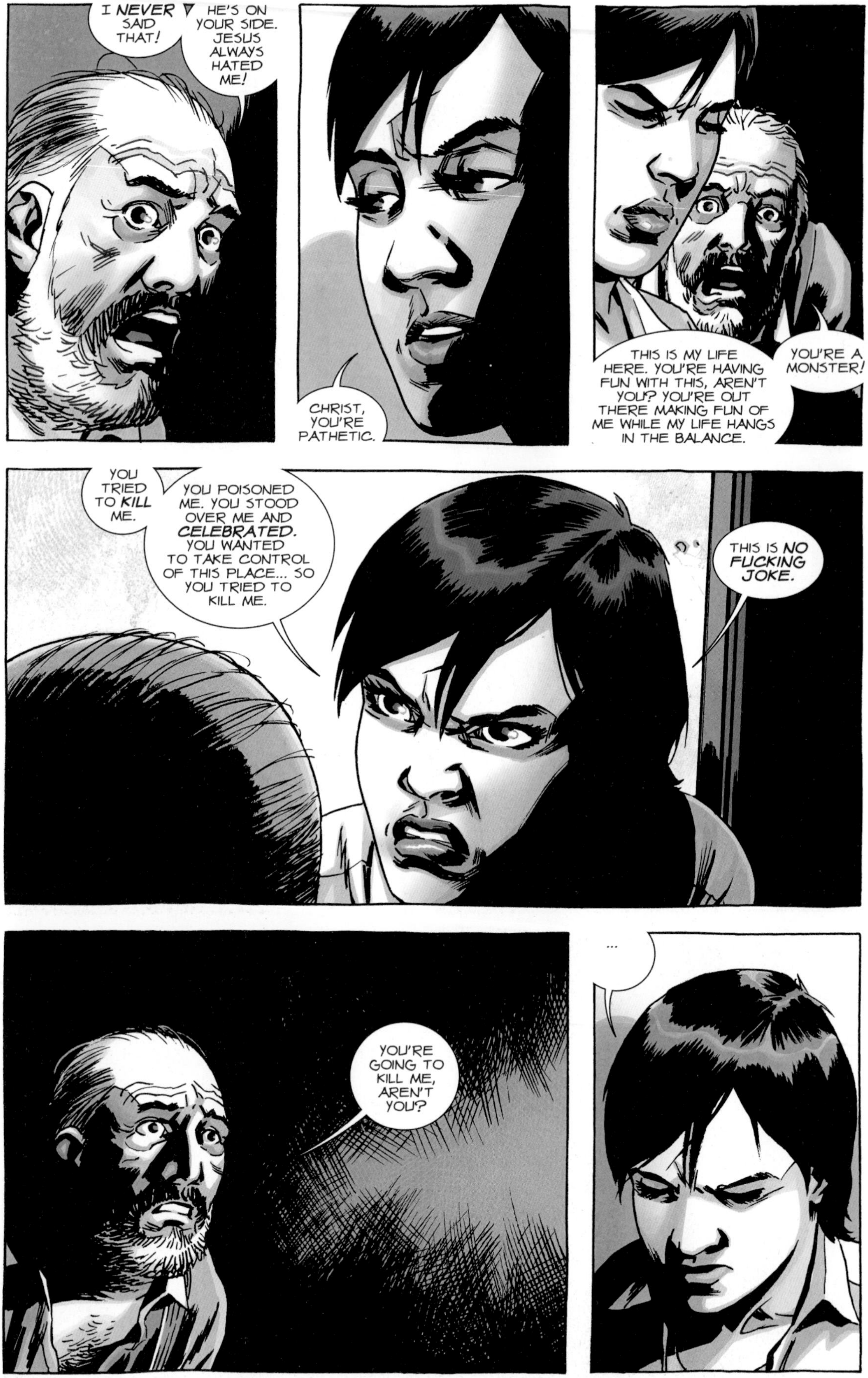
I NEVER SAID THAT!
HE'S ON YOUR SIDE. JESUS ALWAYS HATED ME!
CHRIST, YOU'RE PATHETIC.
THIS IS MY LIFE HERE. YOU'RE HAVING FUN WITH THIS, AREN'T YOU? YOU'RE OUT THERE MAKING FUN OF ME WHILE MY LIFE HANGS IN THE BALANCE.
YOU'RE A MONSTER!
YOU TRIED TO KILL ME.
YOU POISONED ME. YOU STOOD OVER ME AND CELEBRATED. YOU WANTED TO TAKE CONTROL OF THIS PLACE... SO YOU TRIED TO KILL ME.
THIS IS NO FUCKING JOKE.
YOU'RE GOING TO KILL ME, AREN'T YOU?
...

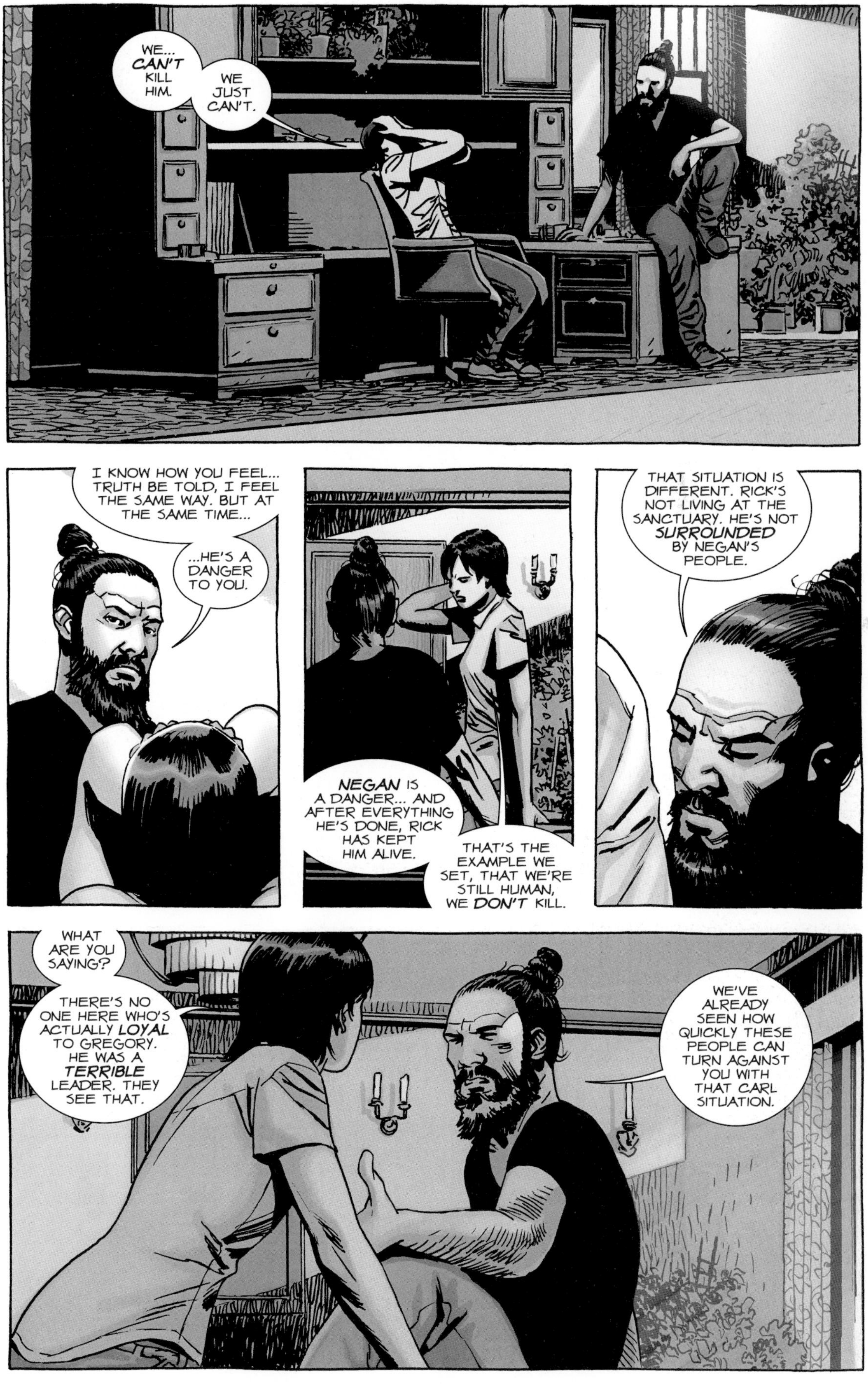
WE... CAN'T KILL HIM.
WE JUST CAN'T.
I KNOW HOW YOU FEEL... TRUTH BE TOLD, I FEEL THE SAME WAY. BUT AT THE SAME TIME...
...HE'S A DANGER TO YOU.
NEGAN IS A DANGER... AND AFTER EVERYTHING HE'S DONE, RICK HAS KEPT HIM ALIVE.
THAT'S THE EXAMPLE WE SET, THAT WE'RE STILL HUMAN, WE DON'T KILL.
THAT SITUATION IS DIFFERENT. RICK'S NOT LIVING AT THE SANCTUARY. HE'S NOT SURROUNDED BY NEGAN'S PEOPLE.
WHAT ARE YOU SAYING?
THERE'S NO ONE HERE WHO'S ACTUALLY LOYAL TO GREGORY. HE WAS A TERRIBLE LEADER. THEY SEE THAT.
WE'VE ALREADY SEEN HOW QUICKLY THESE PEOPLE CAN TURN AGAINST YOU WITH THAT CARL SITUATION.

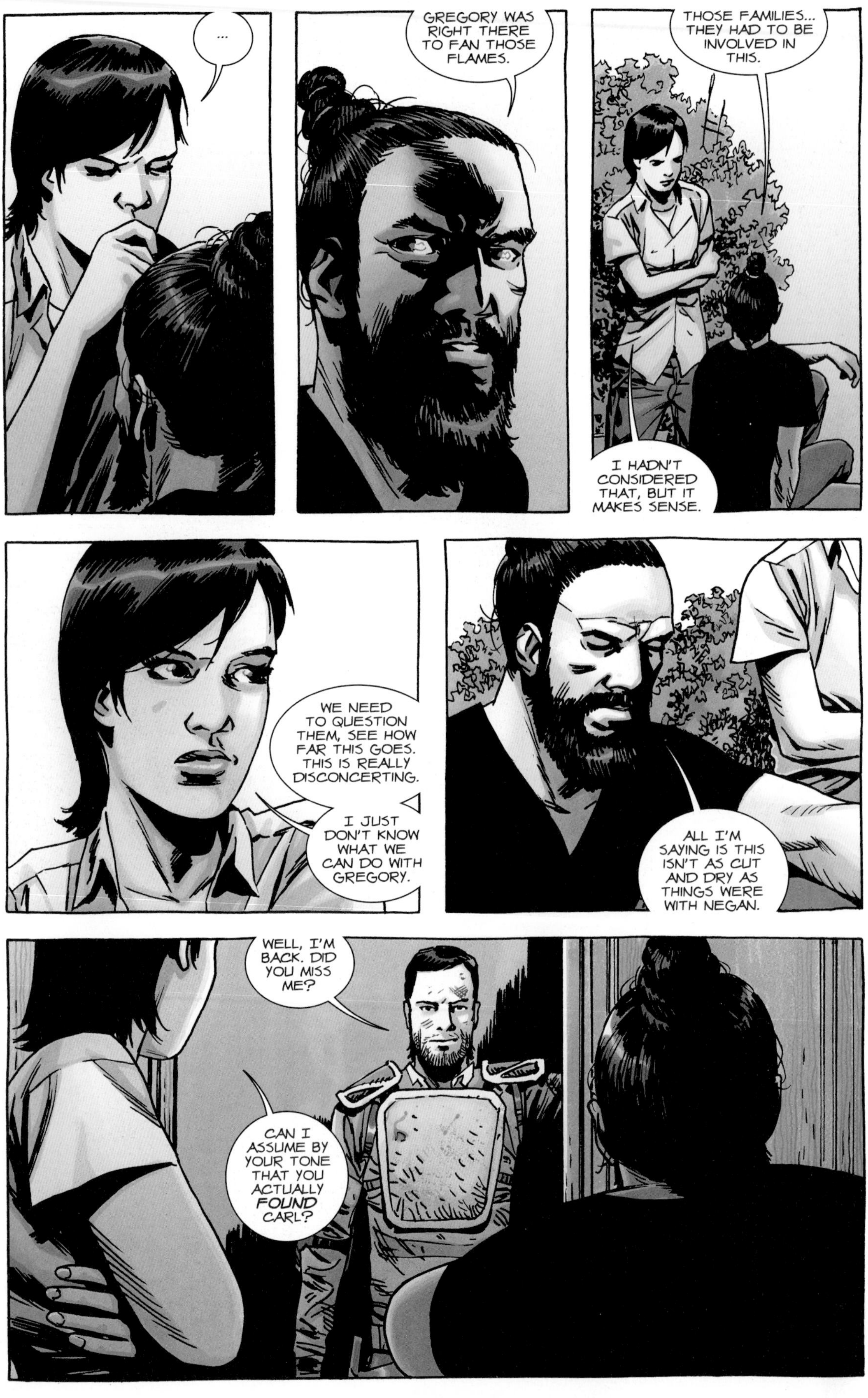
...
GREGORY WAS RIGHT THERE TO FAN THOSE FLAMES.
THOSE FAMILIES... THEY HAD TO BE INVOLVED IN THIS.
I HADN'T CONSIDERED THAT, BUT IT MAKES SENSE.
WE NEED TO QUESTION THEM, SEE HOW FAR THIS GOES. THIS IS REALLY DISCONCERTING.
I JUST DON'T KNOW WHAT WE CAN DO WITH GREGORY.
ALL I'M SAYING IS THIS ISN'T AS CUT AND DRY AS THINGS WERE WITH NEGAN.
WELL, I'M BACK. DID YOU MISS ME?
CAN I ASSUME BY YOUR TONE THAT YOU ACTUALLY FOUND CARL?

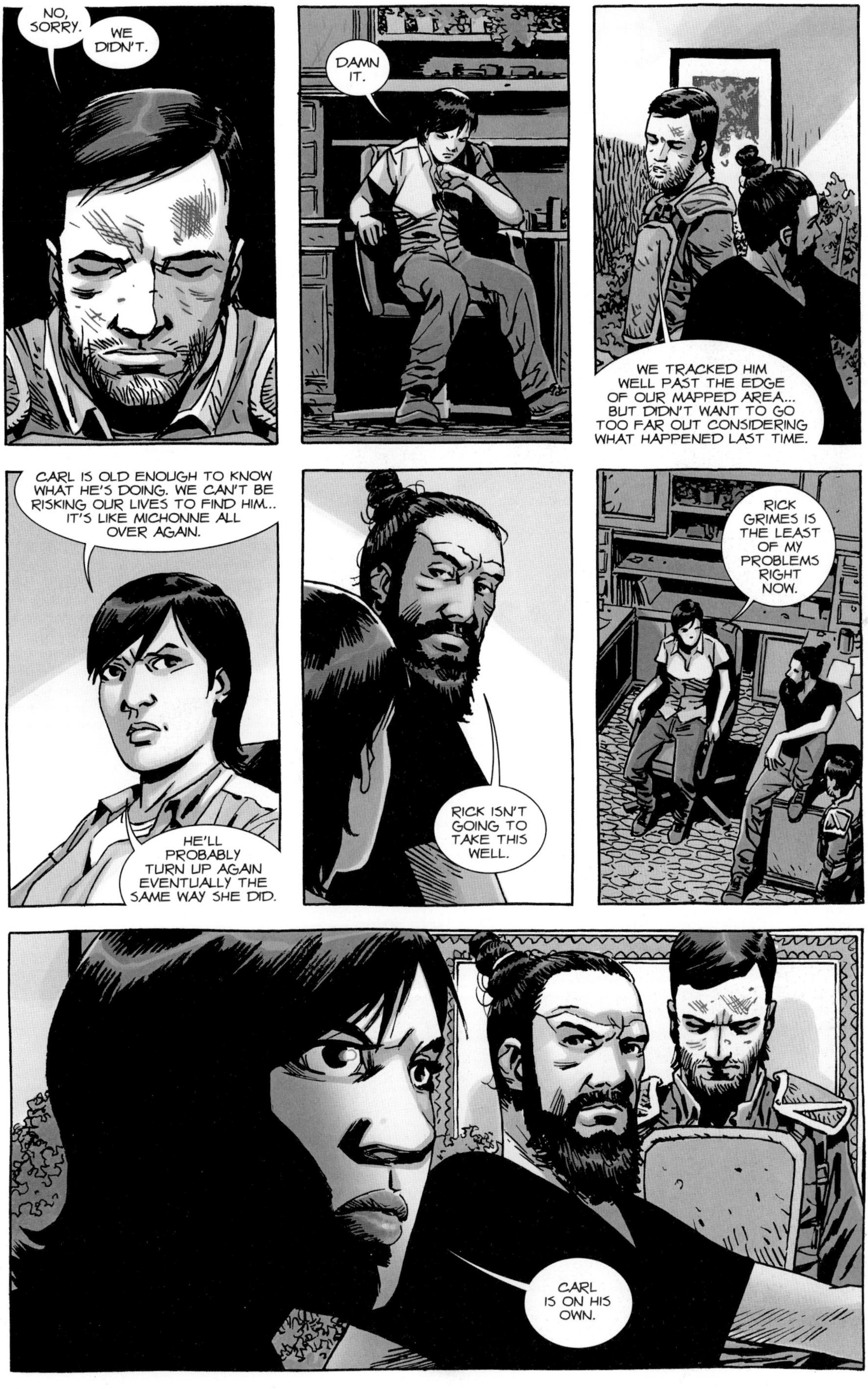
NO, SORRY.
WE DIDN'T.
DAMN IT.
WE TRACKED HIM WELL PAST THE EDGE OF OUR MAPPED AREA... BUT DIDN'T WANT TO GO TOO FAR OUT CONSIDERING WHAT HAPPENED LAST TIME.
CARL IS OLD ENOUGH TO KNOW WHAT HE'S DOING. WE CAN'T BE RISKING OUR LIVES TO FIND HIM... IT'S LIKE MICHONNE ALL OVER AGAIN.
HE'LL PROBABLY TURN UP AGAIN EVENTUALLY THE SAME WAY SHE DID.
RICK ISN'T GOING TO TAKE THIS WELL.
RICK GRIMES IS THE LEAST OF MY PROBLEMS RIGHT NOW.
CARL IS ON HIS OWN.

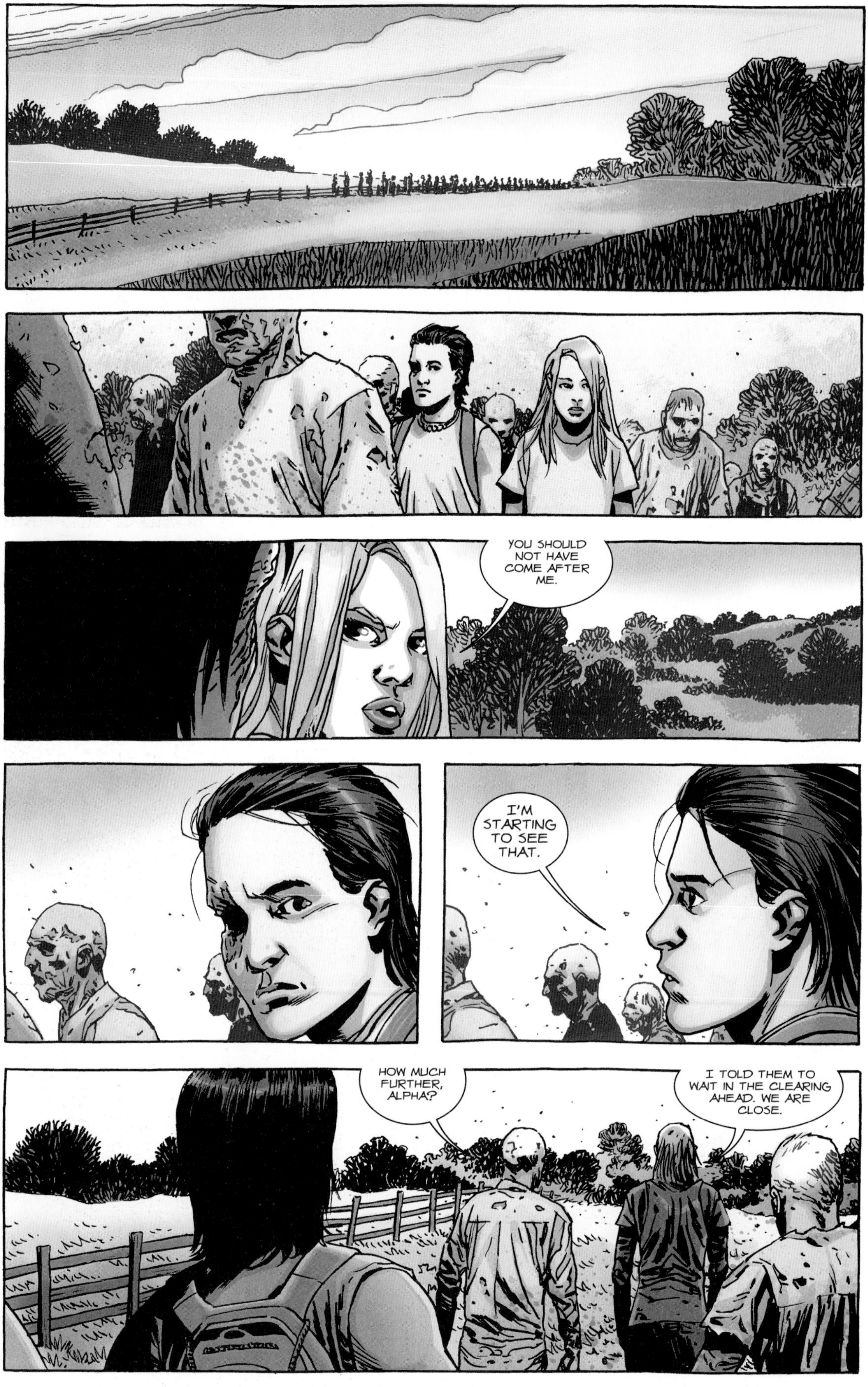
YOU SHOULD NOT HAVE COME AFTER ME.
I'M STARTING TO SEE THAT.
HOW MUCH FURTHER, ALPHA?
I TOLD THEM TO WAIT IN THE CLEARING AHEAD. WE ARE CLOSE.

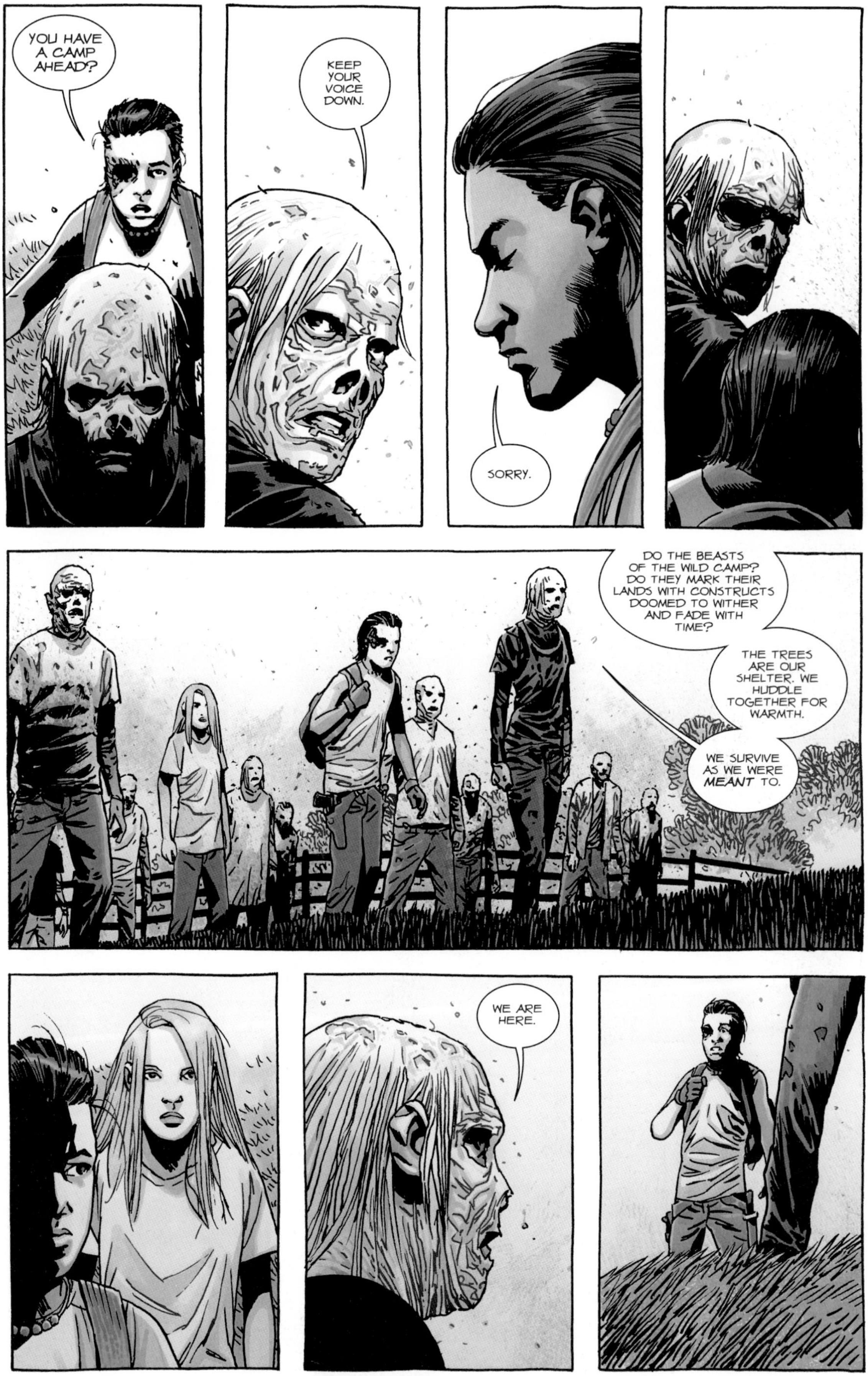
YOU HAVE A CAMP AHEAD?
KEEP YOUR VOICE DOWN.
SORRY.
DO THE BEASTS OF THE WILD CAMP? DO THEY MARK THEIR LANDS WITH CONSTRUCTS DOOMED TO WITHER AND FADE WITH TIME?
THE TREES ARE OUR SHELTER. WE HUDDLE TOGETHER FOR WARMTH.
WE SURVIVE AS WE WERE *MEANT* TO.
WE ARE HERE.

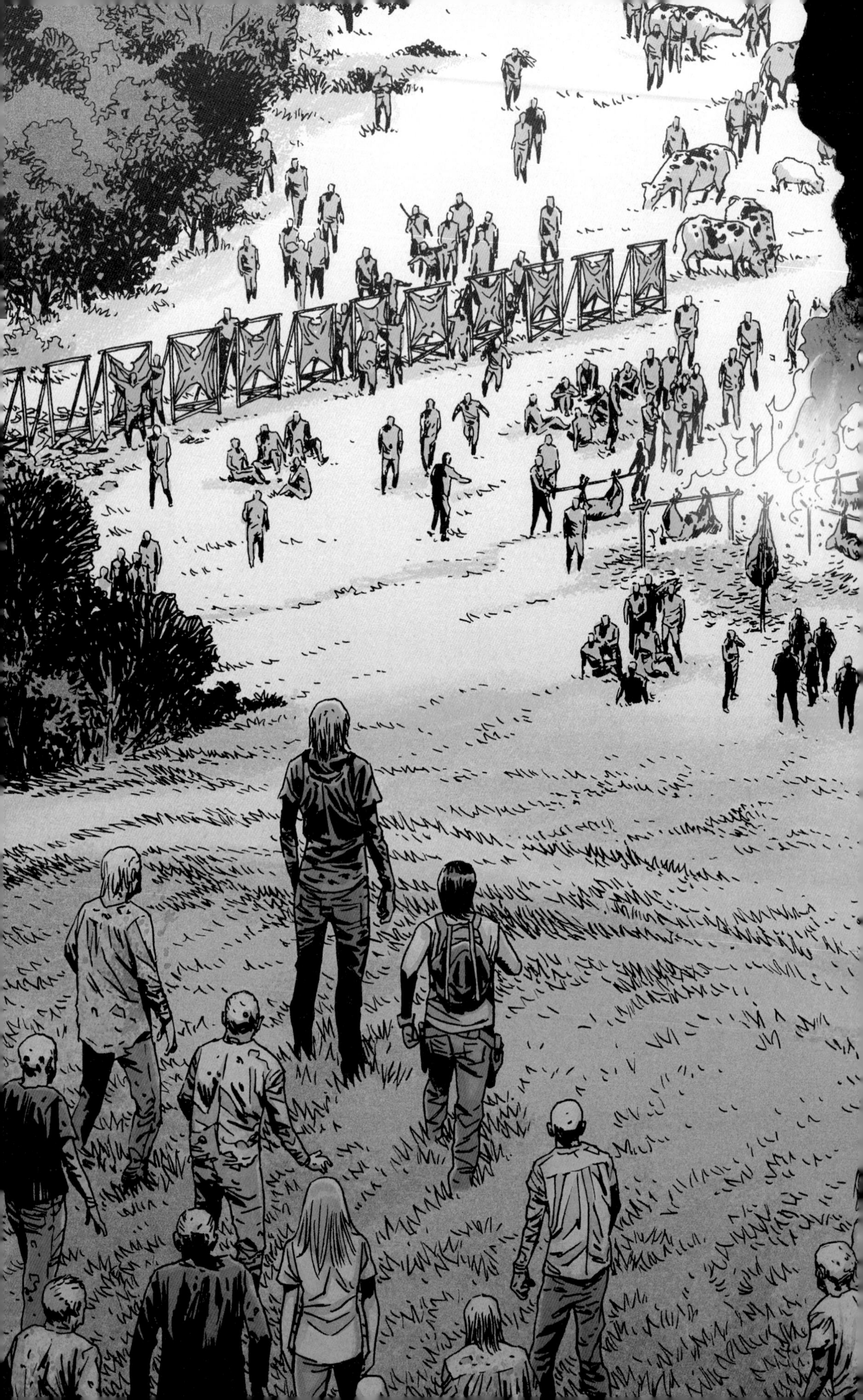

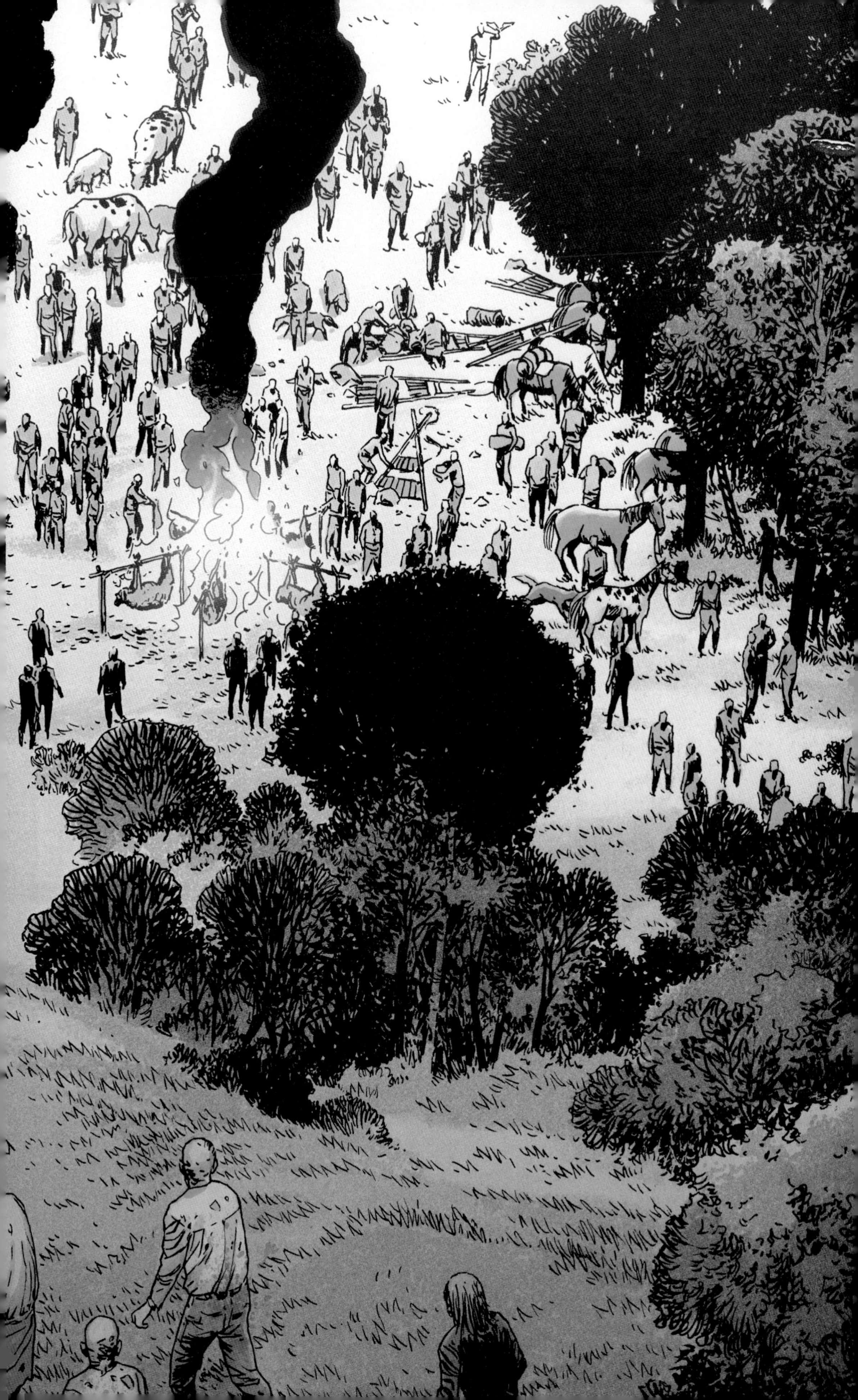

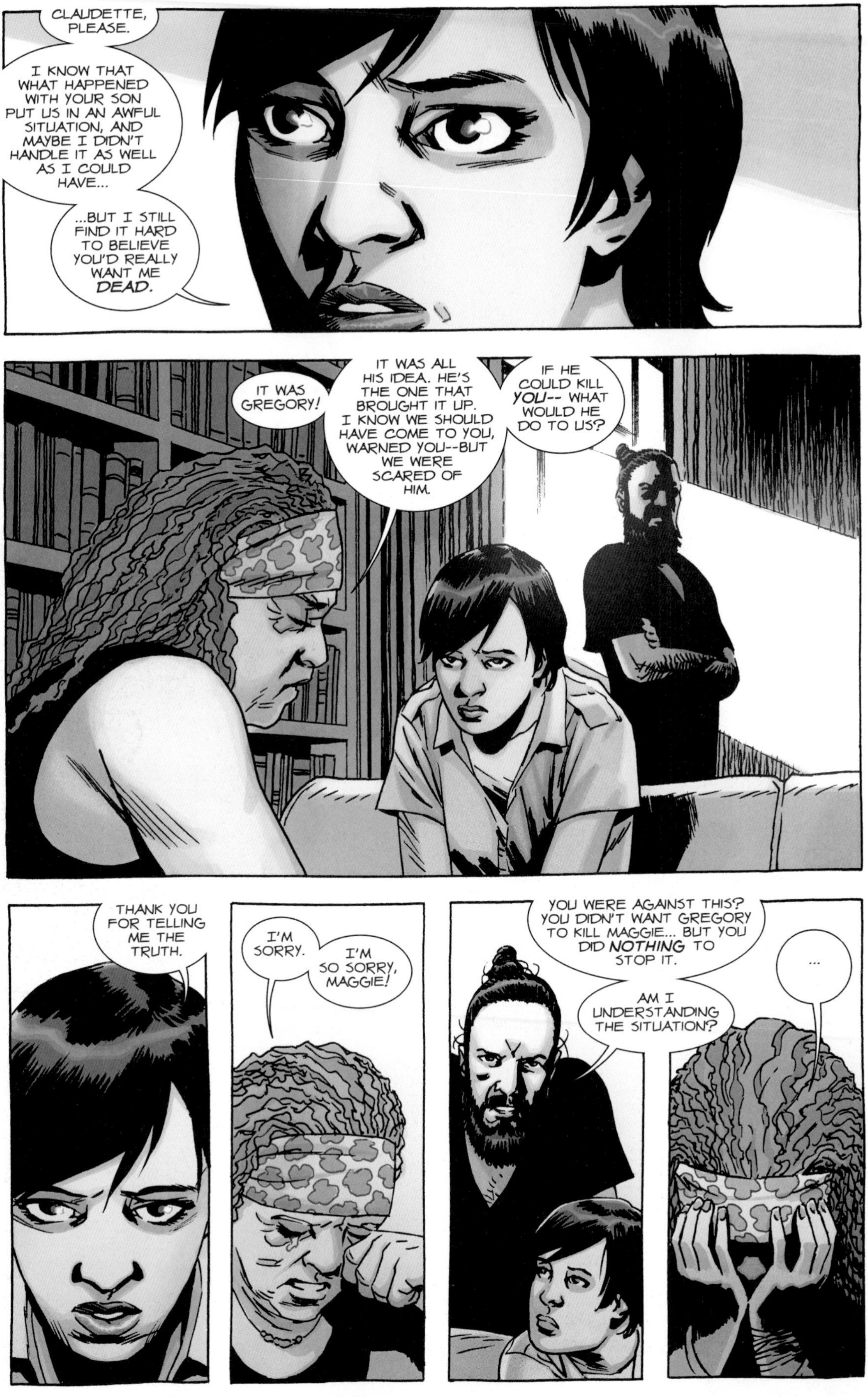
CLAUDETTE, PLEASE.
I KNOW THAT WHAT HAPPENED WITH YOUR SON PUT US IN AN AWFUL SITUATION, AND MAYBE I DIDN'T HANDLE IT AS WELL AS I COULD HAVE...
...BUT I STILL FIND IT HARD TO BELIEVE YOU'D REALLY WANT ME DEAD.
IT WAS GREGORY!
IT WAS ALL HIS IDEA. HE'S THE ONE THAT BROUGHT IT UP. I KNOW WE SHOULD HAVE COME TO YOU, WARNED YOU--BUT WE WERE SCARED OF HIM.
IF HE COULD KILL YOU-- WHAT WOULD HE DO TO US?
THANK YOU FOR TELLING ME THE TRUTH.
I'M SORRY.
I'M SO SORRY, MAGGIE!
YOU WERE AGAINST THIS? YOU DIDN'T WANT GREGORY TO KILL MAGGIE... BUT YOU DID NOTHING TO STOP IT.
AM I UNDERSTANDING THE SITUATION?
...

I WAS ANGRY.

MY SON WAS HURT, YOU WERE ACTING LIKE IT WAS HIS FAULT. I THOUGHT I WAS GOING TO *LOSE* HIM.

SO... I WOULDN'T HAVE BEEN UPSET IF YOU'D DIED.

THAT SOUNDS *AWFUL.*

NO. WHAT I MEAN TO SAY IS IN THE MOMENT, AS ANGRY AS I WAS... I JUST WASN'T THINKING STRAIGHT.

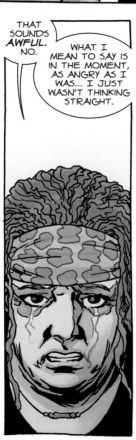

I GET THAT WAY.

ALWAYS HAD A TEMPER.

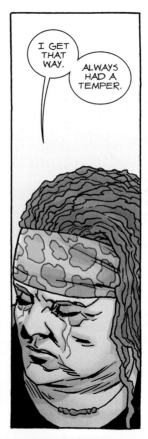

AND YOUR HUSBAND, MORTON? AND THE HARLAN FAMILY?

THEY HAVE THE SAME TEMPER?

WELL...

GREGORY CAN BE REALLY PERSUASIVE.

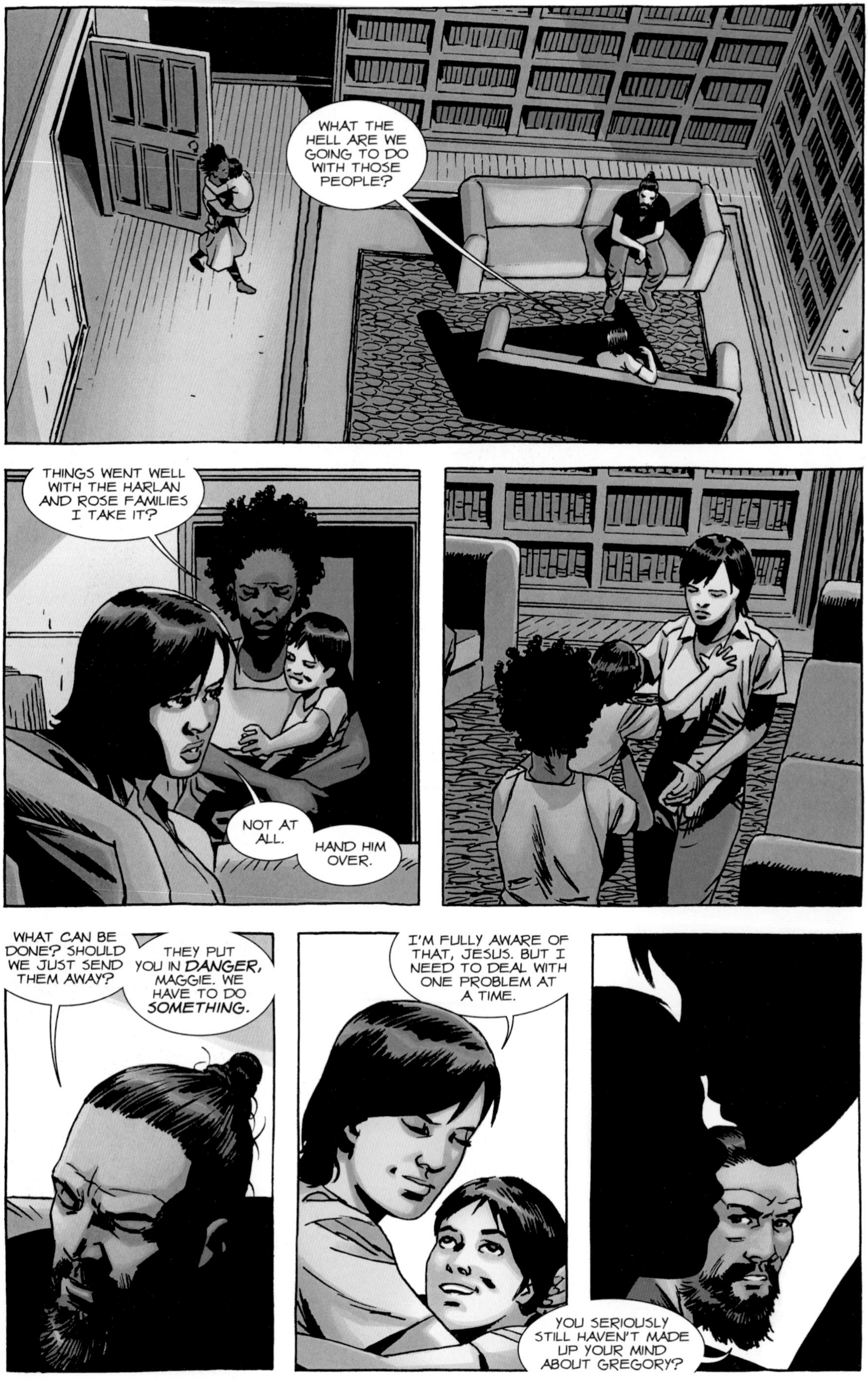
WHAT THE HELL ARE WE GOING TO DO WITH THOSE PEOPLE?
THINGS WENT WELL WITH THE HARLAN AND ROSE FAMILIES I TAKE IT?
NOT AT ALL.
HAND HIM OVER.
WHAT CAN BE DONE? SHOULD WE JUST SEND THEM AWAY?
THEY PUT YOU IN DANGER, MAGGIE. WE HAVE TO DO SOMETHING.
I'M FULLY AWARE OF THAT, JESUS. BUT I NEED TO DEAL WITH ONE PROBLEM AT A TIME.
YOU SERIOUSLY STILL HAVEN'T MADE UP YOUR MIND ABOUT GREGORY?

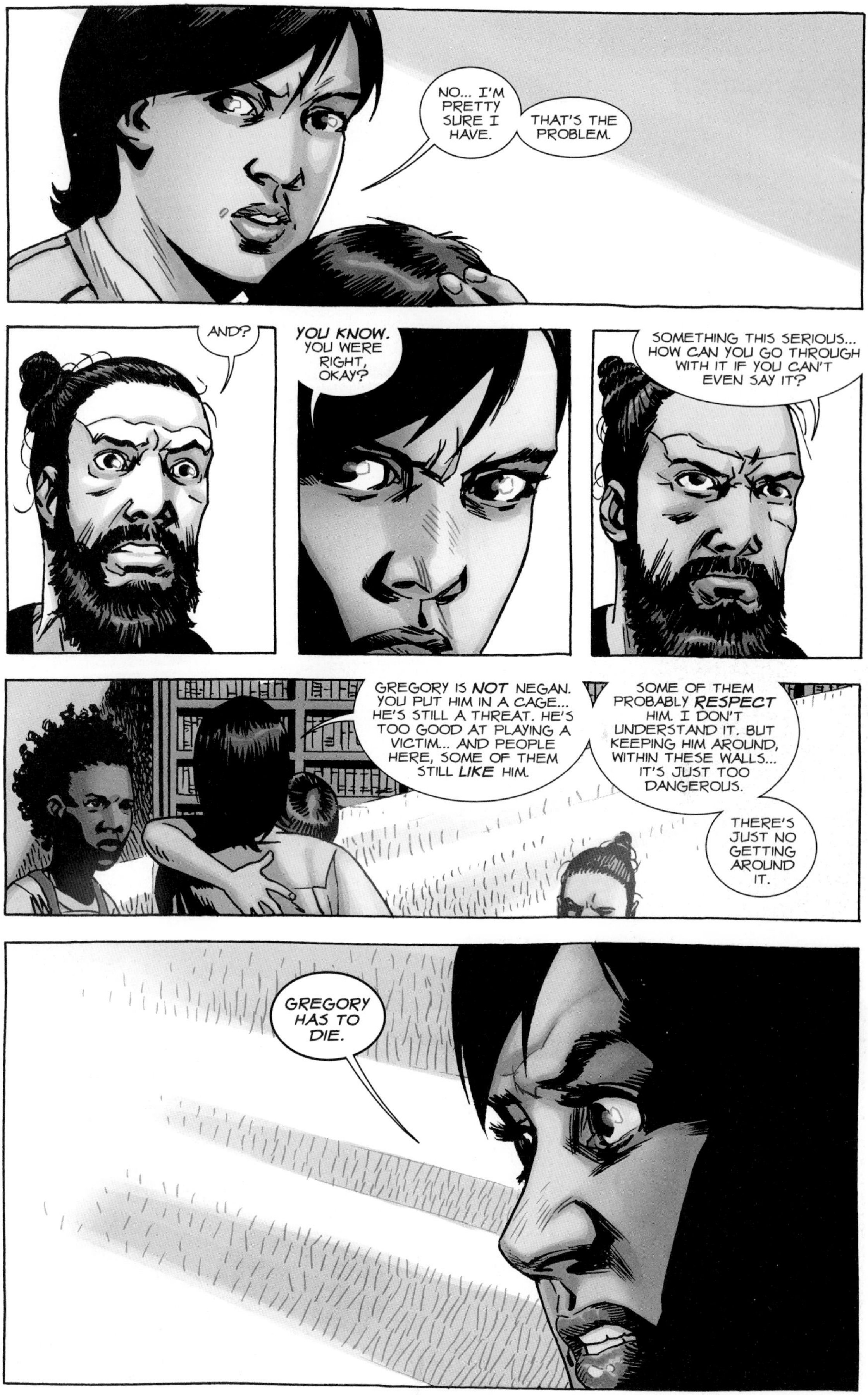
NO... I'M PRETTY SURE I HAVE.
THAT'S THE PROBLEM.
AND?
YOU KNOW. YOU WERE RIGHT, OKAY?
SOMETHING THIS SERIOUS... HOW CAN YOU GO THROUGH WITH IT IF YOU CAN'T EVEN SAY IT?
GREGORY IS NOT NEGAN. YOU PUT HIM IN A CAGE... HE'S STILL A THREAT. HE'S TOO GOOD AT PLAYING A VICTIM... AND PEOPLE HERE, SOME OF THEM STILL LIKE HIM.
SOME OF THEM PROBABLY RESPECT HIM. I DON'T UNDERSTAND IT. BUT KEEPING HIM AROUND, WITHIN THESE WALLS... IT'S JUST TOO DANGEROUS.
THERE'S JUST NO GETTING AROUND IT.
GREGORY HAS TO DIE.

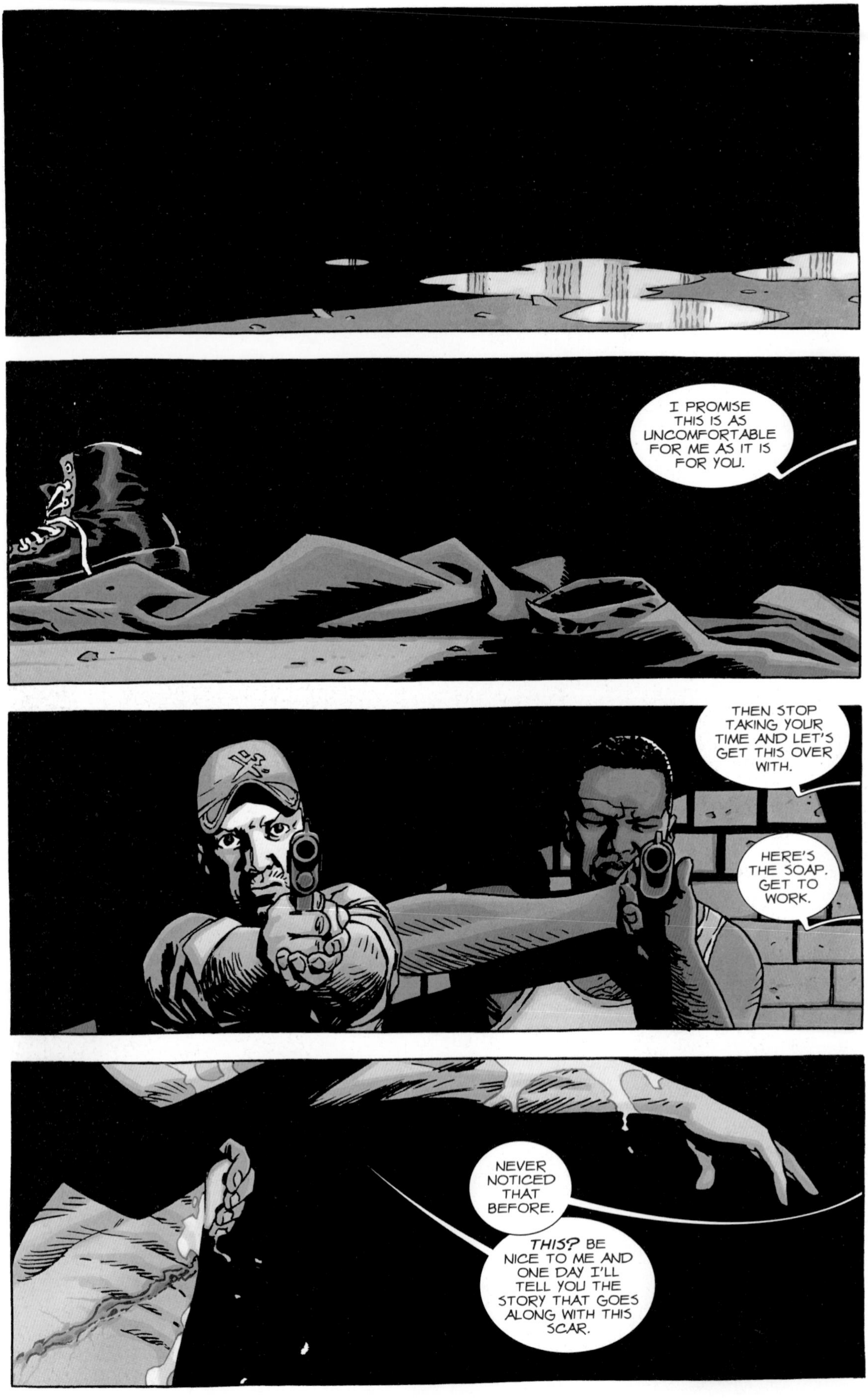
I PROMISE THIS IS AS UNCOMFORTABLE FOR ME AS IT IS FOR YOU.
THEN STOP TAKING YOUR TIME AND LET'S GET THIS OVER WITH.
HERE'S THE SOAP. GET TO WORK.
NEVER NOTICED THAT BEFORE.
THIS? BE NICE TO ME AND ONE DAY I'LL TELL YOU THE STORY THAT GOES ALONG WITH THIS SCAR.

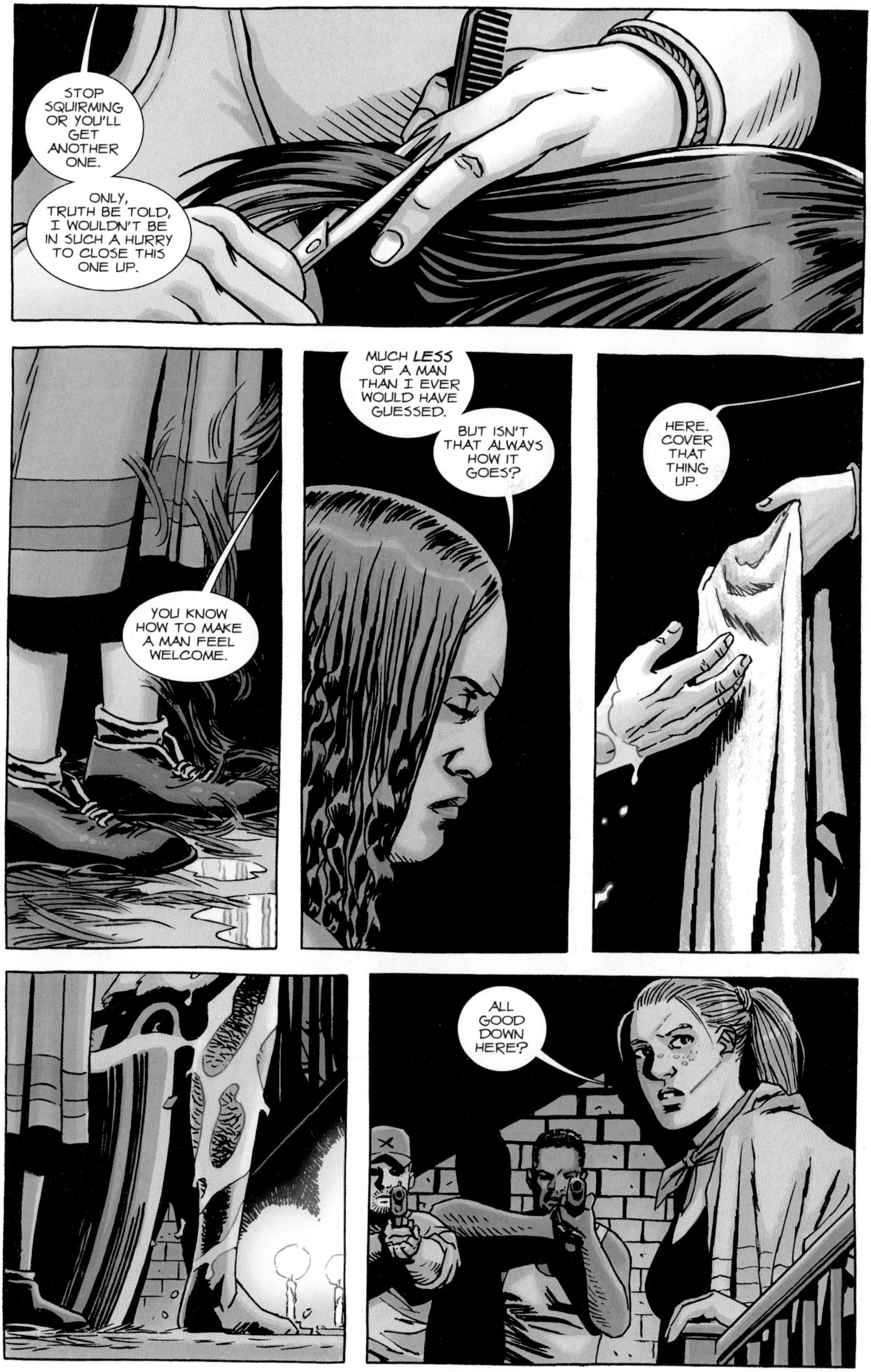
STOP SQUIRMING OR YOU'LL GET ANOTHER ONE.
ONLY, TRUTH BE TOLD, I WOULDN'T BE IN SUCH A HURRY TO CLOSE THIS ONE UP.
YOU KNOW HOW TO MAKE A MAN FEEL WELCOME.
MUCH LESS OF A MAN THAN I EVER WOULD HAVE GUESSED.
BUT ISN'T THAT ALWAYS HOW IT GOES?
HERE. COVER THAT THING UP.
ALL GOOD DOWN HERE?

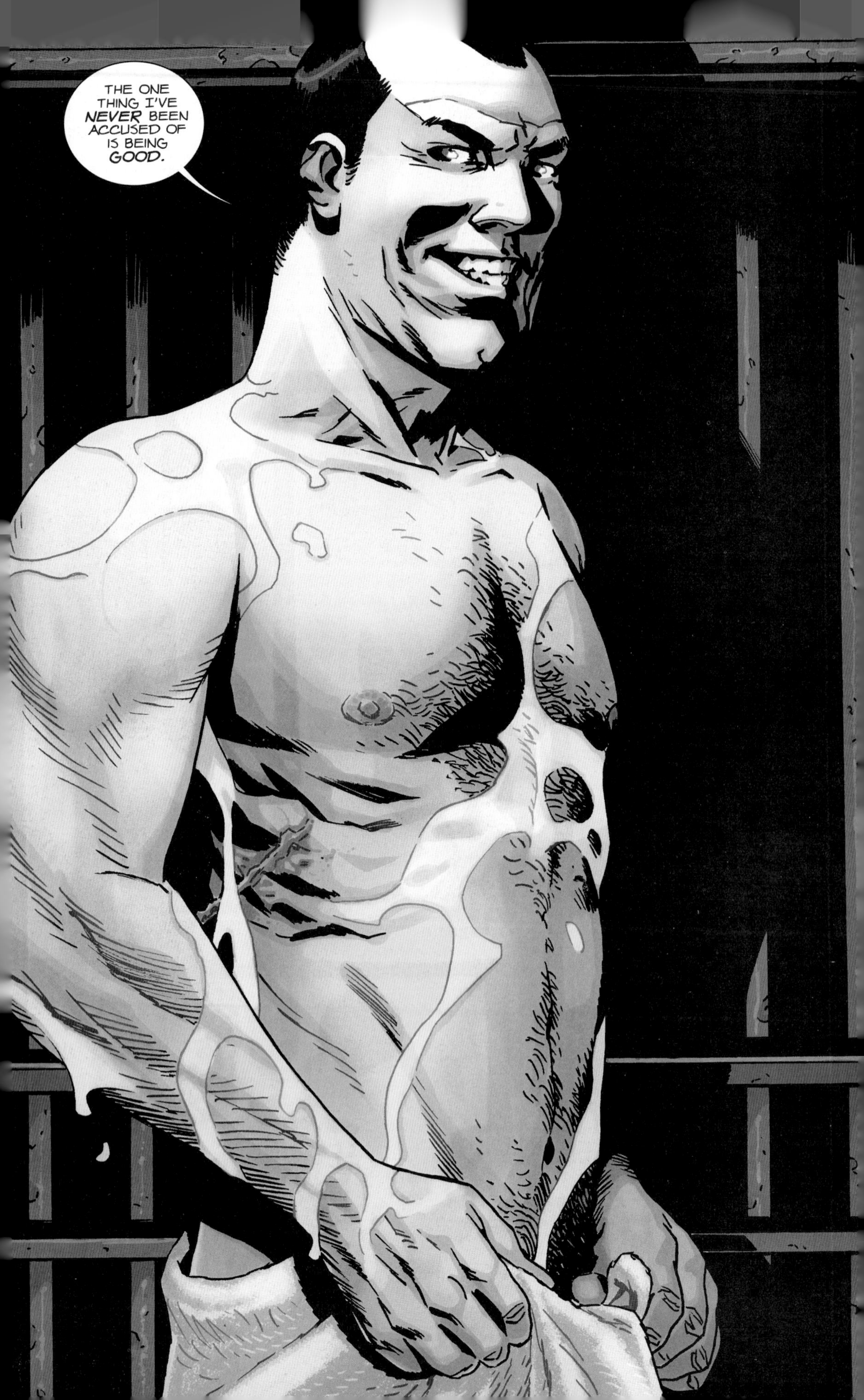
THE ONE THING I'VE NEVER BEEN ACCUSED OF IS BEING GOOD.

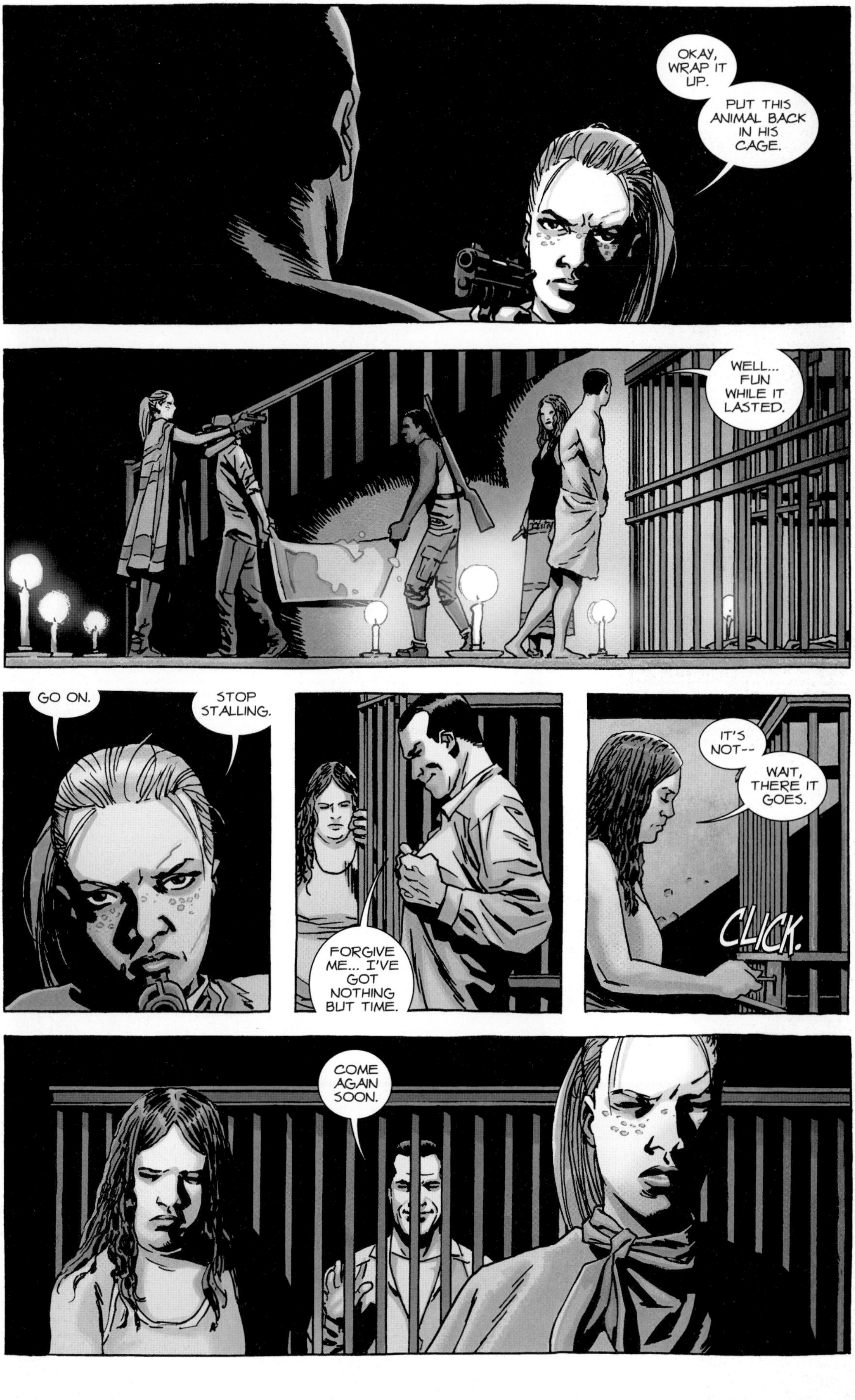
OKAY, WRAP IT UP.
PUT THIS ANIMAL BACK IN HIS CAGE.
WELL... FUN WHILE IT LASTED.
GO ON.
STOP STALLING.
FORGIVE ME... I'VE GOT NOTHING BUT TIME.
IT'S NOT--
WAIT, THERE IT GOES.
CLICK.
COME AGAIN SOON.

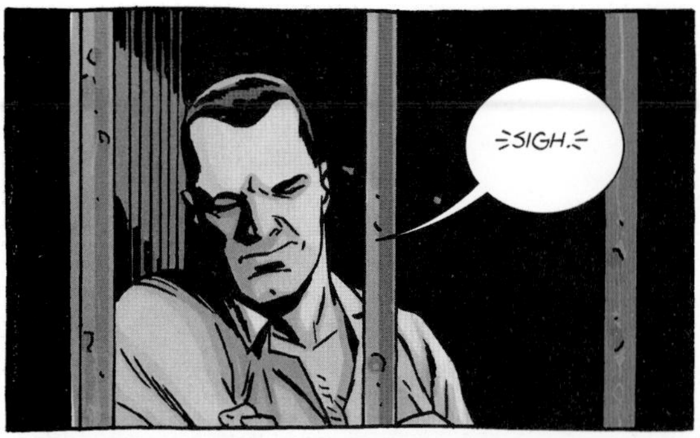
SIGH.

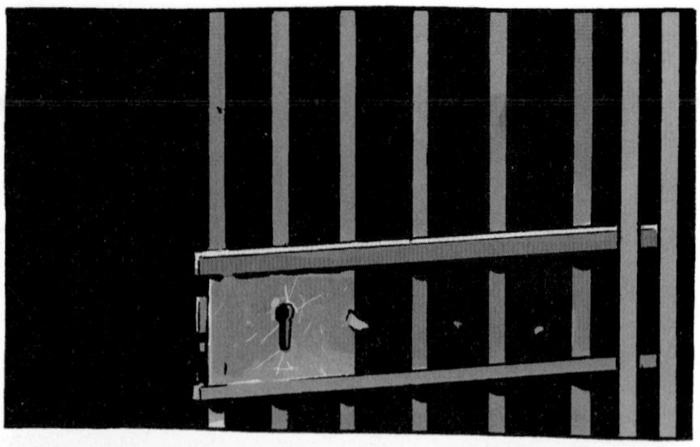

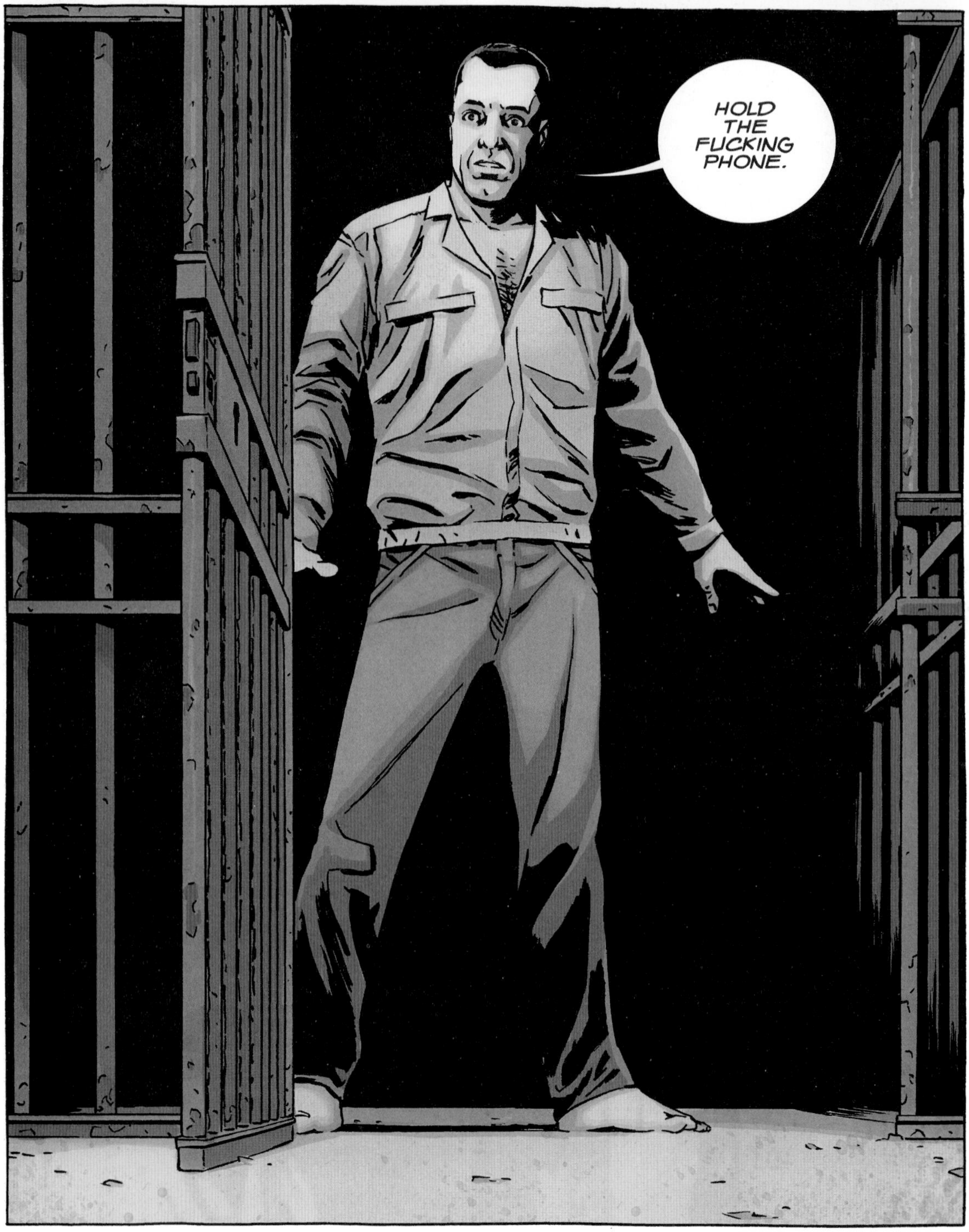
HOLD THE FUCKING PHONE.

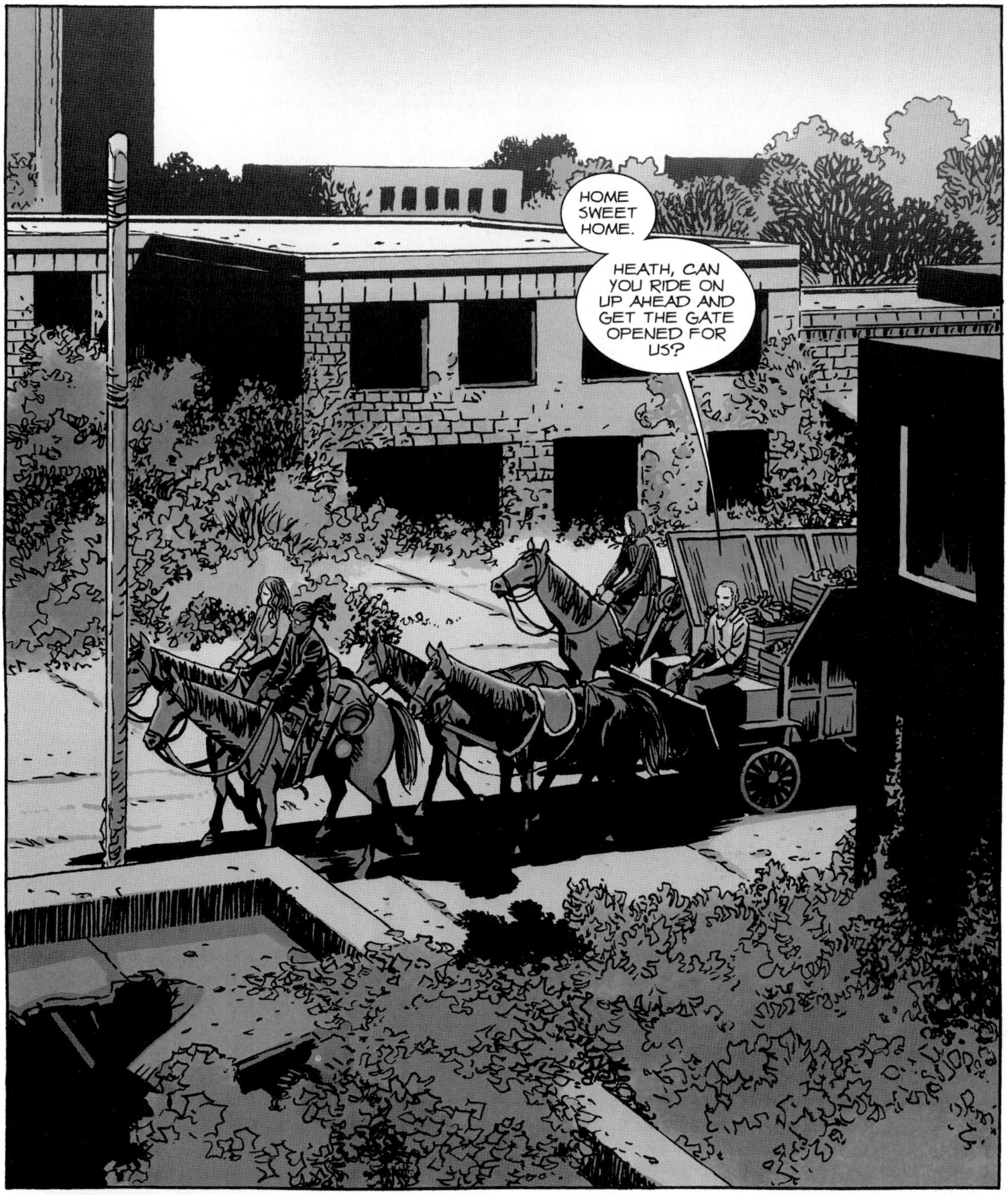
HOME SWEET HOME.
HEATH, CAN YOU RIDE ON UP AHEAD AND GET THE GATE OPENED FOR US?

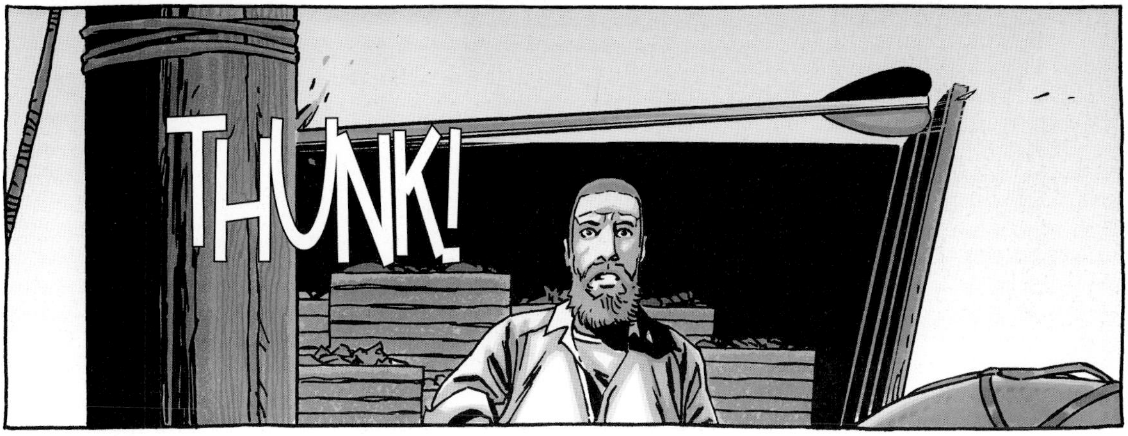
THUNK!

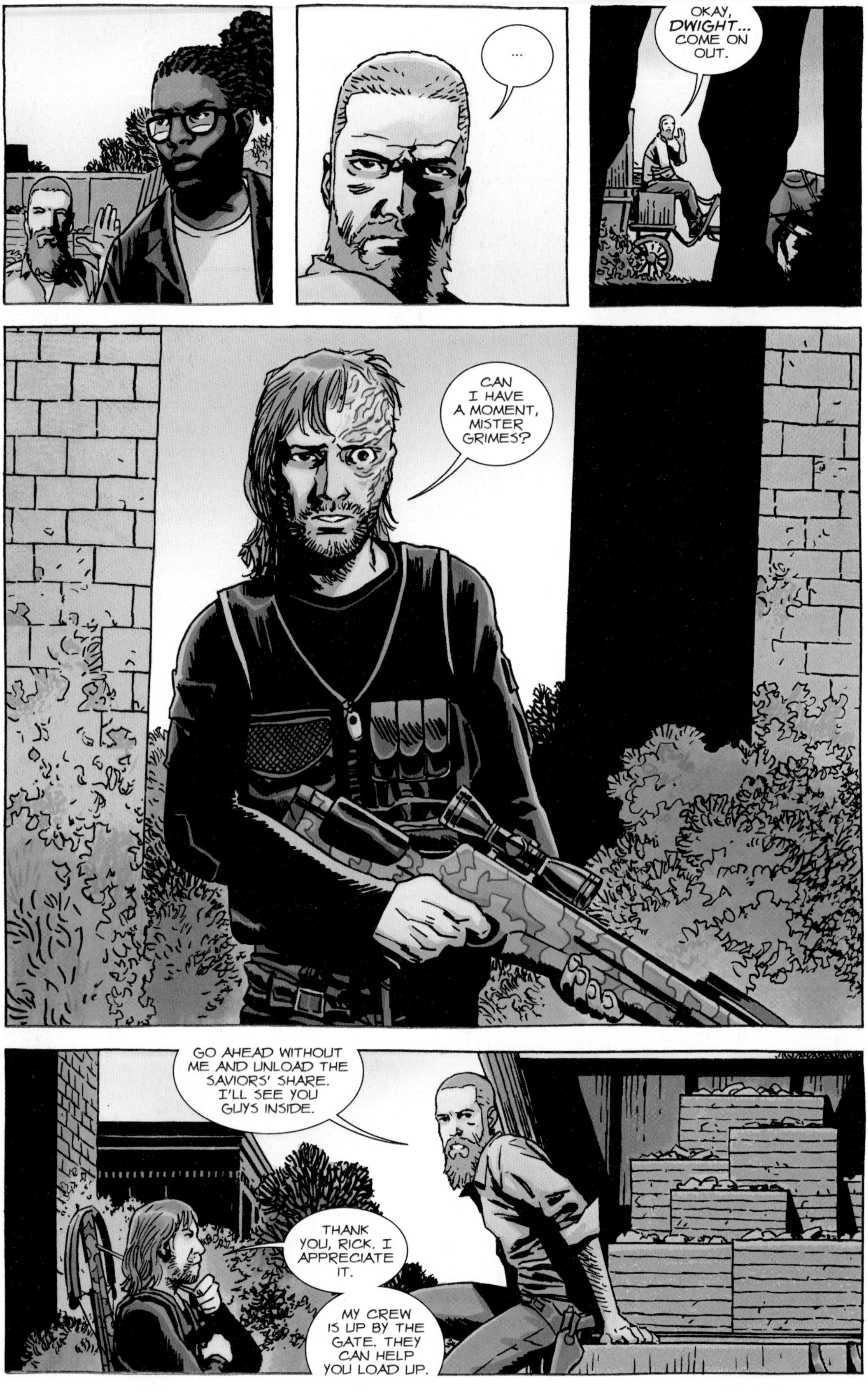
...
OKAY, DWIGHT... COME ON OUT.
CAN I HAVE A MOMENT, MISTER GRIMES?
GO AHEAD WITHOUT ME AND UNLOAD THE SAVIORS' SHARE. I'LL SEE YOU GUYS INSIDE.
THANK YOU, RICK. I APPRECIATE IT.
MY CREW IS UP BY THE GATE. THEY CAN HELP YOU LOAD UP.

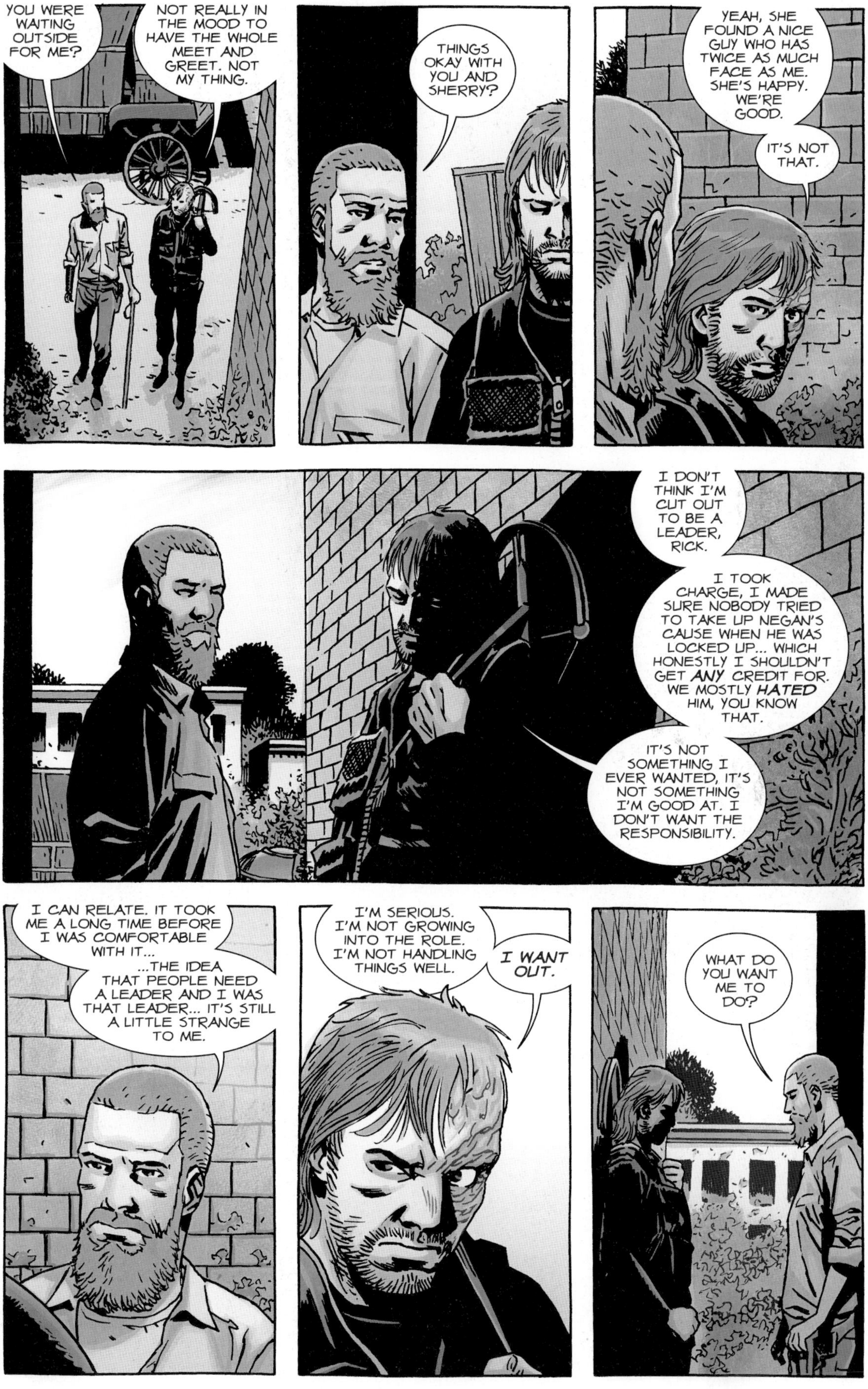
YOU WERE WAITING OUTSIDE FOR ME?
NOT REALLY IN THE MOOD TO HAVE THE WHOLE MEET AND GREET. NOT MY THING.
THINGS OKAY WITH YOU AND SHERRY?
YEAH, SHE FOUND A NICE GUY WHO HAS TWICE AS MUCH FACE AS ME. SHE'S HAPPY. WE'RE GOOD.
IT'S NOT THAT.
I DON'T THINK I'M CUT OUT TO BE A LEADER, RICK.
I TOOK CHARGE, I MADE SURE NOBODY TRIED TO TAKE UP NEGAN'S CAUSE WHEN HE WAS LOCKED UP... WHICH HONESTLY I SHOULDN'T GET ANY CREDIT FOR. WE MOSTLY HATED HIM, YOU KNOW THAT.
IT'S NOT SOMETHING I EVER WANTED, IT'S NOT SOMETHING I'M GOOD AT. I DON'T WANT THE RESPONSIBILITY.
I CAN RELATE. IT TOOK ME A LONG TIME BEFORE I WAS COMFORTABLE WITH IT...
...THE IDEA THAT PEOPLE NEED A LEADER AND I WAS THAT LEADER... IT'S STILL A LITTLE STRANGE TO ME.
I'M SERIOUS. I'M NOT GROWING INTO THE ROLE. I'M NOT HANDLING THINGS WELL.
I WANT OUT.
WHAT DO YOU WANT ME TO DO?

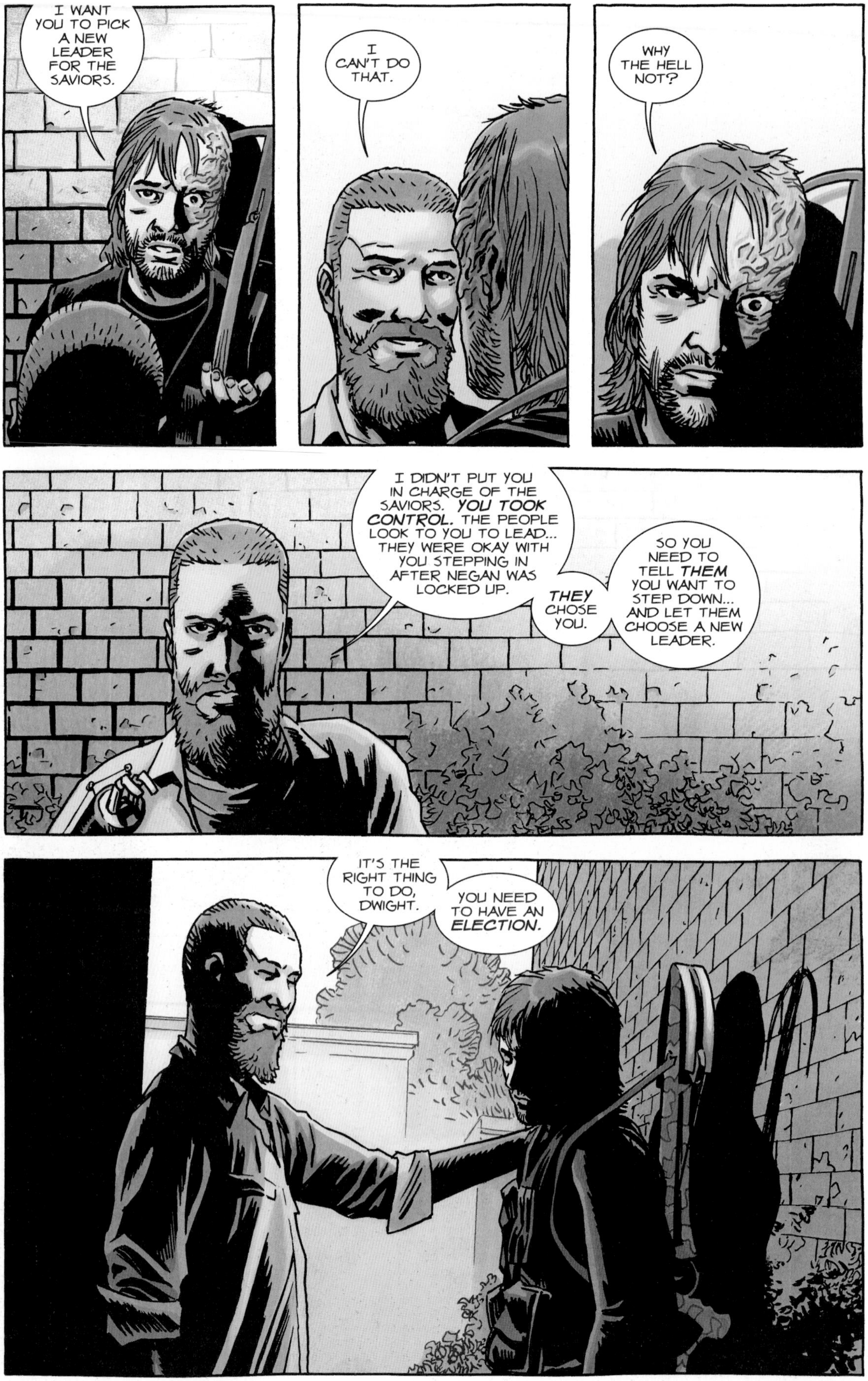
I WANT YOU TO PICK A NEW LEADER FOR THE SAVIORS.
I CAN'T DO THAT.
WHY THE HELL NOT?
I DIDN'T PUT YOU IN CHARGE OF THE SAVIORS. YOU TOOK CONTROL. THE PEOPLE LOOK TO YOU TO LEAD... THEY WERE OKAY WITH YOU STEPPING IN AFTER NEGAN WAS LOCKED UP.
THEY CHOSE YOU.
SO YOU NEED TO TELL THEM YOU WANT TO STEP DOWN... AND LET THEM CHOOSE A NEW LEADER.
IT'S THE RIGHT THING TO DO, DWIGHT.
YOU NEED TO HAVE AN ELECTION.

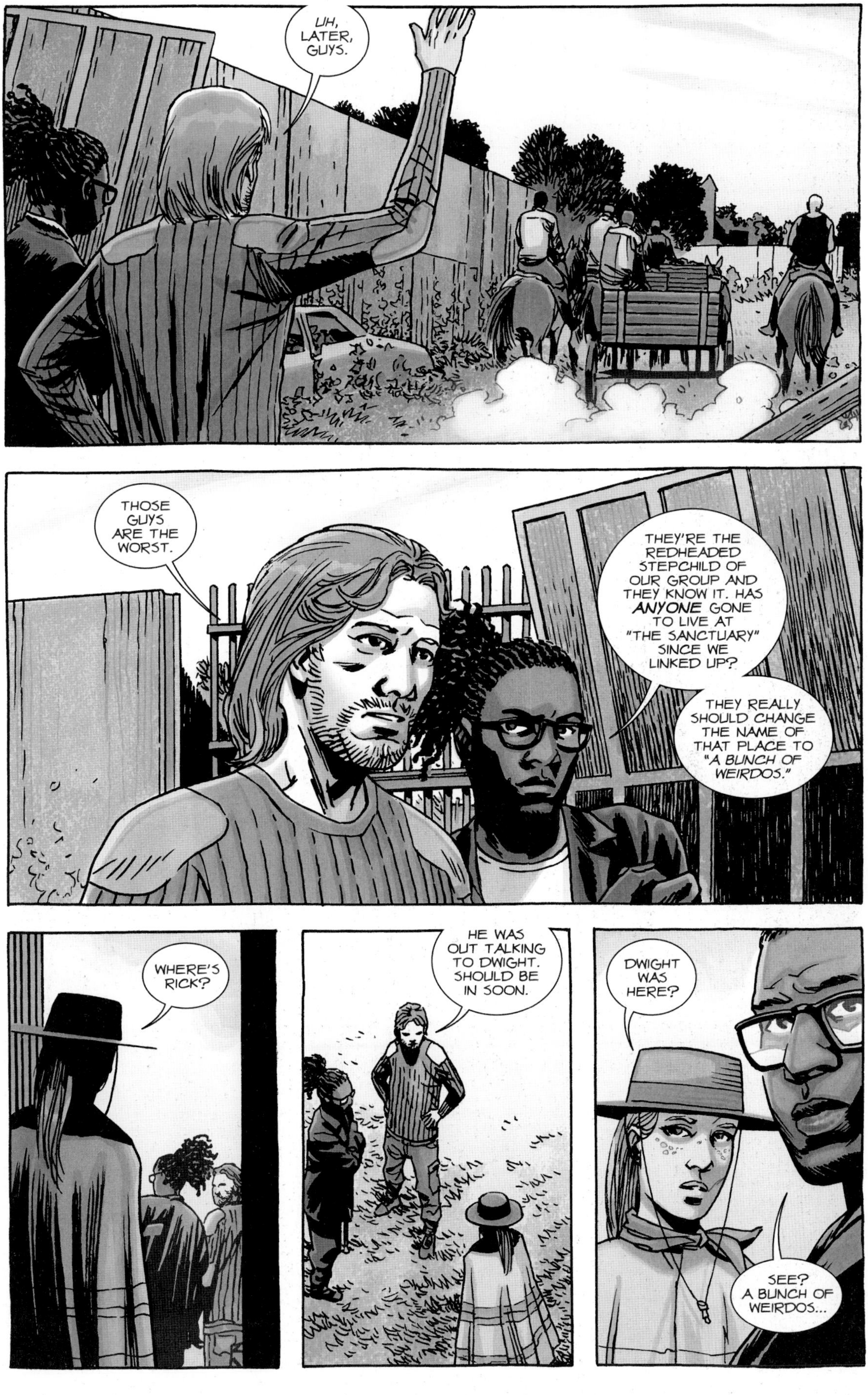
UH, LATER, GUYS.
THOSE GUYS ARE THE WORST.
THEY'RE THE REDHEADED STEPCHILD OF OUR GROUP AND THEY KNOW IT. HAS ANYONE GONE TO LIVE AT "THE SANCTUARY" SINCE WE LINKED UP?
THEY REALLY SHOULD CHANGE THE NAME OF THAT PLACE TO "A BUNCH OF WEIRDOS."
WHERE'S RICK?
HE WAS OUT TALKING TO DWIGHT. SHOULD BE IN SOON.
DWIGHT WAS HERE?
SEE? A BUNCH OF WEIRDOS...

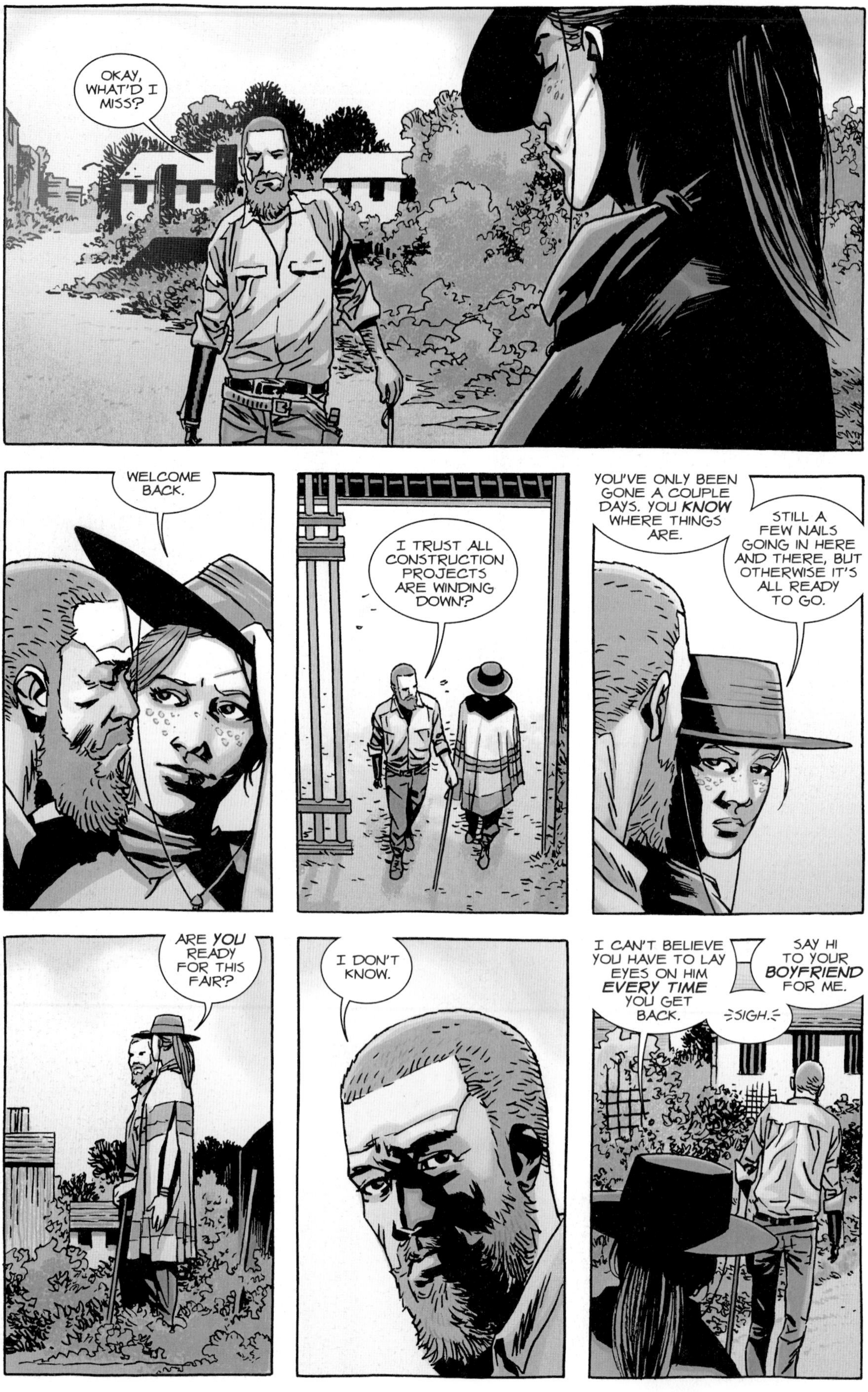
OKAY, WHAT'D I MISS?
WELCOME BACK.
I TRUST ALL CONSTRUCTION PROJECTS ARE WINDING DOWN?
YOU'VE ONLY BEEN GONE A COUPLE DAYS. YOU KNOW WHERE THINGS ARE.
STILL A FEW NAILS GOING IN HERE AND THERE, BUT OTHERWISE IT'S ALL READY TO GO.
ARE YOU READY FOR THIS FAIR?
I DON'T KNOW.
SAY HI TO YOUR BOYFRIEND FOR ME.
SIGH.
I CAN'T BELIEVE YOU HAVE TO LAY EYES ON HIM EVERY TIME YOU GET BACK.

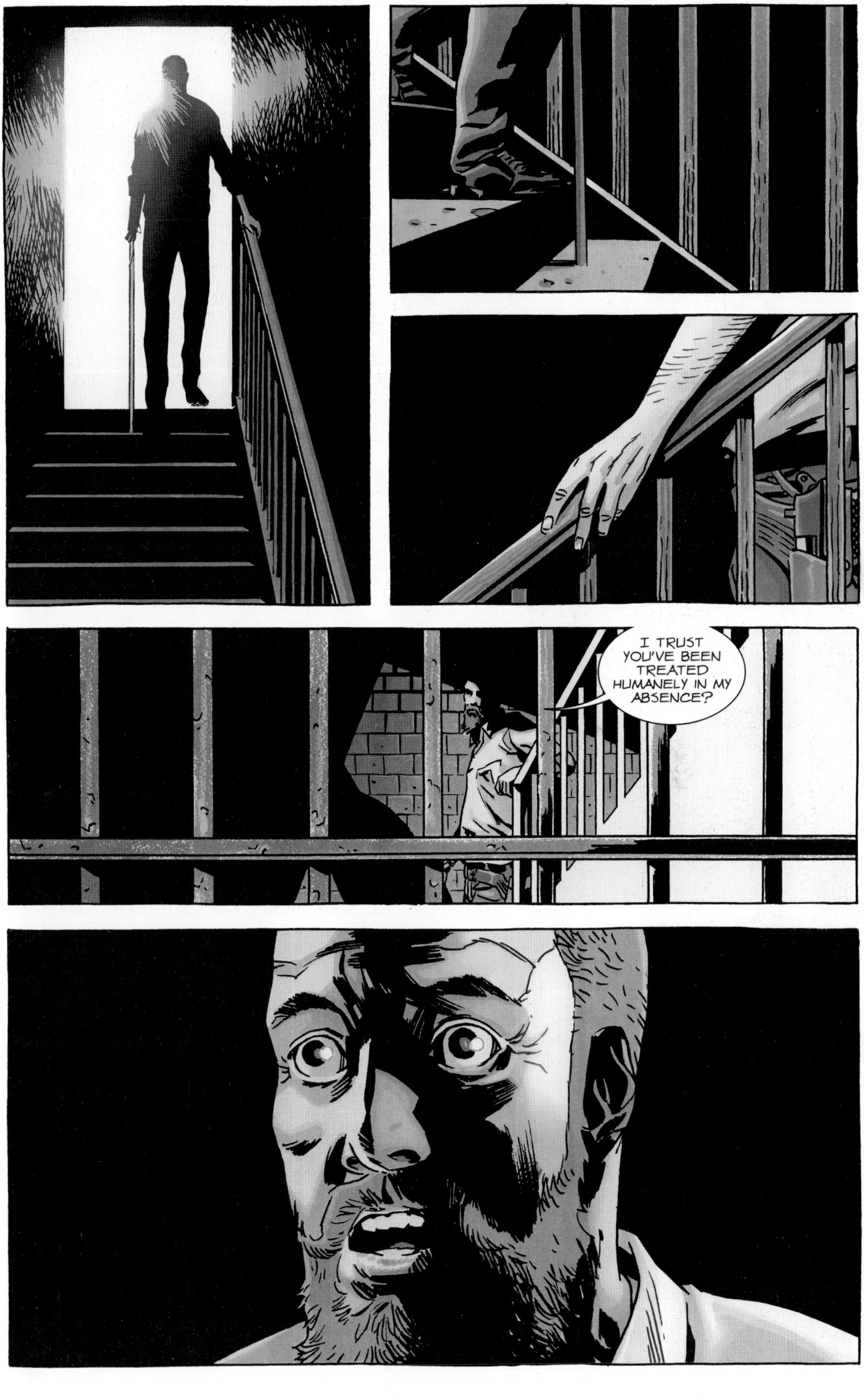
I TRUST YOU'VE BEEN TREATED HUMANELY IN MY ABSENCE?

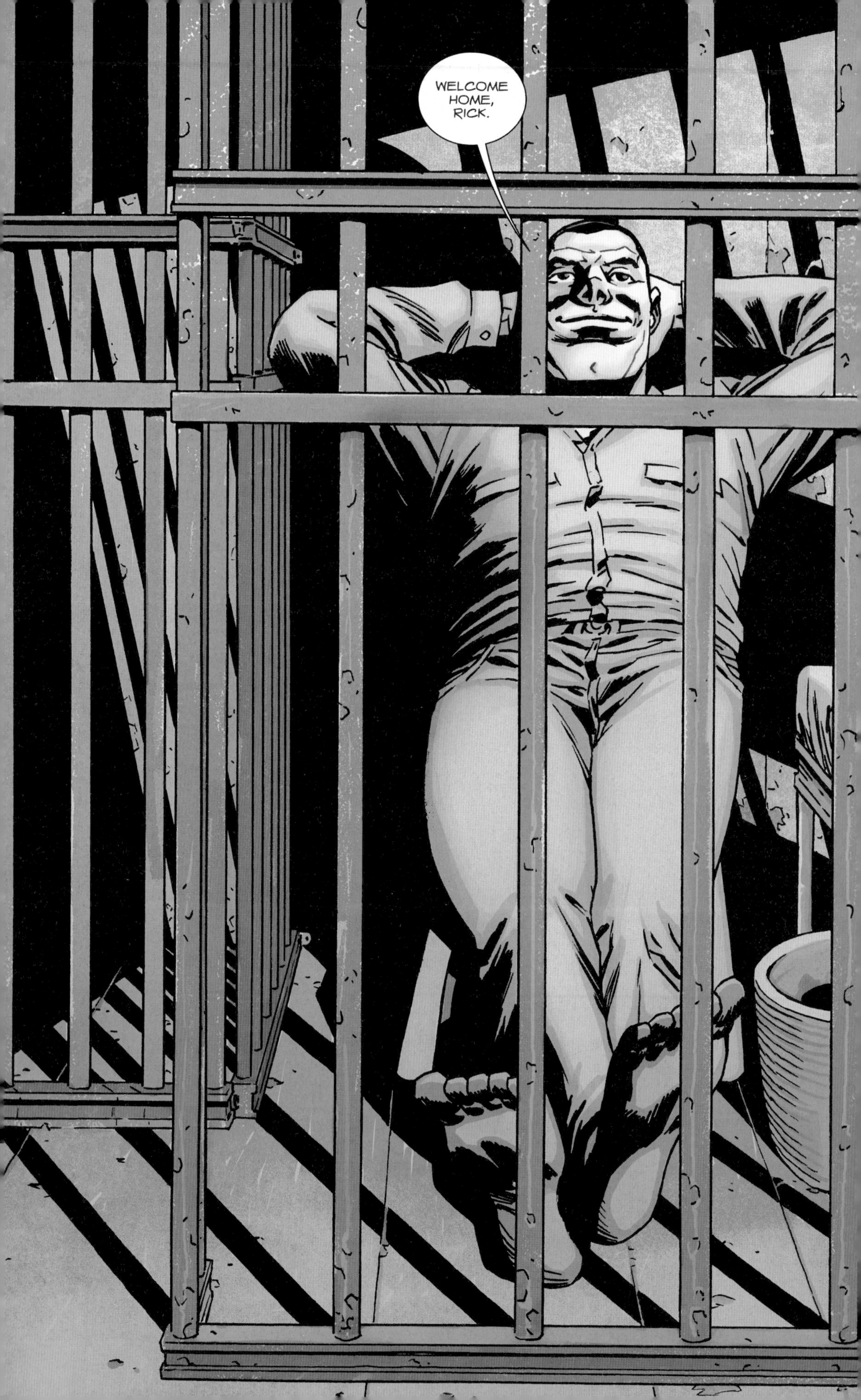
WELCOME HOME, RICK.

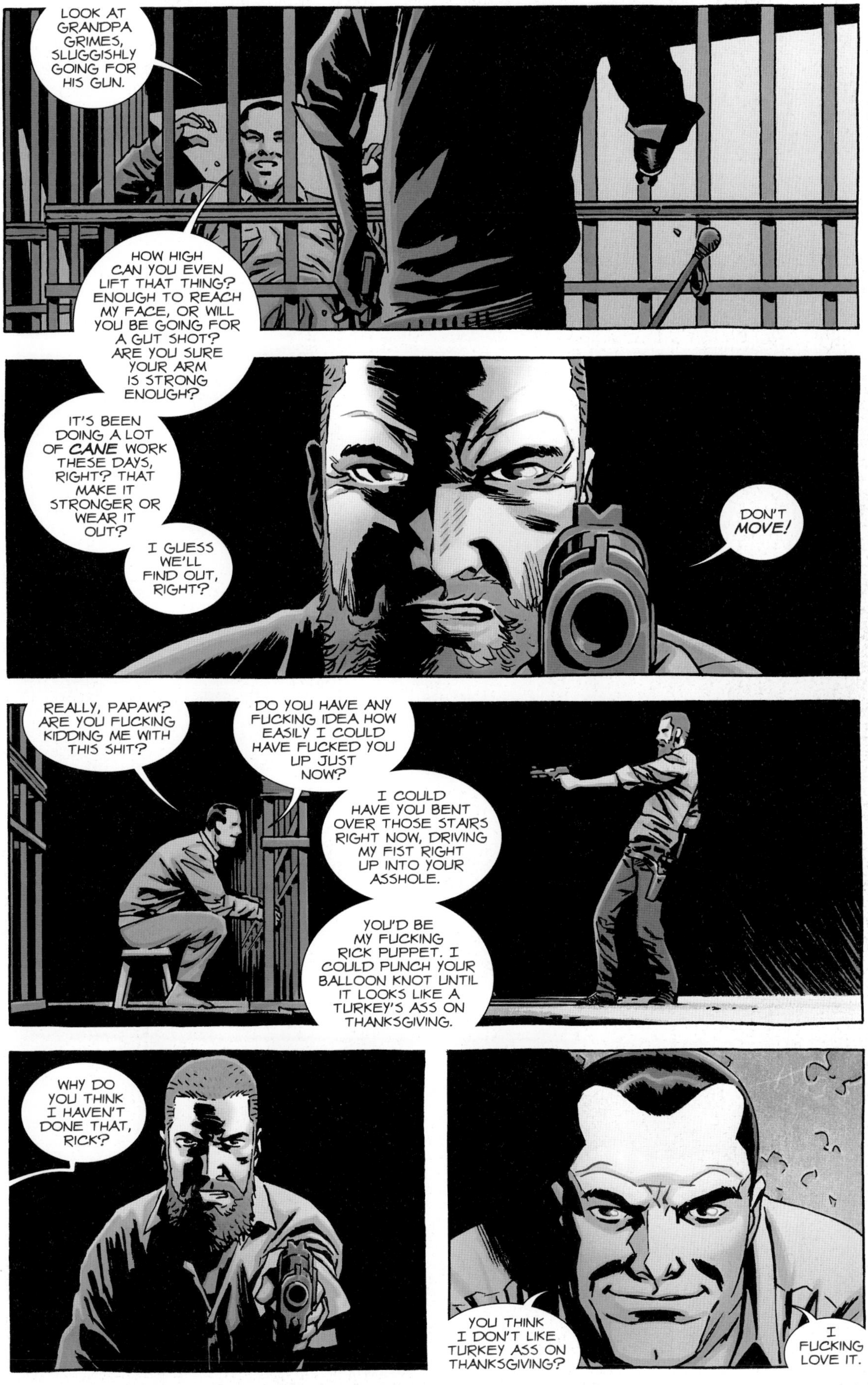
LOOK AT GRANDPA GRIMES, SLUGGISHLY GOING FOR HIS GUN.
HOW HIGH CAN YOU EVEN LIFT THAT THING? ENOUGH TO REACH MY FACE, OR WILL YOU BE GOING FOR A GUT SHOT? ARE YOU SURE YOUR ARM IS STRONG ENOUGH?
IT'S BEEN DOING A LOT OF CANE WORK THESE DAYS, RIGHT? THAT MAKE IT STRONGER OR WEAR IT OUT?
I GUESS WE'LL FIND OUT, RIGHT?
DON'T MOVE!
REALLY, PAPAW? ARE YOU FUCKING KIDDING ME WITH THIS SHIT?
DO YOU HAVE ANY FUCKING IDEA HOW EASILY I COULD HAVE FUCKED YOU UP JUST NOW?
I COULD HAVE YOU BENT OVER THOSE STAIRS RIGHT NOW, DRIVING MY FIST RIGHT UP INTO YOUR ASSHOLE.
YOU'D BE MY FUCKING RICK PUPPET. I COULD PUNCH YOUR BALLOON KNOT UNTIL IT LOOKS LIKE A TURKEY'S ASS ON THANKSGIVING.
WHY DO YOU THINK I HAVEN'T DONE THAT, RICK?
YOU THINK I DON'T LIKE TURKEY ASS ON THANKSGIVING?
I FUCKING LOVE IT.

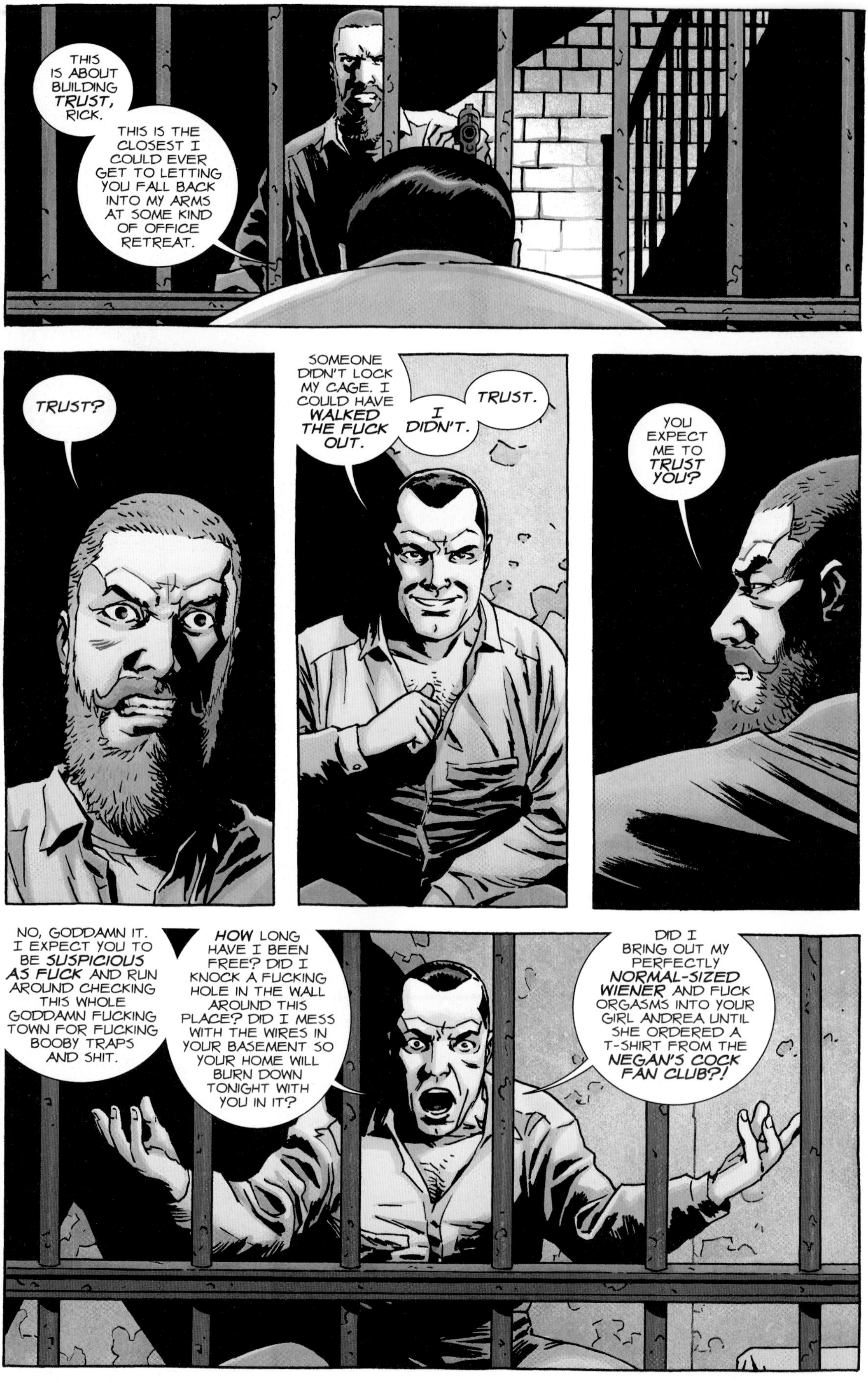
THIS IS ABOUT BUILDING TRUST, RICK.
THIS IS THE CLOSEST I COULD EVER GET TO LETTING YOU FALL BACK INTO MY ARMS AT SOME KIND OF OFFICE RETREAT.
TRUST?
SOMEONE DIDN'T LOCK MY CAGE. I COULD HAVE WALKED THE FUCK OUT.
I DIDN'T.
TRUST.
YOU EXPECT ME TO TRUST YOU?
NO, GODDAMN IT. I EXPECT YOU TO BE SUSPICIOUS AS FUCK AND RUN AROUND CHECKING THIS WHOLE GODDAMN FUCKING TOWN FOR FUCKING BOOBY TRAPS AND SHIT.
HOW LONG HAVE I BEEN FREE? DID I KNOCK A FUCKING HOLE IN THE WALL AROUND THIS PLACE? DID I MESS WITH THE WIRES IN YOUR BASEMENT SO YOUR HOME WILL BURN DOWN TONIGHT WITH YOU IN IT?
DID I BRING OUT MY PERFECTLY NORMAL-SIZED WIENER AND FUCK ORGASMS INTO YOUR GIRL ANDREA UNTIL SHE ORDERED A T-SHIRT FROM THE NEGAN'S COCK FAN CLUB?!

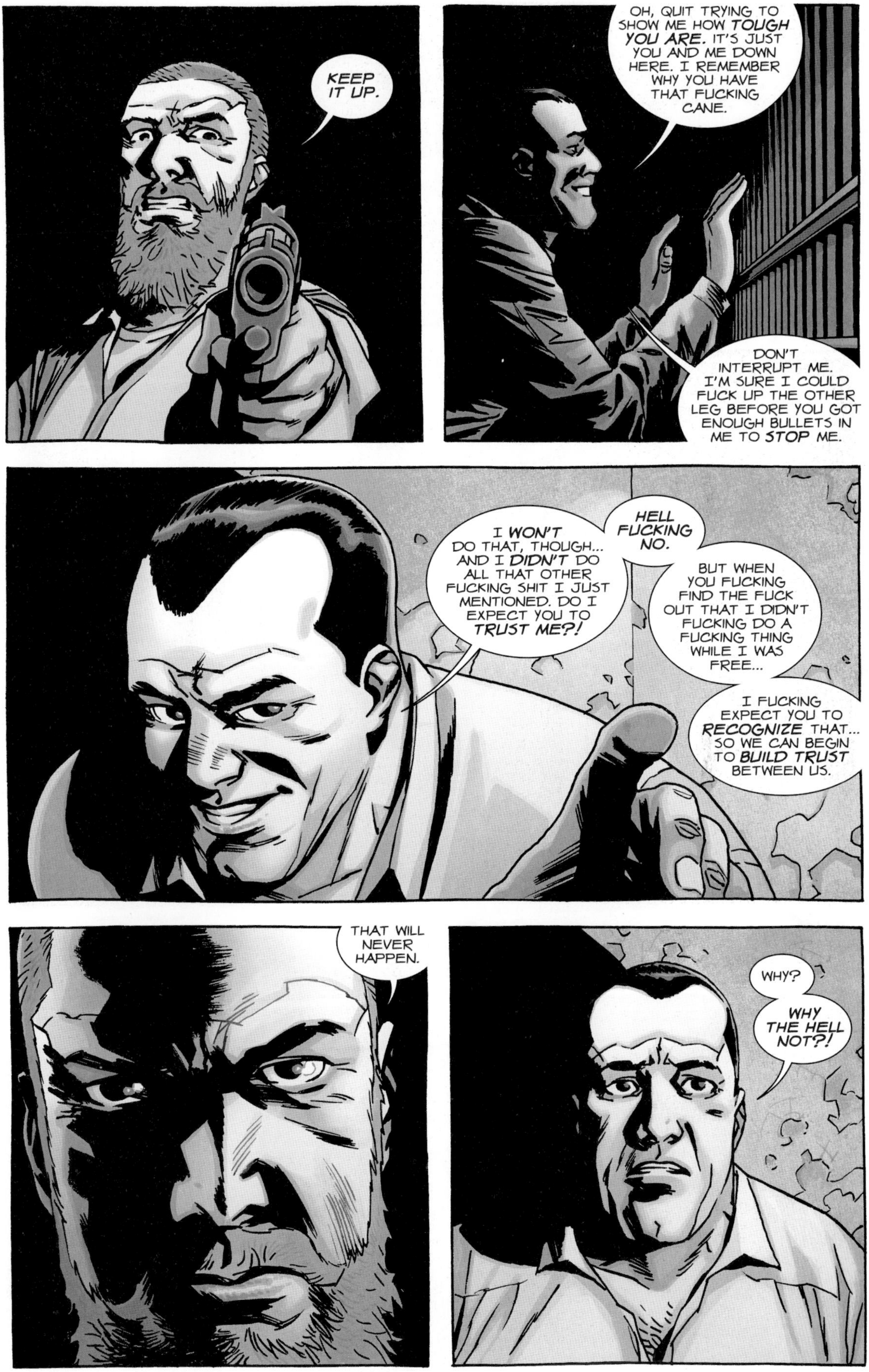
KEEP IT UP.
OH, QUIT TRYING TO SHOW ME HOW TOUGH YOU ARE. IT'S JUST YOU AND ME DOWN HERE. I REMEMBER WHY YOU HAVE THAT FUCKING CANE.
DON'T INTERRUPT ME. I'M SURE I COULD FUCK UP THE OTHER LEG BEFORE YOU GOT ENOUGH BULLETS IN ME TO STOP ME.
I WON'T DO THAT, THOUGH... AND I DIDN'T DO ALL THAT OTHER FUCKING SHIT I JUST MENTIONED. DO I EXPECT YOU TO TRUST ME?!
HELL FUCKING NO.
BUT WHEN YOU FUCKING FIND THE FUCK OUT THAT I DIDN'T FUCKING DO A FUCKING THING WHILE I WAS FREE...
I FUCKING EXPECT YOU TO RECOGNIZE THAT... SO WE CAN BEGIN TO BUILD TRUST BETWEEN US.
THAT WILL NEVER HAPPEN.
WHY?
WHY THE HELL NOT?!

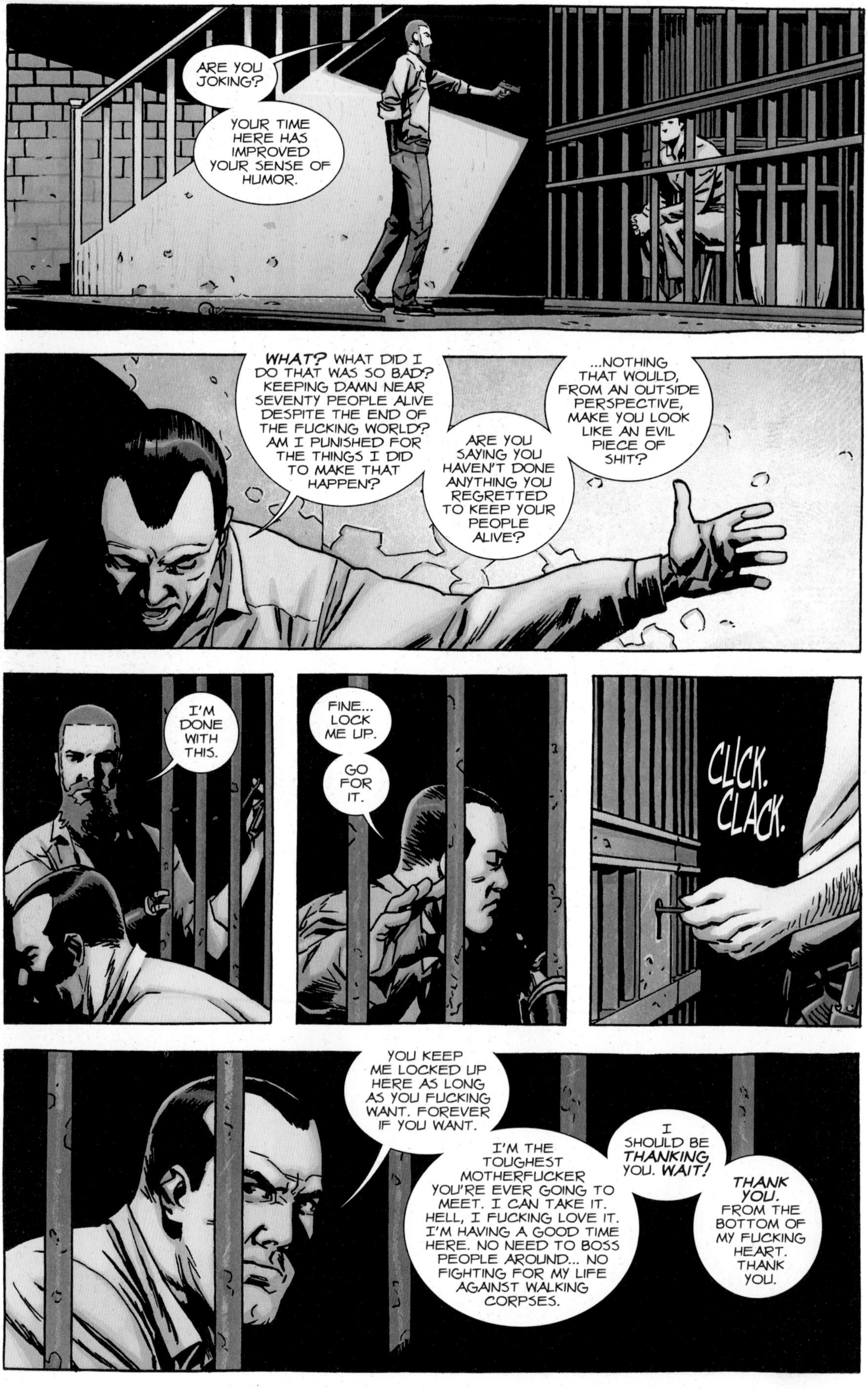
ARE YOU JOKING?
YOUR TIME HERE HAS IMPROVED YOUR SENSE OF HUMOR.
WHAT? WHAT DID I DO THAT WAS SO BAD? KEEPING DAMN NEAR SEVENTY PEOPLE ALIVE DESPITE THE END OF THE FUCKING WORLD? AM I PUNISHED FOR THE THINGS I DID TO MAKE THAT HAPPEN?
ARE YOU SAYING YOU HAVEN'T DONE ANYTHING YOU REGRETTED TO KEEP YOUR PEOPLE ALIVE?
...NOTHING THAT WOULD, FROM AN OUTSIDE PERSPECTIVE, MAKE YOU LOOK LIKE AN EVIL PIECE OF SHIT?
I'M DONE WITH THIS.
FINE... LOCK ME UP.
GO FOR IT.
CLICK. CLACK.
YOU KEEP ME LOCKED UP HERE AS LONG AS YOU FUCKING WANT. FOREVER IF YOU WANT.
I'M THE TOUGHEST MOTHERFUCKER YOU'RE EVER GOING TO MEET. I CAN TAKE IT. HELL, I FUCKING LOVE IT. I'M HAVING A GOOD TIME HERE. NO NEED TO BOSS PEOPLE AROUND... NO FIGHTING FOR MY LIFE AGAINST WALKING CORPSES.
I SHOULD BE THANKING YOU. WAIT!
THANK YOU. FROM THE BOTTOM OF MY FUCKING HEART. THANK YOU.

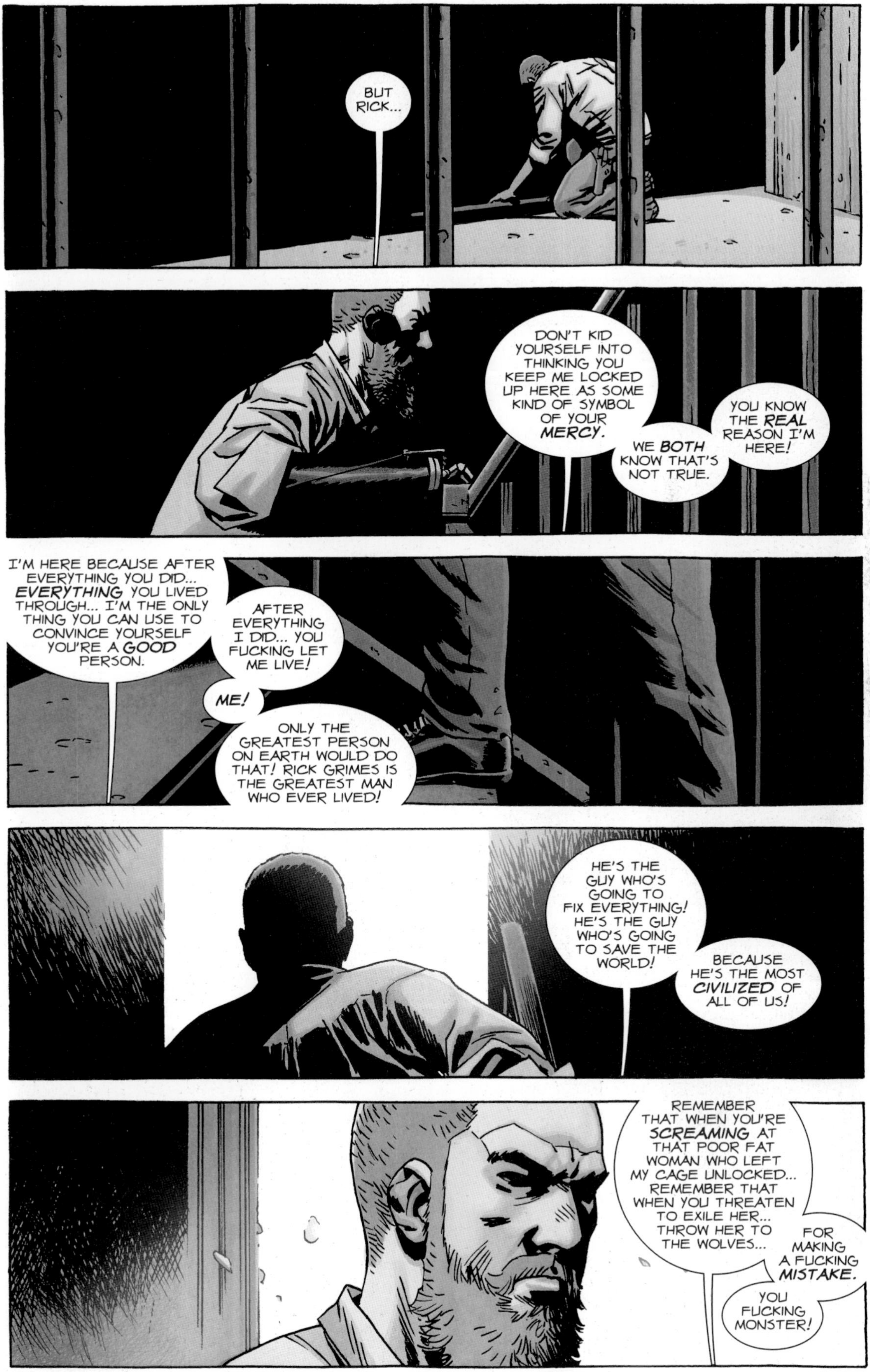
BUT RICK...
DON'T KID YOURSELF INTO THINKING YOU KEEP ME LOCKED UP HERE AS SOME KIND OF YOUR SYMBOL OF YOUR MERCY.
WE BOTH KNOW THAT'S NOT TRUE.
YOU KNOW THE REAL REASON I'M HERE!
I'M HERE BECAUSE AFTER EVERYTHING YOU DID... EVERYTHING YOU LIVED THROUGH... I'M THE ONLY THING YOU CAN USE TO CONVINCE YOURSELF YOU'RE A GOOD PERSON.
AFTER EVERYTHING I DID... YOU FUCKING LET ME LIVE!
ME!
ONLY THE GREATEST PERSON ON EARTH WOULD DO THAT! RICK GRIMES IS THE GREATEST MAN WHO EVER LIVED!
HE'S THE GUY WHO'S GOING TO FIX EVERYTHING! HE'S THE GUY WHO'S GOING TO SAVE THE WORLD!
BECAUSE HE'S THE MOST CIVILIZED OF ALL OF US!
REMEMBER THAT WHEN YOU'RE SCREAMING AT THAT POOR FAT WOMAN WHO LEFT MY CAGE UNLOCKED... REMEMBER THAT WHEN YOU THREATEN TO EXILE HER... THROW HER TO THE WOLVES...
FOR MAKING A FUCKING MISTAKE.
YOU FUCKING MONSTER!

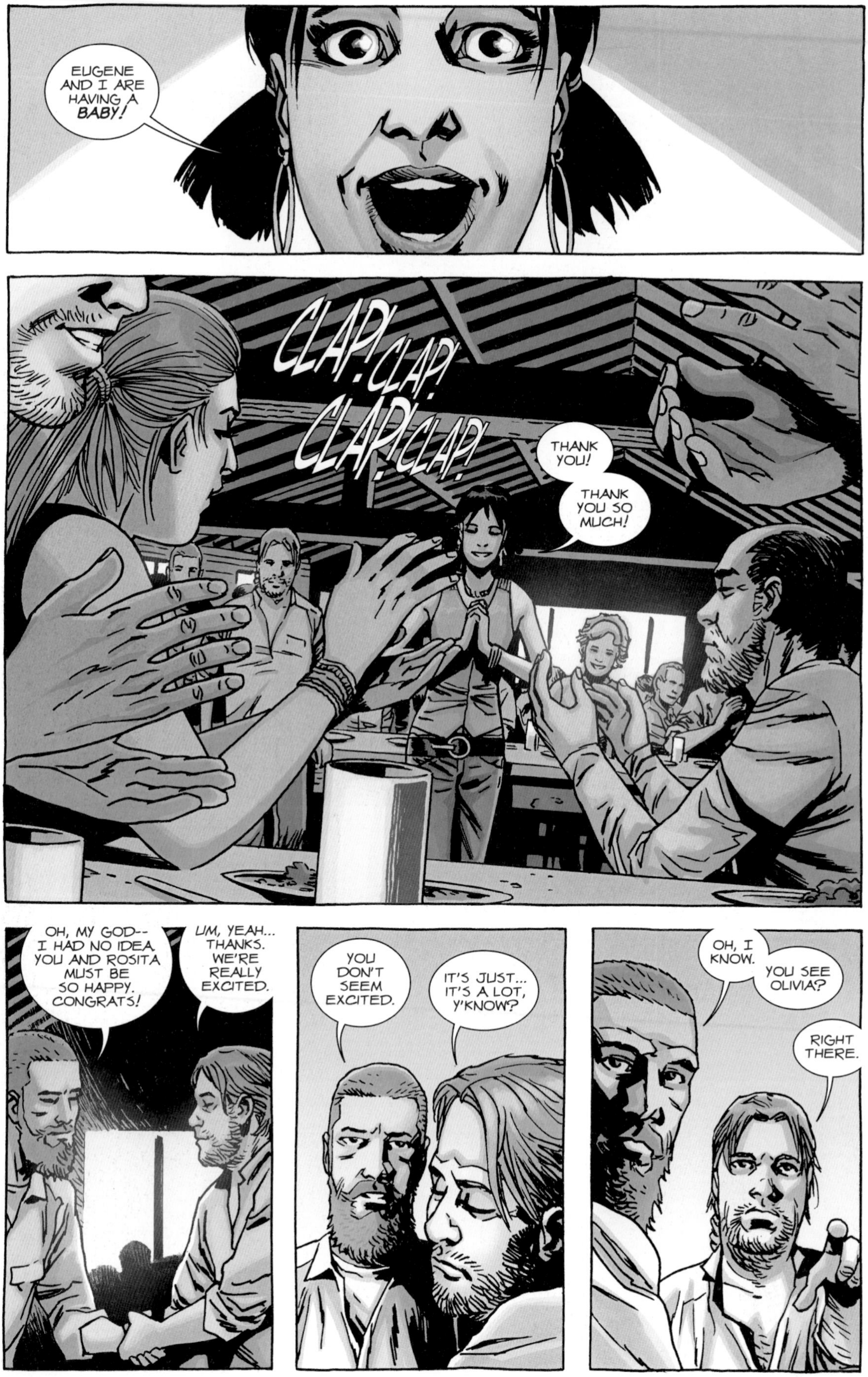
EUGENE AND I ARE HAVING A *BABY!*
CLAP! CLAP! CLAP! CLAP!
THANK YOU!
THANK YOU SO MUCH!
OH, MY GOD-- I HAD NO IDEA. YOU AND ROSITA MUST BE SO HAPPY. CONGRATS!
UM, YEAH... THANKS. WE'RE REALLY EXCITED.
YOU DON'T SEEM EXCITED.
IT'S JUST... IT'S A LOT, Y'KNOW?
OH, I KNOW.
YOU SEE OLIVIA?
RIGHT THERE.

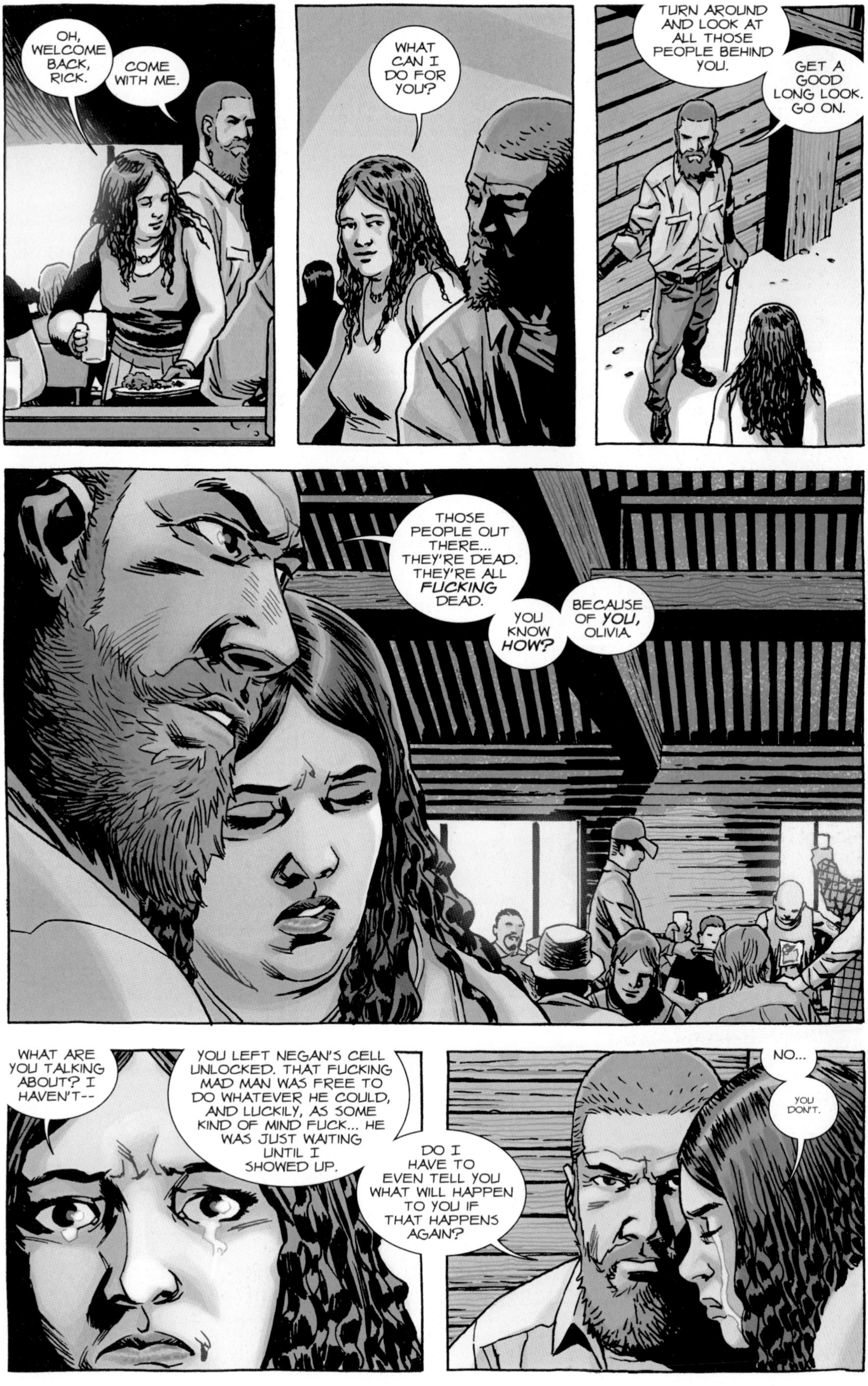
OH, WELCOME BACK, RICK.
COME WITH ME.
WHAT CAN I DO FOR YOU?
TURN AROUND AND LOOK AT ALL THOSE PEOPLE BEHIND YOU.
GET A GOOD LONG LOOK. GO ON.
THOSE PEOPLE OUT THERE... THEY'RE DEAD. THEY'RE ALL FUCKING DEAD.
YOU KNOW HOW?
BECAUSE OF YOU, OLIVIA.
WHAT ARE YOU TALKING ABOUT? I HAVEN'T--
YOU LEFT NEGAN'S CELL UNLOCKED. THAT FUCKING MAD MAN WAS FREE TO DO WHATEVER HE COULD, AND LUCKILY, AS SOME KIND OF MIND FUCK... HE WAS JUST WAITING UNTIL I SHOWED UP.
DO I HAVE TO EVEN TELL YOU WHAT WILL HAPPEN TO YOU IF THAT HAPPENS AGAIN?
NO...
YOU DON'T.

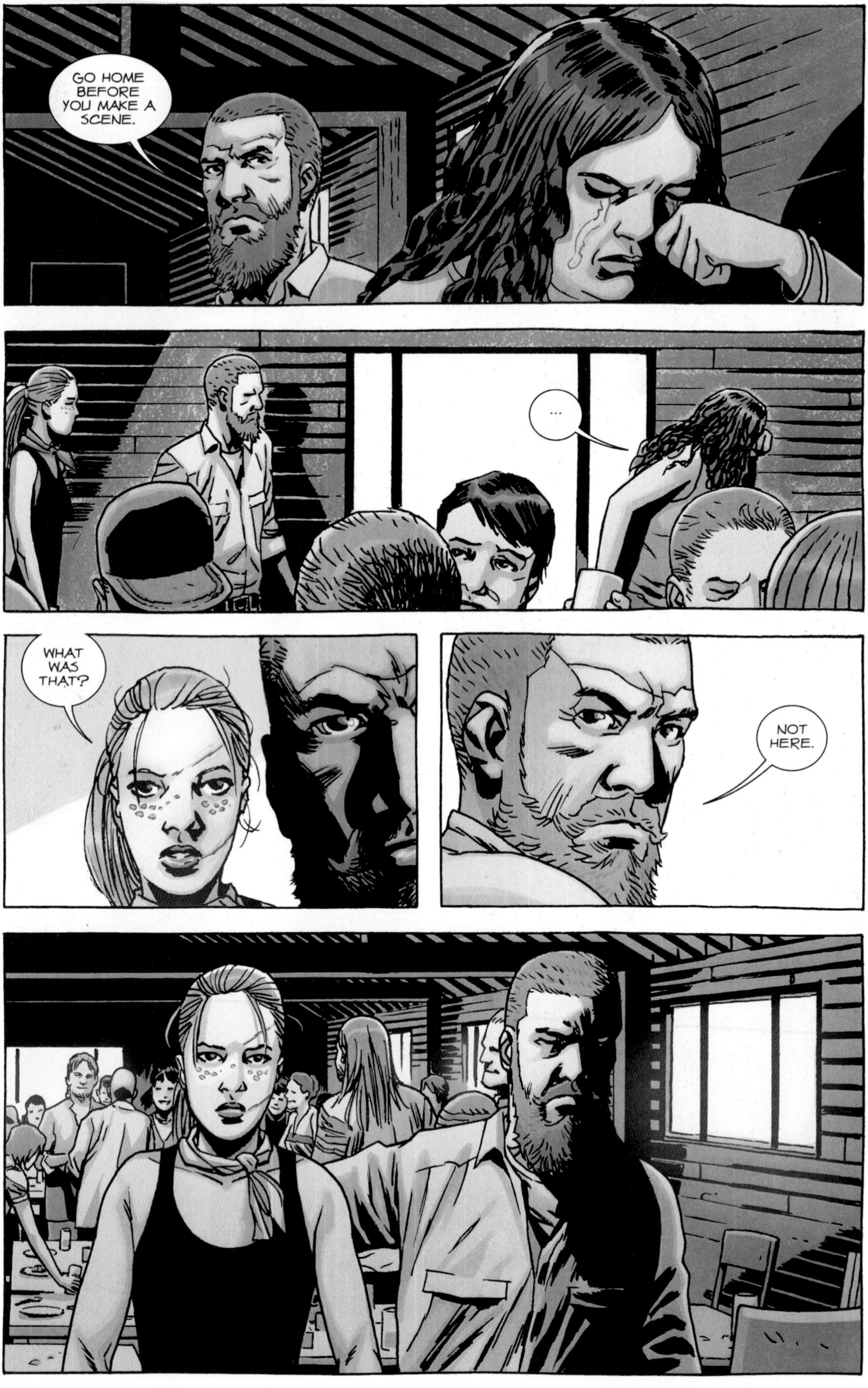
GO HOME BEFORE YOU MAKE A SCENE.
...
WHAT WAS THAT?
NOT HERE.

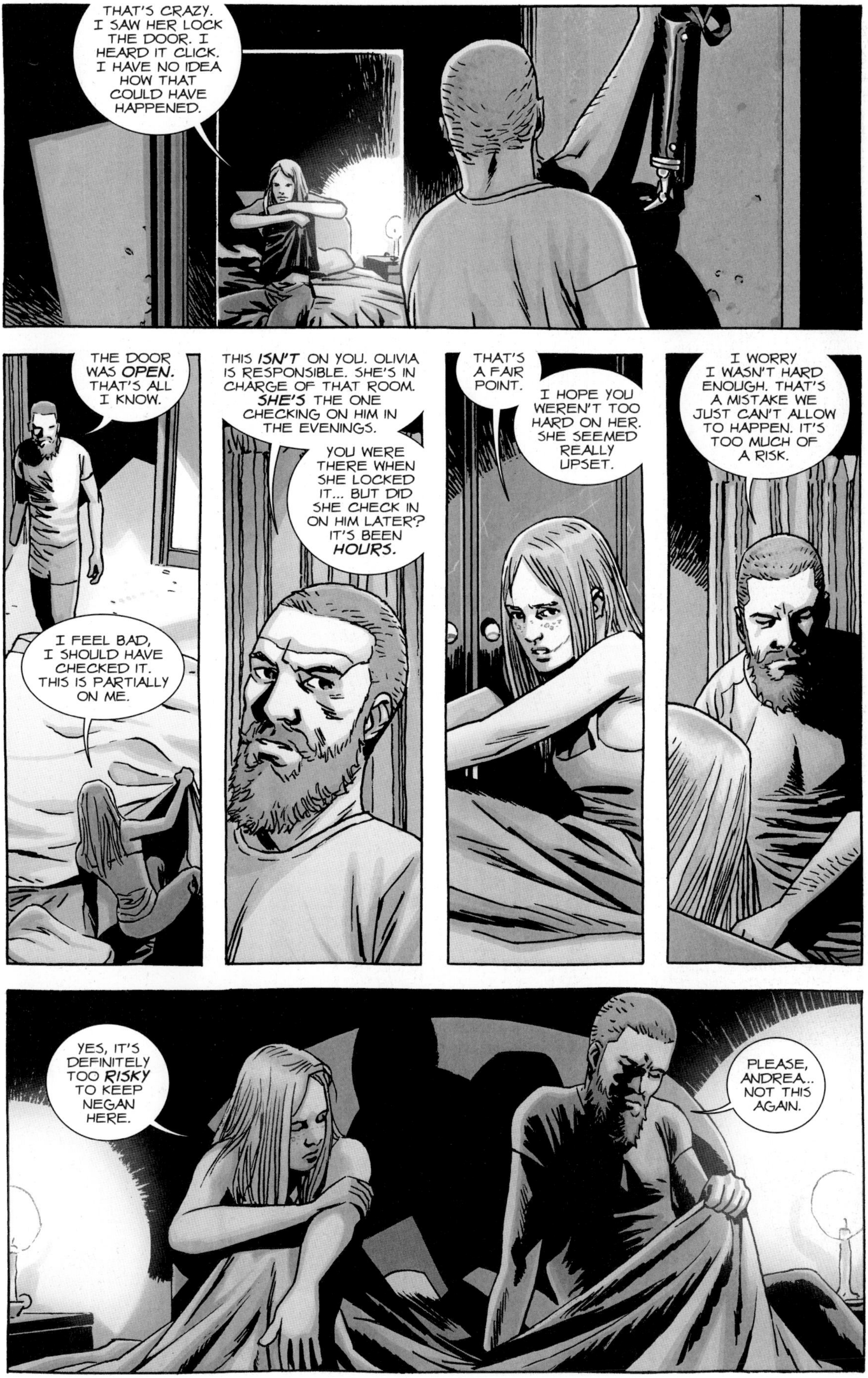
THAT'S CRAZY. I SAW HER LOCK THE DOOR. I HEARD IT CLICK. I HAVE NO IDEA HOW THAT COULD HAVE HAPPENED.
THE DOOR WAS OPEN. THAT'S ALL I KNOW.
I FEEL BAD, I SHOULD HAVE CHECKED IT. THIS IS PARTIALLY ON ME.
THIS ISN'T ON YOU. OLIVIA IS RESPONSIBLE. SHE'S IN CHARGE OF THAT ROOM. SHE'S THE ONE CHECKING ON HIM IN THE EVENINGS.
YOU WERE THERE WHEN SHE LOCKED IT... BUT DID SHE CHECK IN ON HIM LATER? IT'S BEEN HOURS.
THAT'S A FAIR POINT.
I HOPE YOU WEREN'T TOO HARD ON HER. SHE SEEMED REALLY UPSET.
I WORRY I WASN'T HARD ENOUGH. THAT'S A MISTAKE WE JUST CAN'T ALLOW TO HAPPEN. IT'S TOO MUCH OF A RISK.
YES, IT'S DEFINITELY TOO RISKY TO KEEP NEGAN HERE.
PLEASE, ANDREA... NOT THIS AGAIN.

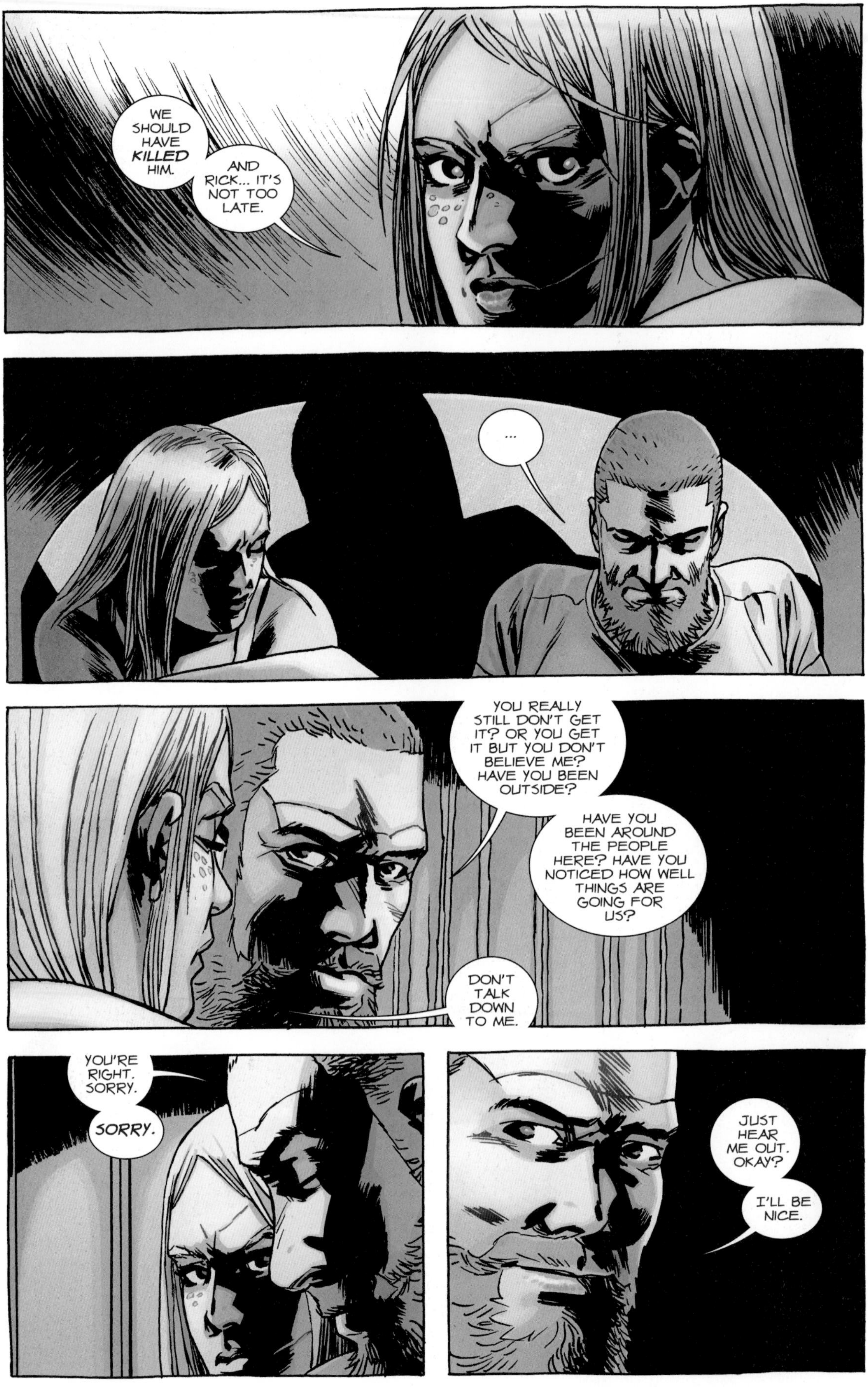

WE SHOULD HAVE **KILLED** HIM.
AND RICK... IT'S NOT TOO LATE.
...
YOU REALLY STILL DON'T GET IT? OR YOU GET IT BUT YOU DON'T BELIEVE ME? HAVE YOU BEEN OUTSIDE?
HAVE YOU BEEN AROUND THE PEOPLE HERE? HAVE YOU NOTICED HOW WELL THINGS ARE GOING FOR US?
DON'T TALK DOWN TO ME.
YOU'RE RIGHT. SORRY.
SORRY.
JUST HEAR ME OUT. OKAY?
I'LL BE NICE.

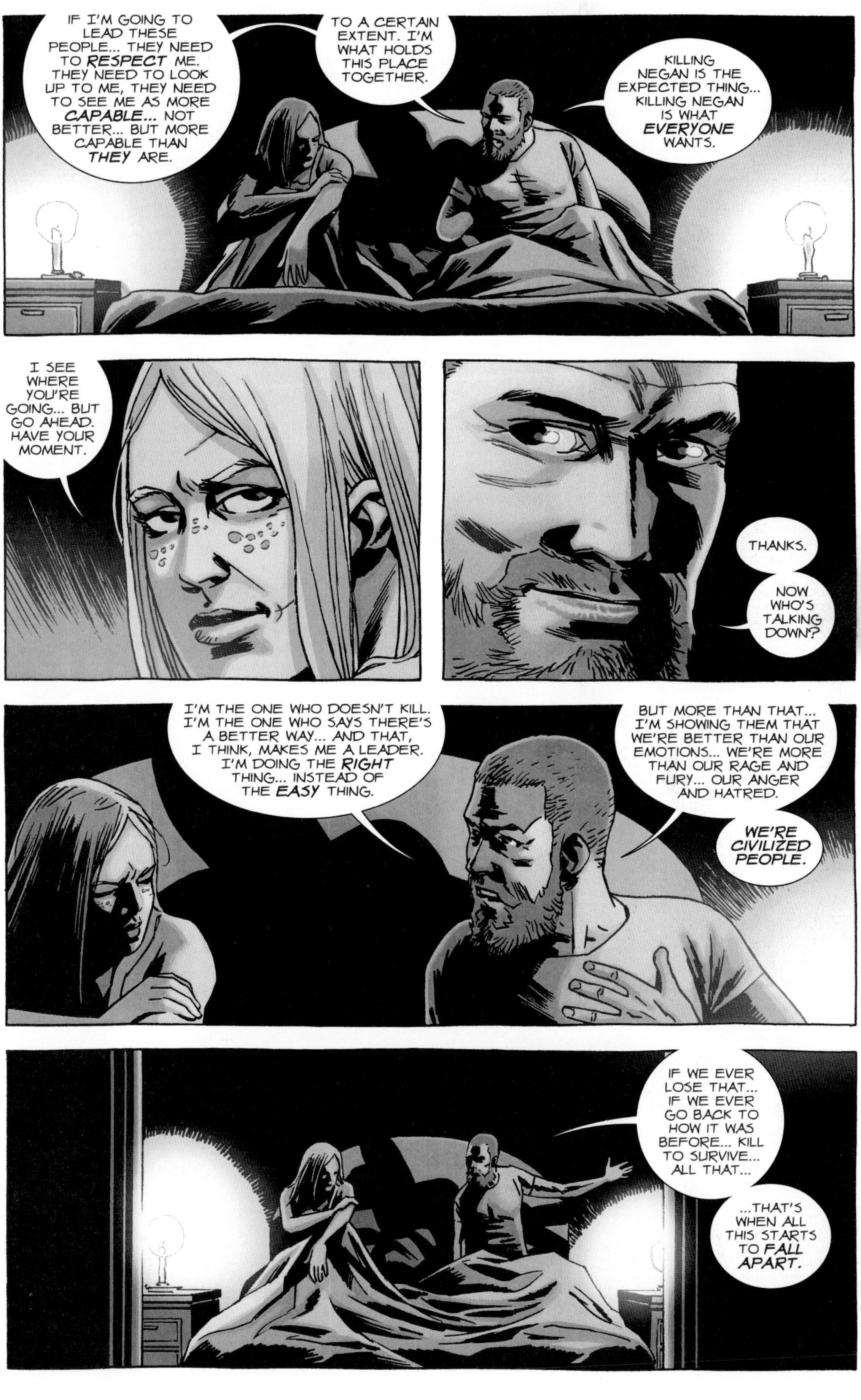
IF I'M GOING TO LEAD THESE PEOPLE... THEY NEED TO RESPECT ME. THEY NEED TO LOOK UP TO ME, THEY NEED TO SEE ME AS MORE CAPABLE... NOT BETTER... BUT MORE CAPABLE THAN THEY ARE.
TO A CERTAIN EXTENT. I'M WHAT HOLDS THIS PLACE TOGETHER.
KILLING NEGAN IS THE EXPECTED THING... KILLING NEGAN IS WHAT EVERYONE WANTS.
I SEE WHERE YOU'RE GOING... BUT GO AHEAD. HAVE YOUR MOMENT.
THANKS.
NOW WHO'S TALKING DOWN?
I'M THE ONE WHO DOESN'T KILL. I'M THE ONE WHO SAYS THERE'S A BETTER WAY... AND THAT, I THINK, MAKES ME A LEADER. I'M DOING THE RIGHT THING... INSTEAD OF THE EASY THING.
BUT MORE THAN THAT... I'M SHOWING THEM THAT WE'RE BETTER THAN OUR EMOTIONS... WE'RE MORE THAN OUR RAGE AND FURY... OUR ANGER AND HATRED.
WE'RE CIVILIZED PEOPLE.
IF WE EVER LOSE THAT... IF WE EVER GO BACK TO HOW IT WAS BEFORE... KILL TO SURVIVE... ALL THAT...
...THAT'S WHEN ALL THIS STARTS TO FALL APART.

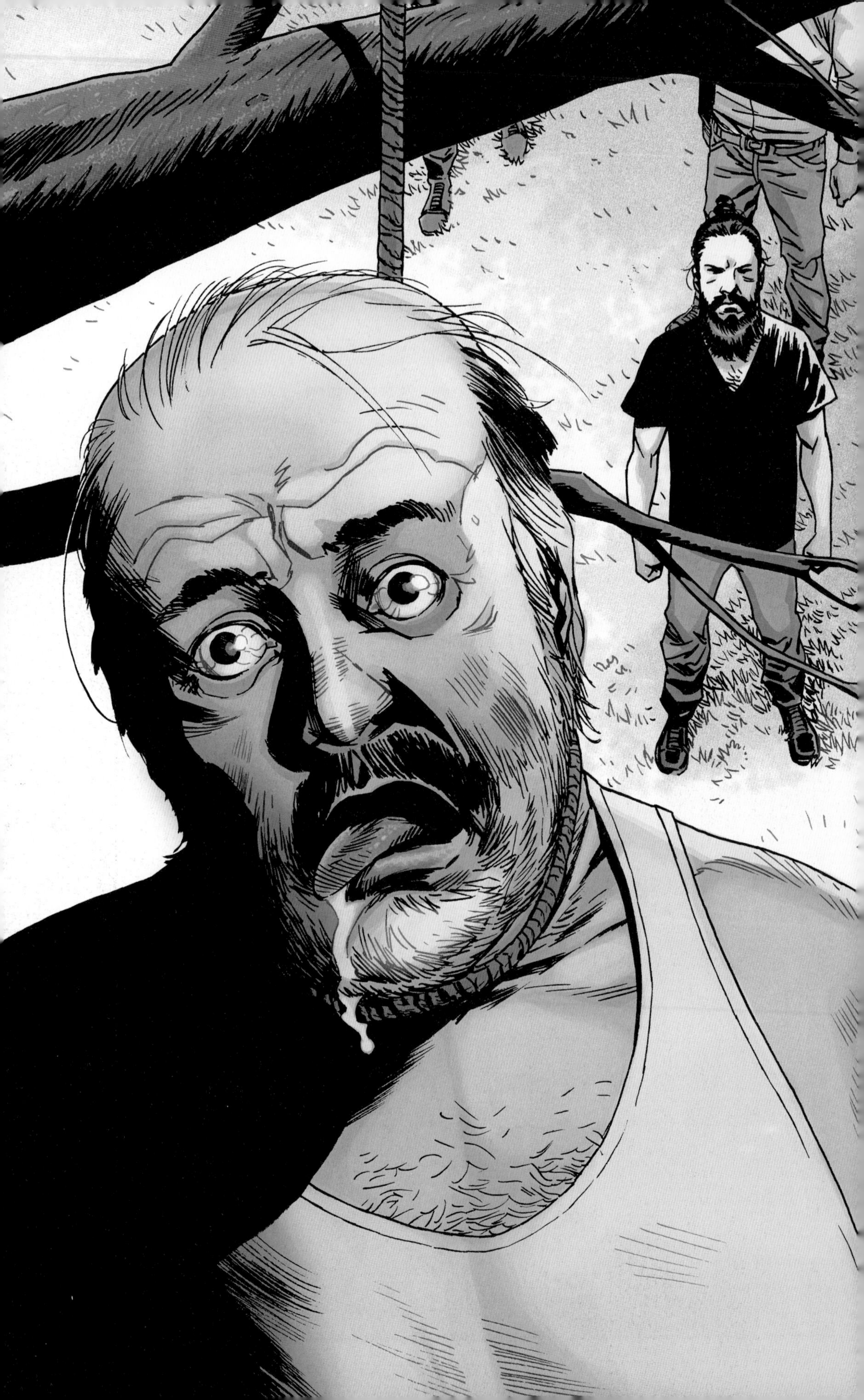

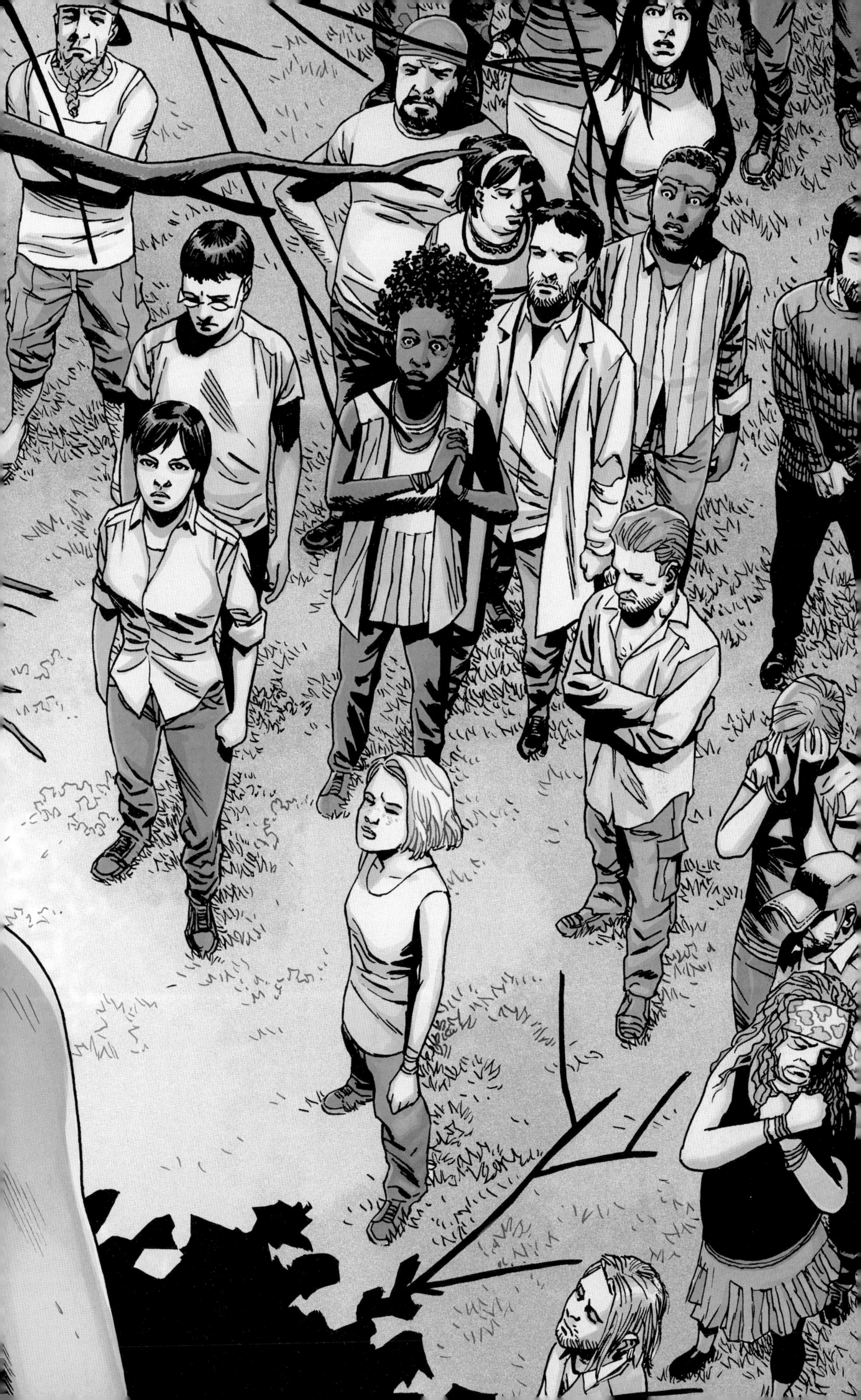

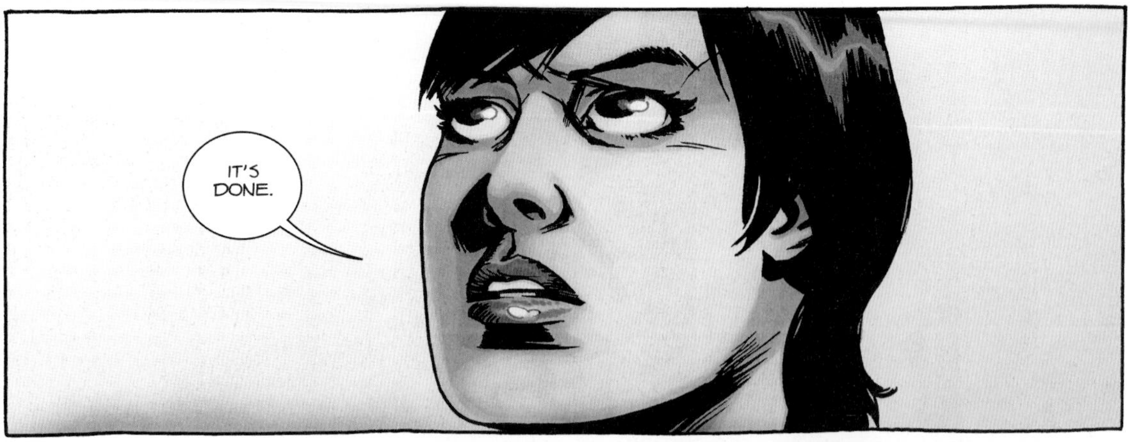
IT'S DONE.

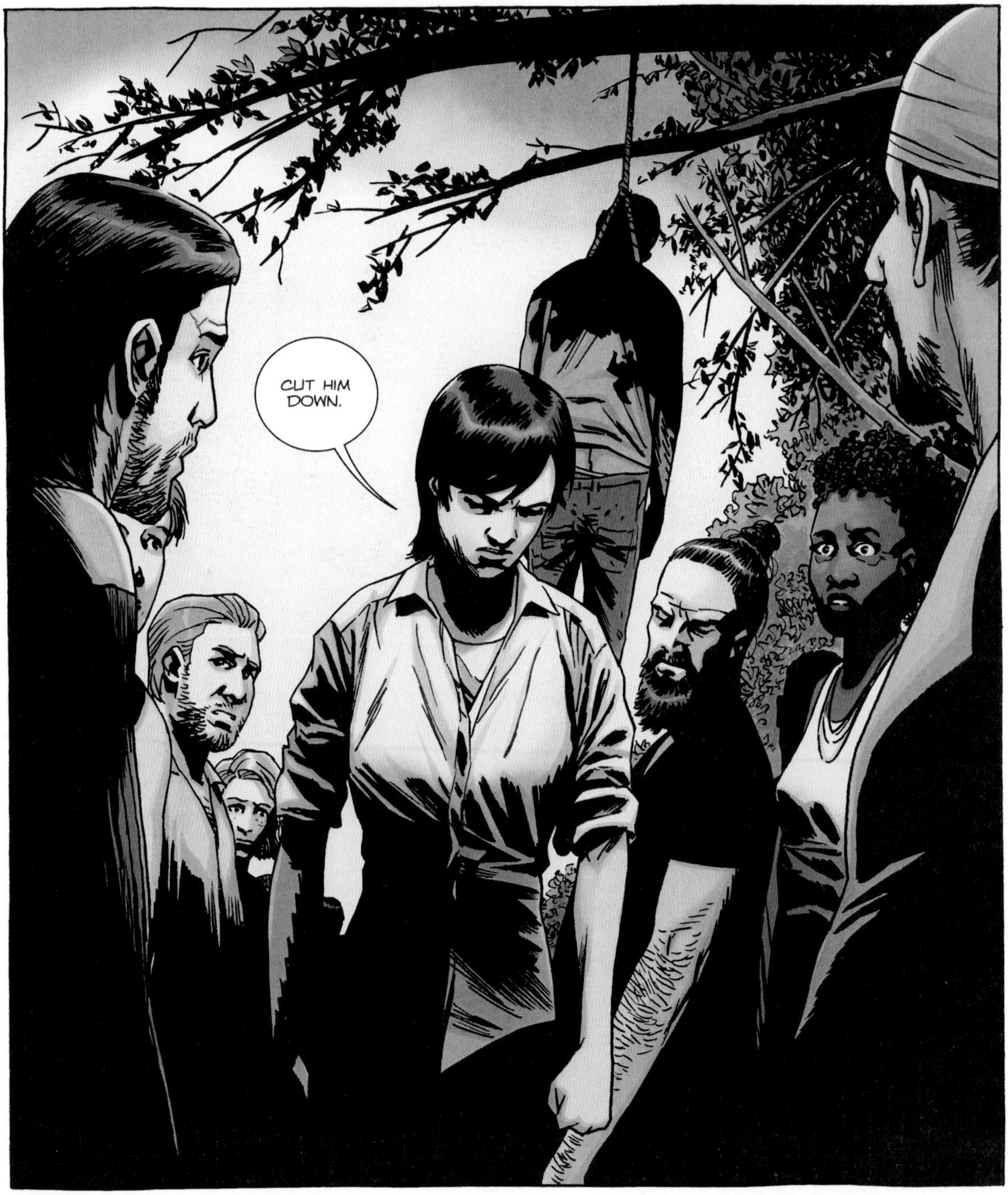
CUT HIM DOWN.

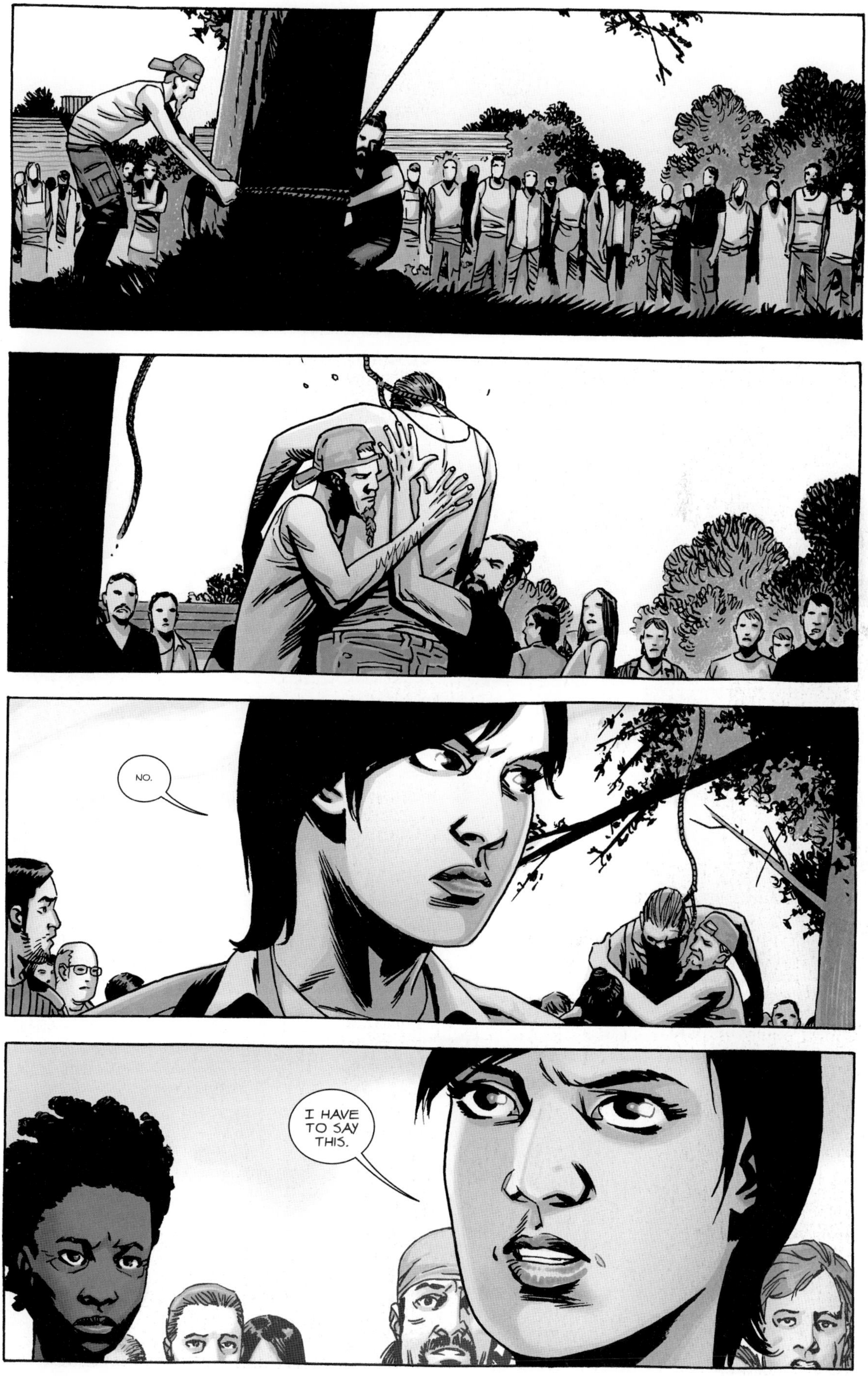
NO.
I HAVE TO SAY THIS.

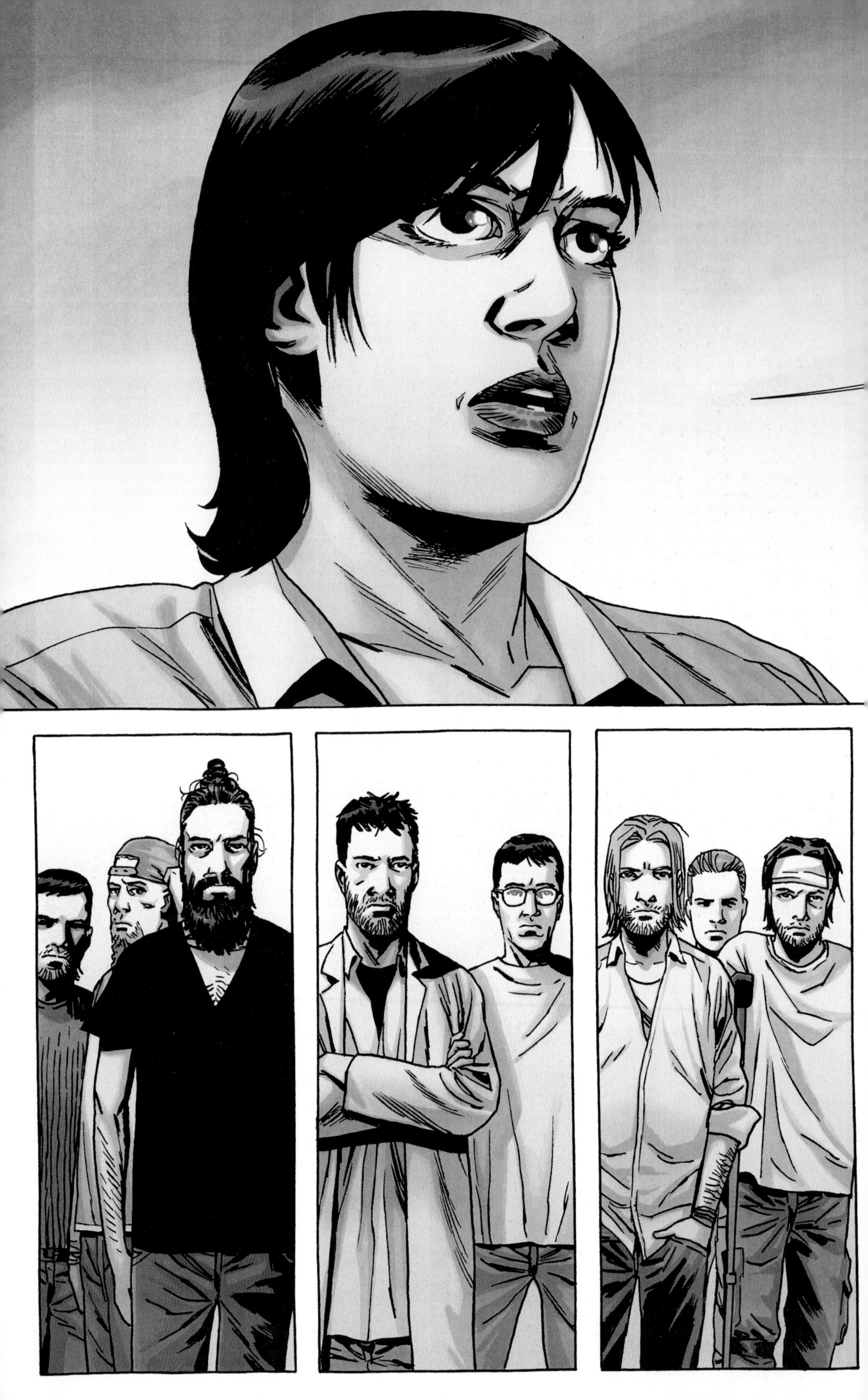

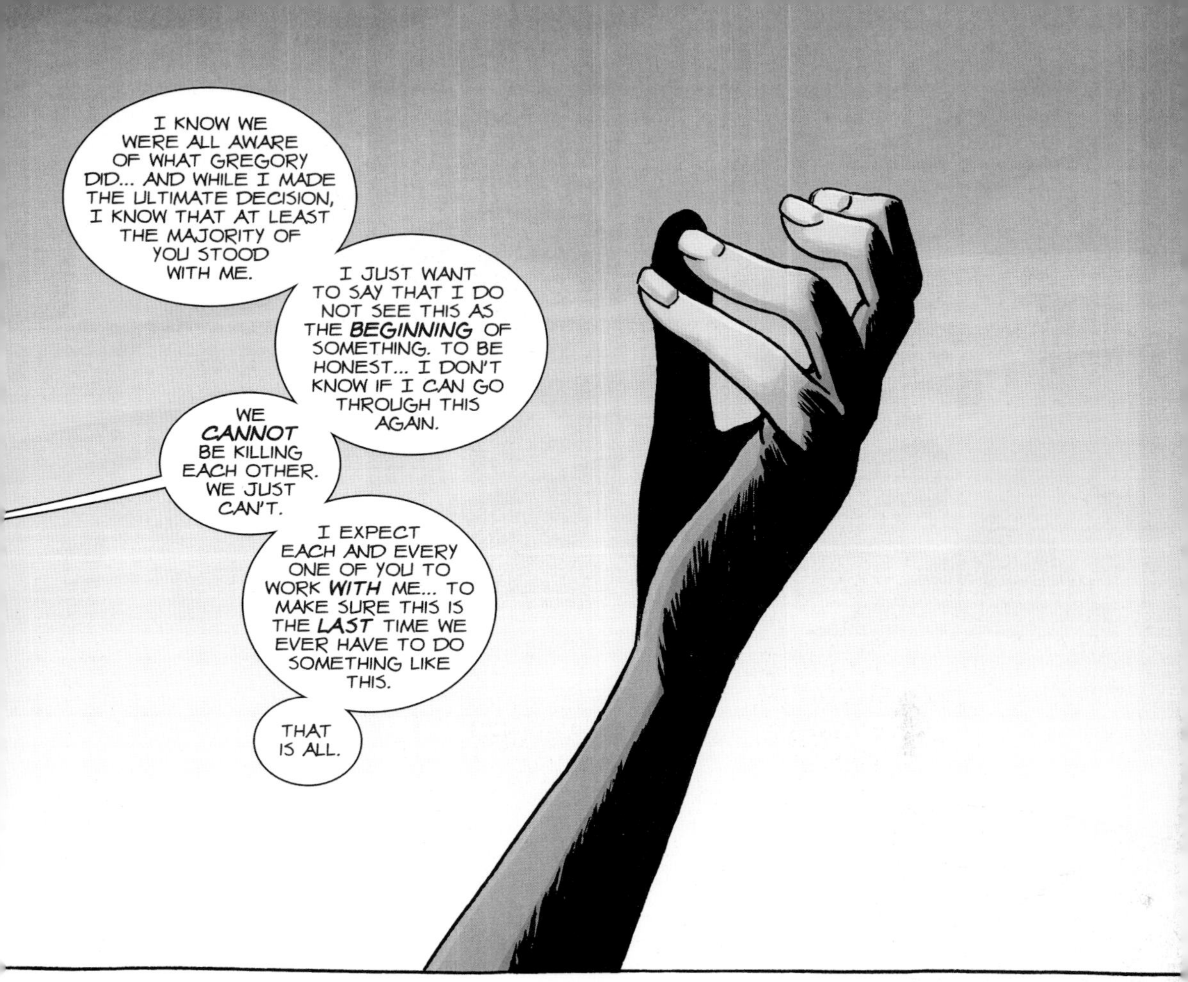
I KNOW WE WERE ALL AWARE OF WHAT GREGORY DID... AND WHILE I MADE THE ULTIMATE DECISION, I KNOW THAT AT LEAST THE MAJORITY OF YOU STOOD WITH ME.
I JUST WANT TO SAY THAT I DO NOT SEE THIS AS THE BEGINNING OF SOMETHING. TO BE HONEST... I DON'T KNOW IF I CAN GO THROUGH THIS AGAIN.
WE CANNOT BE KILLING EACH OTHER. WE JUST CAN'T.
I EXPECT EACH AND EVERY ONE OF YOU TO WORK WITH ME... TO MAKE SURE THIS IS THE LAST TIME WE EVER HAVE TO DO SOMETHING LIKE THIS.
THAT IS ALL.
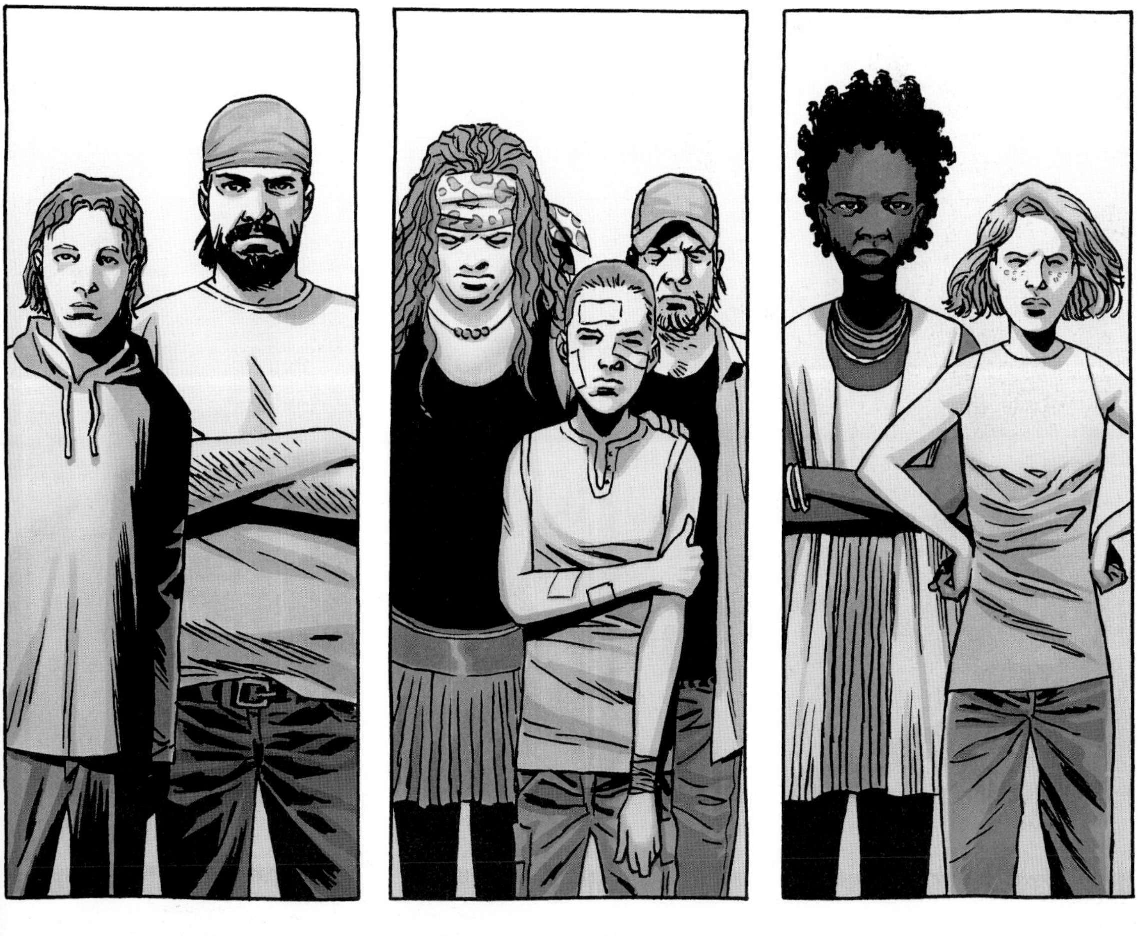

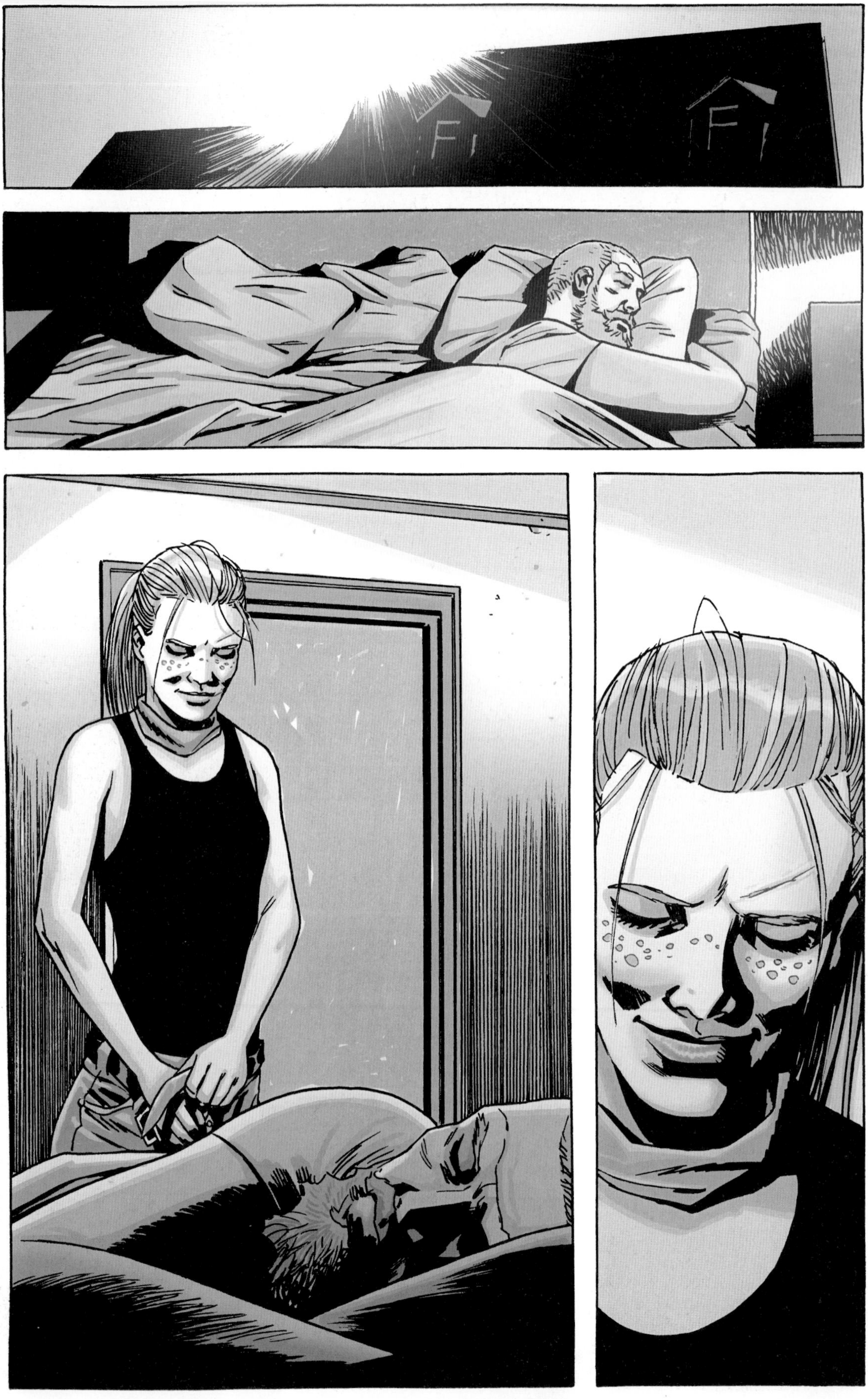
F
F

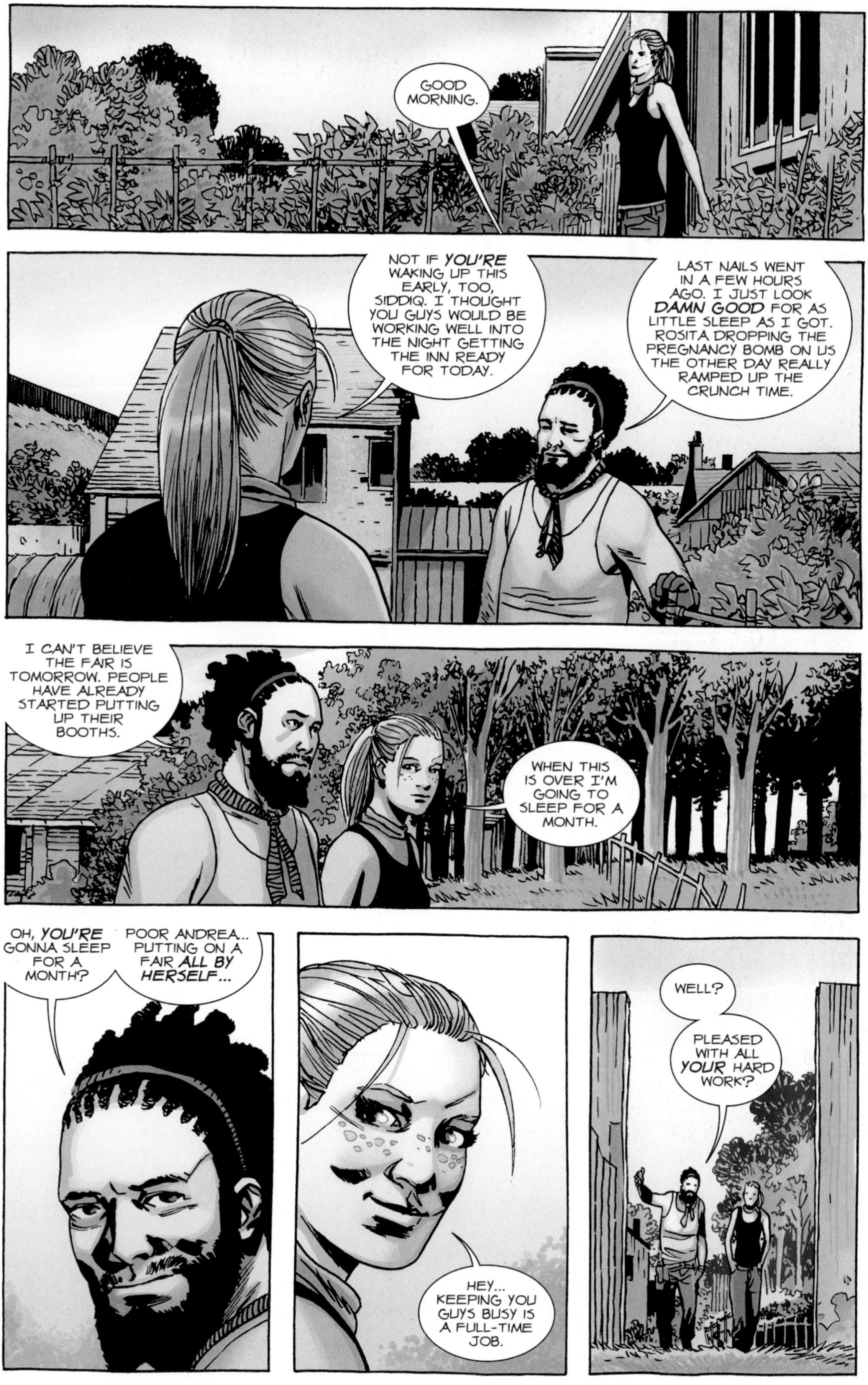
GOOD MORNING.
NOT IF YOU'RE WAKING UP THIS EARLY, TOO, SIDDIQ. I THOUGHT YOU GUYS WOULD BE WORKING WELL INTO THE NIGHT GETTING THE INN READY FOR TODAY.
LAST NAILS WENT IN A FEW HOURS AGO. I JUST LOOK DAMN GOOD FOR AS LITTLE SLEEP AS I GOT. ROSITA DROPPING THE PREGNANCY BOMB ON US THE OTHER DAY REALLY RAMPED UP THE CRUNCH TIME.
I CAN'T BELIEVE THE FAIR IS TOMORROW. PEOPLE HAVE ALREADY STARTED PUTTING UP THEIR BOOTHS.
WHEN THIS IS OVER I'M GOING TO SLEEP FOR A MONTH.
OH, YOU'RE GONNA SLEEP FOR A MONTH?
POOR ANDREA... PUTTING ON A FAIR ALL BY HERSELF...
HEY... KEEPING YOU GUYS BUSY IS A FULL-TIME JOB.
WELL?
PLEASED WITH ALL YOUR HARD WORK?

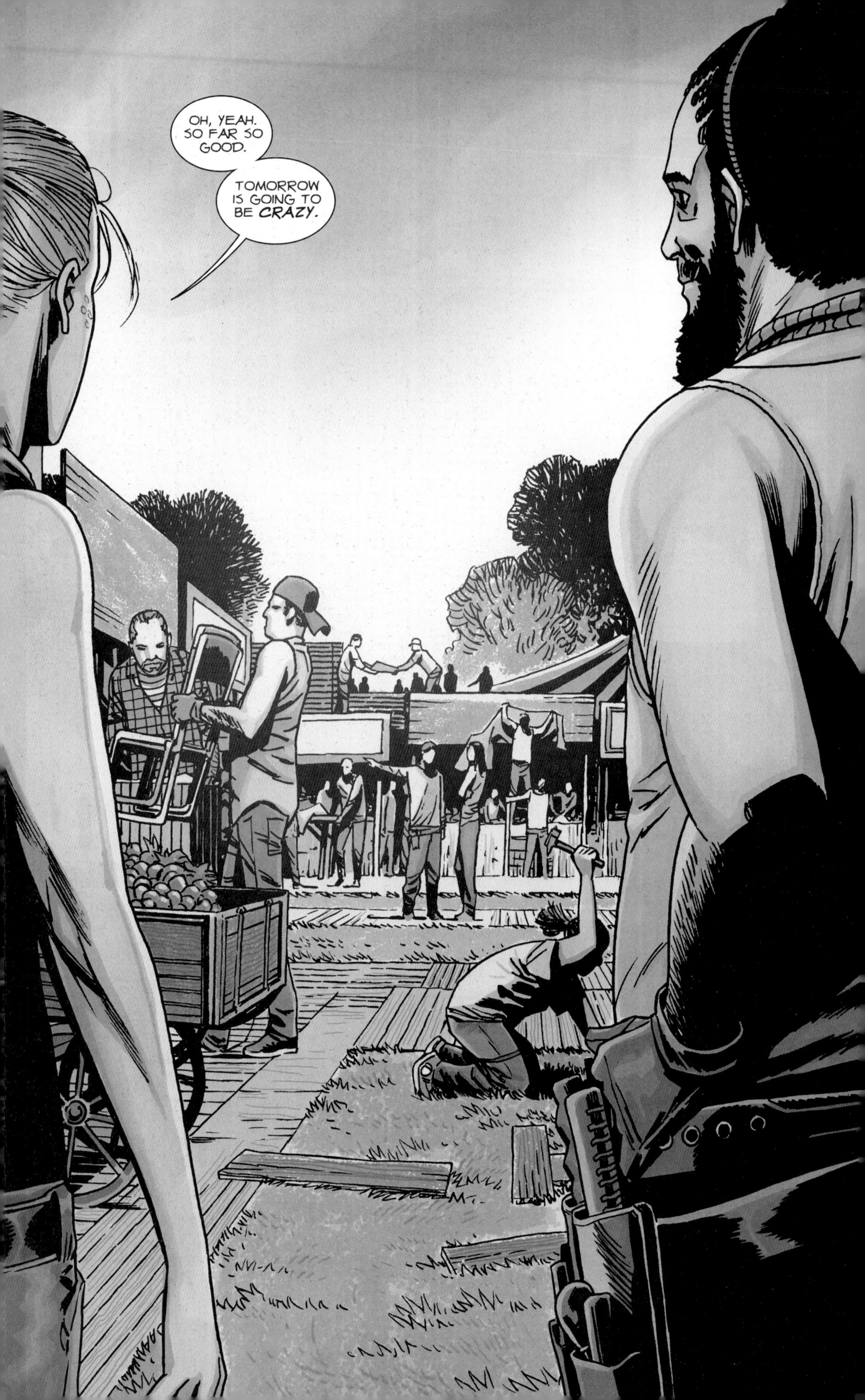
OH, YEAH. SO FAR SO GOOD.
TOMORROW IS GOING TO BE CRAZY.

EVERYTHING OKAY?

YEAH... OF COURSE. THIS IS JUST... THIS IS *STRANGE*... SEEING ALL THIS.

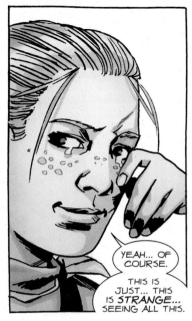

IT'S GOING TO TAKE SOME GETTING USED TO.

WELL, GET USED TO IT... DOESN'T RICK WANT TO DO THIS, WHAT-- TWICE A YEAR?

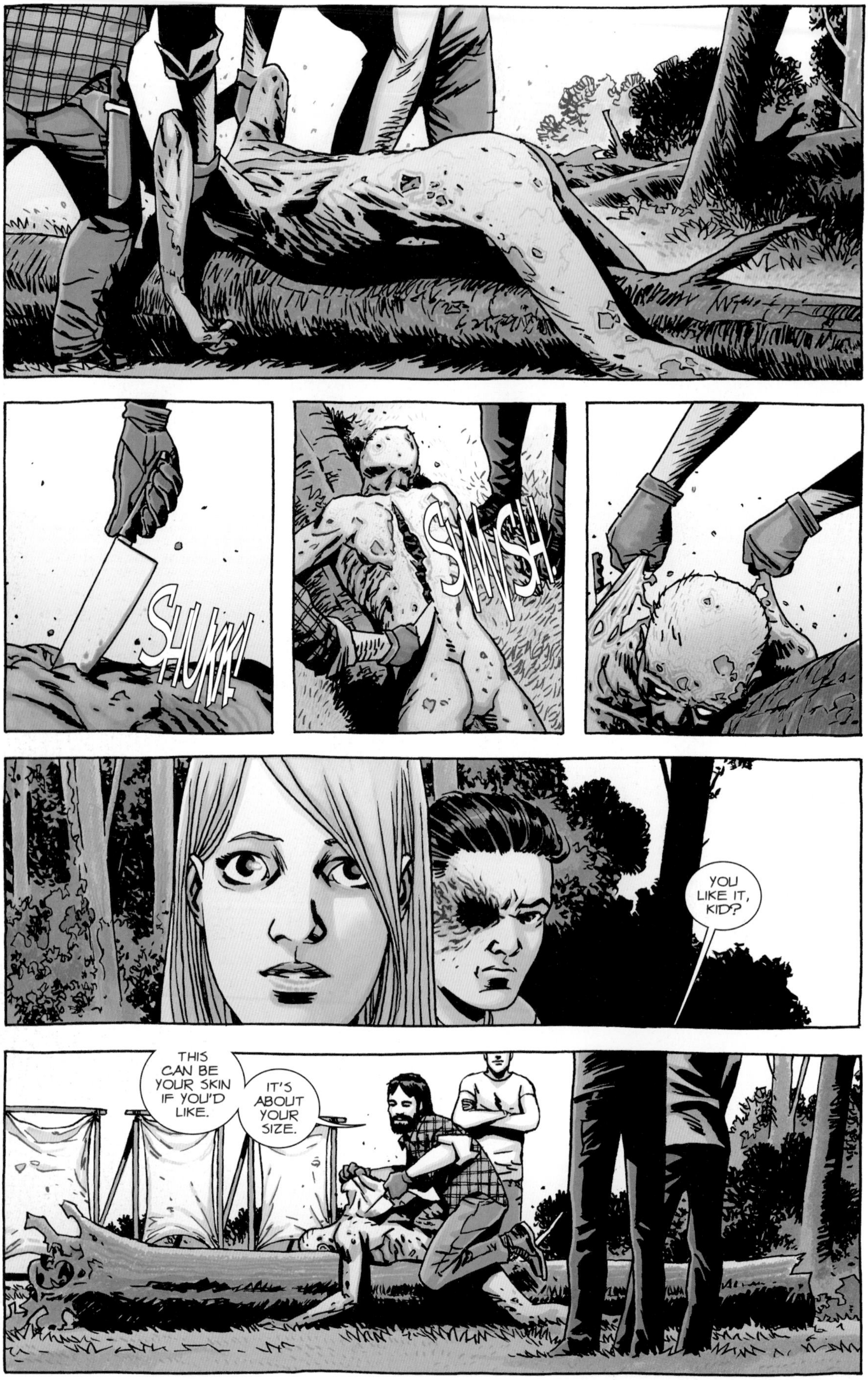
SHUKK!
SWISH!
YOU LIKE IT, KID?
THIS CAN BE YOUR SKIN IF YOU'D LIKE.
IT'S ABOUT YOUR SIZE.

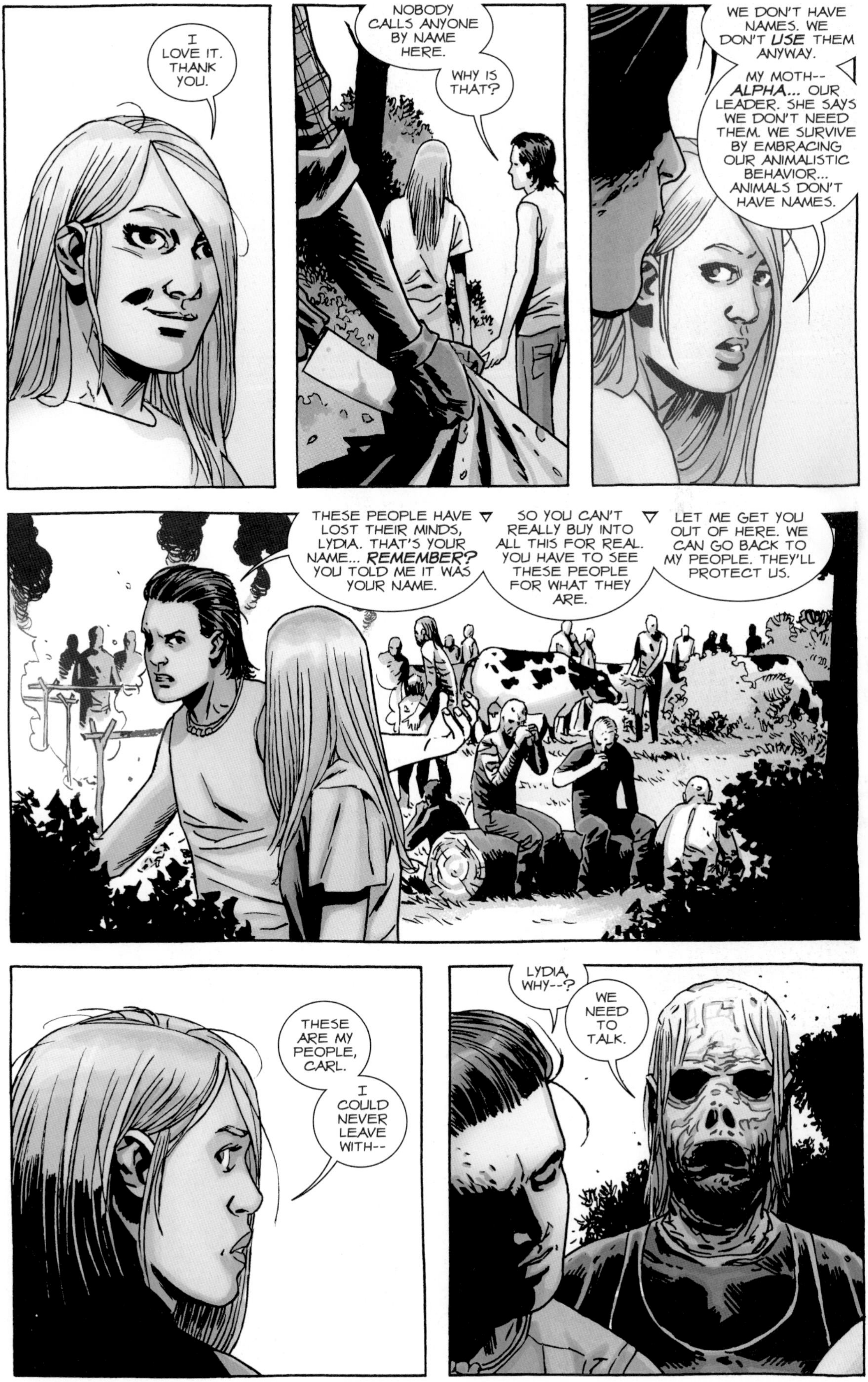
I LOVE IT. THANK YOU.
NOBODY CALLS ANYONE BY NAME HERE.
WHY IS THAT?
WE DON'T HAVE NAMES. WE DON'T USE THEM ANYWAY.
MY MOTH-- ALPHA... OUR LEADER. SHE SAYS WE DON'T NEED THEM. WE SURVIVE BY EMBRACING OUR ANIMALISTIC BEHAVIOR... ANIMALS DON'T HAVE NAMES.
THESE PEOPLE HAVE LOST THEIR MINDS, LYDIA. THAT'S YOUR NAME... REMEMBER? YOU TOLD ME IT WAS YOUR NAME.
SO YOU CAN'T REALLY BUY INTO ALL THIS FOR REAL. YOU HAVE TO SEE THESE PEOPLE FOR WHAT THEY ARE.
LET ME GET YOU OUT OF HERE. WE CAN GO BACK TO MY PEOPLE. THEY'LL PROTECT US.
THESE ARE MY PEOPLE, CARL.
I COULD NEVER LEAVE WITH--
LYDIA, WHY--?
WE NEED TO TALK.

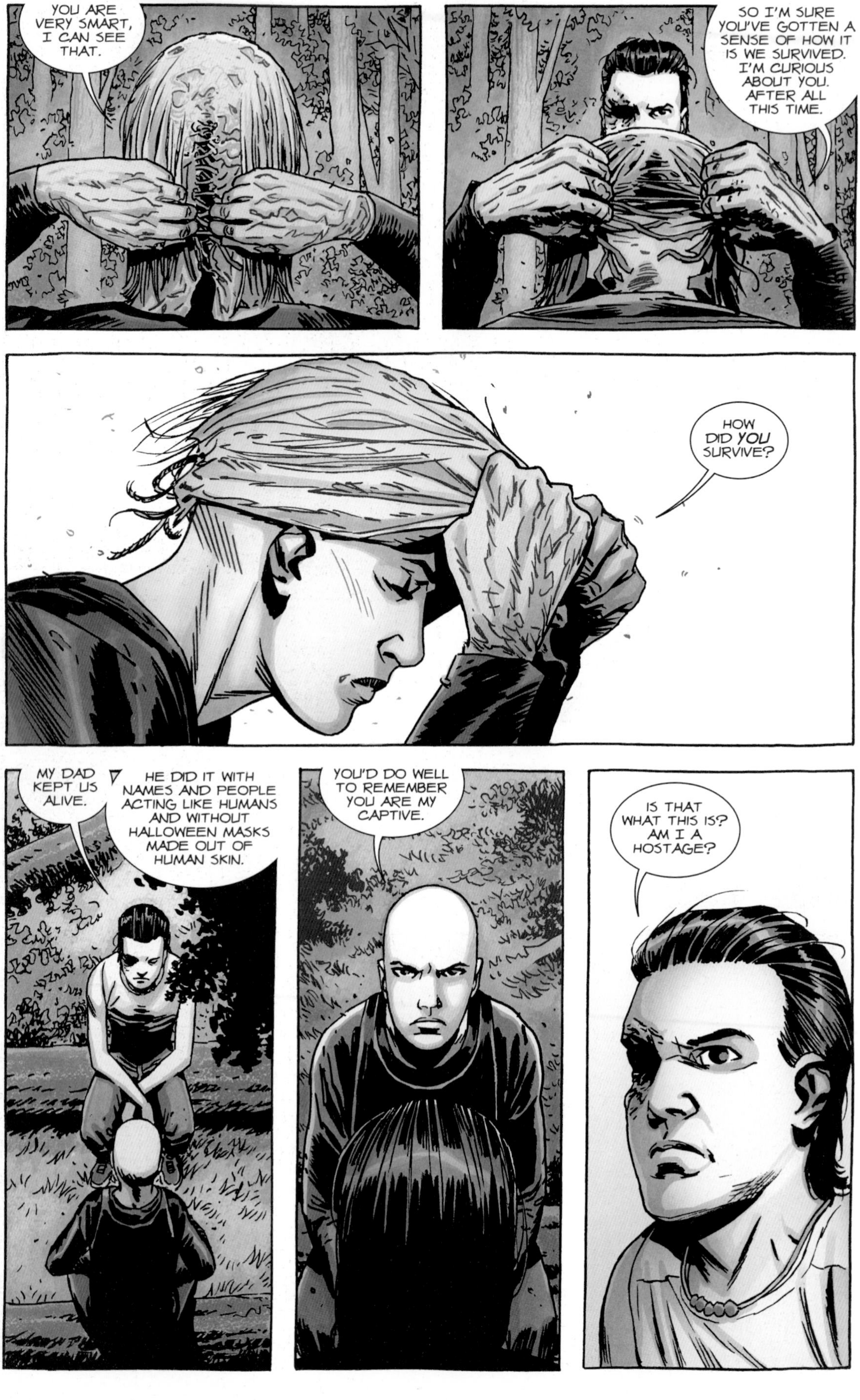
YOU ARE VERY SMART, I CAN SEE THAT.
SO I'M SURE YOU'VE GOTTEN A SENSE OF HOW IT IS WE SURVIVED. I'M CURIOUS ABOUT YOU. AFTER ALL THIS TIME.
HOW DID *YOU* SURVIVE?
MY DAD KEPT US ALIVE.
HE DID IT WITH NAMES AND PEOPLE ACTING LIKE HUMANS AND WITHOUT HALLOWEEN MASKS MADE OUT OF HUMAN SKIN.
YOU'D DO WELL TO REMEMBER YOU ARE MY CAPTIVE.
IS THAT WHAT THIS IS? AM I A HOSTAGE?

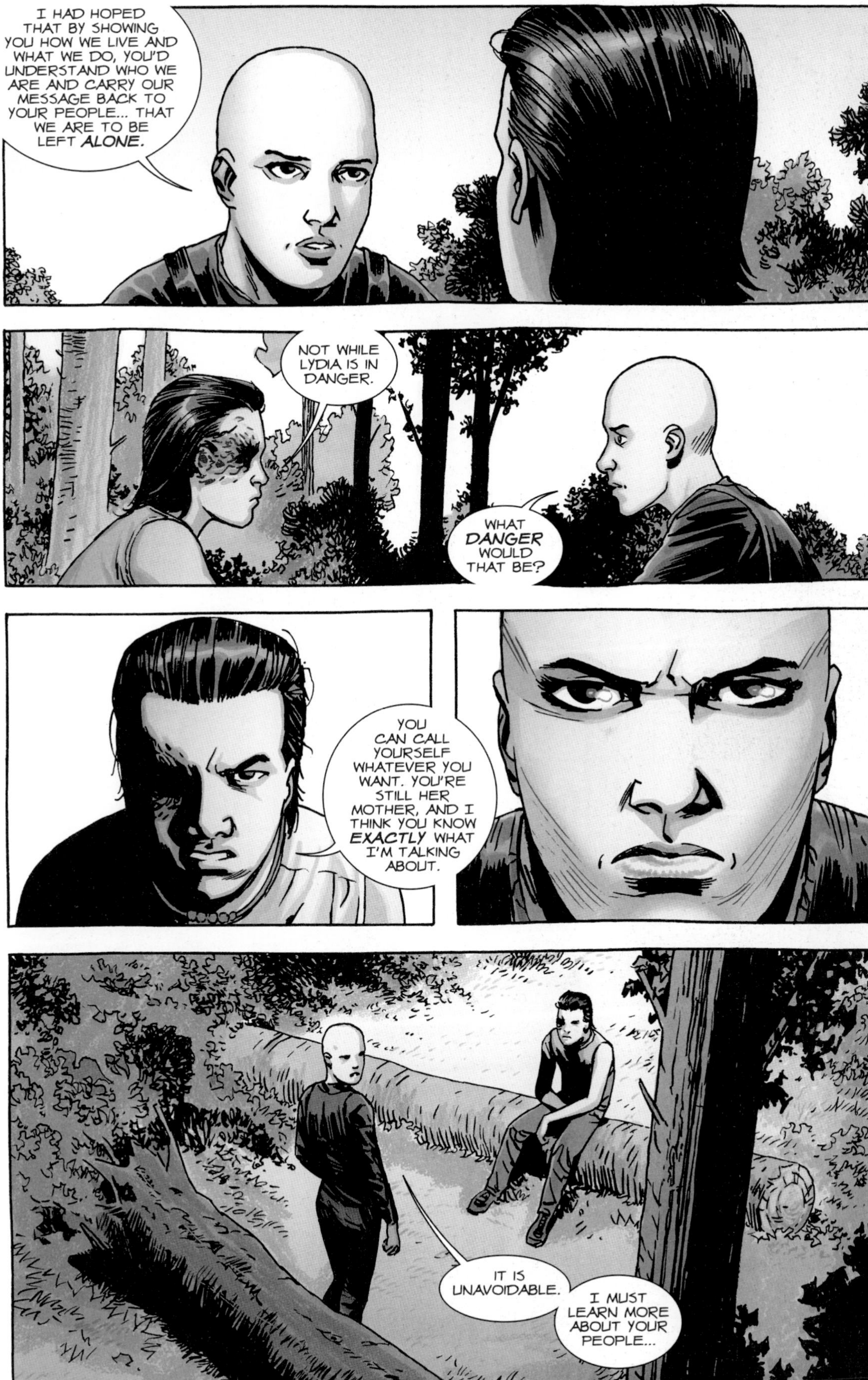
I HAD HOPED THAT BY SHOWING YOU HOW WE LIVE AND WHAT WE DO, YOU'D UNDERSTAND WHO WE ARE AND CARRY OUR MESSAGE BACK TO YOUR PEOPLE... THAT WE ARE TO BE LEFT ALONE.
NOT WHILE LYDIA IS IN DANGER.
WHAT DANGER WOULD THAT BE?
YOU CAN CALL YOURSELF WHATEVER YOU WANT. YOU'RE STILL HER MOTHER, AND I THINK YOU KNOW EXACTLY WHAT I'M TALKING ABOUT.
IT IS UNAVOIDABLE.
I MUST LEARN MORE ABOUT YOUR PEOPLE...

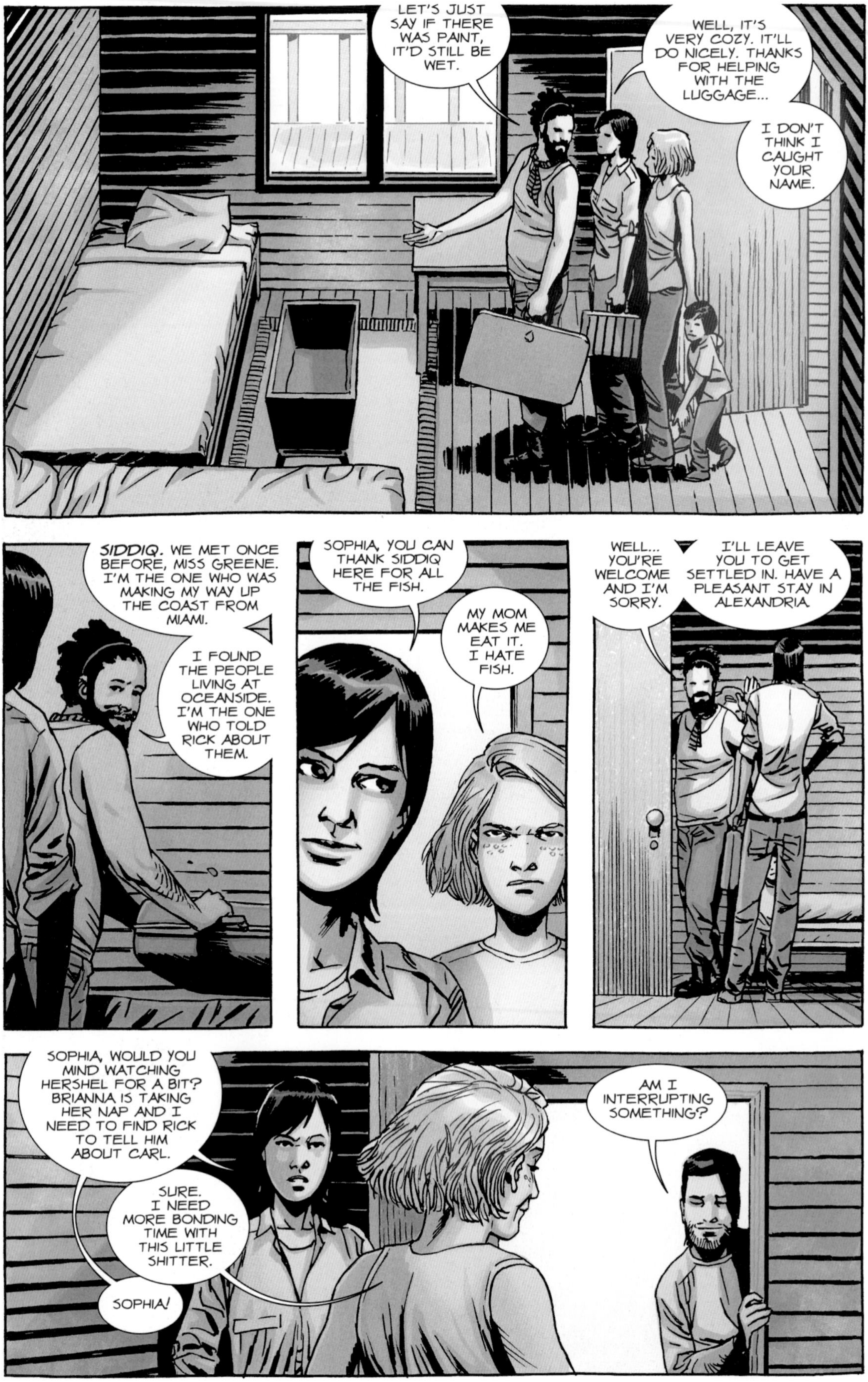
LET'S JUST SAY IF THERE WAS PAINT, IT'D STILL BE WET.
WELL, IT'S VERY COZY. IT'LL DO NICELY. THANKS FOR HELPING WITH THE LUGGAGE...
I DON'T THINK I CAUGHT YOUR NAME.
SIDDIQ. WE MET ONCE BEFORE, MISS GREENE. I'M THE ONE WHO WAS MAKING MY WAY UP THE COAST FROM MIAMI.
I FOUND THE PEOPLE LIVING AT OCEANSIDE. I'M THE ONE WHO TOLD RICK ABOUT THEM.
SOPHIA, YOU CAN THANK SIDDIQ HERE FOR ALL THE FISH.
MY MOM MAKES ME EAT IT. I HATE FISH.
WELL... YOU'RE WELCOME AND I'M SORRY.
I'LL LEAVE YOU TO GET SETTLED IN. HAVE A PLEASANT STAY IN ALEXANDRIA.
SOPHIA, WOULD YOU MIND WATCHING HERSHEL FOR A BIT? BRIANNA IS TAKING HER NAP AND I NEED TO FIND RICK TO TELL HIM ABOUT CARL.
SURE. I NEED MORE BONDING TIME WITH THIS LITTLE SHITTER.
SOPHIA!
AM I INTERRUPTING SOMETHING?

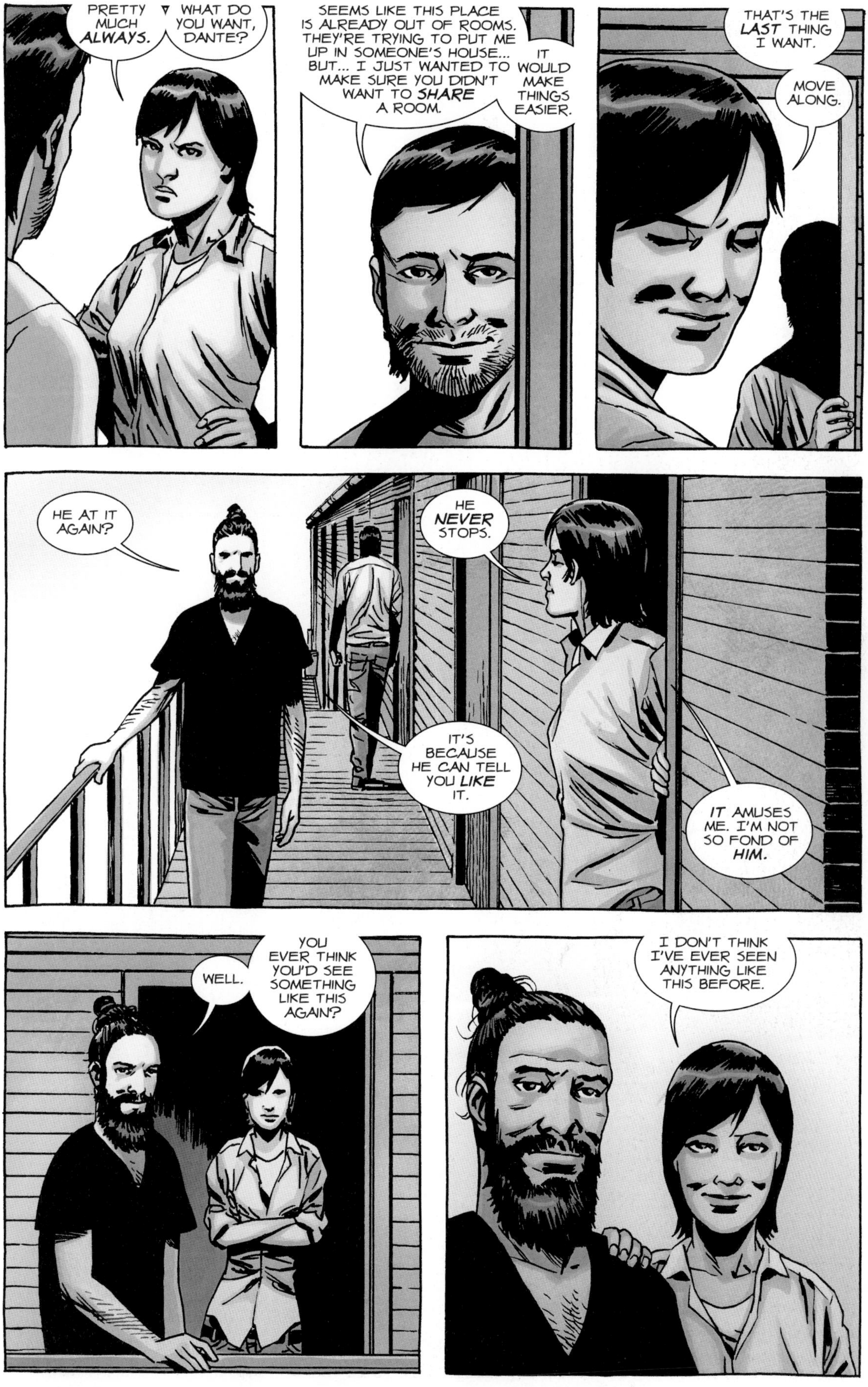

PRETTY MUCH ALWAYS.
WHAT DO YOU WANT, DANTE?
SEEMS LIKE THIS PLACE IS ALREADY OUT OF ROOMS. THEY'RE TRYING TO PUT ME UP IN SOMEONE'S HOUSE... BUT... I JUST WANTED TO MAKE SURE YOU DIDN'T WANT TO SHARE A ROOM.
IT WOULD MAKE THINGS EASIER.
THAT'S THE LAST THING I WANT.
MOVE ALONG.
HE AT IT AGAIN?
HE NEVER STOPS.
IT'S BECAUSE HE CAN TELL YOU LIKE IT.
IT AMUSES ME. I'M NOT SO FOND OF HIM.
WELL.
YOU EVER THINK YOU'D SEE SOMETHING LIKE THIS AGAIN?
I DON'T THINK I'VE EVER SEEN ANYTHING LIKE THIS BEFORE.

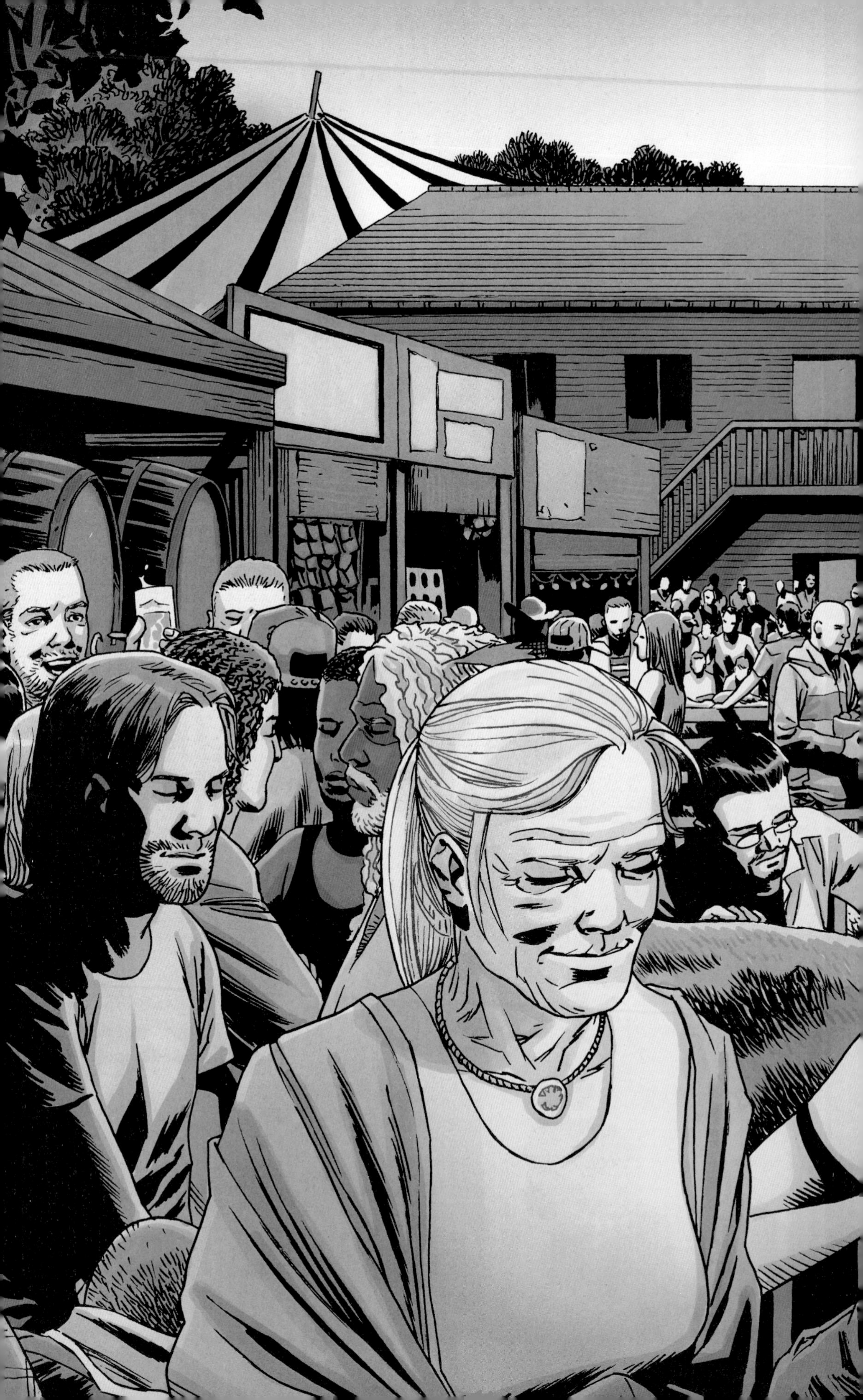

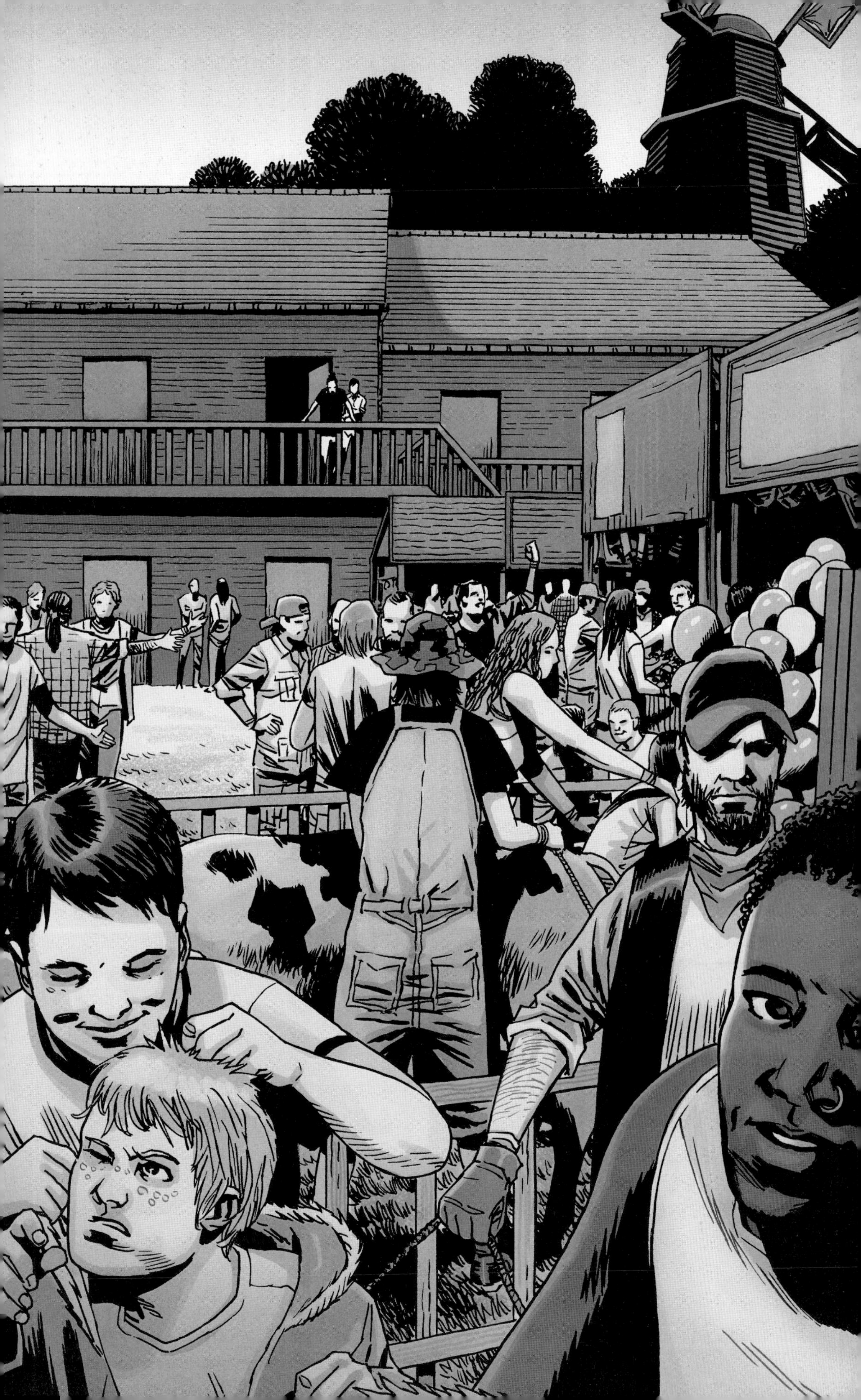

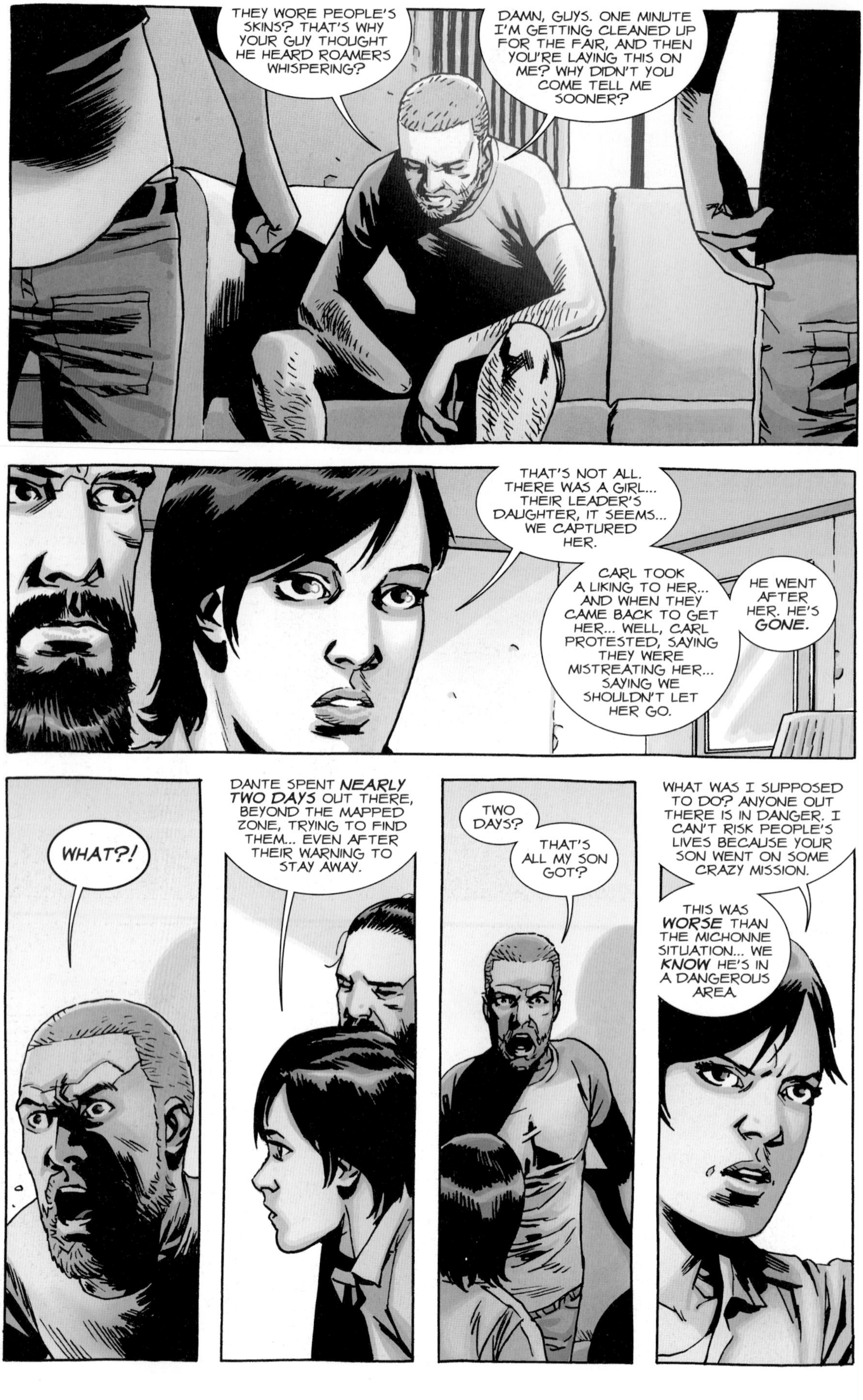

THEY WORE PEOPLE'S SKINS? THAT'S WHY YOUR GUY THOUGHT HE HEARD ROAMERS WHISPERING?
DAMN, GUYS. ONE MINUTE I'M GETTING CLEANED UP FOR THE FAIR, AND THEN YOU'RE LAYING THIS ON ME? WHY DIDN'T YOU COME TELL ME SOONER?
THAT'S NOT ALL. THERE WAS A GIRL... THEIR LEADER'S DAUGHTER, IT SEEMS... WE CAPTURED HER.
CARL TOOK A LIKING TO HER... AND WHEN THEY CAME BACK TO GET HER... WELL, CARL PROTESTED, SAYING THEY WERE MISTREATING HER... SAYING WE SHOULDN'T LET HER GO.
HE WENT AFTER HER. HE'S ***GONE.***
WHAT?!
DANTE SPENT ***NEARLY TWO DAYS*** OUT THERE, BEYOND THE MAPPED ZONE, TRYING TO FIND THEM... EVEN AFTER THEIR WARNING TO STAY AWAY.
TWO DAYS?
THAT'S ALL MY SON GOT?
WHAT WAS I SUPPOSED TO DO? ANYONE OUT THERE IS IN DANGER. I CAN'T RISK PEOPLE'S LIVES BECAUSE YOUR SON WENT ON SOME CRAZY MISSION.
THIS WAS ***WORSE*** THAN THE MICHONNE SITUATION... WE ***KNOW*** HE'S IN A DANGEROUS AREA

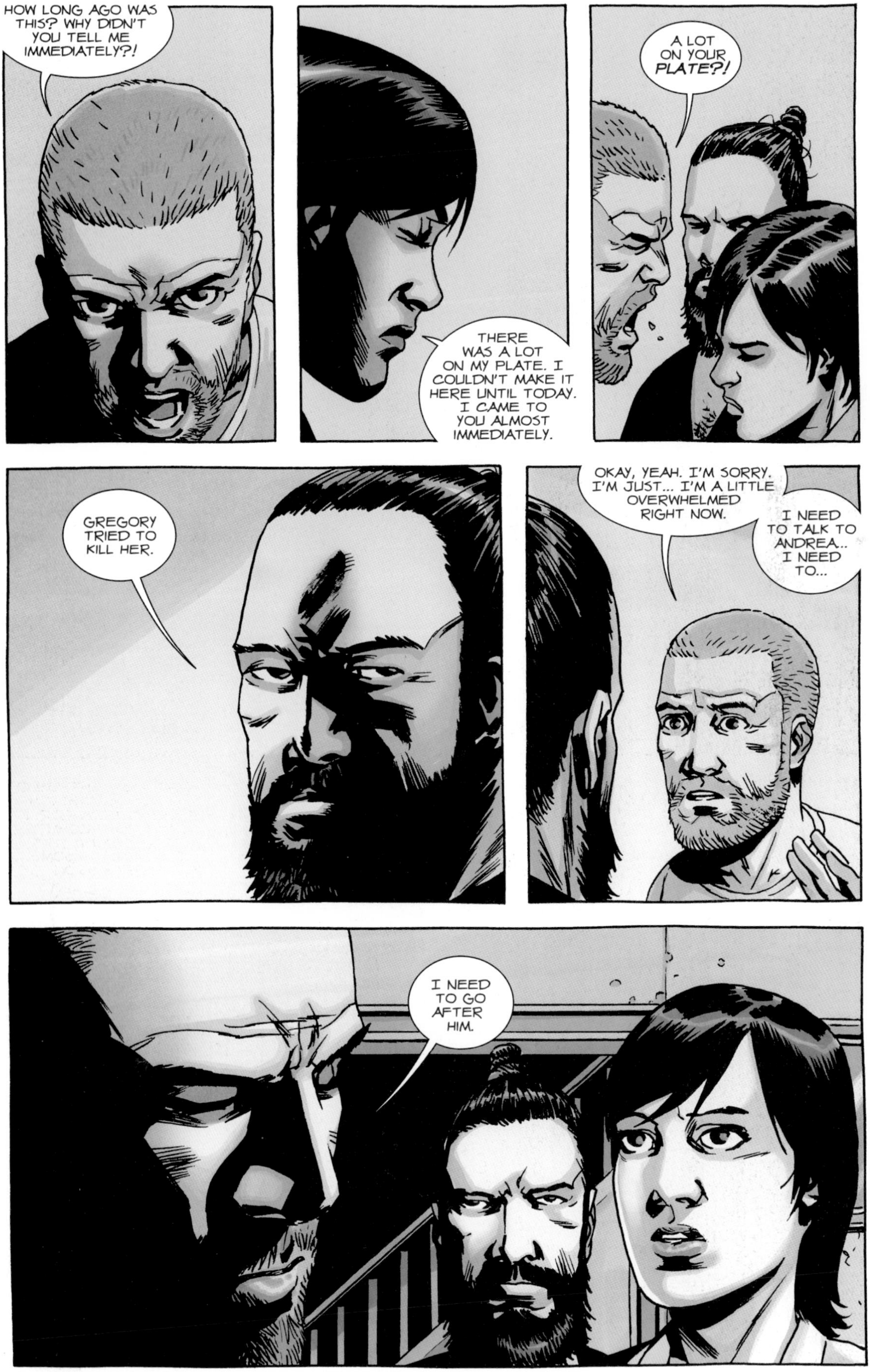
HOW LONG AGO WAS THIS? WHY DIDN'T YOU TELL ME IMMEDIATELY?!
THERE WAS A LOT ON MY PLATE. I COULDN'T MAKE IT HERE UNTIL TODAY. I CAME TO YOU ALMOST IMMEDIATELY.
A LOT ON YOUR PLATE?!
GREGORY TRIED TO KILL HER.
OKAY, YEAH. I'M SORRY. I'M JUST... I'M A LITTLE OVERWHELMED RIGHT NOW.
I NEED TO TALK TO ANDREA... I NEED TO...
I NEED TO GO AFTER HIM.

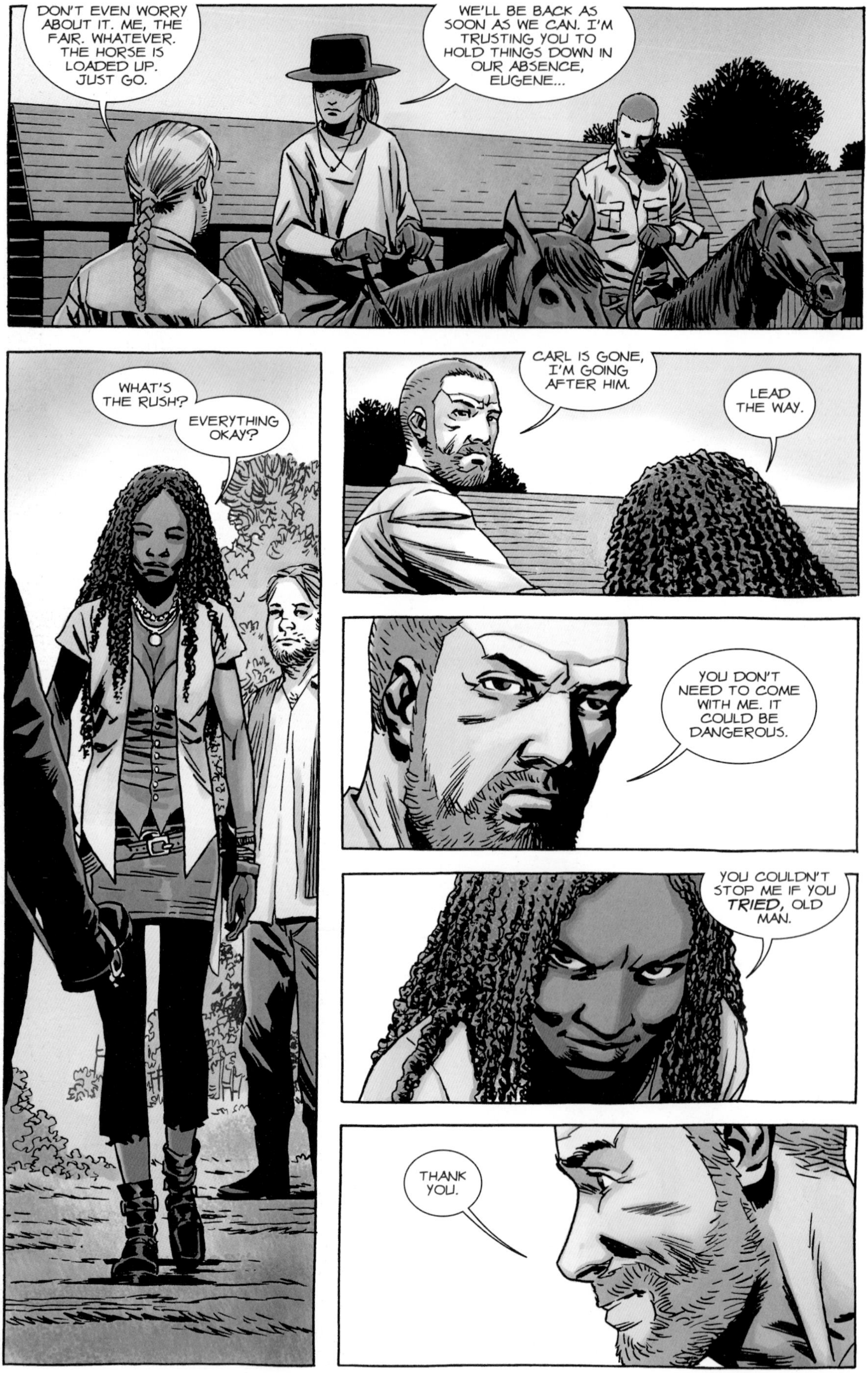
DON'T EVEN WORRY ABOUT IT. ME, THE FAIR. WHATEVER. THE HORSE IS LOADED UP. JUST GO.
WE'LL BE BACK AS SOON AS WE CAN. I'M TRUSTING YOU TO HOLD THINGS DOWN IN OUR ABSENCE, EUGENE...
WHAT'S THE RUSH?
EVERYTHING OKAY?
CARL IS GONE, I'M GOING AFTER HIM.
LEAD THE WAY.
YOU DON'T NEED TO COME WITH ME. IT COULD BE DANGEROUS.
YOU COULDN'T STOP ME IF YOU *TRIED,* OLD MAN.
THANK YOU.

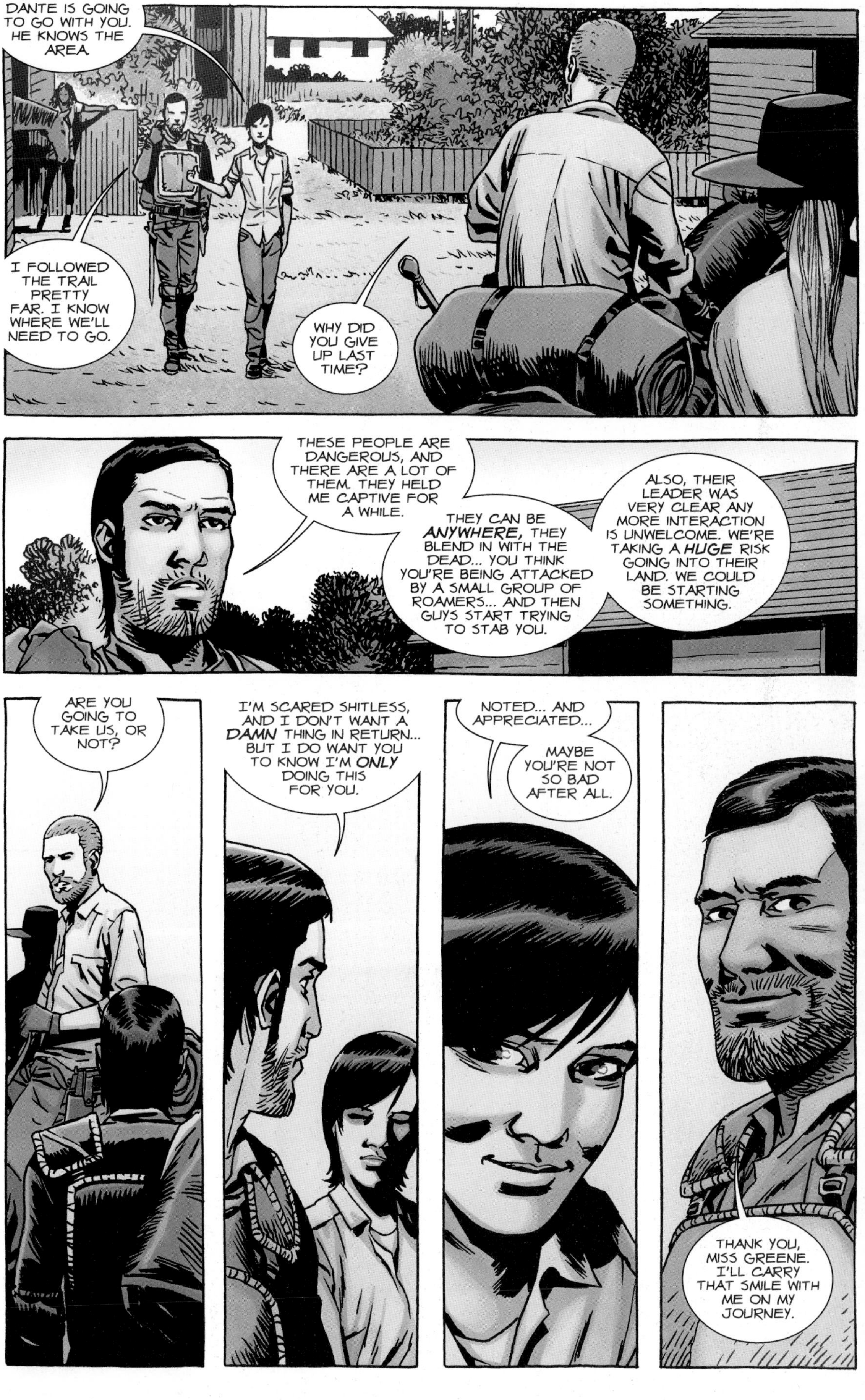
DANTE IS GOING TO GO WITH YOU. HE KNOWS THE AREA.
I FOLLOWED THE TRAIL PRETTY FAR. I KNOW WHERE WE'LL NEED TO GO.
WHY DID YOU GIVE UP LAST TIME?
THESE PEOPLE ARE DANGEROUS, AND THERE ARE A LOT OF THEM. THEY HELD ME CAPTIVE FOR A WHILE.
THEY CAN BE ANYWHERE, THEY BLEND IN WITH THE DEAD... YOU THINK YOU'RE BEING ATTACKED BY A SMALL GROUP OF ROAMERS... AND THEN GUYS START TRYING TO STAB YOU.
ALSO, THEIR LEADER WAS VERY CLEAR ANY MORE INTERACTION IS UNWELCOME. WE'RE TAKING A HUGE RISK GOING INTO THEIR LAND. WE COULD BE STARTING SOMETHING.
ARE YOU GOING TO TAKE US, OR NOT?
I'M SCARED SHITLESS, AND I DON'T WANT A DAMN THING IN RETURN... BUT I DO WANT YOU TO KNOW I'M ONLY DOING THIS FOR YOU.
NOTED... AND APPRECIATED...
MAYBE YOU'RE NOT SO BAD AFTER ALL.
THANK YOU, MISS GREENE. I'LL CARRY THAT SMILE WITH ME ON MY JOURNEY.

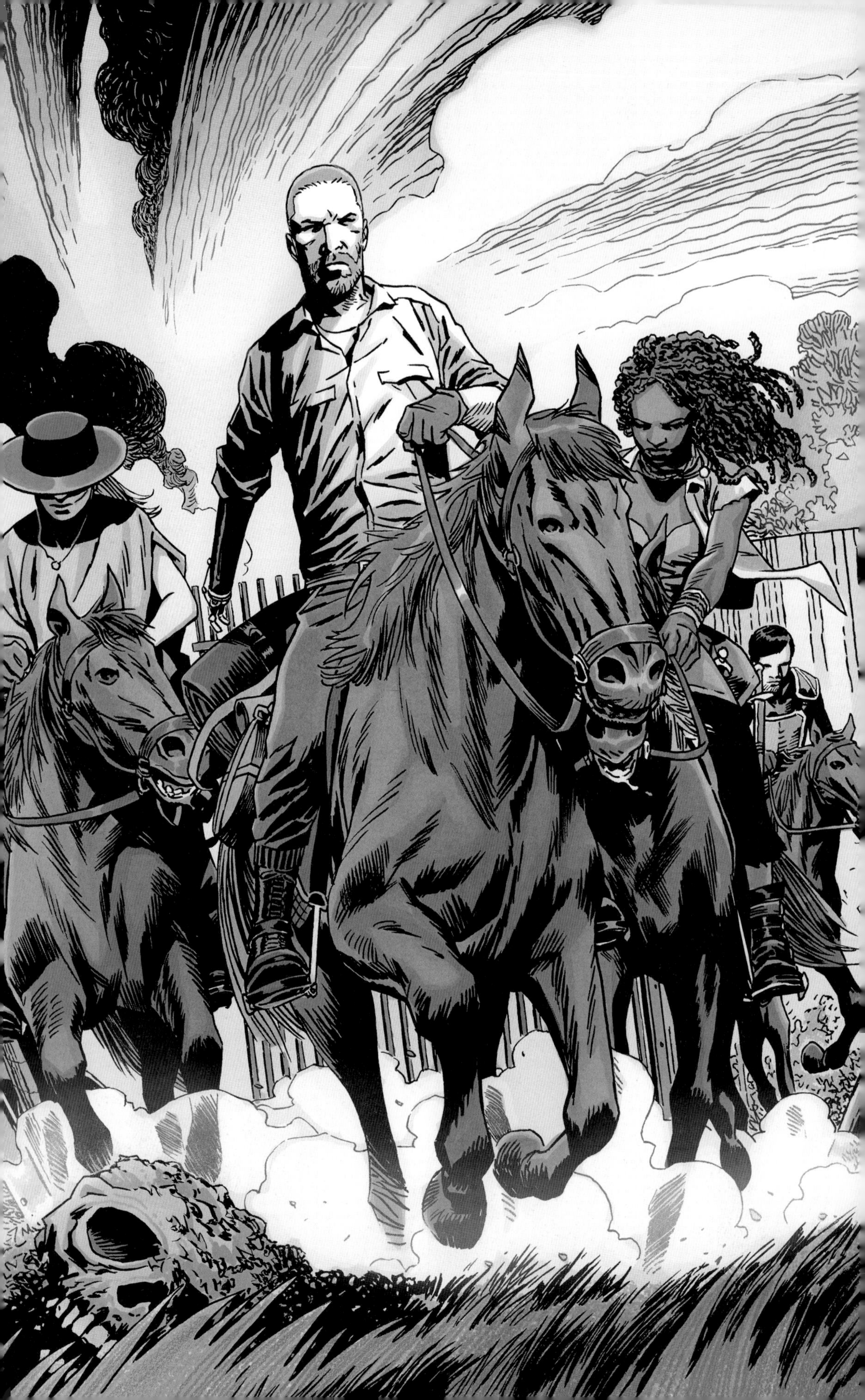

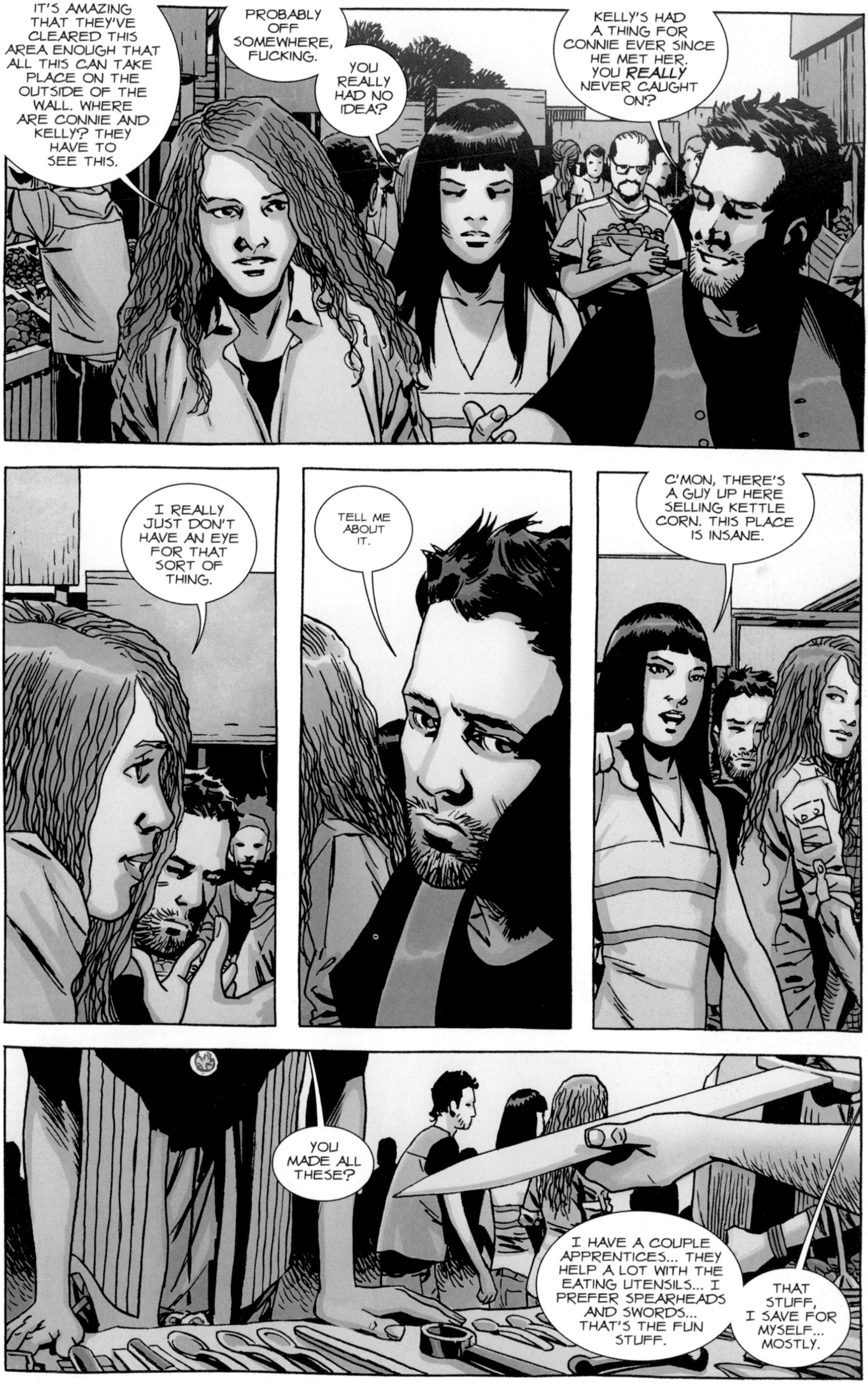
IT'S AMAZING THAT THEY'VE CLEARED THIS AREA ENOUGH THAT ALL THIS CAN TAKE PLACE ON THE OUTSIDE OF THE WALL. WHERE ARE CONNIE AND KELLY? THEY HAVE TO SEE THIS.
PROBABLY OFF SOMEWHERE, FUCKING.
YOU REALLY HAD NO IDEA?
KELLY'S HAD A THING FOR CONNIE EVER SINCE HE MET HER. YOU REALLY NEVER CAUGHT ON?
I REALLY JUST DON'T HAVE AN EYE FOR THAT SORT OF THING.
TELL ME ABOUT IT.
C'MON, THERE'S A GUY UP HERE SELLING KETTLE CORN. THIS PLACE IS INSANE.
YOU MADE ALL THESE?
I HAVE A COUPLE APPRENTICES... THEY HELP A LOT WITH THE EATING UTENSILS... I PREFER SPEARHEADS AND SWORDS... THAT'S THE FUN STUFF.
THAT STUFF, I SAVE FOR MYSELF... MOSTLY.

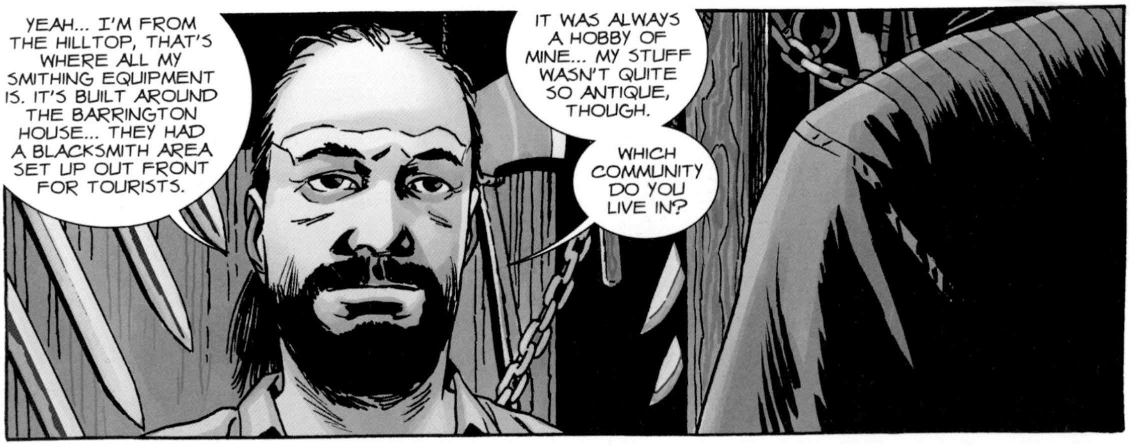
YEAH... I'M FROM THE HILLTOP, THAT'S WHERE ALL MY SMITHING EQUIPMENT IS. IT'S BUILT AROUND THE BARRINGTON HOUSE... THEY HAD A BLACKSMITH AREA SET UP OUT FRONT FOR TOURISTS.
IT WAS ALWAYS A HOBBY OF MINE... MY STUFF WASN'T QUITE SO ANTIQUE, THOUGH.
WHICH COMMUNITY DO YOU LIVE IN?

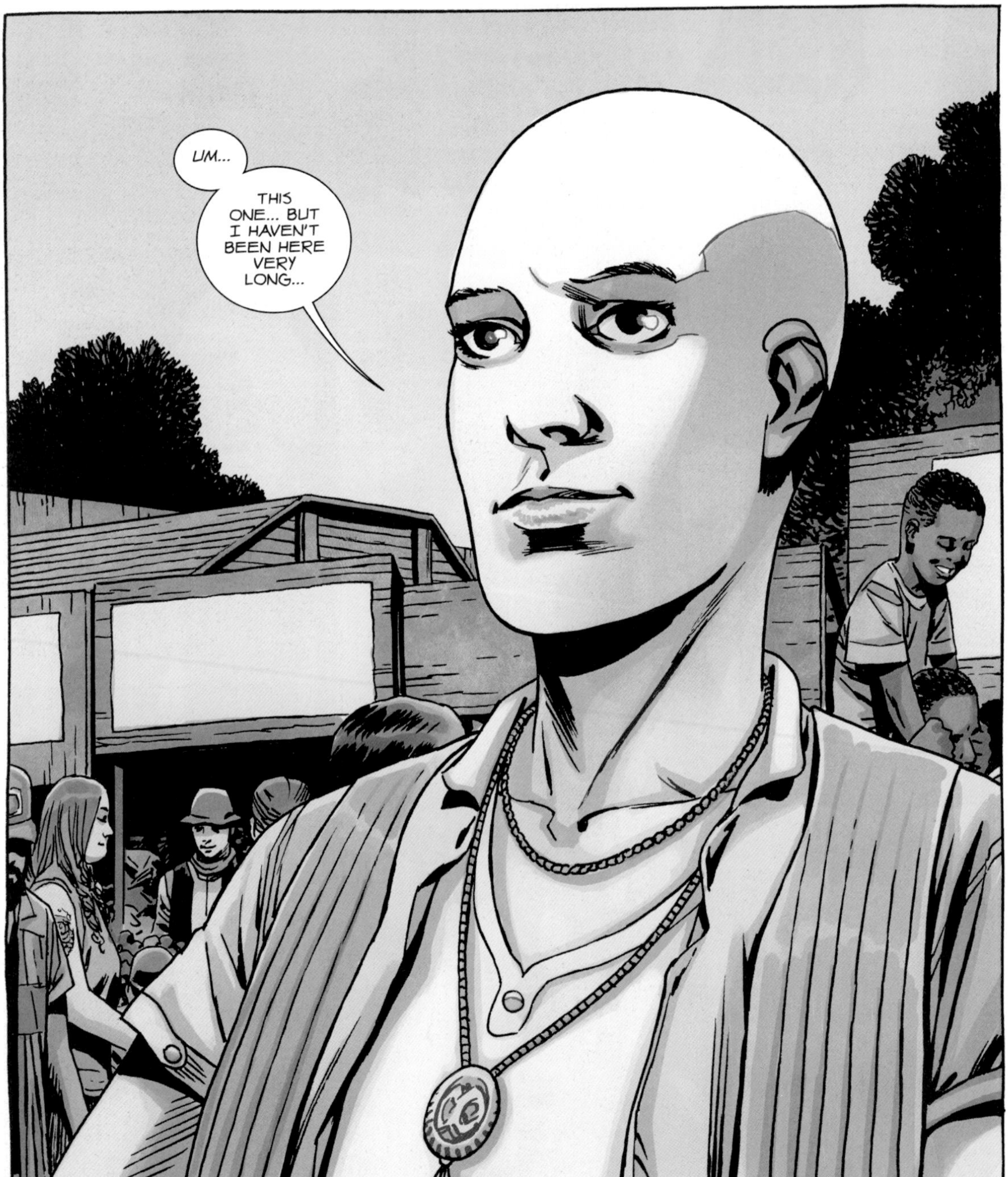
UM...
THIS ONE... BUT I HAVEN'T BEEN HERE VERY LONG...

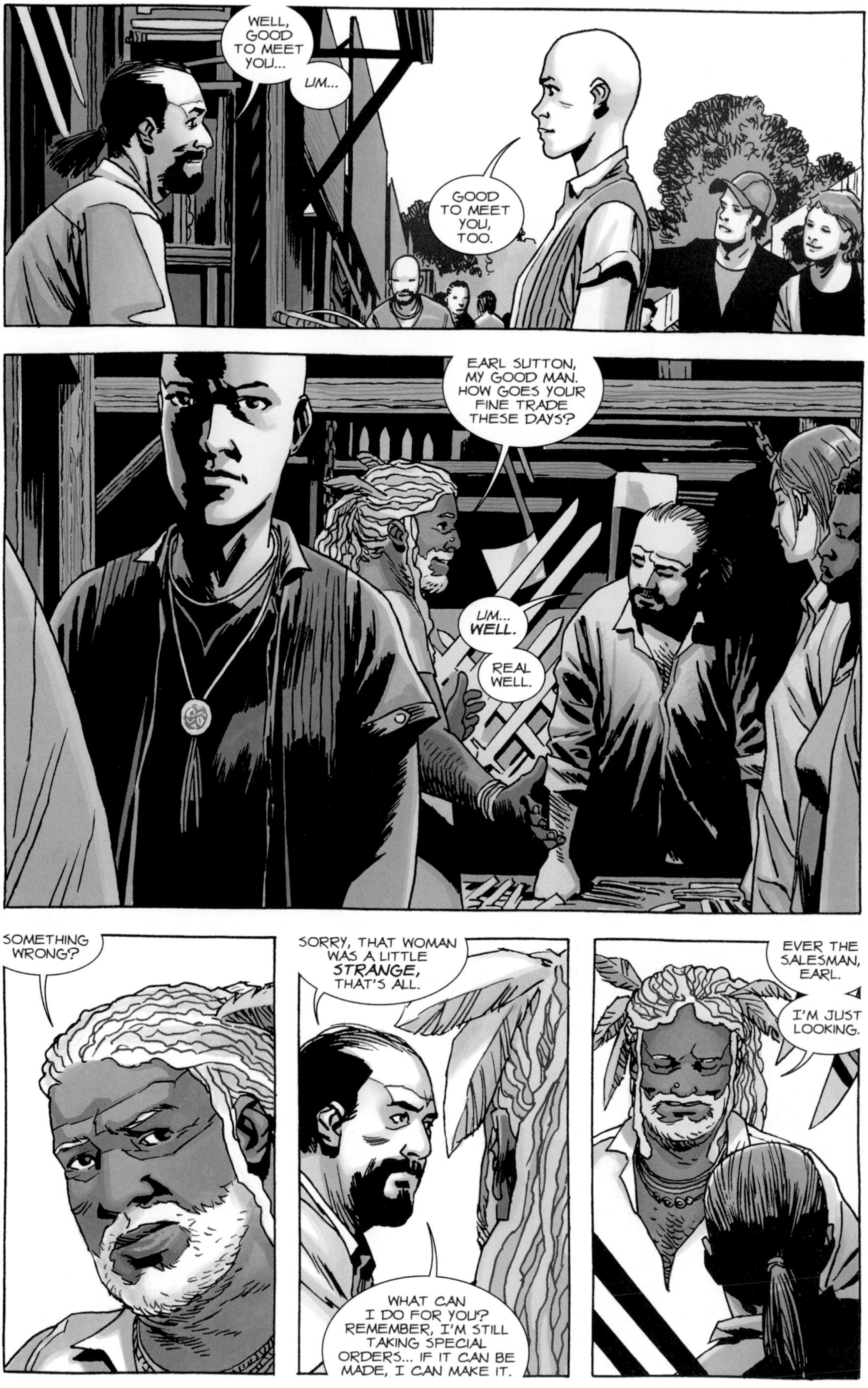
WELL, GOOD TO MEET YOU...
UM...
GOOD TO MEET YOU, TOO.
EARL SUTTON, MY GOOD MAN. HOW GOES YOUR FINE TRADE THESE DAYS?
UM... WELL.
REAL WELL.
SOMETHING WRONG?
SORRY, THAT WOMAN WAS A LITTLE STRANGE, THAT'S ALL.
WHAT CAN I DO FOR YOU? REMEMBER, I'M STILL TAKING SPECIAL ORDERS... IF IT CAN BE MADE, I CAN MAKE IT.
EVER THE SALESMAN, EARL.
I'M JUST LOOKING.

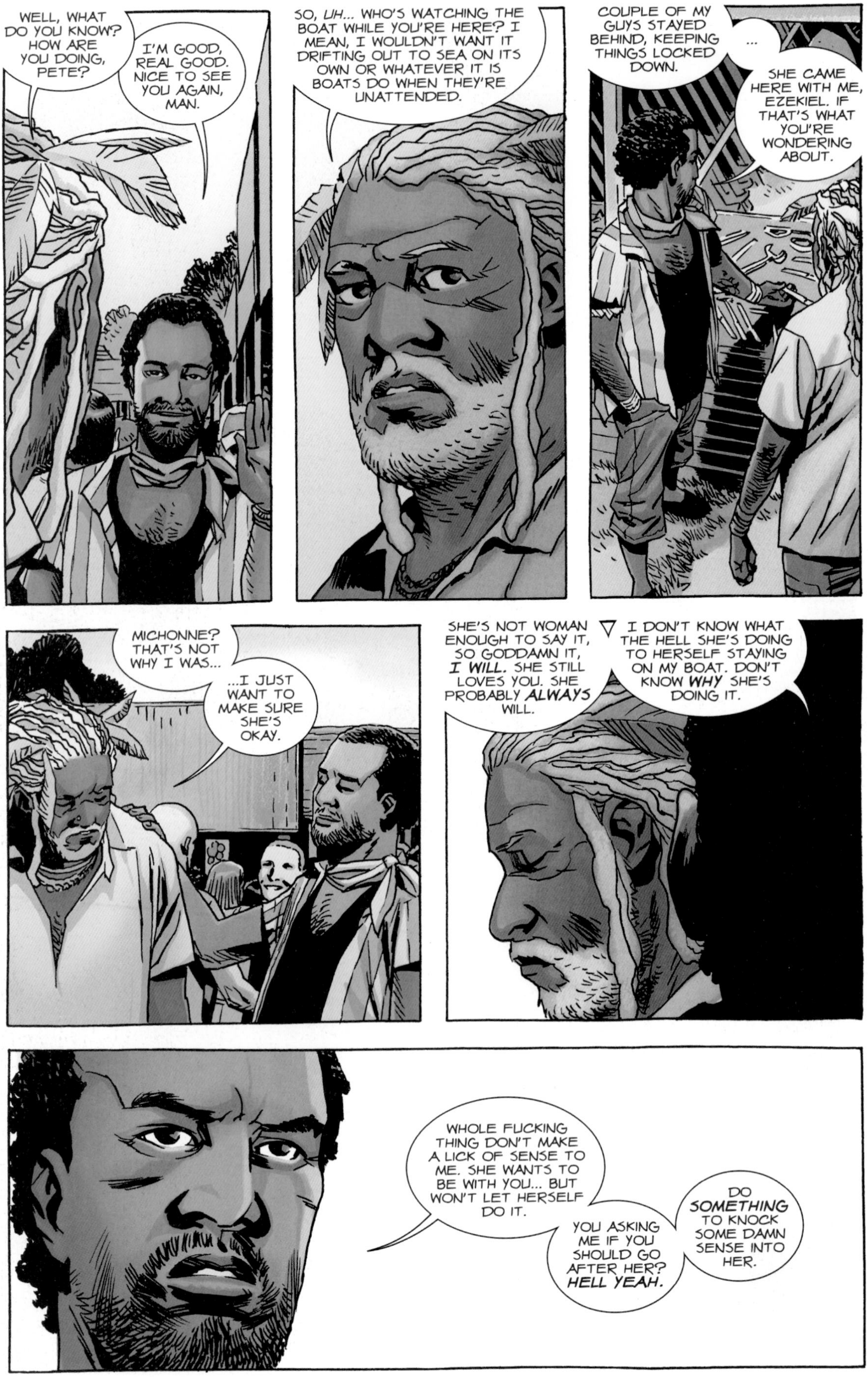
WELL, WHAT DO YOU KNOW? HOW ARE YOU DOING, PETE?
I'M GOOD, REAL GOOD. NICE TO SEE YOU AGAIN, MAN.
SO, UH... WHO'S WATCHING THE BOAT WHILE YOU'RE HERE? I MEAN, I WOULDN'T WANT IT DRIFTING OUT TO SEA ON ITS OWN OR WHATEVER IT IS BOATS DO WHEN THEY'RE UNATTENDED.
COUPLE OF MY GUYS STAYED BEHIND, KEEPING THINGS LOCKED DOWN.
...
SHE CAME HERE WITH ME, EZEKIEL. IF THAT'S WHAT YOU'RE WONDERING ABOUT.
MICHONNE? THAT'S NOT WHY I WAS...
...I JUST WANT TO MAKE SURE SHE'S OKAY.
I DON'T KNOW WHAT THE HELL SHE'S DOING TO HERSELF STAYING ON MY BOAT. DON'T KNOW WHY SHE'S DOING IT.
SHE'S NOT WOMAN ENOUGH TO SAY IT, SO GODDAMN IT, I WILL. SHE STILL LOVES YOU. SHE PROBABLY ALWAYS WILL.
WHOLE FUCKING THING DON'T MAKE A LICK OF SENSE TO ME. SHE WANTS TO BE WITH YOU... BUT WON'T LET HERSELF DO IT.
YOU ASKING ME IF YOU SHOULD GO AFTER HER? HELL YEAH.
DO SOMETHING TO KNOCK SOME DAMN SENSE INTO HER.

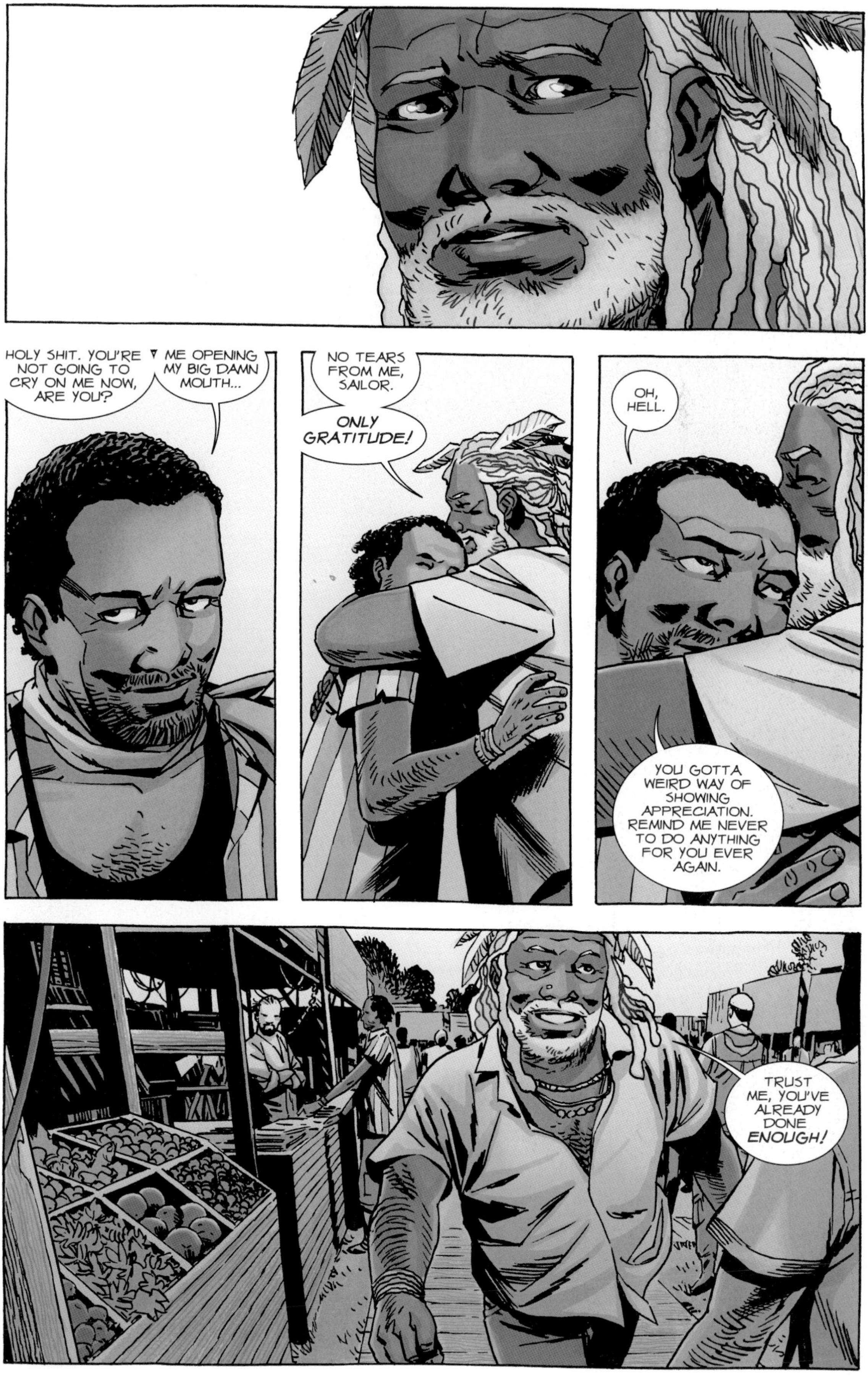
HOLY SHIT. YOU'RE NOT GOING TO CRY ON ME NOW, ARE YOU?
ME OPENING MY BIG DAMN MOUTH...
NO TEARS FROM ME, SAILOR.
ONLY GRATITUDE!
OH, HELL.
YOU GOTTA WEIRD WAY OF SHOWING APPRECIATION. REMIND ME NEVER TO DO ANYTHING FOR YOU EVER AGAIN.
TRUST ME, YOU'VE ALREADY DONE ENOUGH!

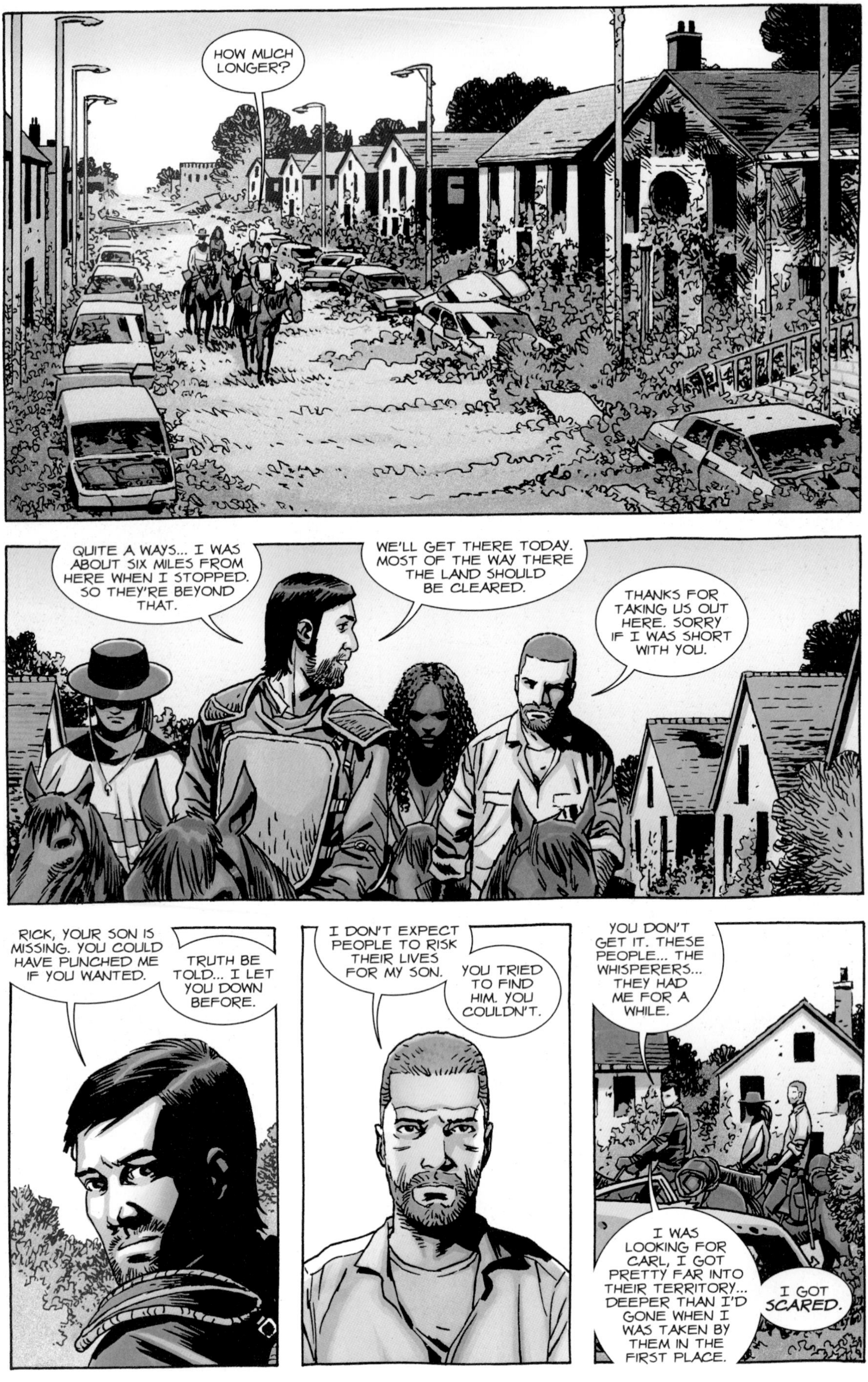
HOW MUCH LONGER?
QUITE A WAYS... I WAS ABOUT SIX MILES FROM HERE WHEN I STOPPED. SO THEY'RE BEYOND THAT.
WE'LL GET THERE TODAY. MOST OF THE WAY THERE THE LAND SHOULD BE CLEARED.
THANKS FOR TAKING US OUT HERE. SORRY IF I WAS SHORT WITH YOU.
RICK, YOUR SON IS MISSING. YOU COULD HAVE PUNCHED ME IF YOU WANTED.
TRUTH BE TOLD... I LET YOU DOWN BEFORE.
I DON'T EXPECT PEOPLE TO RISK THEIR LIVES FOR MY SON.
YOU TRIED TO FIND HIM. YOU COULDN'T.
YOU DON'T GET IT. THESE PEOPLE... THE WHISPERERS... THEY HAD ME FOR A WHILE.
I WAS LOOKING FOR CARL, I GOT PRETTY FAR INTO THEIR TERRITORY... DEEPER THAN I'D GONE WHEN I WAS TAKEN BY THEM IN THE FIRST PLACE.
I GOT *SCARED.*

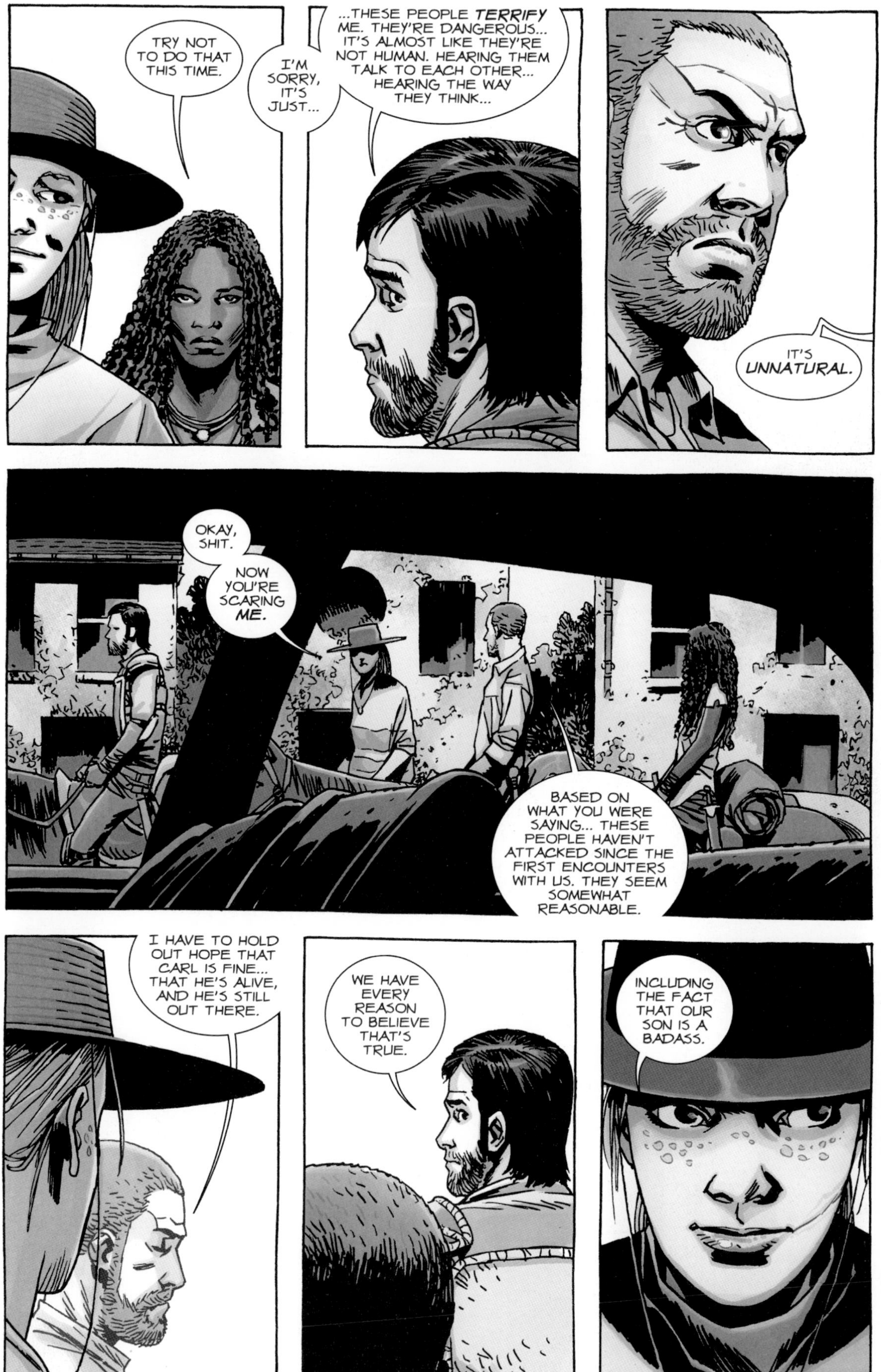

TRY NOT TO DO THAT THIS TIME.
I'M SORRY, IT'S JUST...
...THESE PEOPLE TERRIFY ME. THEY'RE DANGEROUS... IT'S ALMOST LIKE THEY'RE NOT HUMAN. HEARING THEM TALK TO EACH OTHER... HEARING THE WAY THEY THINK...
IT'S UNNATURAL.
OKAY, SHIT.
NOW YOU'RE SCARING ME.
BASED ON WHAT YOU WERE SAYING... THESE PEOPLE HAVEN'T ATTACKED SINCE THE FIRST ENCOUNTERS WITH US. THEY SEEM SOMEWHAT REASONABLE.
I HAVE TO HOLD OUT HOPE THAT CARL IS FINE... THAT HE'S ALIVE, AND HE'S STILL OUT THERE.
WE HAVE EVERY REASON TO BELIEVE THAT'S TRUE.
INCLUDING THE FACT THAT OUR SON IS A BADASS.

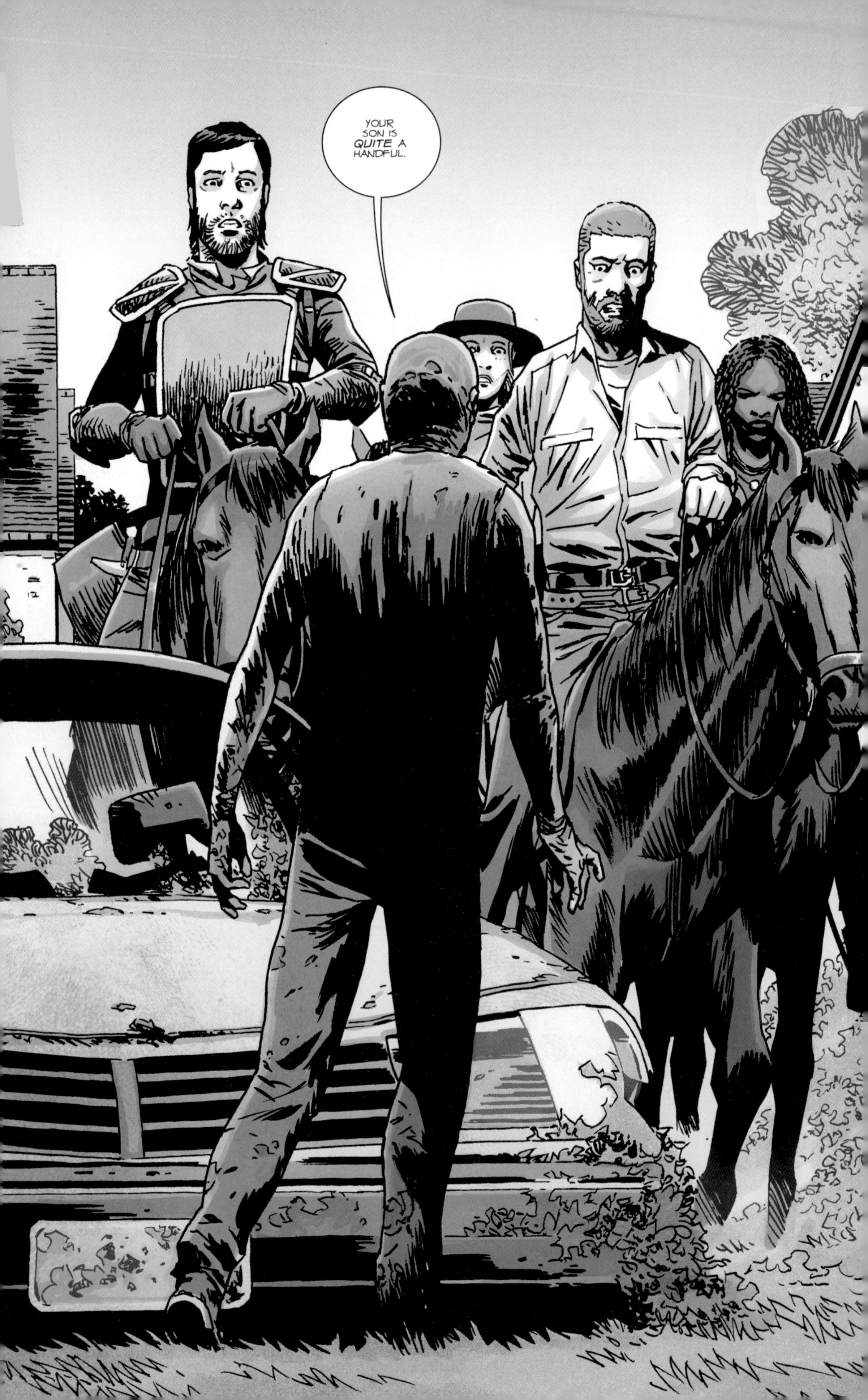
YOUR SON IS QUITE A HANDFUL.

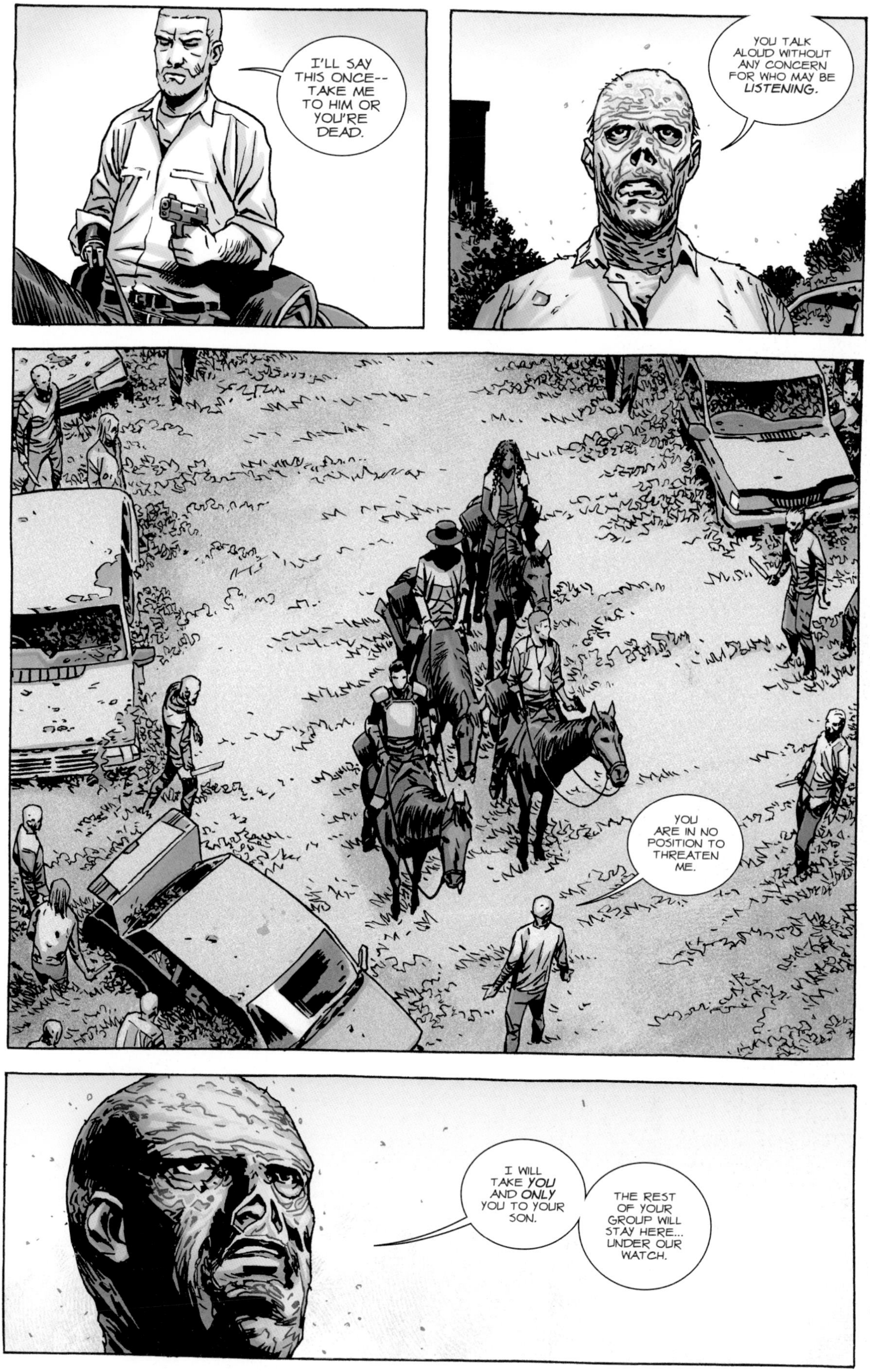
I'LL SAY THIS ONCE-- TAKE ME TO HIM OR YOU'RE DEAD.
YOU TALK ALOUD WITHOUT ANY CONCERN FOR WHO MAY BE *LISTENING.*
YOU ARE IN NO POSITION TO THREATEN ME.
I WILL TAKE *YOU* AND *ONLY* YOU TO YOUR SON.
THE REST OF YOUR GROUP WILL STAY HERE... UNDER OUR WATCH.

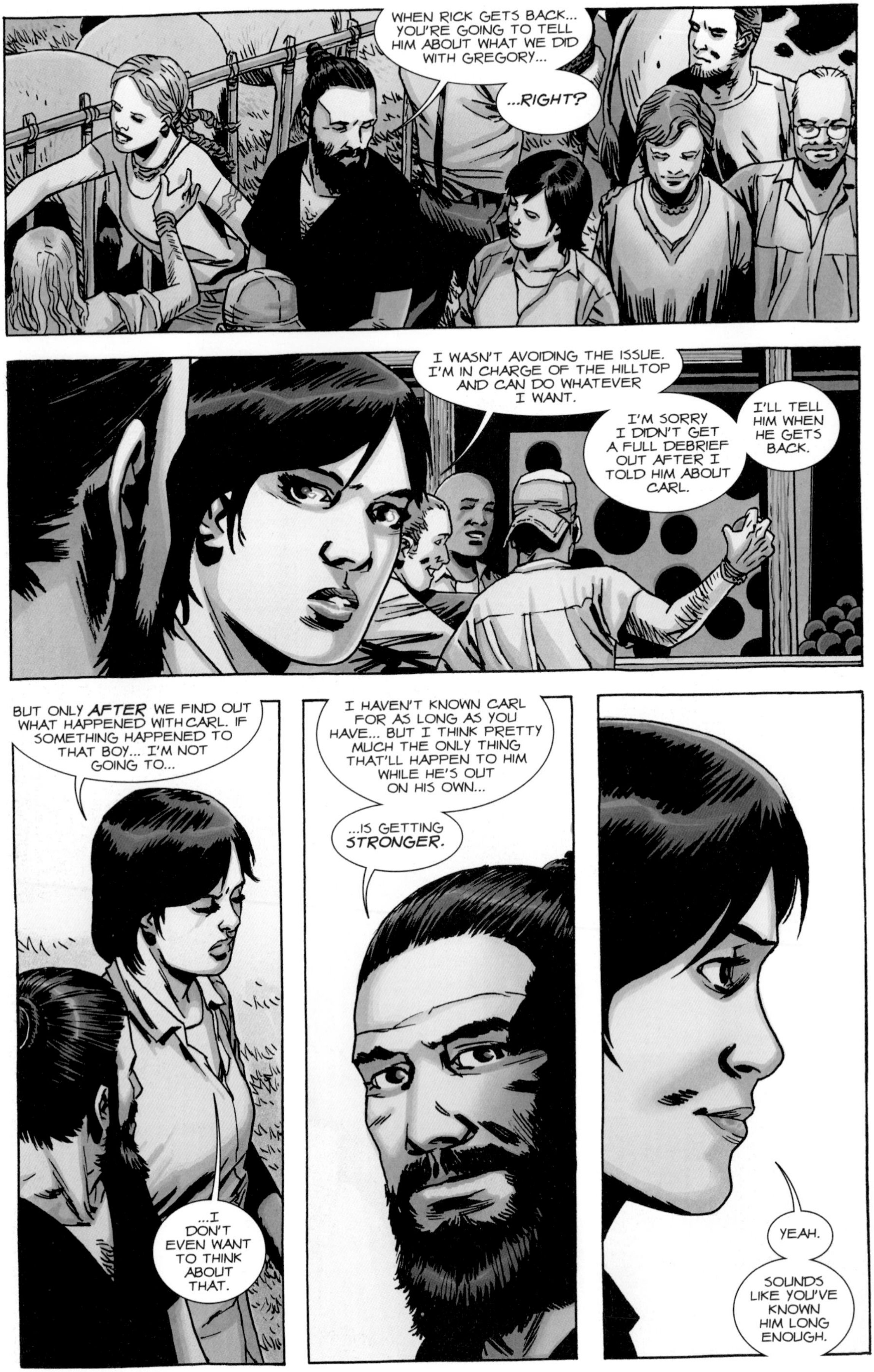
WHEN RICK GETS BACK... YOU'RE GOING TO TELL HIM ABOUT WHAT WE DID WITH GREGORY...
...RIGHT?
I WASN'T AVOIDING THE ISSUE. I'M IN CHARGE OF THE HILLTOP AND CAN DO WHATEVER I WANT.
I'M SORRY I DIDN'T GET A FULL DEBRIEF OUT AFTER I TOLD HIM ABOUT CARL.
I'LL TELL HIM WHEN HE GETS BACK.
BUT ONLY AFTER WE FIND OUT WHAT HAPPENED WITH CARL. IF SOMETHING HAPPENED TO THAT BOY... I'M NOT GOING TO...
...I DON'T EVEN WANT TO THINK ABOUT THAT.
I HAVEN'T KNOWN CARL FOR AS LONG AS YOU HAVE... BUT I THINK PRETTY MUCH THE ONLY THING THAT'LL HAPPEN TO HIM WHILE HE'S OUT ON HIS OWN...
...IS GETTING STRONGER.
YEAH.
SOUNDS LIKE YOU'VE KNOWN HIM LONG ENOUGH.

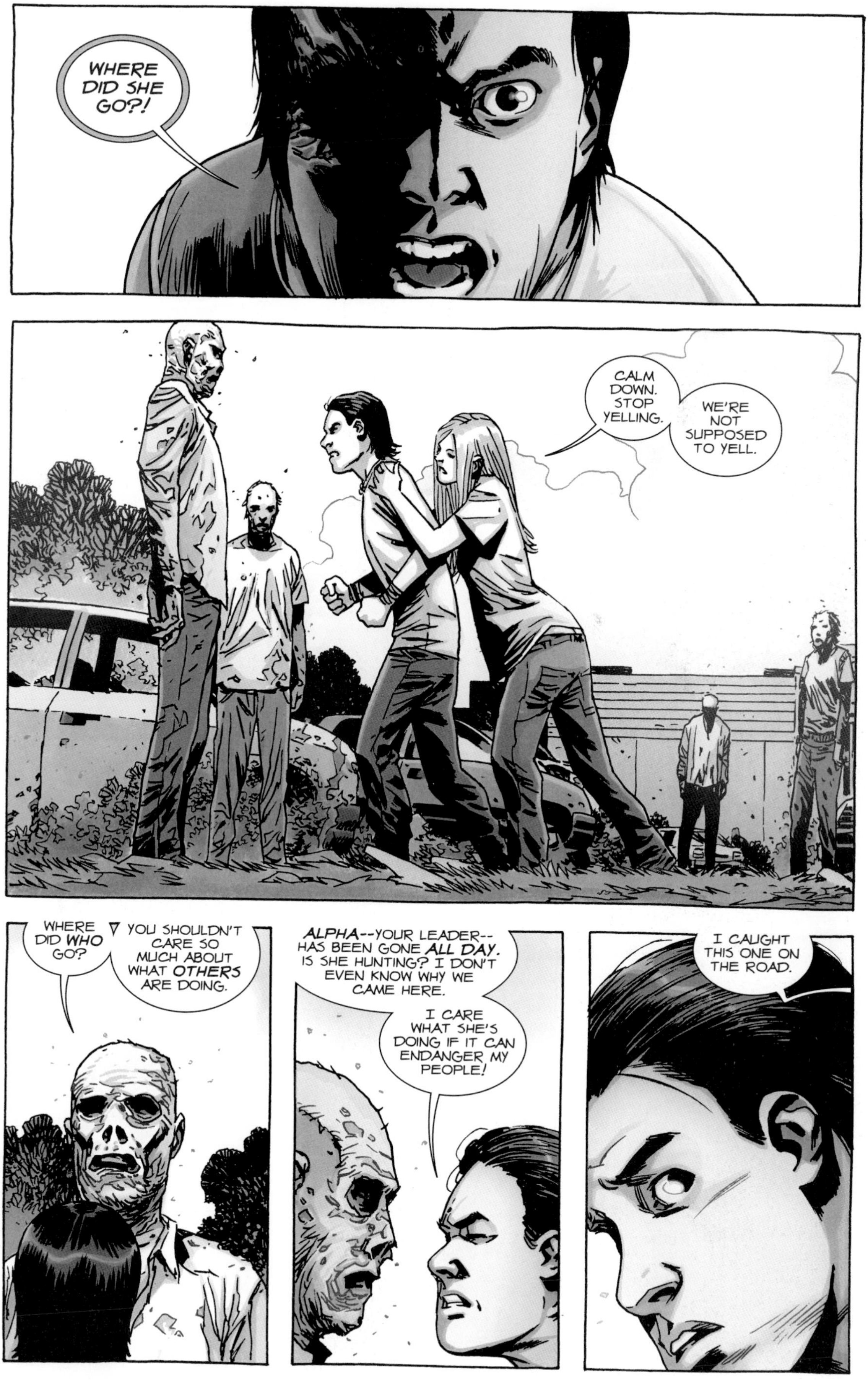
WHERE DID SHE GO?!
CALM DOWN. STOP YELLING.
WE'RE NOT SUPPOSED TO YELL.
WHERE DID WHO GO?
YOU SHOULDN'T CARE SO MUCH ABOUT WHAT OTHERS ARE DOING.
ALPHA--YOUR LEADER--HAS BEEN GONE ALL DAY. IS SHE HUNTING? I DON'T EVEN KNOW WHY WE CAME HERE.
I CARE WHAT SHE'S DOING IF IT CAN ENDANGER MY PEOPLE!
I CAUGHT THIS ONE ON THE ROAD.

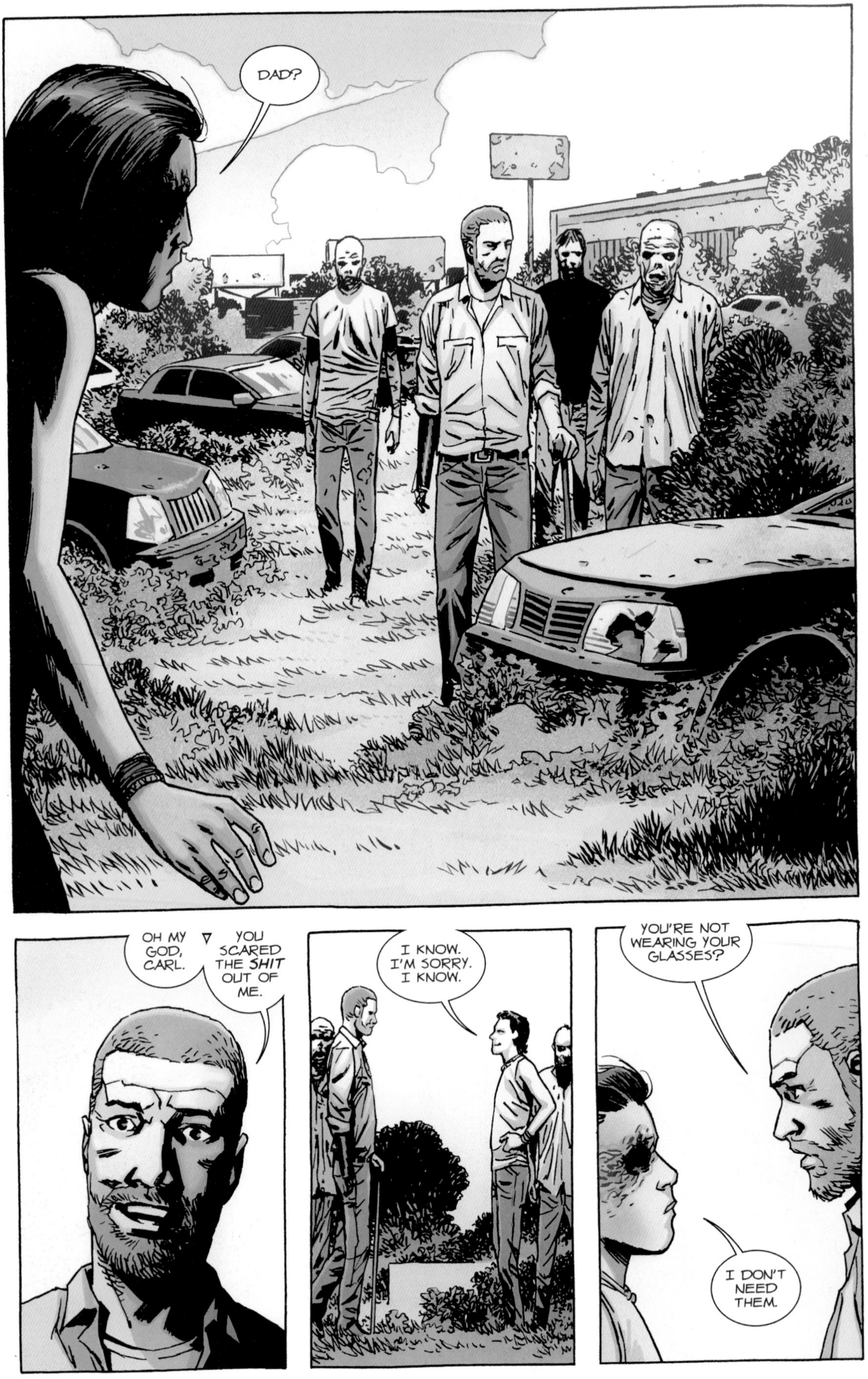
DAD?
OH MY GOD, CARL.
YOU SCARED THE *SHIT* OUT OF ME.
I KNOW. I'M SORRY. I KNOW.
YOU'RE NOT WEARING YOUR GLASSES?
I DON'T NEED THEM.

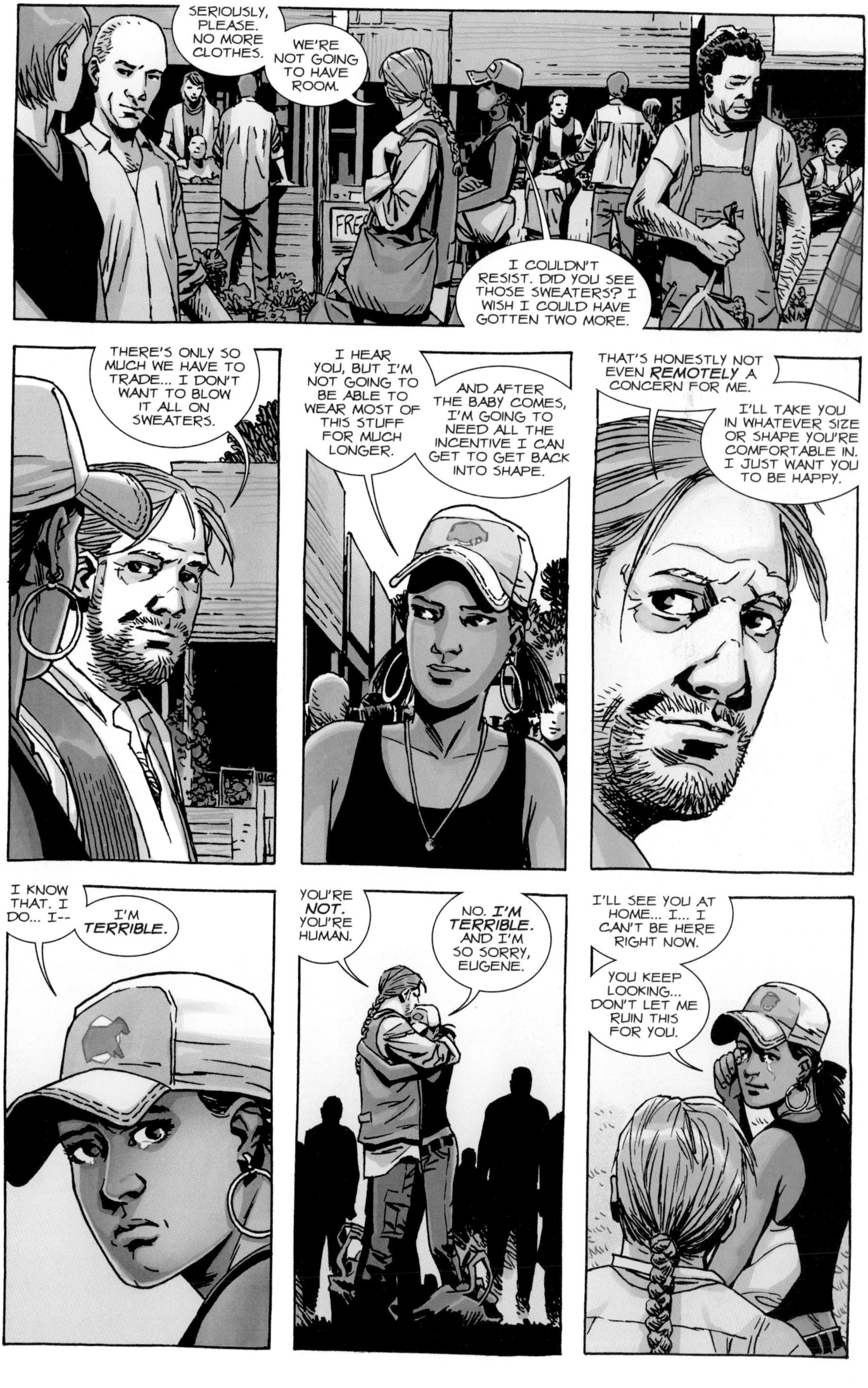

SERIOUSLY, PLEASE. NO MORE CLOTHES.
WE'RE NOT GOING TO HAVE ROOM.
I COULDN'T RESIST. DID YOU SEE THOSE SWEATERS? I WISH I COULD HAVE GOTTEN TWO MORE.
THERE'S ONLY SO MUCH WE HAVE TO TRADE... I DON'T WANT TO BLOW IT ALL ON SWEATERS.
I HEAR YOU, BUT I'M NOT GOING TO BE ABLE TO WEAR MOST OF THIS STUFF FOR MUCH LONGER.
AND AFTER THE BABY COMES, I'M GOING TO NEED ALL THE INCENTIVE I CAN GET TO GET BACK INTO SHAPE.
THAT'S HONESTLY NOT EVEN REMOTELY A CONCERN FOR ME.
I'LL TAKE YOU IN WHATEVER SIZE OR SHAPE YOU'RE COMFORTABLE IN. I JUST WANT YOU TO BE HAPPY.
I KNOW THAT. I DO... I--
I'M TERRIBLE.
YOU'RE NOT. YOU'RE HUMAN.
NO. I'M TERRIBLE. AND I'M SO SORRY, EUGENE.
I'LL SEE YOU AT HOME... I... I CAN'T BE HERE RIGHT NOW.
YOU KEEP LOOKING... DON'T LET ME RUIN THIS FOR YOU.

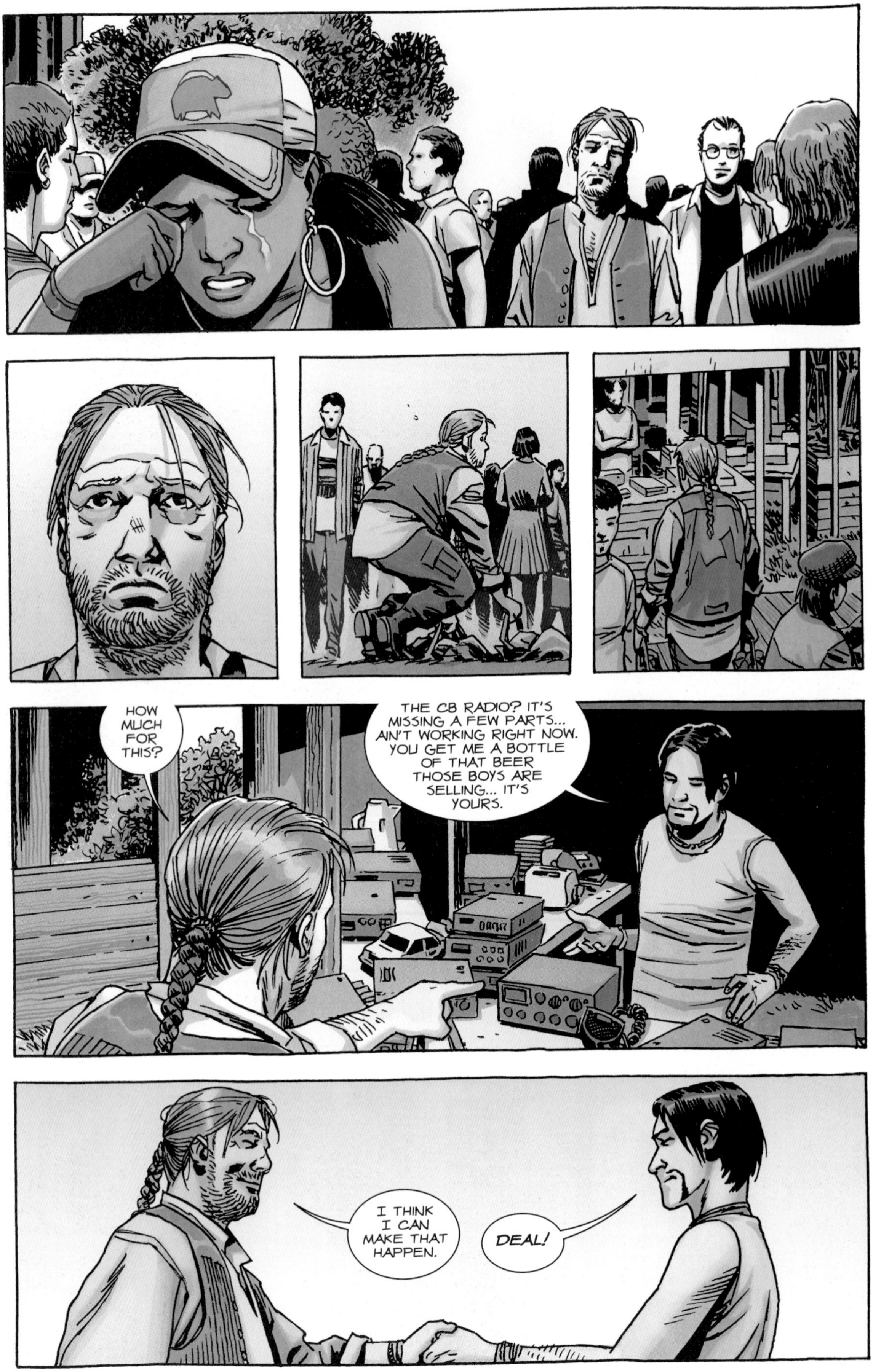
HOW MUCH FOR THIS?
THE CB RADIO? IT'S MISSING A FEW PARTS... AIN'T WORKING RIGHT NOW. YOU GET ME A BOTTLE OF THAT BEER THOSE BOYS ARE SELLING... IT'S YOURS.
I THINK I CAN MAKE THAT HAPPEN.
DEAL!

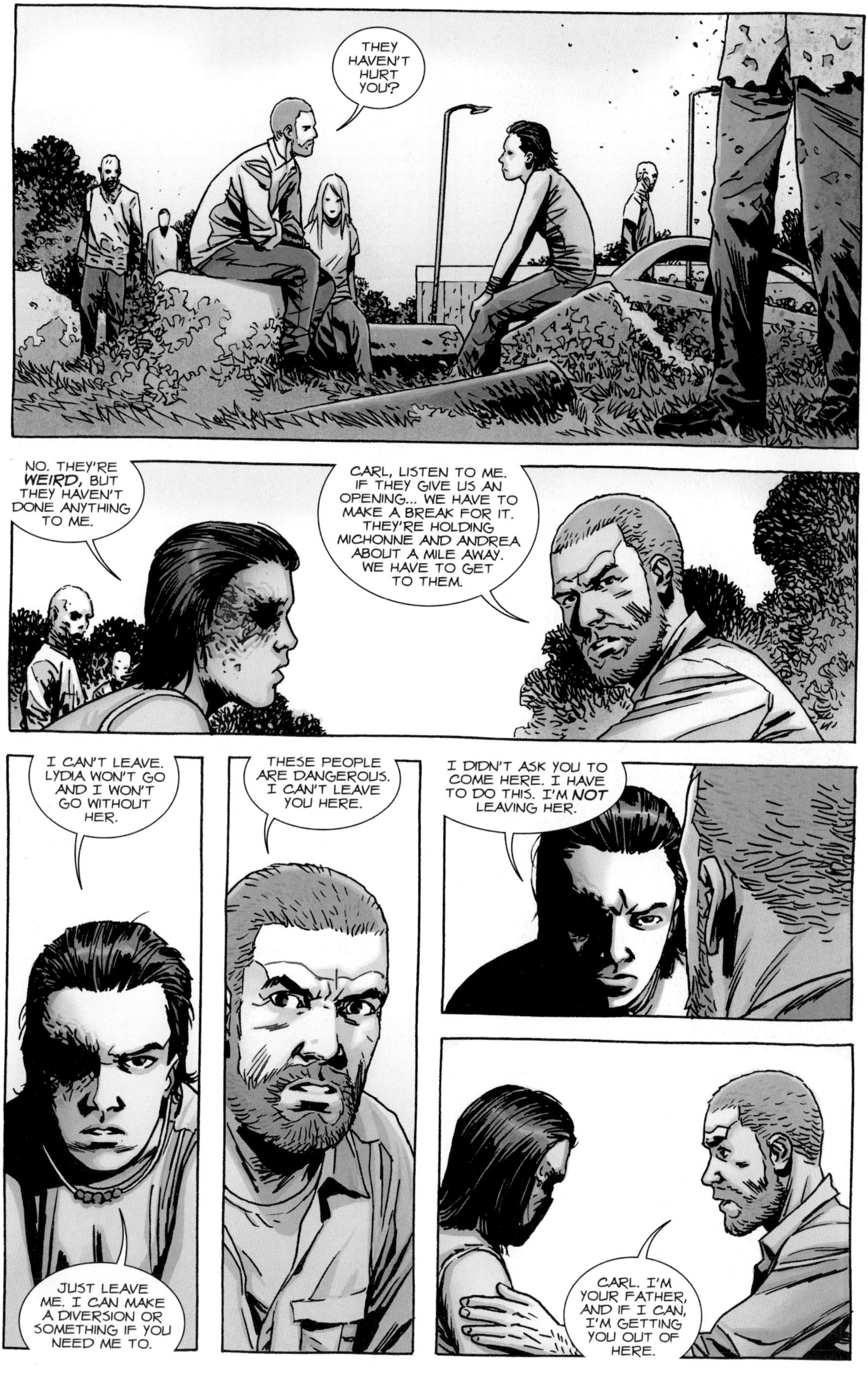
THEY HAVEN'T HURT YOU?
NO. THEY'RE WEIRD, BUT THEY HAVEN'T DONE ANYTHING TO ME.
CARL, LISTEN TO ME. IF THEY GIVE US AN OPENING... WE HAVE TO MAKE A BREAK FOR IT. THEY'RE HOLDING MICHONNE AND ANDREA ABOUT A MILE AWAY. WE HAVE TO GET TO THEM.
I CAN'T LEAVE. LYDIA WON'T GO AND I WON'T GO WITHOUT HER.
JUST LEAVE ME. I CAN MAKE A DIVERSION OR SOMETHING IF YOU NEED ME TO.
THESE PEOPLE ARE DANGEROUS. I CAN'T LEAVE YOU HERE.
I DIDN'T ASK YOU TO COME HERE. I HAVE TO DO THIS. I'M NOT LEAVING HER.
CARL. I'M YOUR FATHER, AND IF I CAN, I'M GETTING YOU OUT OF HERE.

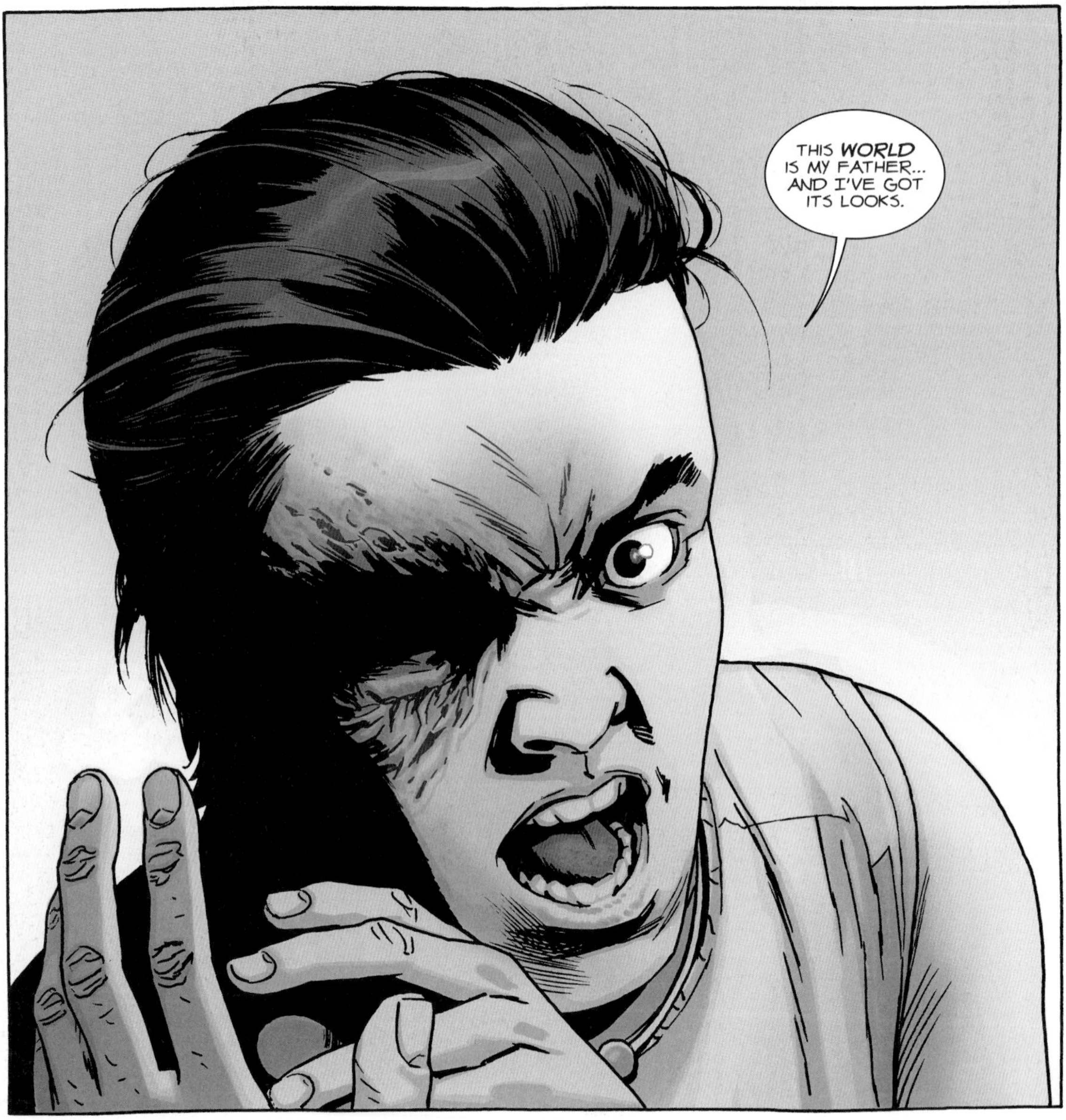
THIS WORLD IS MY FATHER... AND I'VE GOT ITS LOOKS.

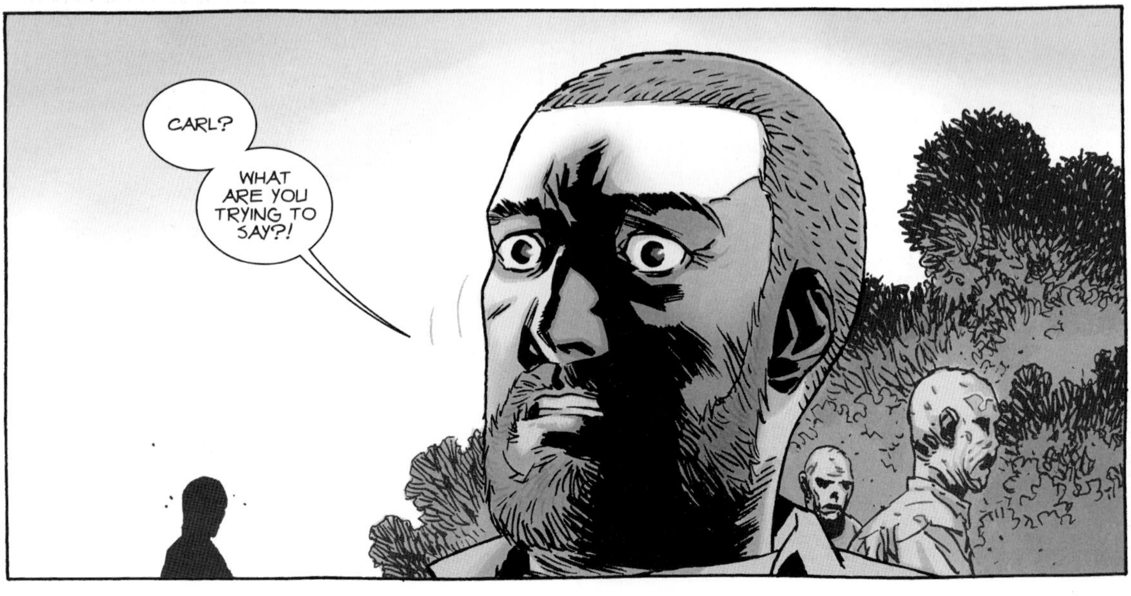
CARL?
WHAT ARE YOU TRYING TO SAY?!

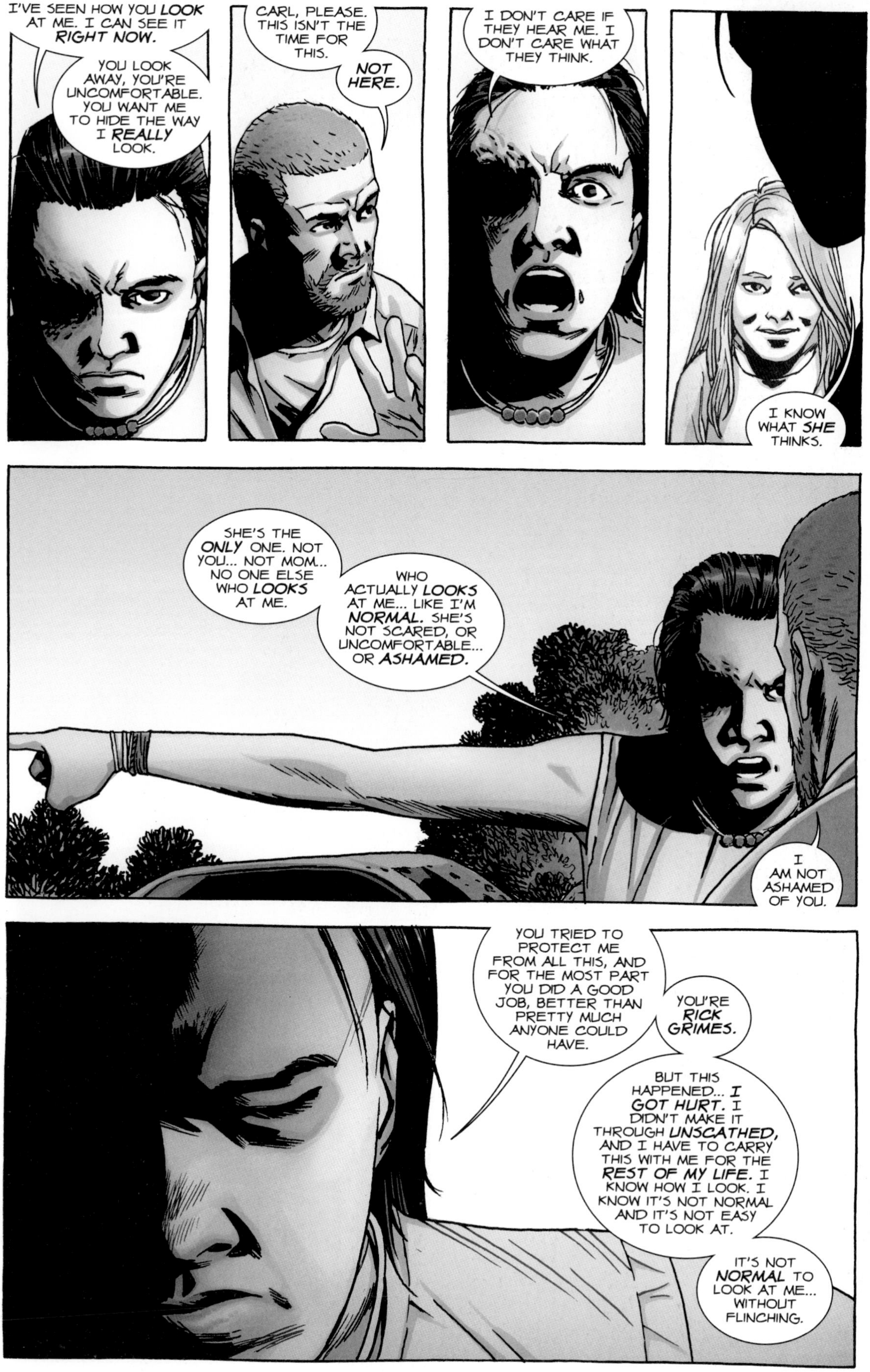
I'VE SEEN HOW YOU LOOK AT ME. I CAN SEE IT RIGHT NOW.
YOU LOOK AWAY, YOU'RE UNCOMFORTABLE. YOU WANT ME TO HIDE THE WAY I REALLY LOOK.
CARL, PLEASE. THIS ISN'T THE TIME FOR THIS.
NOT HERE.
I DON'T CARE IF THEY HEAR ME. I DON'T CARE WHAT THEY THINK.
I KNOW WHAT SHE THINKS.
SHE'S THE ONLY ONE. NOT YOU... NOT MOM... NO ONE ELSE WHO LOOKS AT ME.
WHO ACTUALLY LOOKS AT ME... LIKE I'M NORMAL. SHE'S NOT SCARED, OR UNCOMFORTABLE... OR ASHAMED.
I AM NOT ASHAMED OF YOU.
YOU TRIED TO PROTECT ME FROM ALL THIS, AND FOR THE MOST PART YOU DID A GOOD JOB, BETTER THAN PRETTY MUCH ANYONE COULD HAVE.
YOU'RE RICK GRIMES.
BUT THIS HAPPENED... I GOT HURT. I DIDN'T MAKE IT THROUGH UNSCATHED, AND I HAVE TO CARRY THIS WITH ME FOR THE REST OF MY LIFE. I KNOW HOW I LOOK. I KNOW IT'S NOT NORMAL AND IT'S NOT EASY TO LOOK AT.
IT'S NOT NORMAL TO LOOK AT ME... WITHOUT FLINCHING.

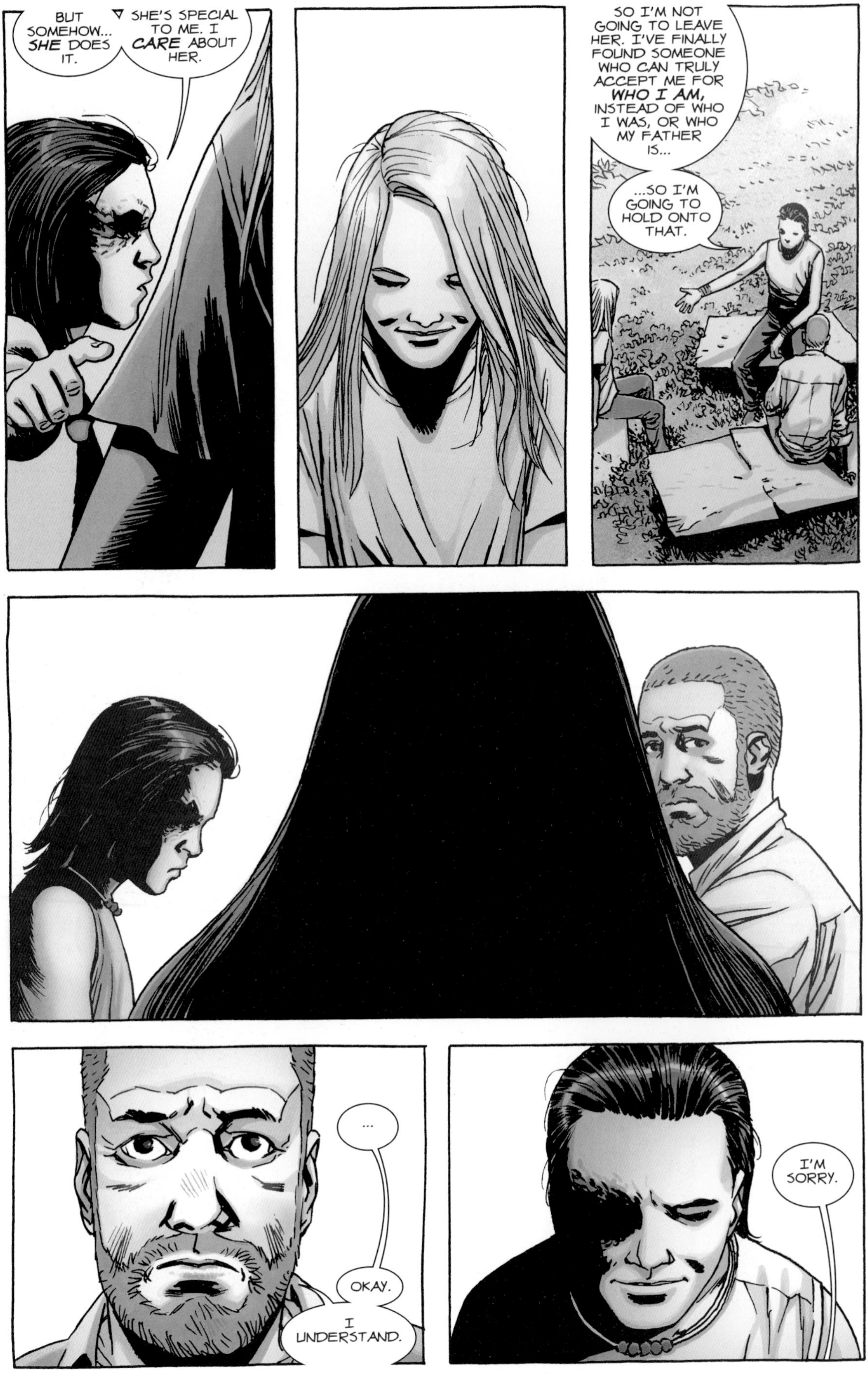
BUT SOMEHOW... SHE DOES IT.
SHE'S SPECIAL TO ME. I CARE ABOUT HER.
SO I'M NOT GOING TO LEAVE HER. I'VE FINALLY FOUND SOMEONE WHO CAN TRULY ACCEPT ME FOR WHO I AM, INSTEAD OF WHO I WAS, OR WHO MY FATHER IS...
...SO I'M GOING TO HOLD ONTO THAT.
...
OKAY.
I UNDERSTAND.
I'M SORRY.

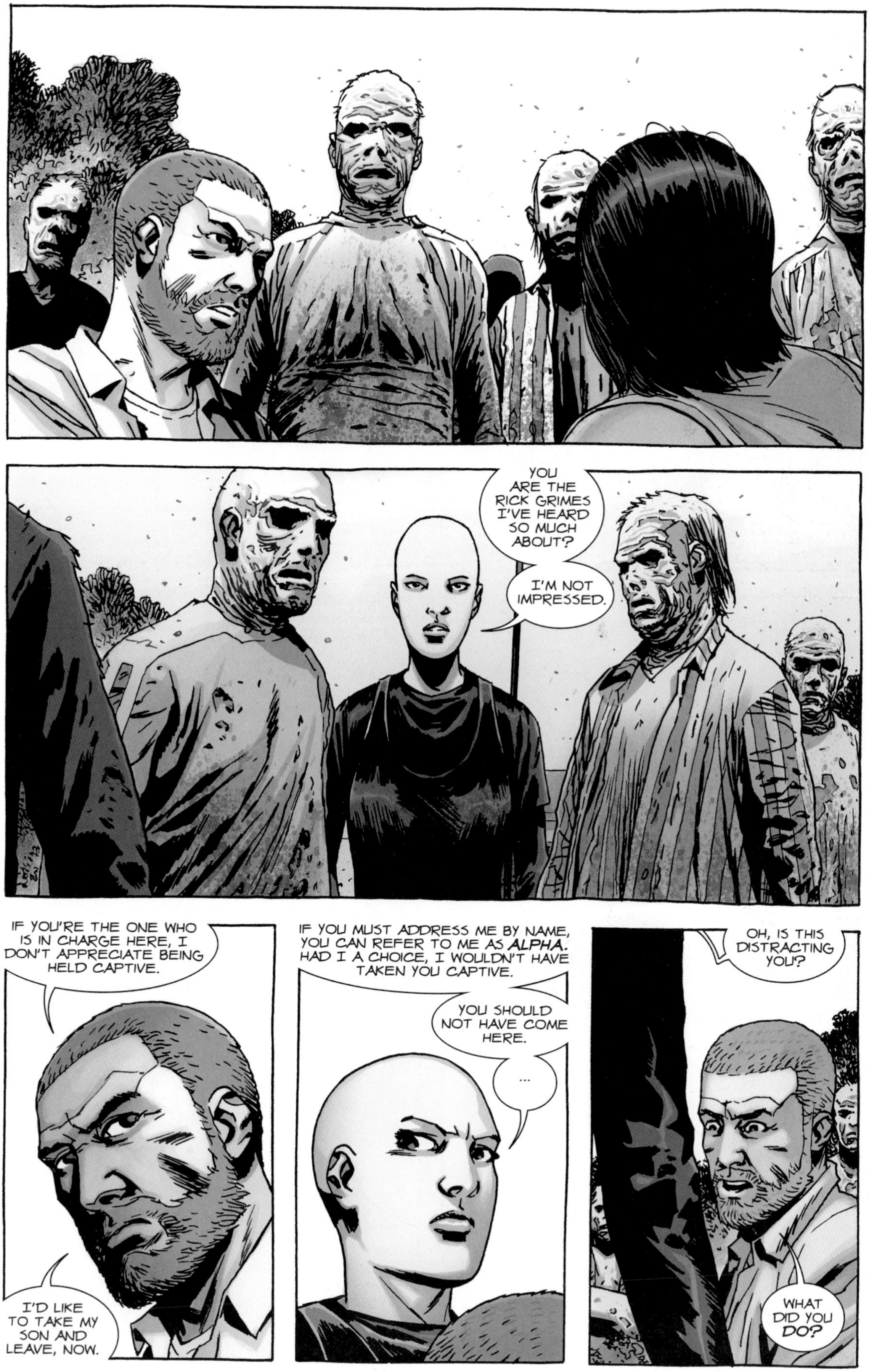
YOU ARE THE RICK GRIMES I'VE HEARD SO MUCH ABOUT?
I'M NOT IMPRESSED.
IF YOU'RE THE ONE WHO IS IN CHARGE HERE, I DON'T APPRECIATE BEING HELD CAPTIVE.
I'D LIKE TO TAKE MY SON AND LEAVE, NOW.
IF YOU MUST ADDRESS ME BY NAME, YOU CAN REFER TO ME AS ALPHA. HAD I A CHOICE, I WOULDN'T HAVE TAKEN YOU CAPTIVE.
YOU SHOULD NOT HAVE COME HERE.
...
OH, IS THIS DISTRACTING YOU?
WHAT DID YOU DO?

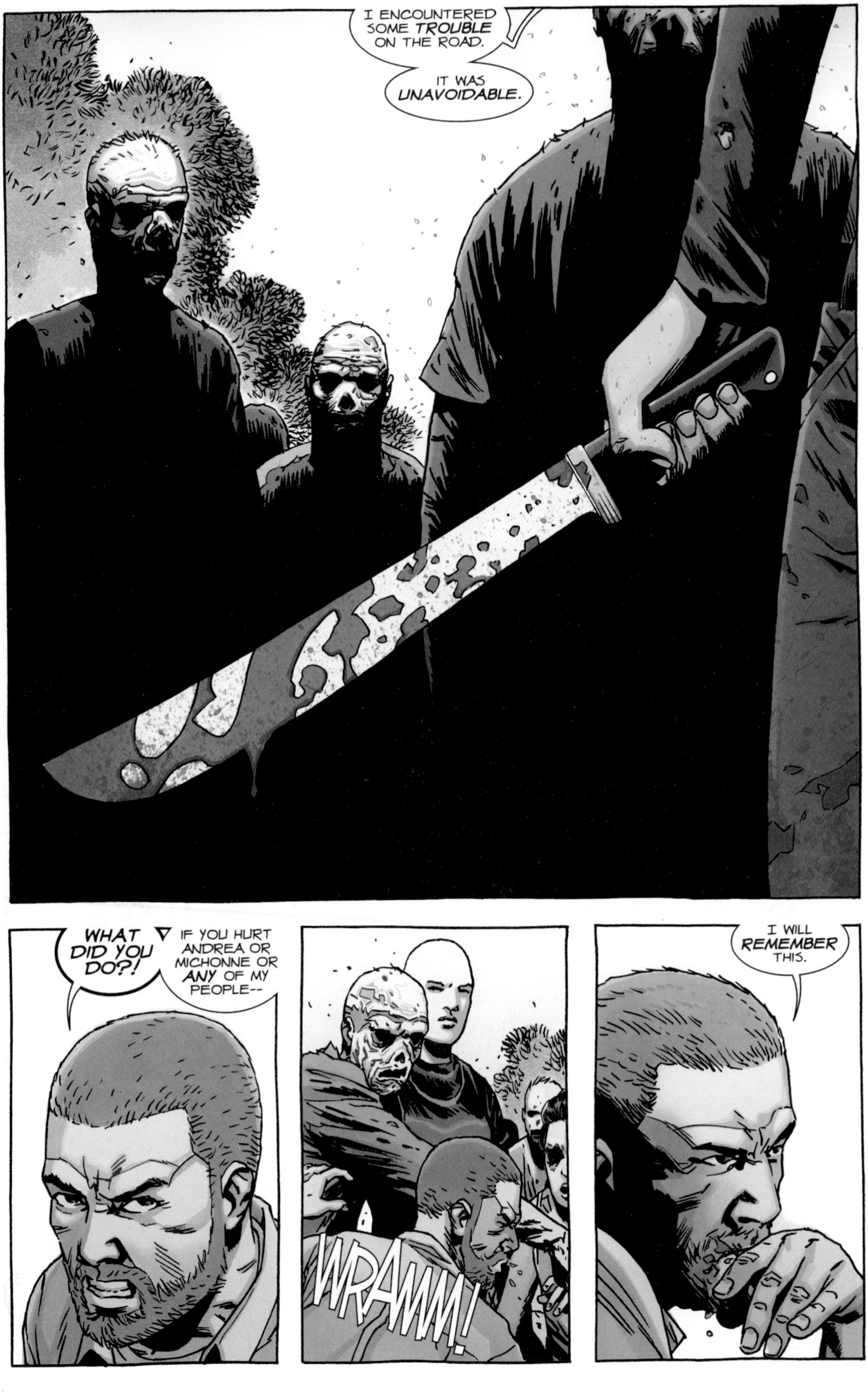
I ENCOUNTERED SOME TROUBLE ON THE ROAD.
IT WAS UNAVOIDABLE.
WHAT DID YOU DO?!
IF YOU HURT ANDREA OR MICHONNE OR ANY OF MY PEOPLE--
WRAMM!
I WILL REMEMBER THIS.

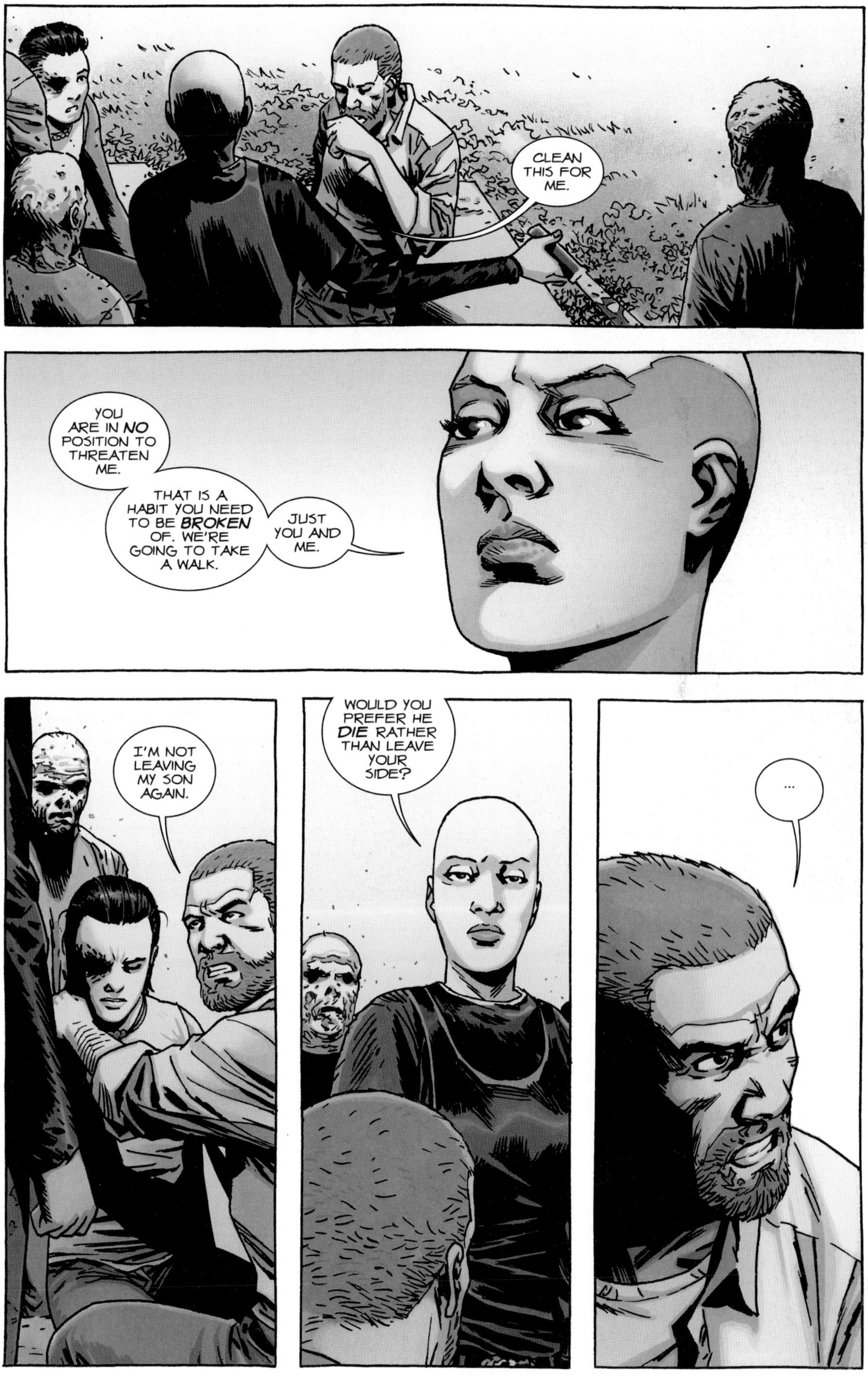
CLEAN THIS FOR ME.
YOU ARE IN NO POSITION TO THREATEN ME.
THAT IS A HABIT YOU NEED TO BE BROKEN OF. WE'RE GOING TO TAKE A WALK.
JUST YOU AND ME.
I'M NOT LEAVING MY SON AGAIN.
WOULD YOU PREFER HE DIE RATHER THAN LEAVE YOUR SIDE?
...

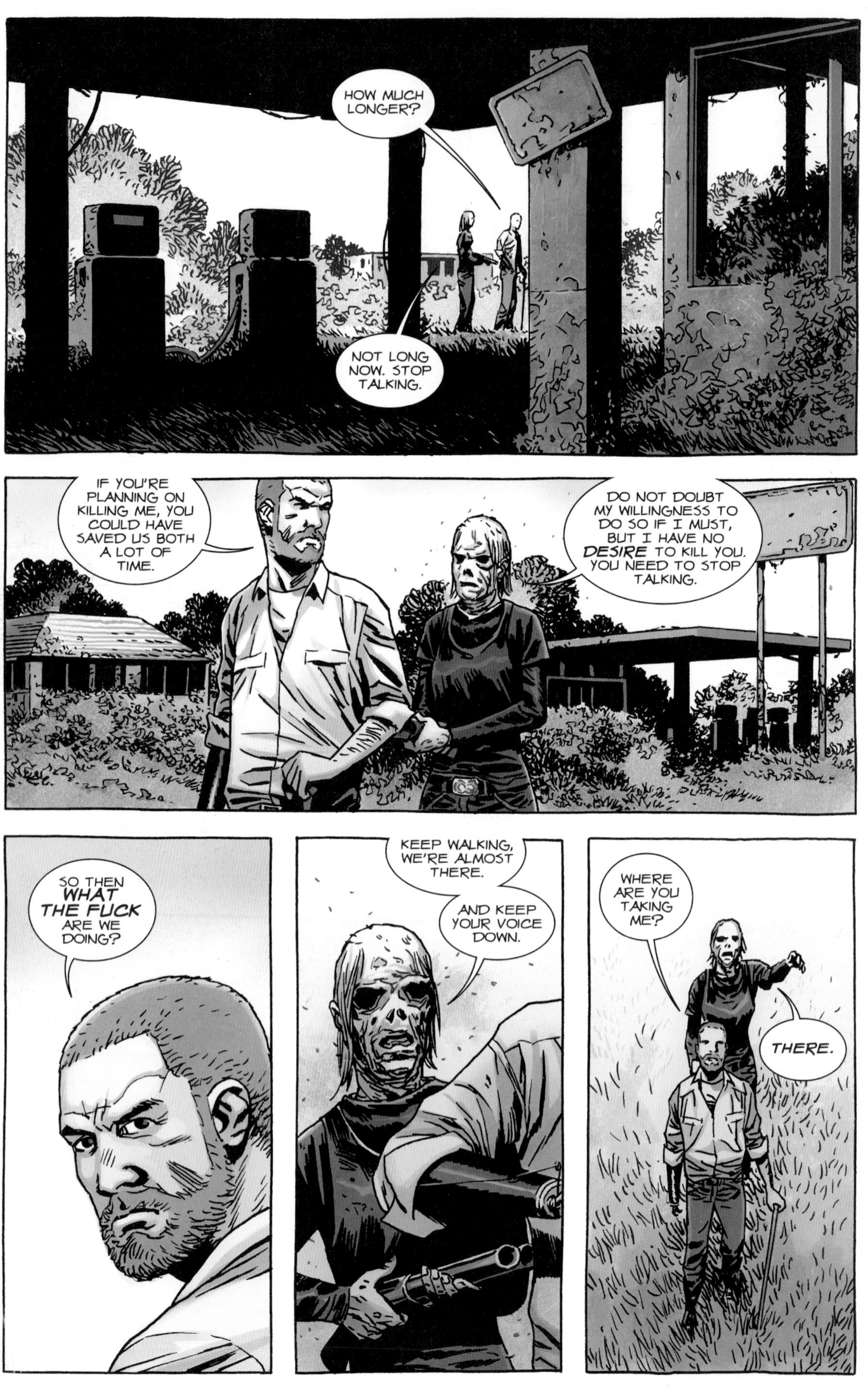
HOW MUCH LONGER?
NOT LONG NOW. STOP TALKING.
IF YOU'RE PLANNING ON KILLING ME, YOU COULD HAVE SAVED US BOTH A LOT OF TIME.
DO NOT DOUBT MY WILLINGNESS TO DO SO IF I MUST, BUT I HAVE NO DESIRE TO KILL YOU. YOU NEED TO STOP TALKING.
SO THEN WHAT THE FUCK ARE WE DOING?
KEEP WALKING, WE'RE ALMOST THERE.
AND KEEP YOUR VOICE DOWN.
WHERE ARE YOU TAKING ME?
THERE.

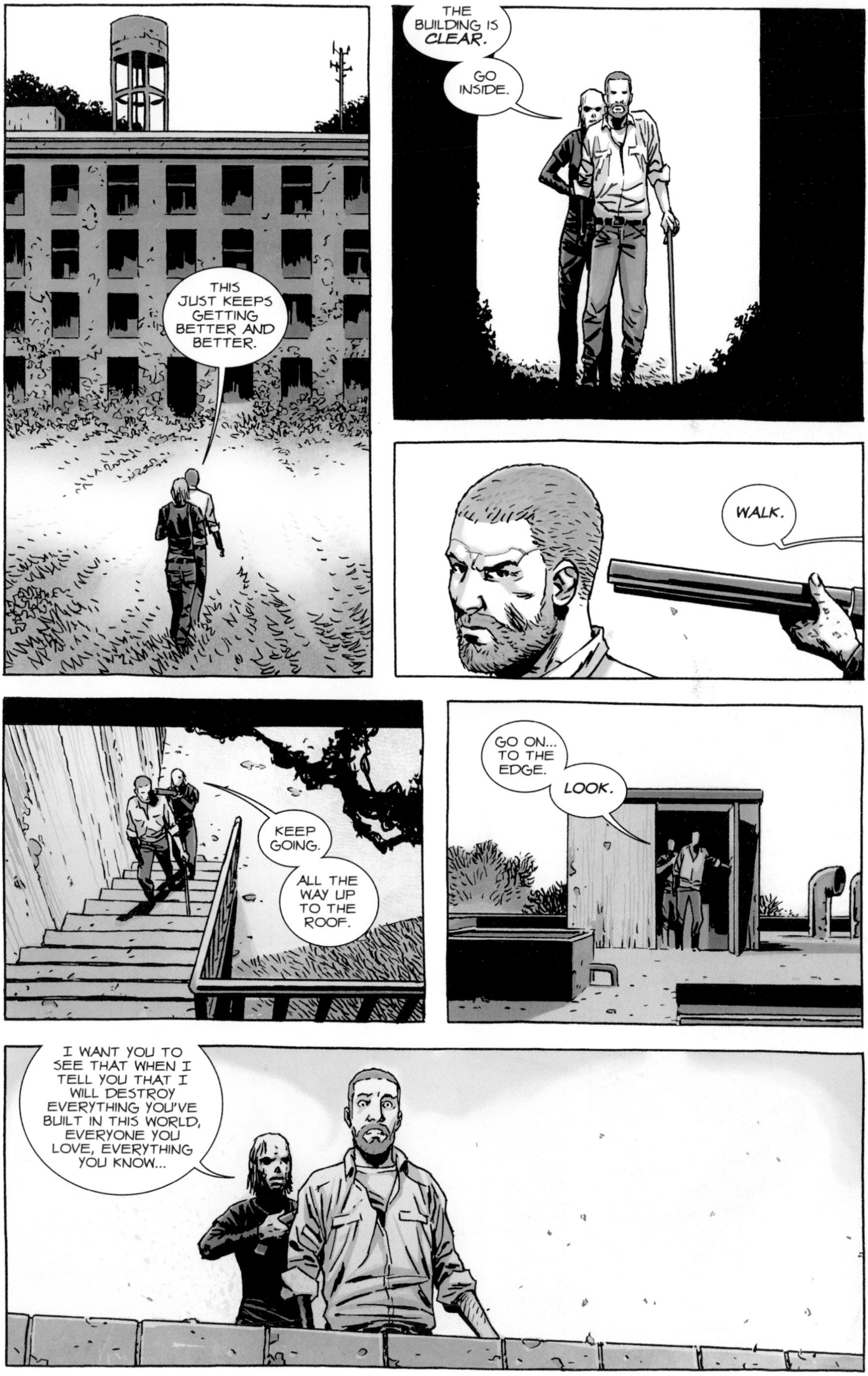
THIS JUST KEEPS GETTING BETTER AND BETTER.
THE BUILDING IS *CLEAR.*
GO INSIDE.
WALK.
KEEP GOING.
ALL THE WAY UP TO THE ROOF.
GO ON... TO THE EDGE.
LOOK.
I WANT YOU TO SEE THAT WHEN I TELL YOU THAT I WILL DESTROY EVERYTHING YOU'VE BUILT IN THIS WORLD, EVERYONE YOU LOVE, EVERYTHING YOU KNOW...

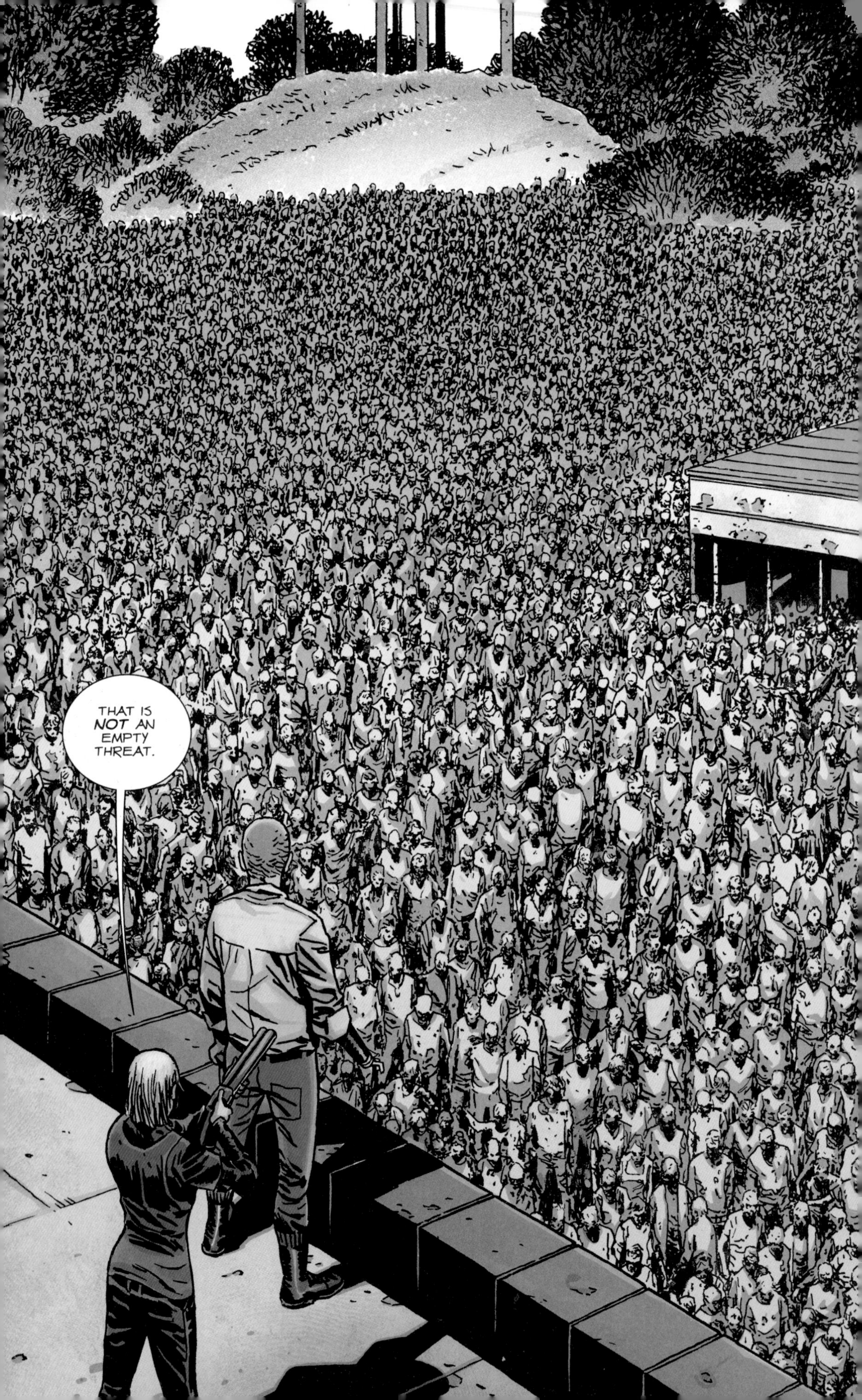
THAT IS NOT AN EMPTY THREAT.

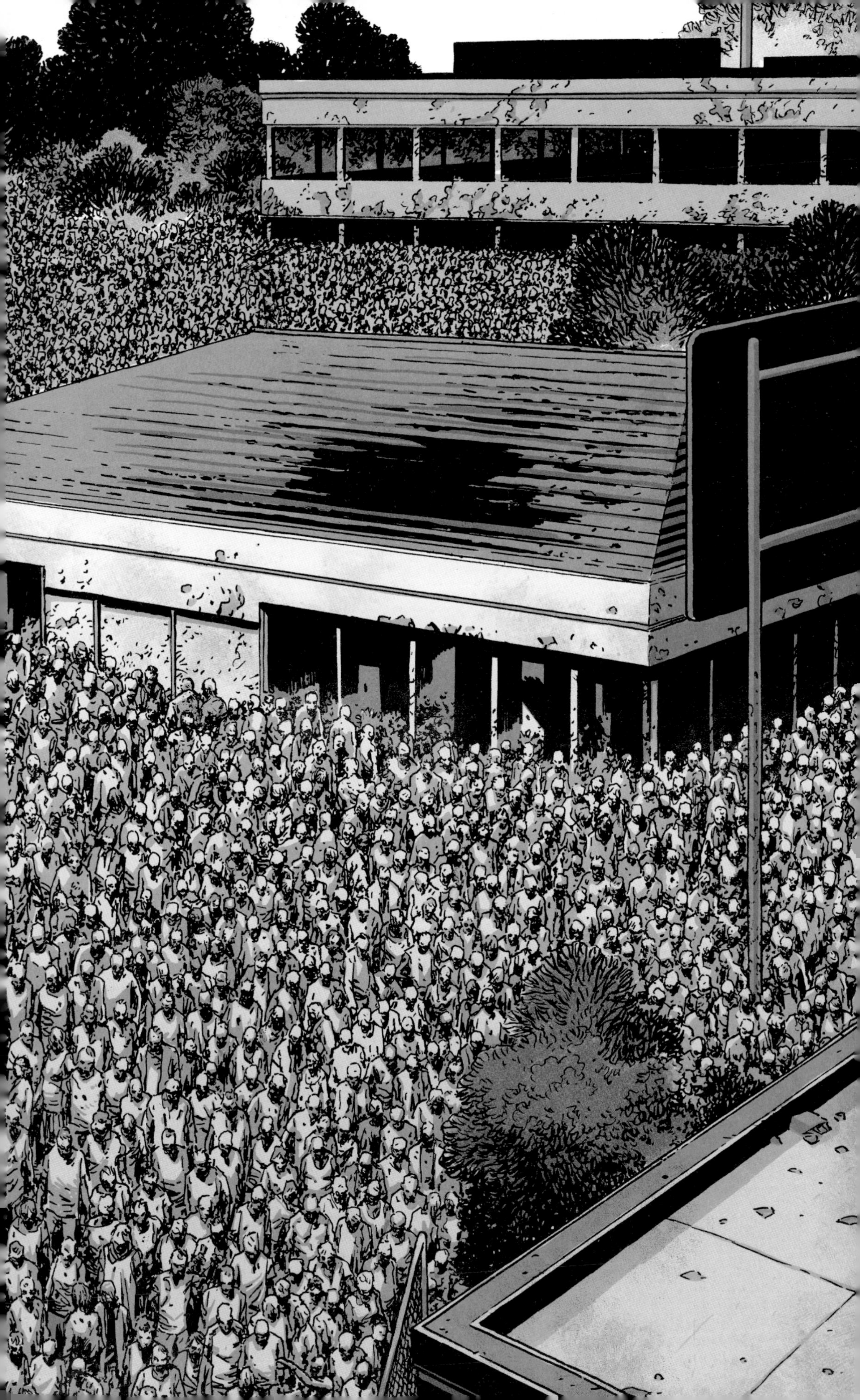

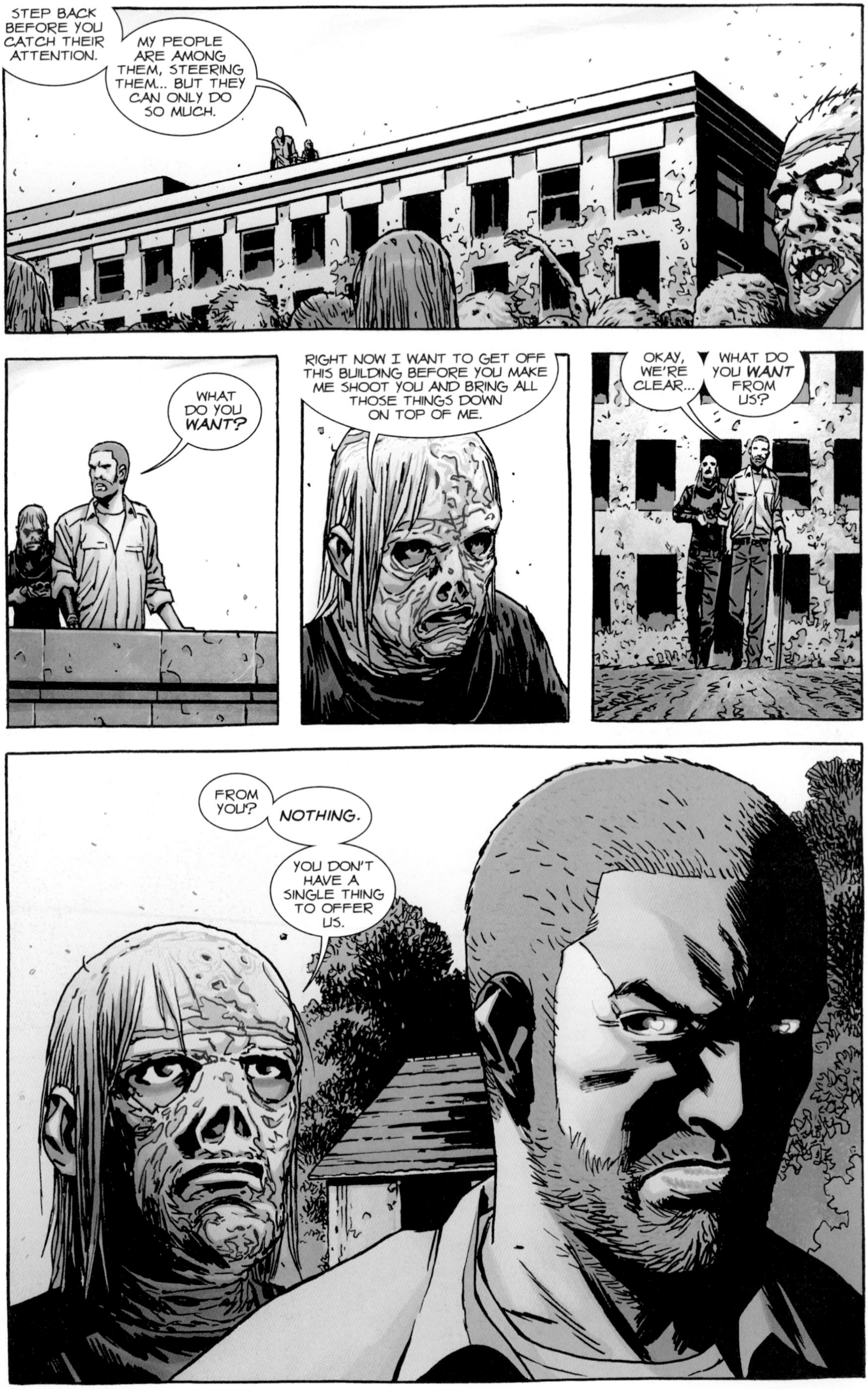
STEP BACK BEFORE YOU CATCH THEIR ATTENTION.
MY PEOPLE ARE AMONG THEM, STEERING THEM... BUT THEY CAN ONLY DO SO MUCH.
WHAT DO YOU *WANT?*
RIGHT NOW I WANT TO GET OFF THIS BUILDING BEFORE YOU MAKE ME SHOOT YOU AND BRING ALL THOSE THINGS DOWN ON TOP OF ME.
OKAY, WE'RE CLEAR...
WHAT DO YOU *WANT* FROM US?
FROM YOU?
NOTHING.
YOU DON'T HAVE A SINGLE THING TO OFFER US.

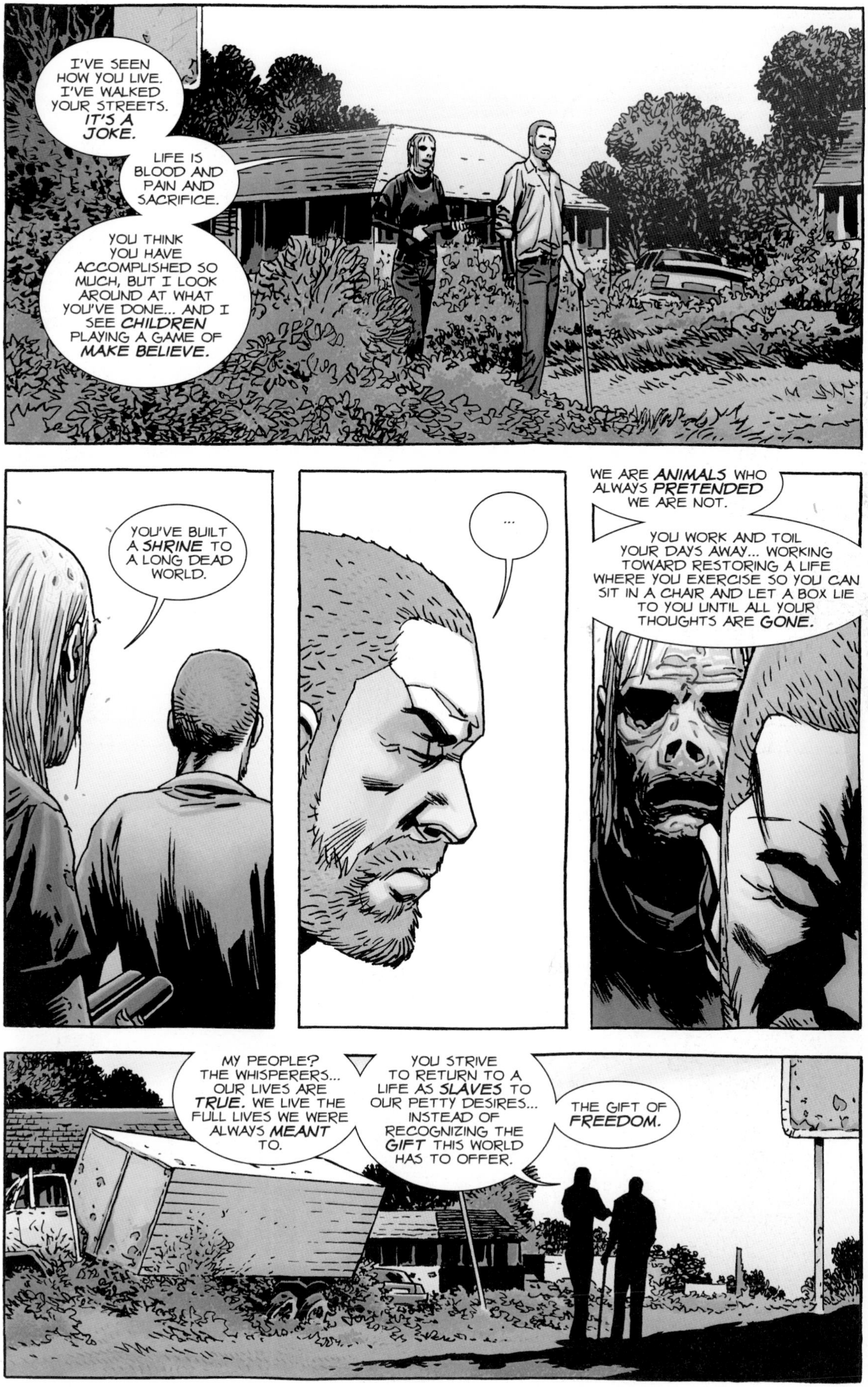
I'VE SEEN HOW YOU LIVE. I'VE WALKED YOUR STREETS. IT'S A JOKE.
LIFE IS BLOOD AND PAIN AND SACRIFICE.
YOU THINK YOU HAVE ACCOMPLISHED SO MUCH, BUT I LOOK AROUND AT WHAT YOU'VE DONE... AND I SEE CHILDREN PLAYING A GAME OF MAKE BELIEVE.
YOU'VE BUILT A SHRINE TO A LONG DEAD WORLD.
...
WE ARE ANIMALS WHO ALWAYS PRETENDED WE ARE NOT.
YOU WORK AND TOIL YOUR DAYS AWAY... WORKING TOWARD RESTORING A LIFE WHERE YOU EXERCISE SO YOU CAN SIT IN A CHAIR AND LET A BOX LIE TO YOU UNTIL ALL YOUR THOUGHTS ARE GONE.
MY PEOPLE? THE WHISPERERS... OUR LIVES ARE TRUE. WE LIVE THE FULL LIVES WE WERE ALWAYS MEANT TO.
YOU STRIVE TO RETURN TO A LIFE AS SLAVES TO OUR PETTY DESIRES... INSTEAD OF RECOGNIZING THE GIFT THIS WORLD HAS TO OFFER.
THE GIFT OF FREEDOM.

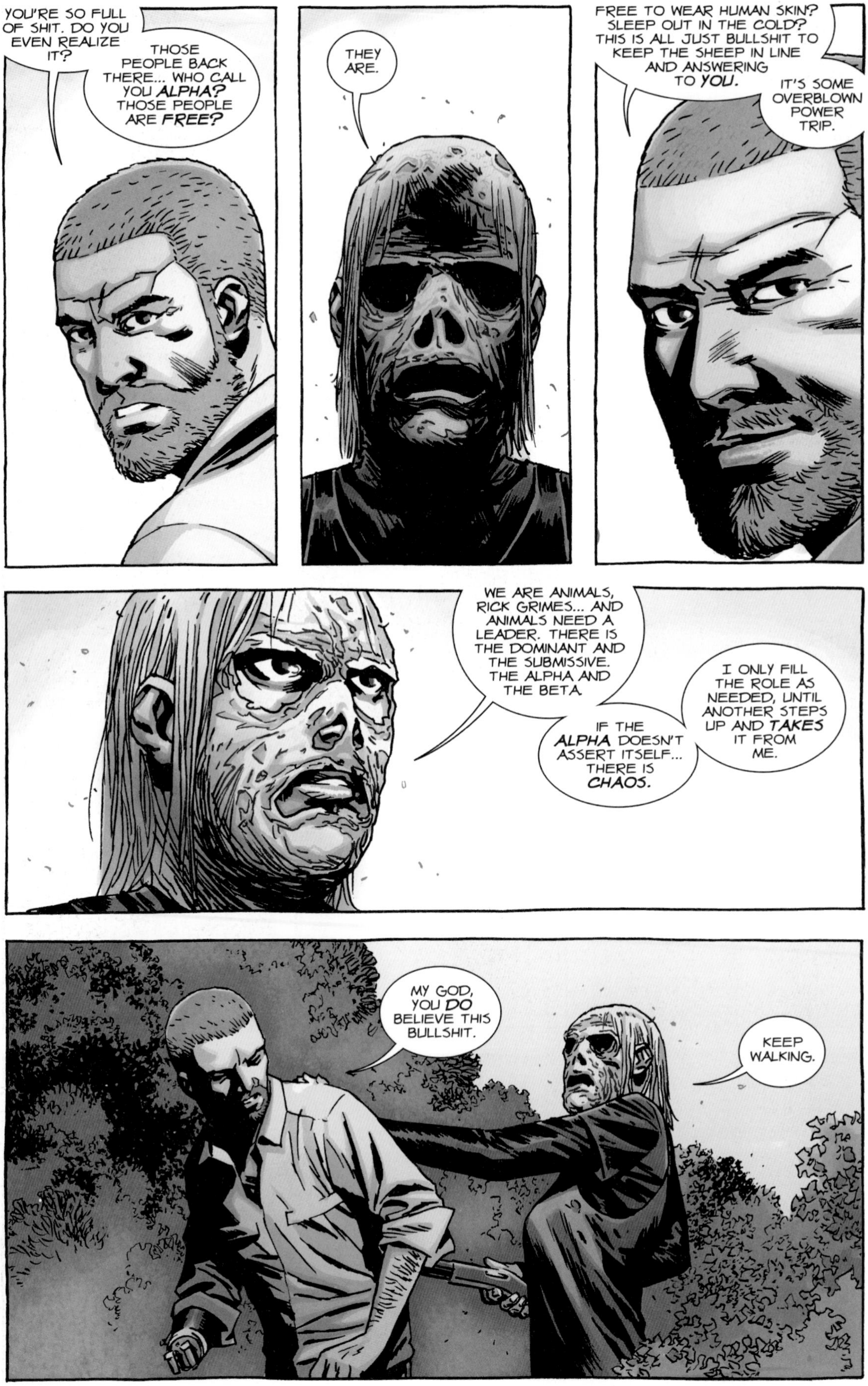
YOU'RE SO FULL OF SHIT. DO YOU EVEN REALIZE IT?
THOSE PEOPLE BACK THERE... WHO CALL YOU ALPHA? THOSE PEOPLE ARE FREE?
THEY ARE.
FREE TO WEAR HUMAN SKIN? SLEEP OUT IN THE COLD? THIS IS ALL JUST BULLSHIT TO KEEP THE SHEEP IN LINE AND ANSWERING TO YOU.
IT'S SOME OVERBLOWN POWER TRIP.
WE ARE ANIMALS, RICK GRIMES... AND ANIMALS NEED A LEADER. THERE IS THE DOMINANT AND THE SUBMISSIVE. THE ALPHA AND THE BETA.
IF THE ALPHA DOESN'T ASSERT ITSELF... THERE IS CHAOS.
I ONLY FILL THE ROLE AS NEEDED, UNTIL ANOTHER STEPS UP AND TAKES IT FROM ME.
MY GOD, YOU DO BELIEVE THIS BULLSHIT.
KEEP WALKING.

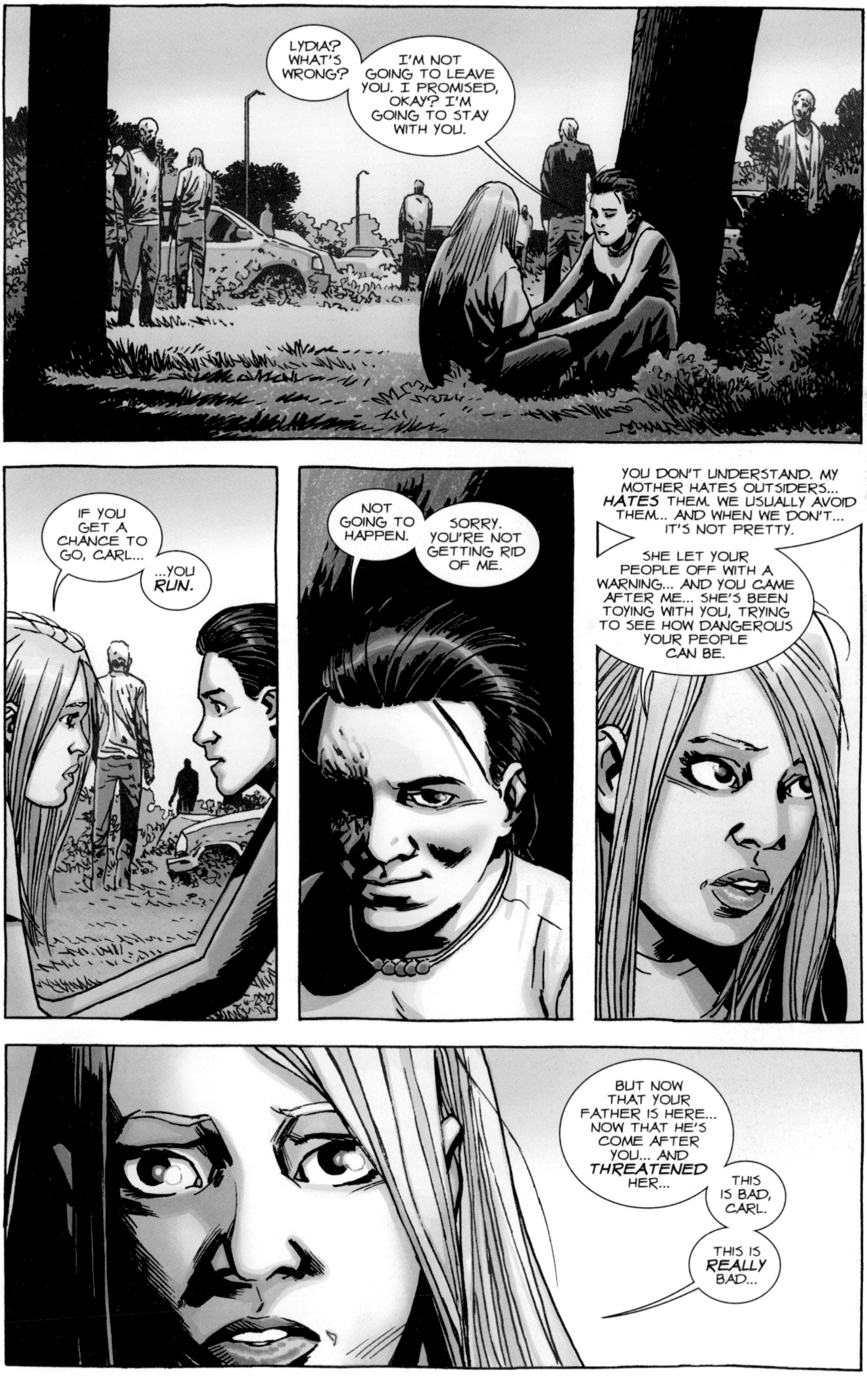

LYDIA? WHAT'S WRONG?
I'M NOT GOING TO LEAVE YOU. I PROMISED, OKAY? I'M GOING TO STAY WITH YOU.
IF YOU GET A CHANCE TO GO, CARL...
...YOU RUN.
NOT GOING TO HAPPEN.
SORRY. YOU'RE NOT GETTING RID OF ME.
YOU DON'T UNDERSTAND. MY MOTHER HATES OUTSIDERS... HATES THEM. WE USUALLY AVOID THEM... AND WHEN WE DON'T... IT'S NOT PRETTY.
SHE LET YOUR PEOPLE OFF WITH A WARNING... AND YOU CAME AFTER ME... SHE'S BEEN TOYING WITH YOU, TRYING TO SEE HOW DANGEROUS YOUR PEOPLE CAN BE.
BUT NOW THAT YOUR FATHER IS HERE... NOW THAT HE'S COME AFTER YOU... AND THREATENED HER...
THIS IS BAD, CARL.
THIS IS REALLY BAD...

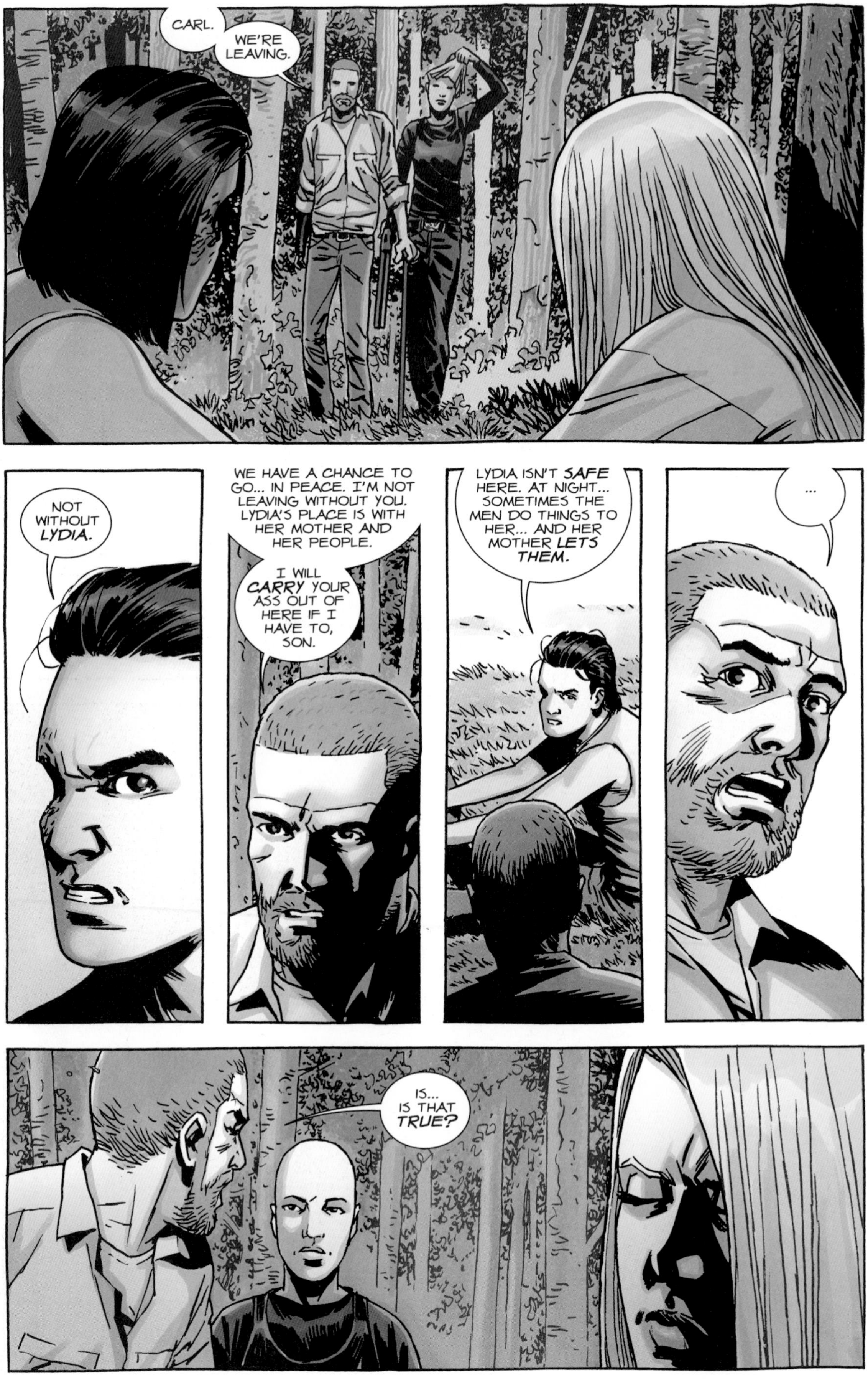
CARL.
WE'RE LEAVING.
NOT WITHOUT LYDIA.
WE HAVE A CHANCE TO GO... IN PEACE. I'M NOT LEAVING WITHOUT YOU. LYDIA'S PLACE IS WITH HER MOTHER AND HER PEOPLE.
I WILL CARRY YOUR ASS OUT OF HERE IF I HAVE TO, SON.
LYDIA ISN'T SAFE HERE. AT NIGHT... SOMETIMES THE MEN DO THINGS TO HER... AND HER MOTHER LETS THEM.
...
IS... IS THAT TRUE?

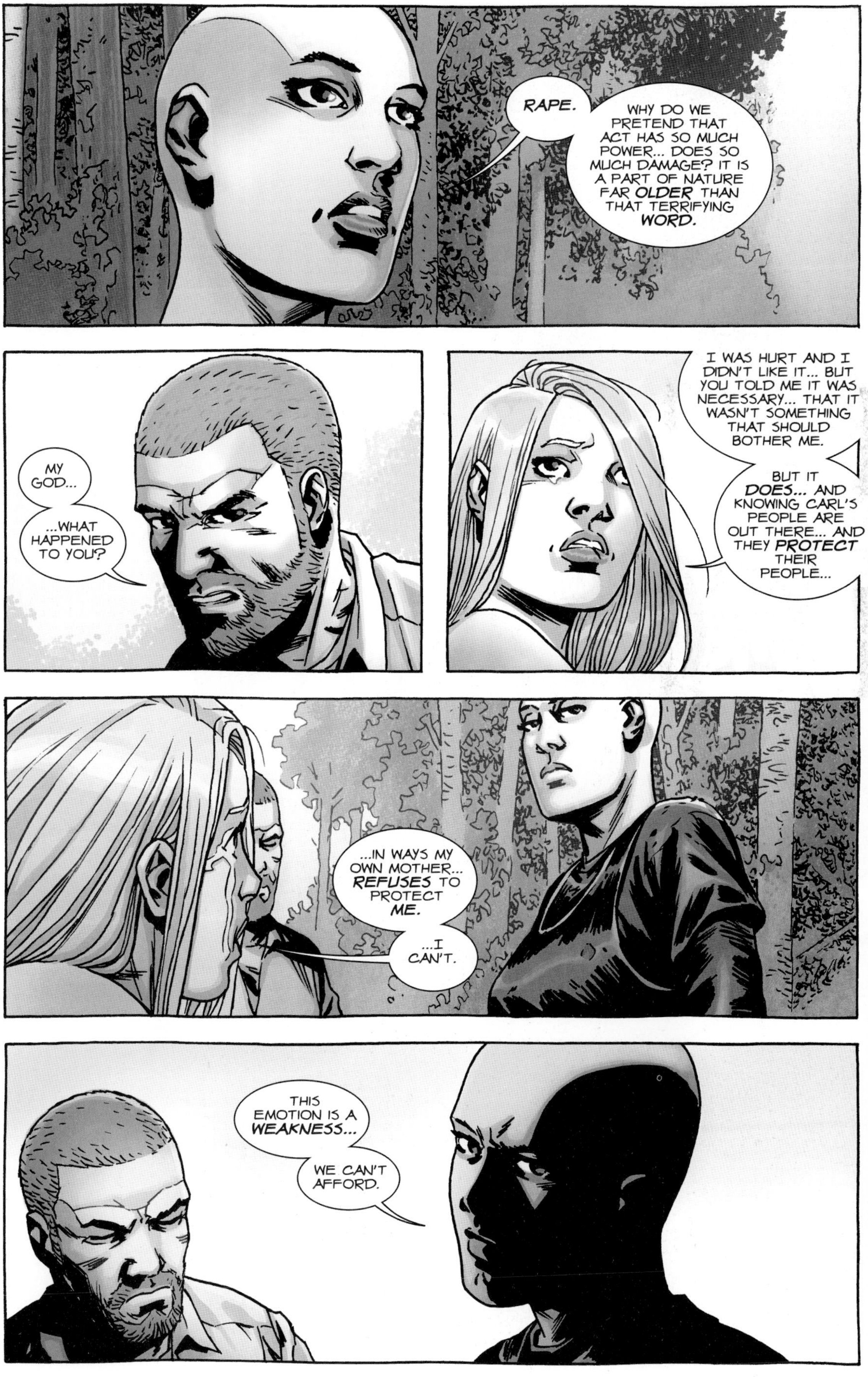
RAPE.
WHY DO WE PRETEND THAT ACT HAS SO MUCH POWER... DOES SO MUCH DAMAGE? IT IS A PART OF NATURE FAR OLDER THAN THAT TERRIFYING WORD.
MY GOD...
...WHAT HAPPENED TO YOU?
I WAS HURT AND I DIDN'T LIKE IT... BUT YOU TOLD ME IT WAS NECESSARY... THAT IT WASN'T SOMETHING THAT SHOULD BOTHER ME.
BUT IT DOES... AND KNOWING CARL'S PEOPLE ARE OUT THERE... AND THEY PROTECT THEIR PEOPLE...
...IN WAYS MY OWN MOTHER... REFUSES TO PROTECT ME.
...I CAN'T.
THIS EMOTION IS A WEAKNESS...
WE CAN'T AFFORD.

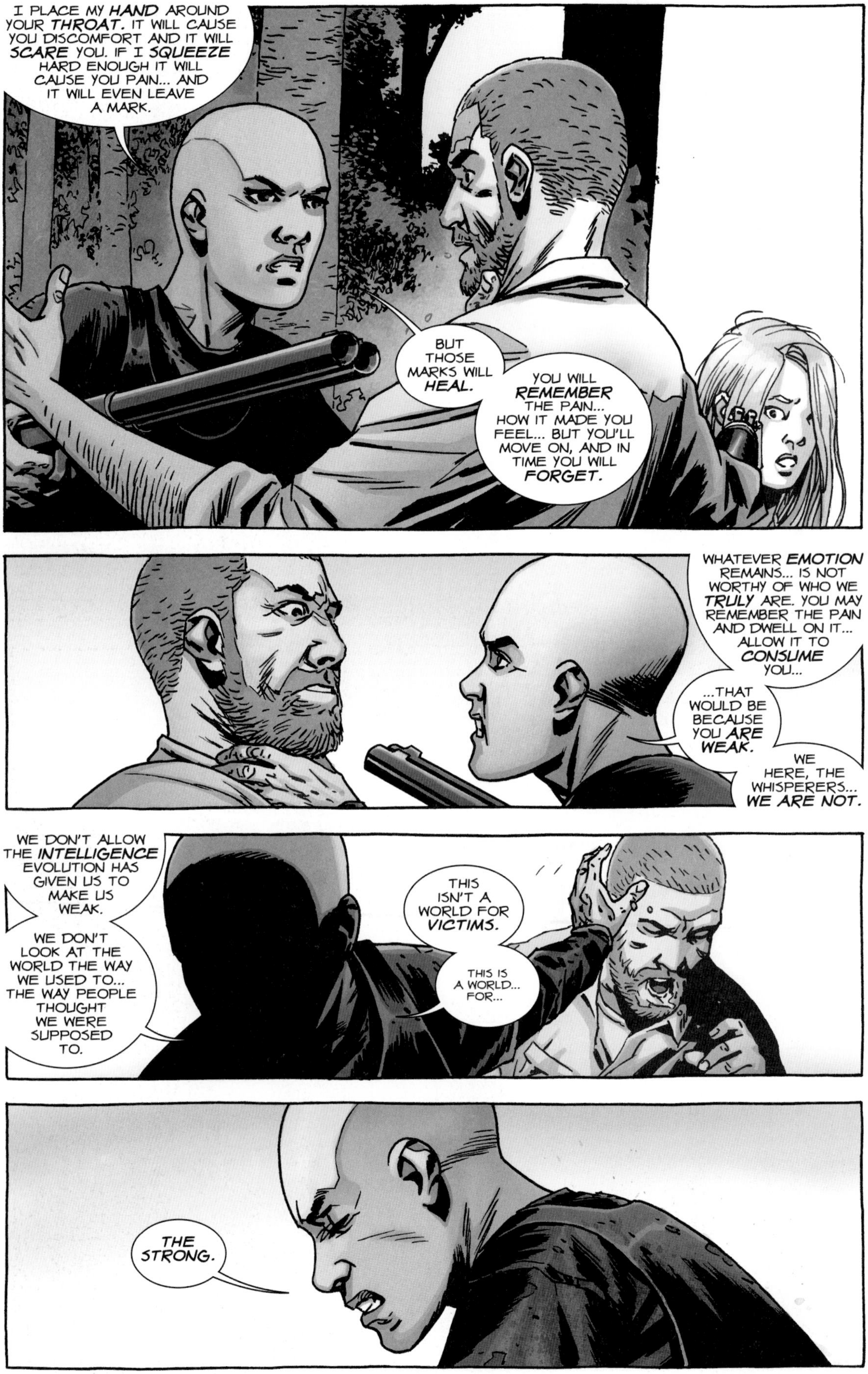
I PLACE MY HAND AROUND YOUR THROAT. IT WILL CAUSE YOU DISCOMFORT AND IT WILL SCARE YOU. IF I SQUEEZE HARD ENOUGH IT WILL CAUSE YOU PAIN... AND IT WILL EVEN LEAVE A MARK.
BUT THOSE MARKS WILL HEAL.
YOU WILL REMEMBER THE PAIN... HOW IT MADE YOU FEEL... BUT YOU'LL MOVE ON, AND IN TIME YOU WILL FORGET.
WHATEVER EMOTION REMAINS... IS NOT WORTHY OF WHO WE TRULY ARE. YOU MAY REMEMBER THE PAIN AND DWELL ON IT... ALLOW IT TO CONSUME YOU...
...THAT WOULD BE BECAUSE YOU ARE WEAK.
WE HERE, THE WHISPERERS... WE ARE NOT.
WE DON'T ALLOW THE INTELLIGENCE EVOLUTION HAS GIVEN US TO MAKE US WEAK.
WE DON'T LOOK AT THE WORLD THE WAY WE USED TO... THE WAY PEOPLE THOUGHT WE WERE SUPPOSED TO.
THIS ISN'T A WORLD FOR VICTIMS.
THIS IS A WORLD... FOR...
THE STRONG.

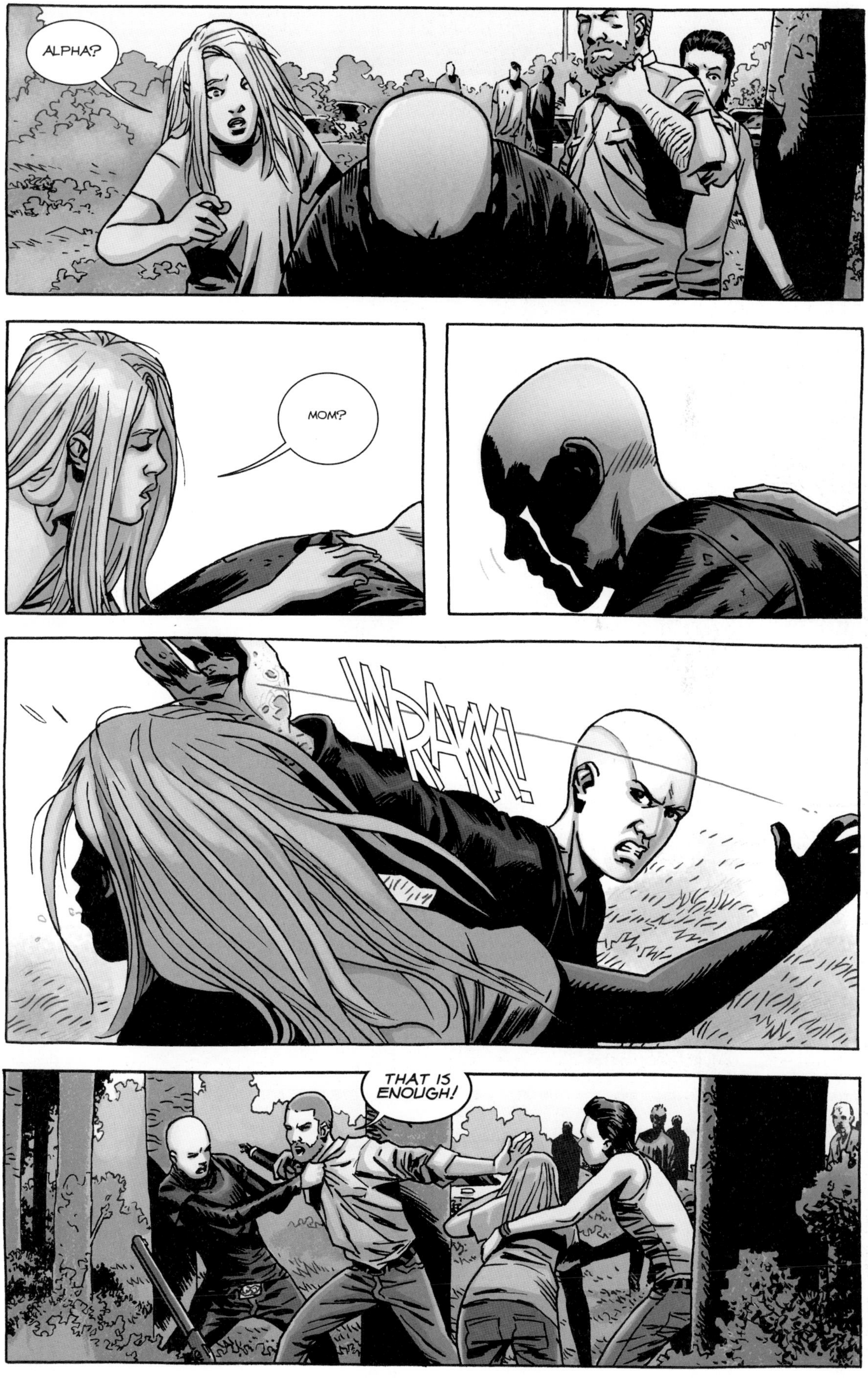
ALPHA?
MOM?
WRAKK!
THAT IS ENOUGH!

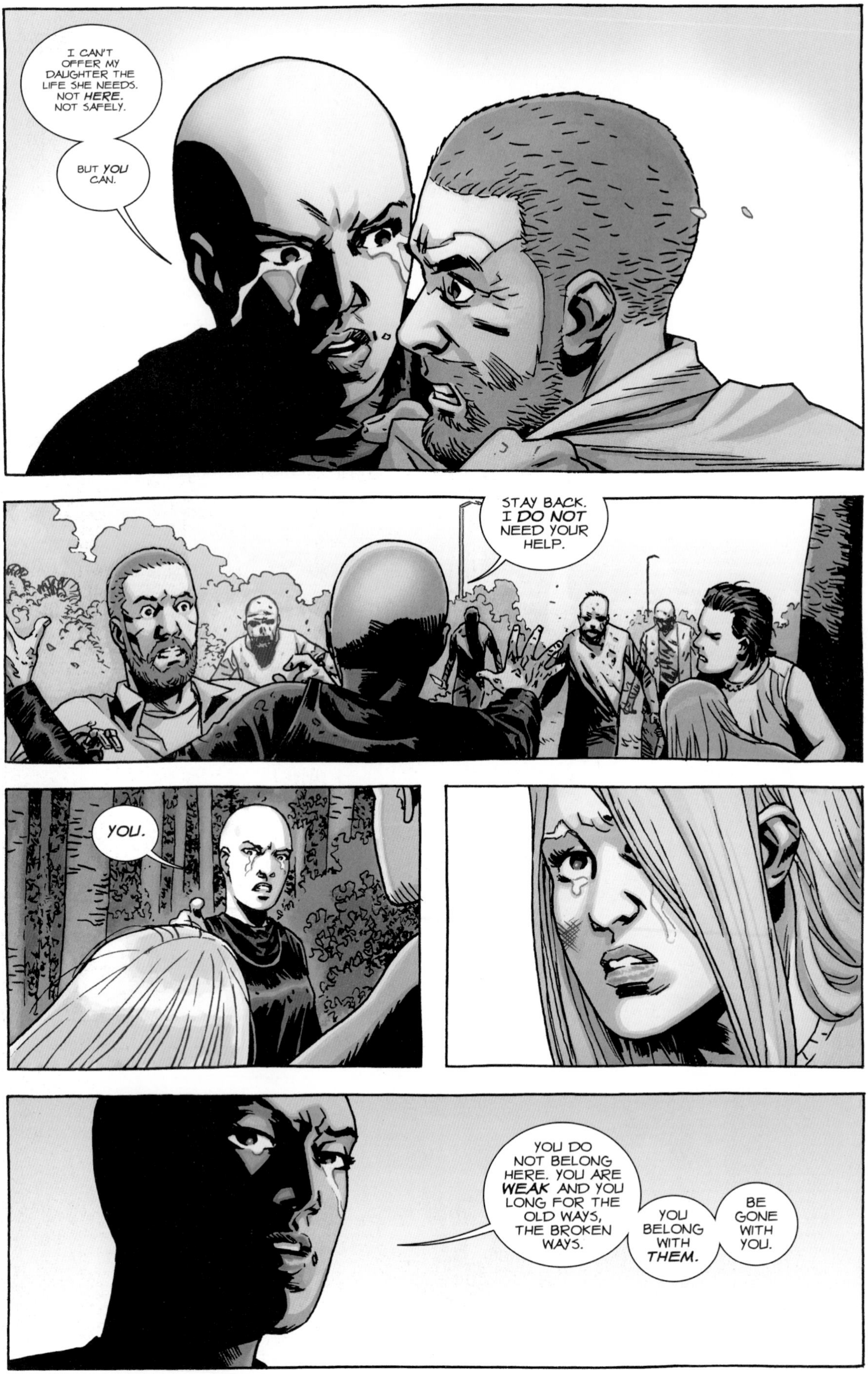
I CAN'T OFFER MY DAUGHTER THE LIFE SHE NEEDS. NOT HERE. NOT SAFELY.
BUT YOU CAN.
STAY BACK. I DO NOT NEED YOUR HELP.
YOU.
YOU DO NOT BELONG HERE. YOU ARE WEAK AND YOU LONG FOR THE OLD WAYS, THE BROKEN WAYS.
YOU BELONG WITH THEM.
BE GONE WITH YOU.

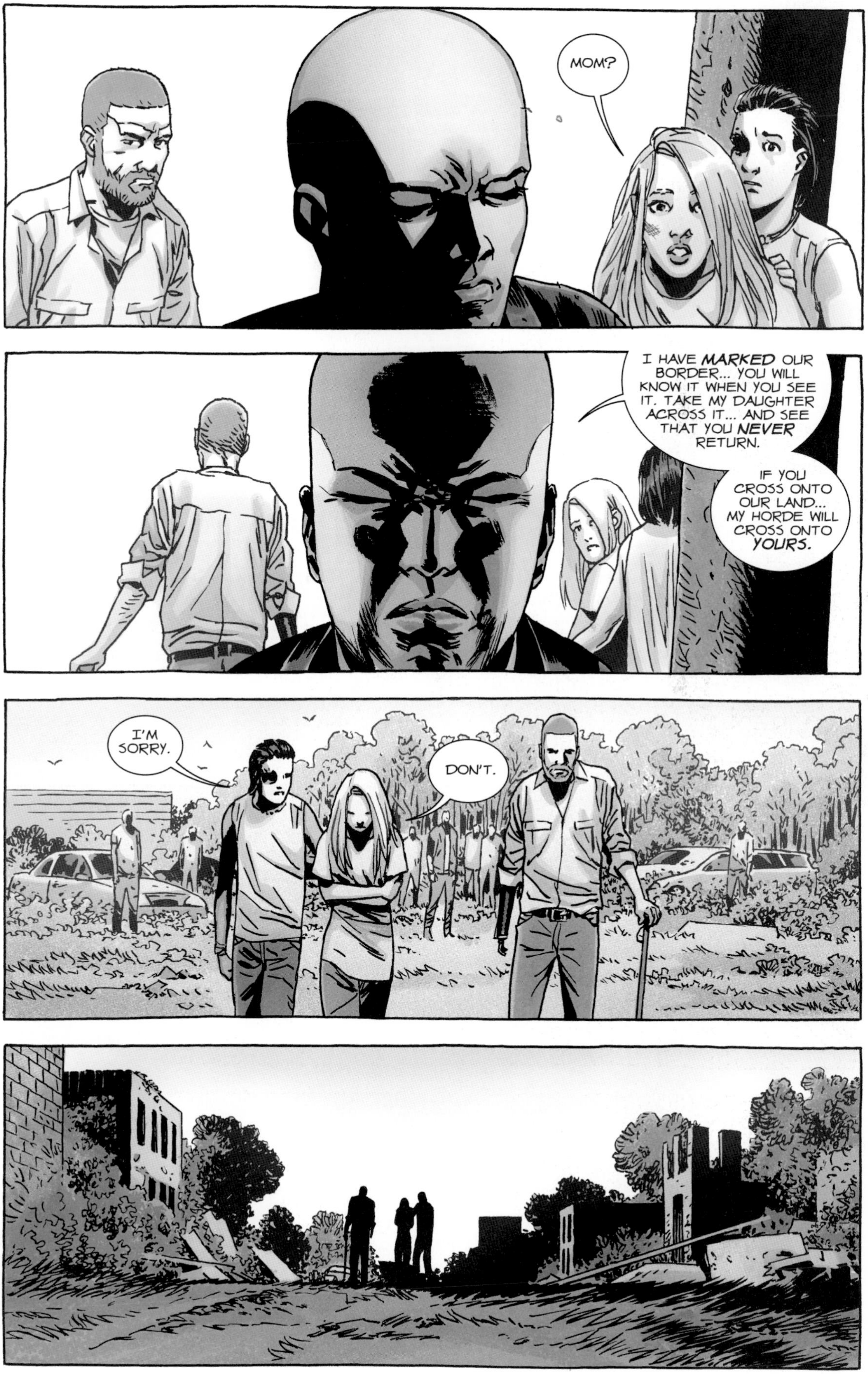
MOM?
I HAVE MARKED OUR BORDER... YOU WILL KNOW IT WHEN YOU SEE IT. TAKE MY DAUGHTER ACROSS IT... AND SEE THAT YOU NEVER RETURN.
IF YOU CROSS ONTO OUR LAND... MY HORDE WILL CROSS ONTO YOURS.
I'M SORRY.
DON'T.

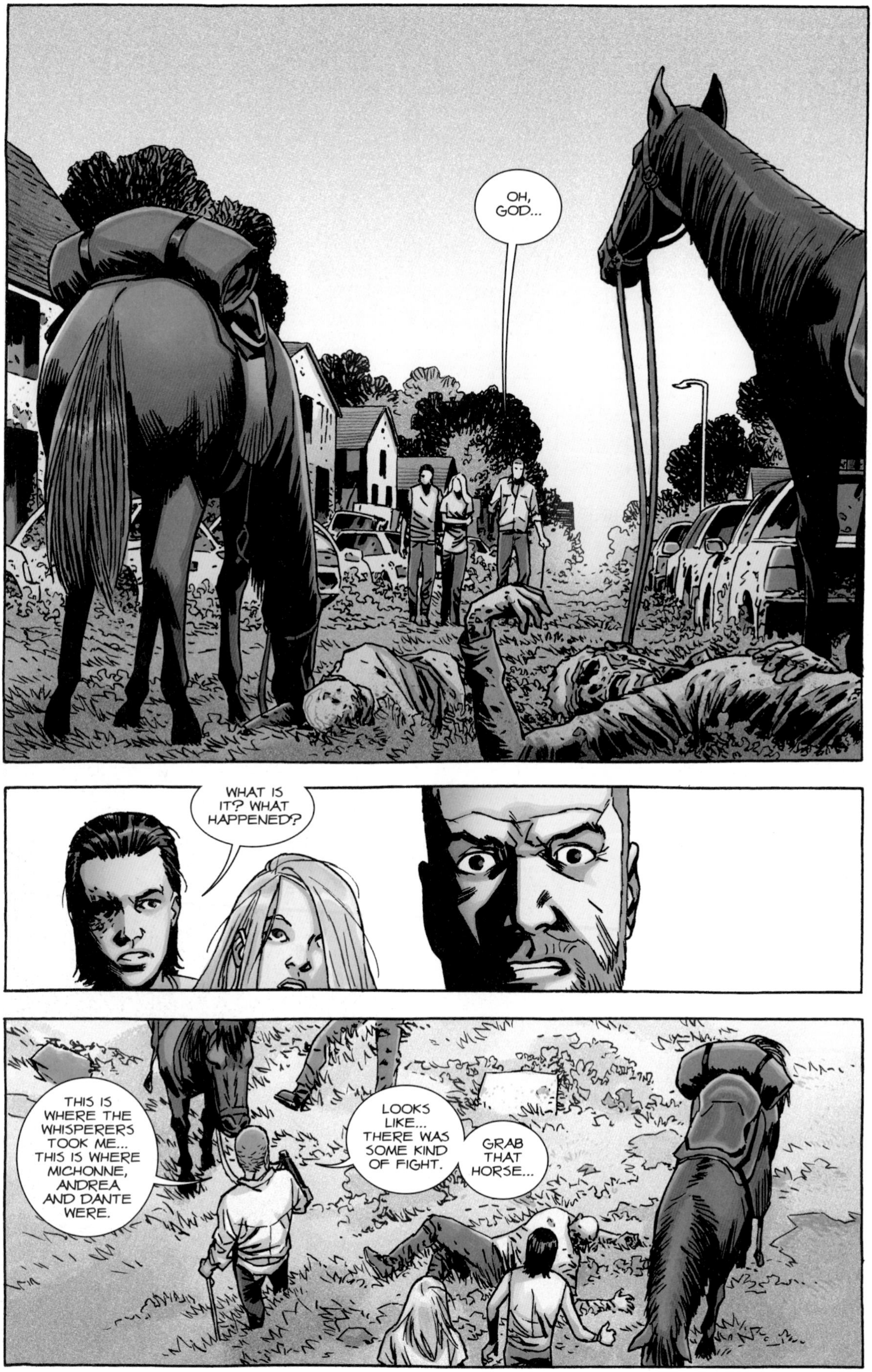
OH, GOD...
WHAT IS IT? WHAT HAPPENED?
THIS IS WHERE THE WHISPERERS TOOK ME... THIS IS WHERE MICHONNE, ANDREA AND DANTE WERE.
LOOKS LIKE... THERE WAS SOME KIND OF FIGHT.
GRAB THAT HORSE...

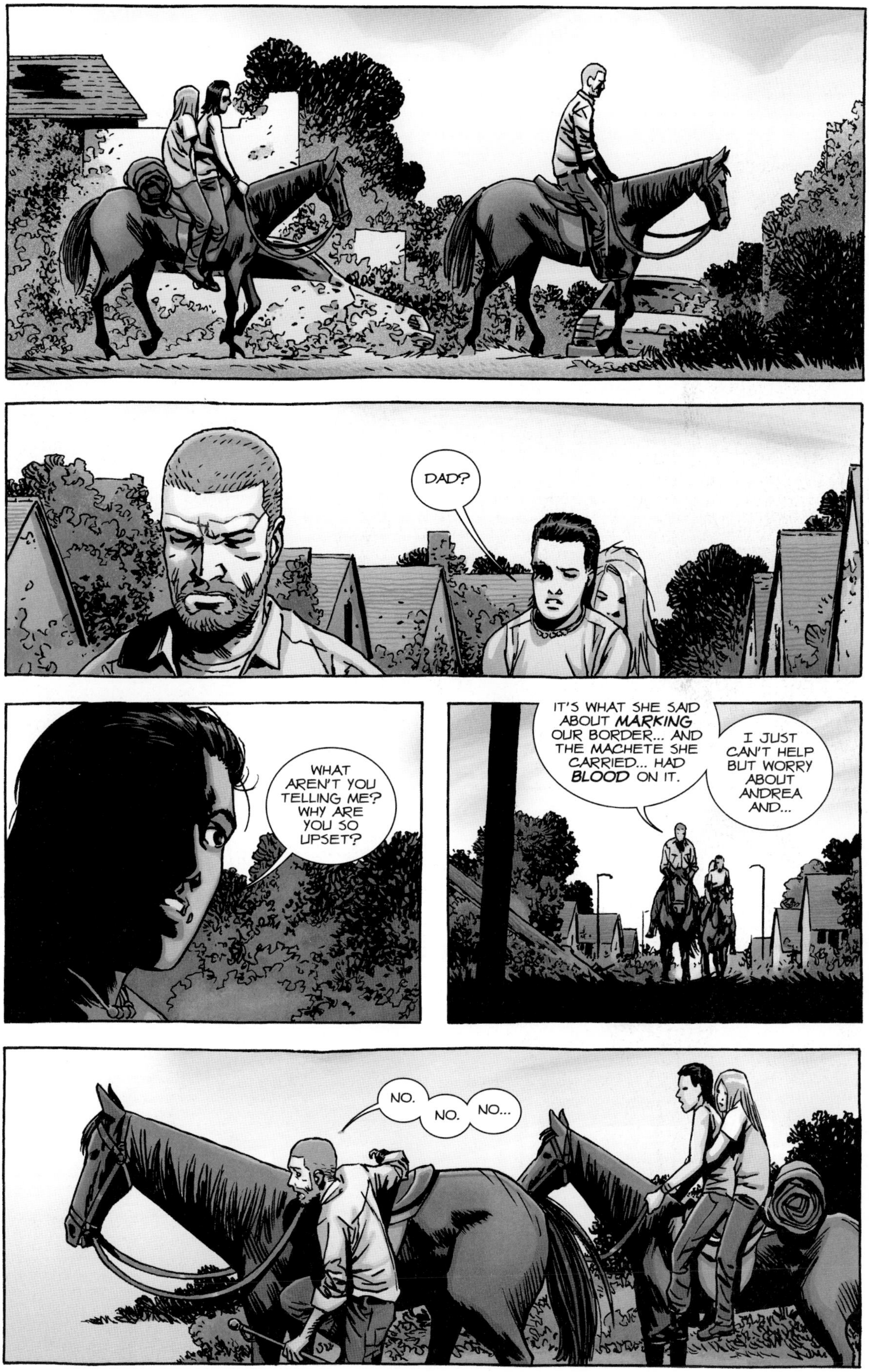
DAD?
WHAT AREN'T YOU TELLING ME? WHY ARE YOU SO UPSET?
IT'S WHAT SHE SAID ABOUT MARKING OUR BORDER... AND THE MACHETE SHE CARRIED... HAD BLOOD ON IT.
I JUST CAN'T HELP BUT WORRY ABOUT ANDREA AND...
NO.
NO.
NO...

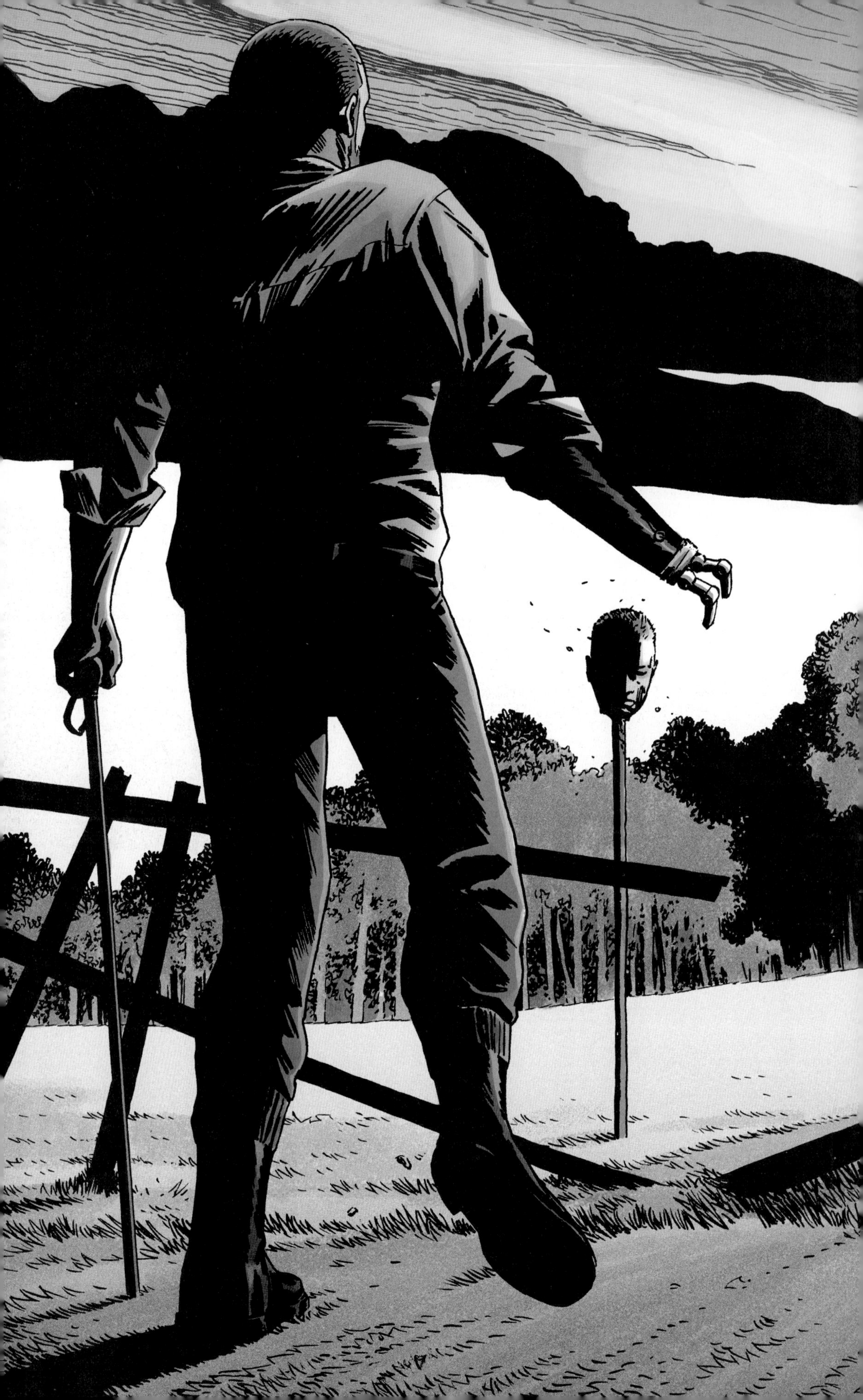

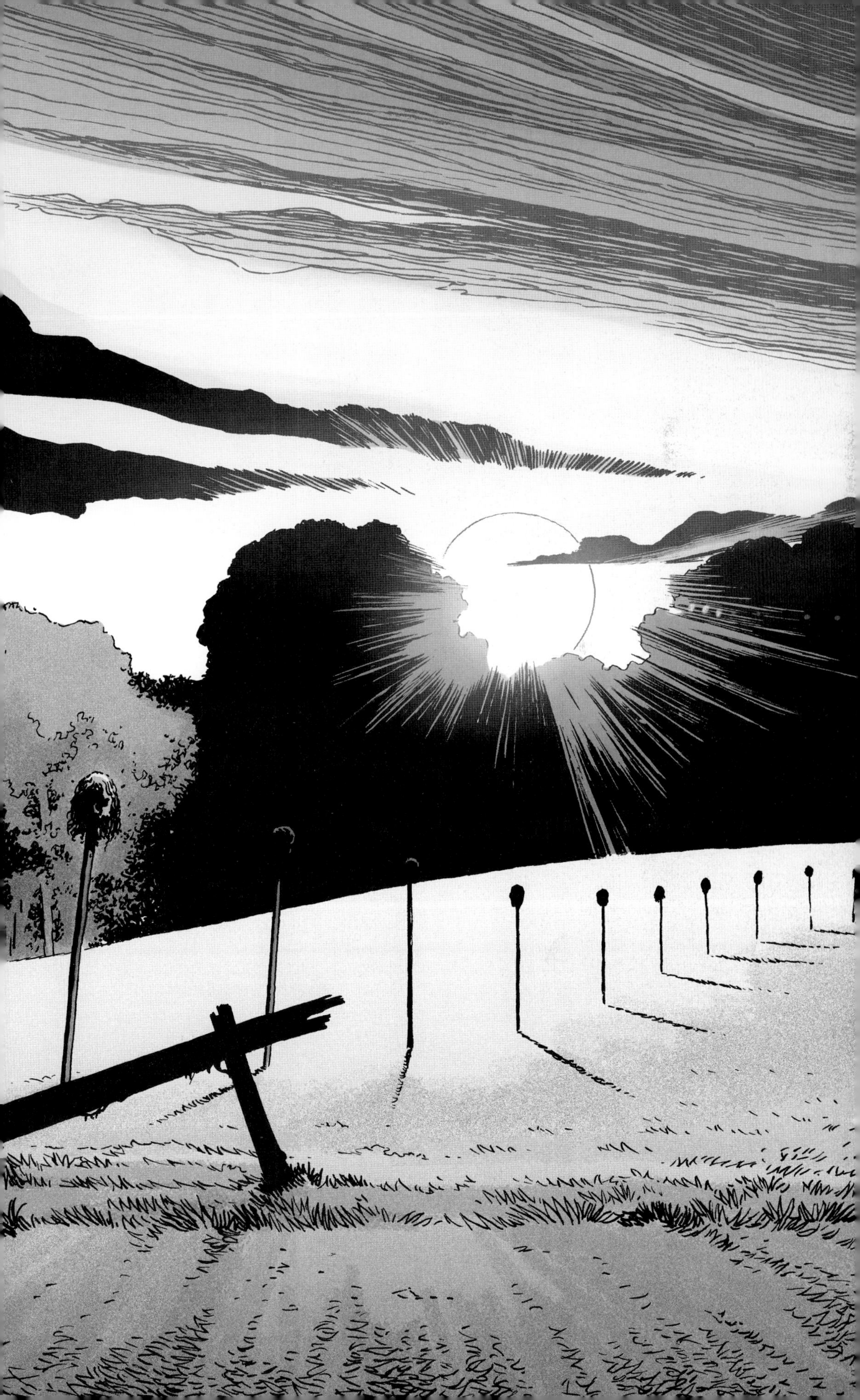

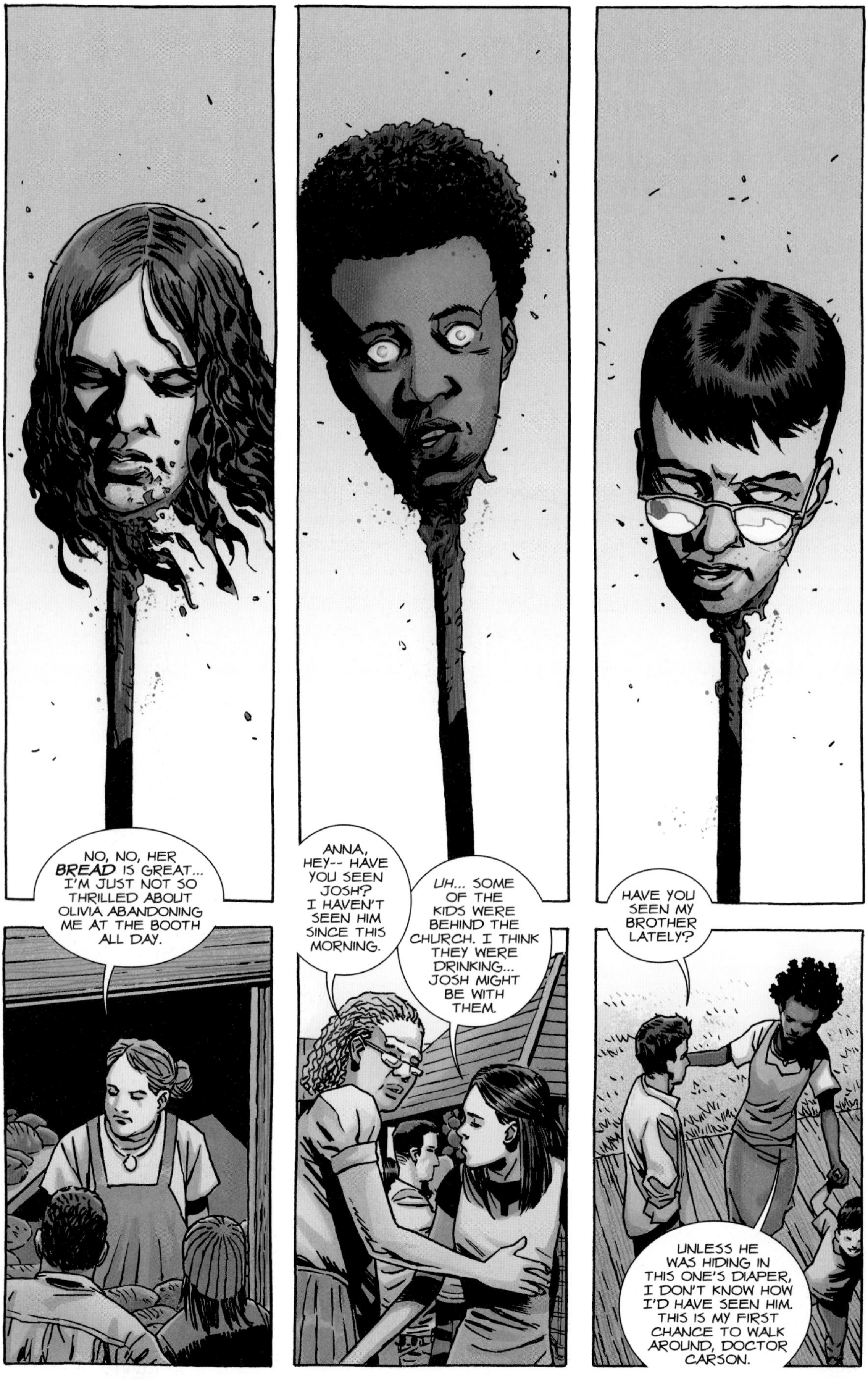
NO, NO, HER BREAD IS GREAT... I'M JUST NOT SO THRILLED ABOUT OLIVIA ABANDONING ME AT THE BOOTH ALL DAY.
ANNA, HEY-- HAVE YOU SEEN JOSH? I HAVEN'T SEEN HIM SINCE THIS MORNING.
UH... SOME OF THE KIDS WERE BEHIND THE CHURCH. I THINK THEY WERE DRINKING... JOSH MIGHT BE WITH THEM.
HAVE YOU SEEN MY BROTHER LATELY?
UNLESS HE WAS HIDING IN THIS ONE'S DIAPER, I DON'T KNOW HOW I'D HAVE SEEN HIM. THIS IS MY FIRST CHANCE TO WALK AROUND, DOCTOR CARSON.

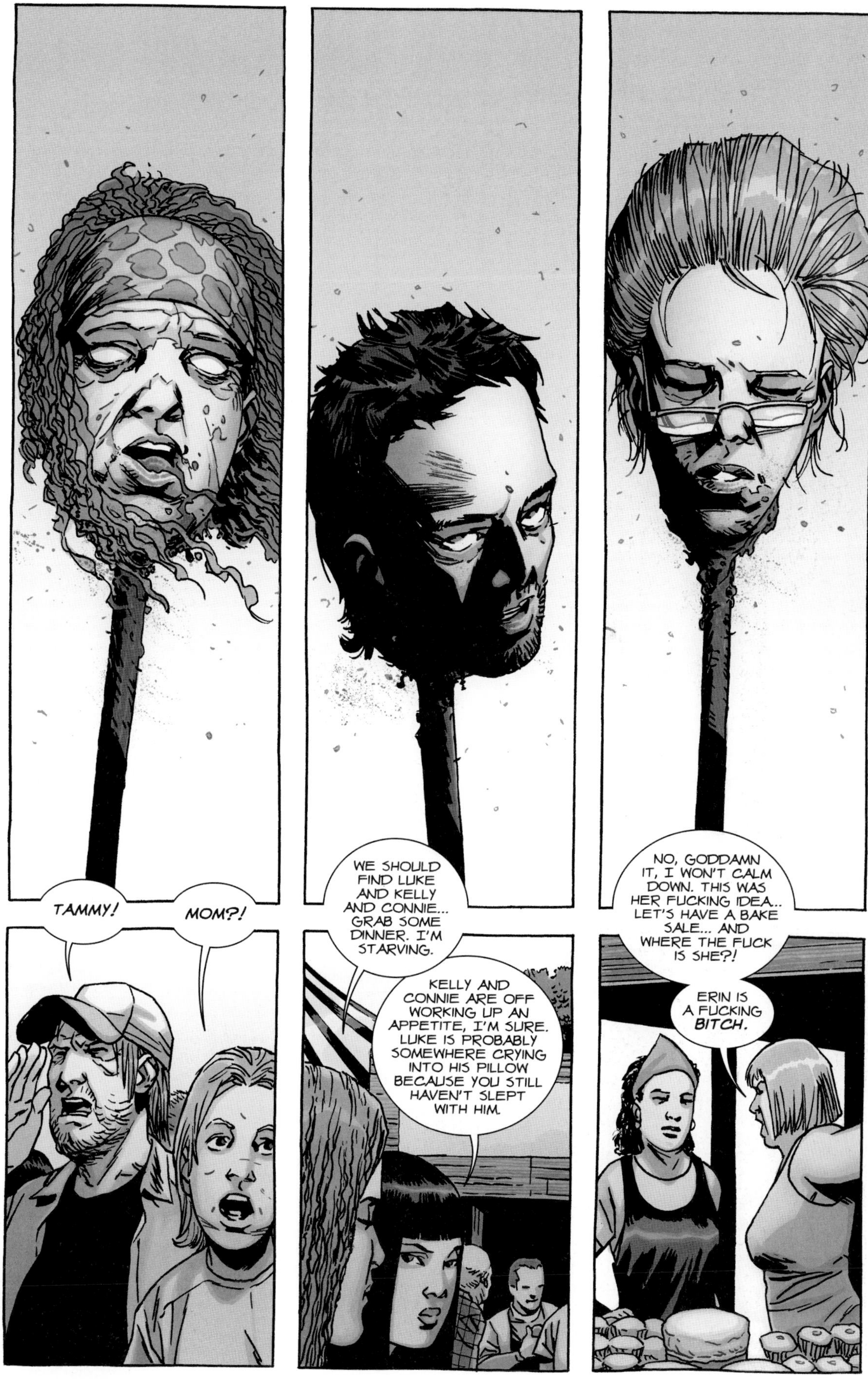
TAMMY!
MOM?!
WE SHOULD FIND LUKE AND KELLY AND CONNIE... GRAB SOME DINNER. I'M STARVING.
KELLY AND CONNIE ARE OFF WORKING UP AN APPETITE, I'M SURE. LUKE IS PROBABLY SOMEWHERE CRYING INTO HIS PILLOW BECAUSE YOU STILL HAVEN'T SLEPT WITH HIM.
NO, GODDAMN IT, I WON'T CALM DOWN. THIS WAS HER FUCKING IDEA.. LET'S HAVE A BAKE SALE... AND WHERE THE FUCK IS SHE?!
ERIN IS A FUCKING *BITCH*.

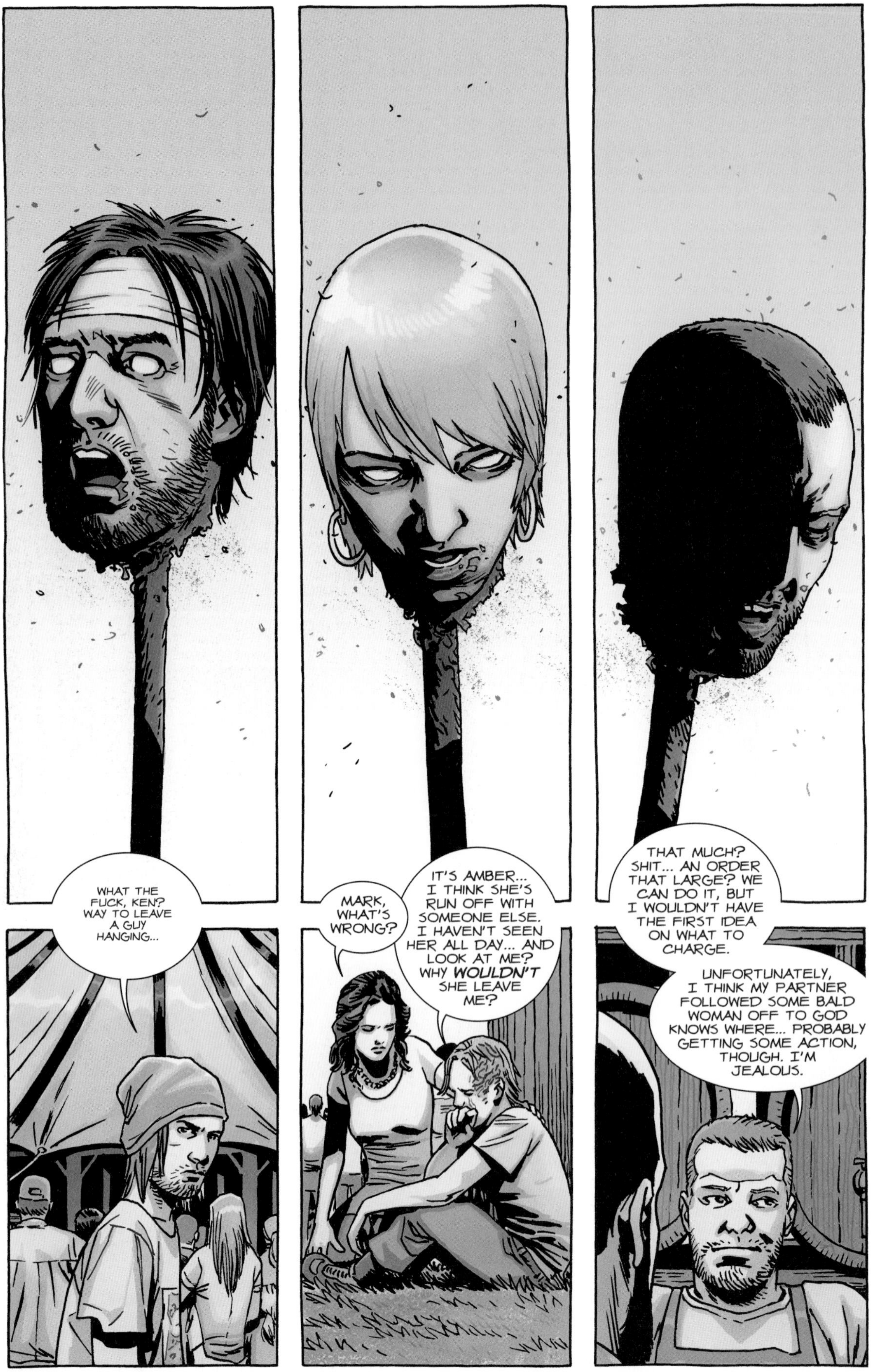
WHAT THE FUCK, KEN? WAY TO LEAVE A GUY HANGING...
MARK, WHAT'S WRONG?
IT'S AMBER... I THINK SHE'S RUN OFF WITH SOMEONE ELSE. I HAVEN'T SEEN HER ALL DAY... AND LOOK AT ME? WHY **WOULDN'T** SHE LEAVE ME?
THAT MUCH? SHIT... AN ORDER THAT LARGE? WE CAN DO IT, BUT I WOULDN'T HAVE THE FIRST IDEA ON WHAT TO CHARGE.
UNFORTUNATELY, I THINK MY PARTNER FOLLOWED SOME BALD WOMAN OFF TO GOD KNOWS WHERE... PROBABLY GETTING SOME ACTION, THOUGH. I'M JEALOUS.

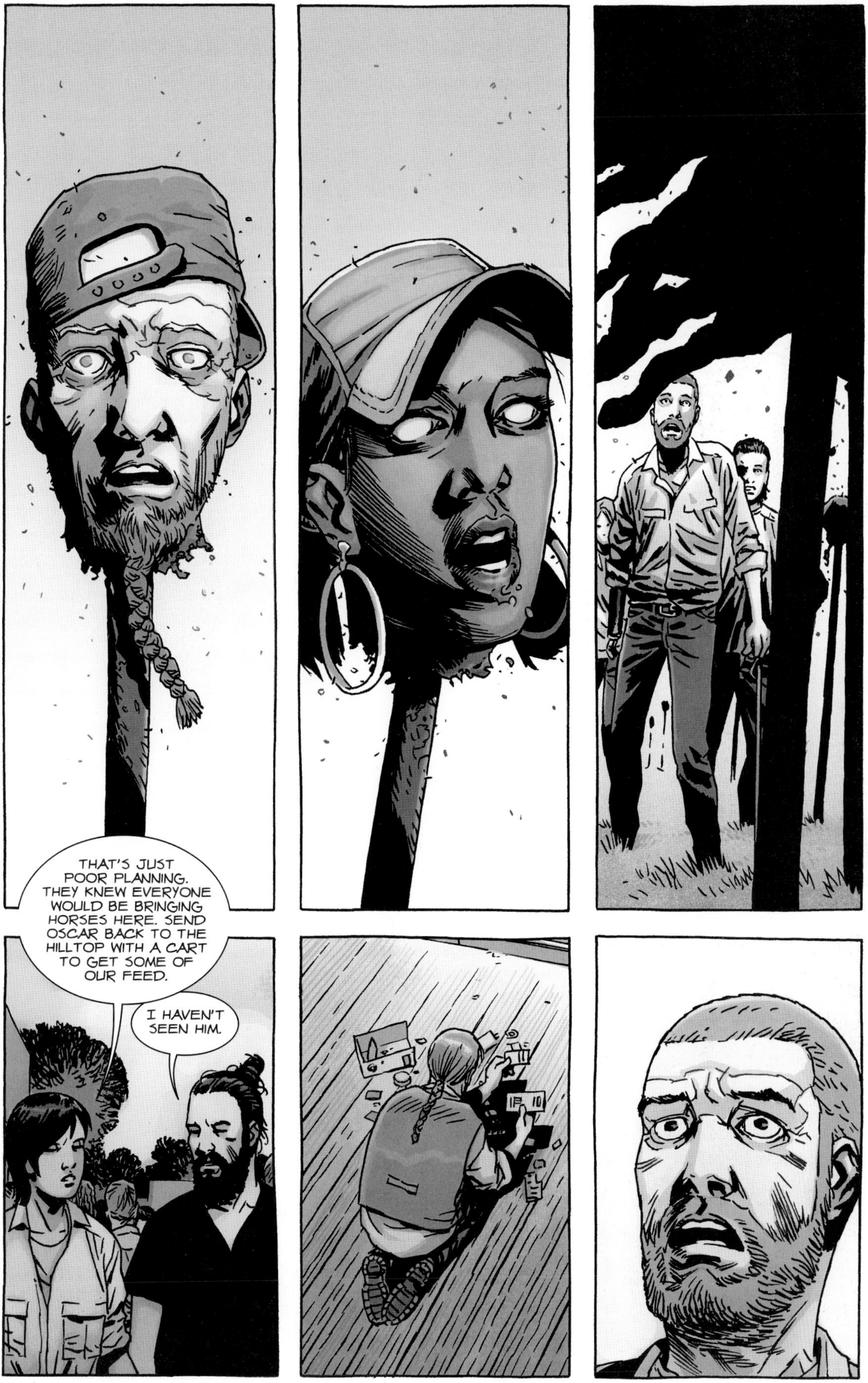
THAT'S JUST POOR PLANNING. THEY KNEW EVERYONE WOULD BE BRINGING HORSES HERE. SEND OSCAR BACK TO THE HILLTOP WITH A CART TO GET SOME OF OUR FEED.
I HAVEN'T SEEN HIM.

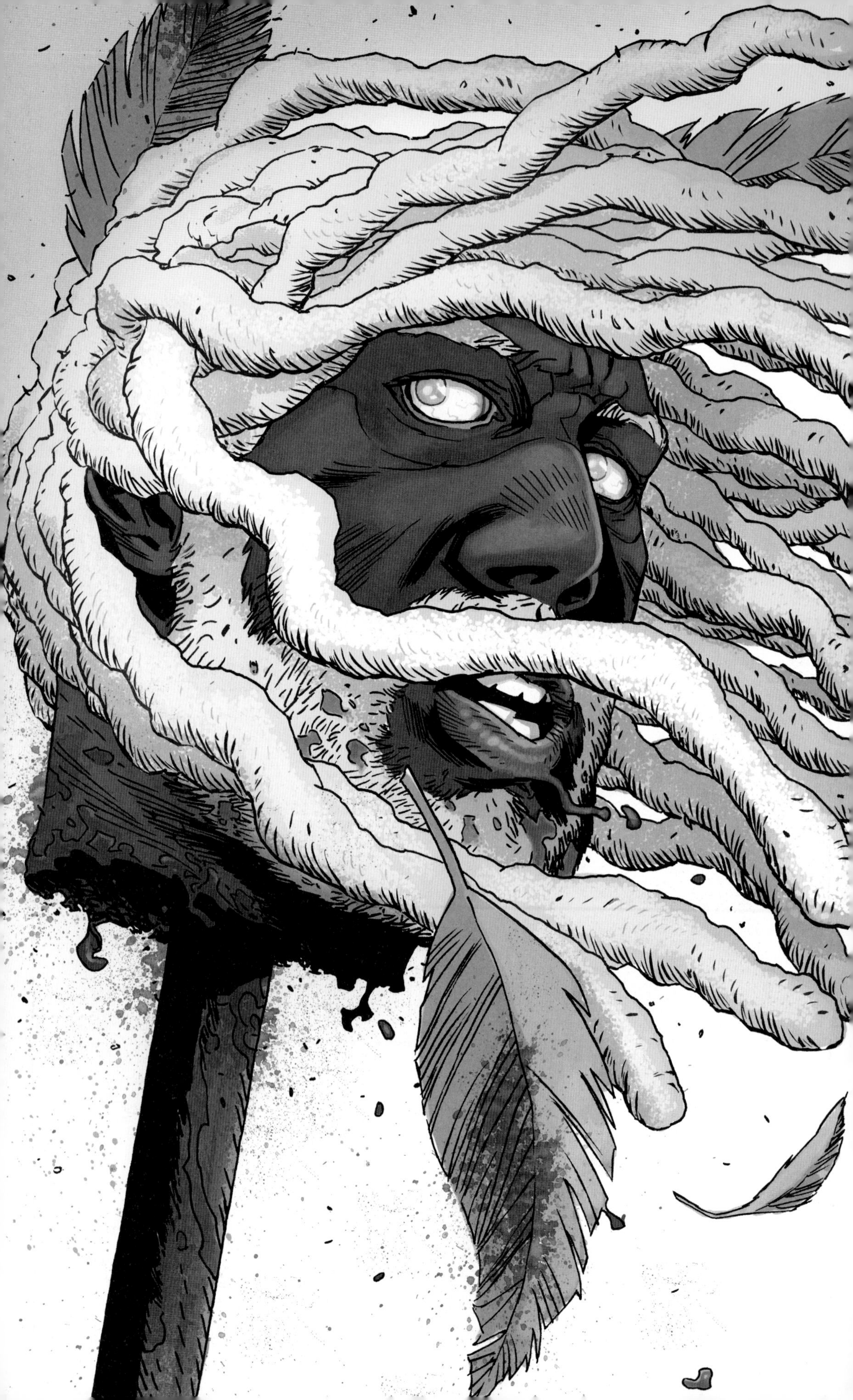

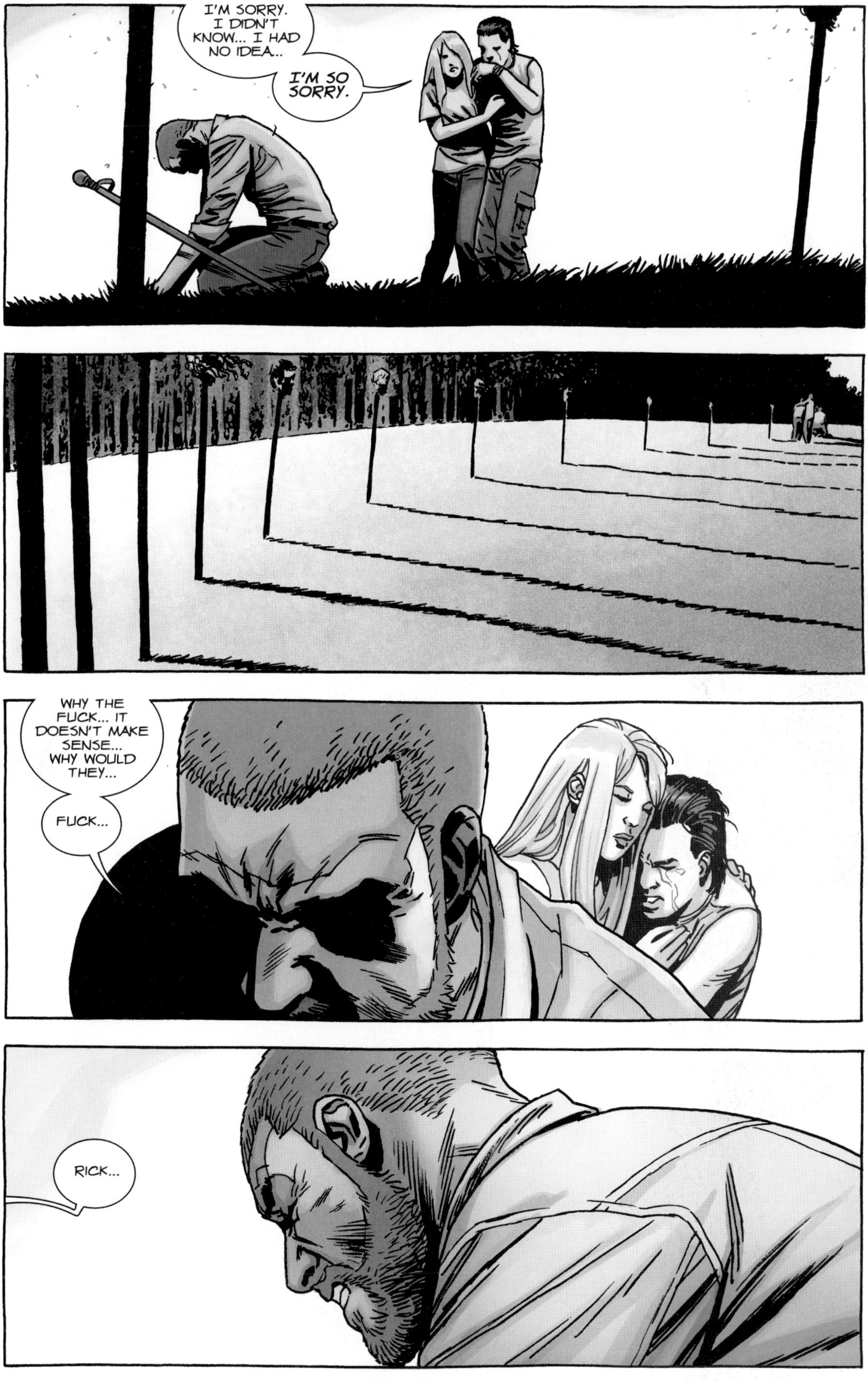
I'M SORRY. I DIDN'T KNOW... I HAD NO IDEA...
I'M SO SORRY.
WHY THE FUCK... IT DOESN'T MAKE SENSE... WHY WOULD THEY...
FUCK...
RICK...

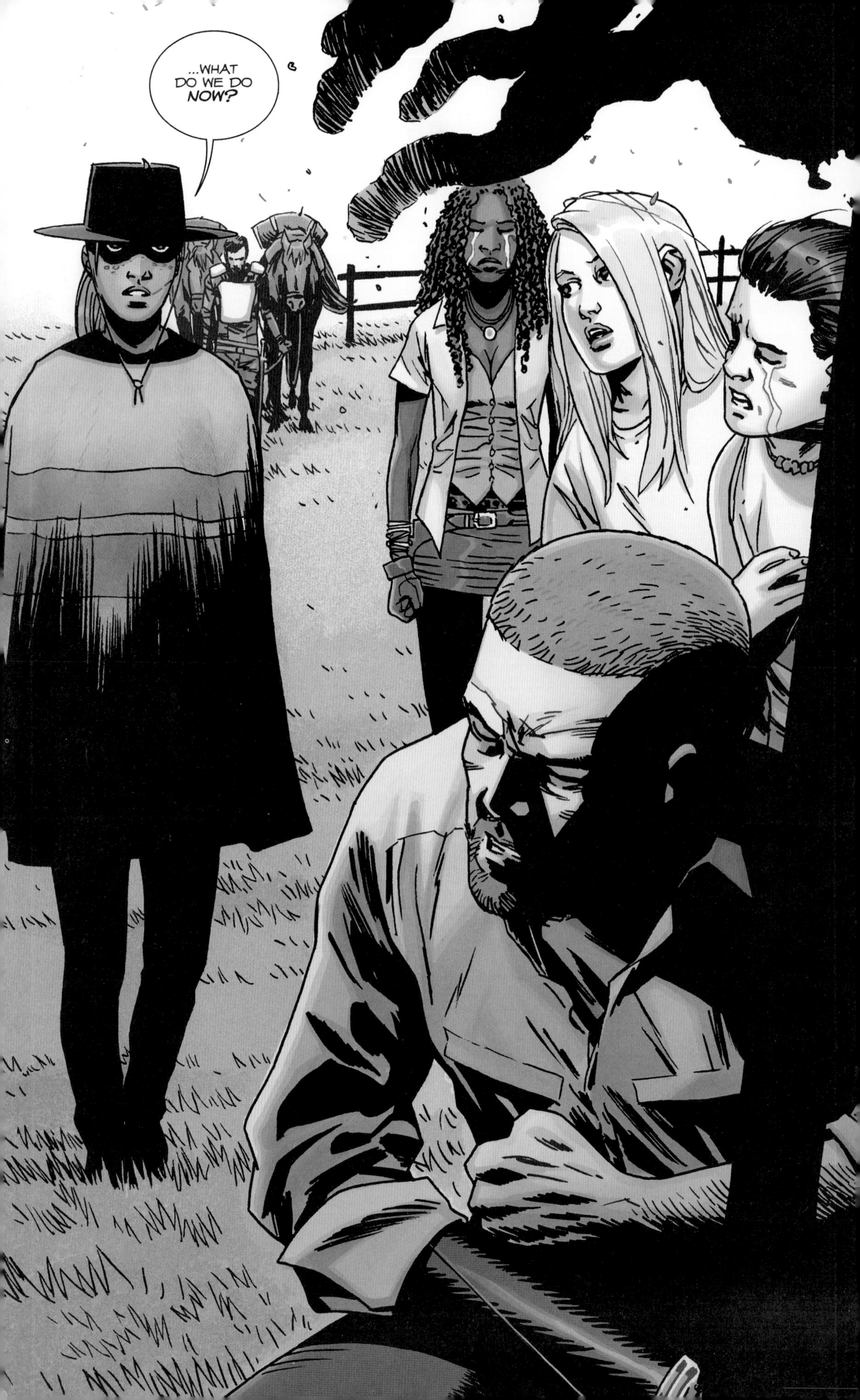
...WHAT DO WE DO NOW?